## More praise for *Shadows over Innsmouth*

"A terrific anthology . . . from some of the best British writers in the field today. Highly recommended."
—*The Year's Best Fantasy and Horror*

"A supremely entertaining volume . . . A very strong anthology."
—*The Scream Factory*

"Horror abounds in *Shadows over Innsmouth.*"
—*Publishers Weekly*

"Addicts of American Gothic will like it."
—*The Times* (London)

"An intelligent, witty anthology."
—*The Good Book Guide*

"Lovecraftians will rejoice."
—*Booklist*

*More Lovecraftian Horror from Del Rey Books:*

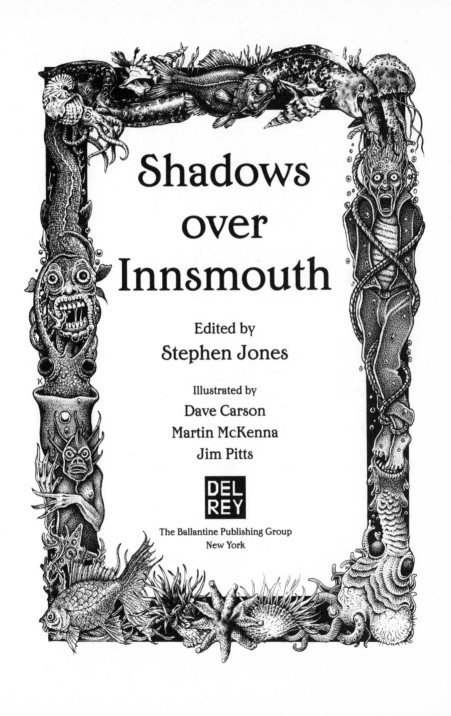

# Shadows over Innsmouth

Edited by
## Stephen Jones

Illustrated by
### Dave Carson
### Martin McKenna
### Jim Pitts

**DEL REY**

The Ballantine Publishing Group
New York

A Del Rey® Book
Published by The Ballantine Publishing Group
Copyright © 1994 by Stephen Jones
Artwork copyright © 1994 by Dave Carson, Martin McKenna and Jim Pitts

"Introduction: Spawn of the Deep Ones" Copyright © 1994 Stephen Jones.

"The Shadow over Innsmouth" Copyright © 1936 Visionary Publishing Company.
Copyright © 1939 August Derleth and Donald Wandrei. Reprinted with permission of the
Author's Estate and Scott Meredith Literary Agency.

"Beyond the Reef" Copyright © 1994 Basil Copper.

"The Big Fish" Copyright © 1993 Jack Yeovil. Originally published in *Interzone* No. 76,
October 1993 (as by Kim Newman). Reprinted by permission of the author.

"Return to Innsmouth" Copyright © 1992 Guy Smith Associates. Originally published
in *Reminiscon 40 Souvenir Programme*. Reprinted by permission of the author.

"The Crossing" Copyright © 1994 Adrian Cole.

"Down to the Boots" Copyright © 1989 D. F. Lewis. Originally published in *Dagon* No.
26, October–December 1989. Reprinted by permission of the author.

"The Church in High Street" Copyright © 1962 Ramsey Campbell. Originally published
in *Dark Mind, Dark Heart* (as by J. Ramsey Campbell). Reprinted by permission of the author.

"Innsmouth Gold" Copyright © 1994 David Sutton.

"Daoine Domhain" Copyright © 1993 Peter Tremayne. Originally published in *Aisling
and Other Irish Tales of Terror*. Reprinted by permission of the author.

"A Quarter to Three" Copyright © 1988 Kim Newman. Originally published in *Fear* No.
2, September–October 1988. Reprinted by permission of the author.

"The Tomb of Priscus" Copyright © 1994 Brian Mooney.

"The Innsmouth Heritage" Copyright © 1992 Brian Stableford. Originally published in
*The Innsmouth Heritage*. Reprinted by permission of the author.

"The Homecoming" Copyright © 1994 Nicholas Royle.

"Deepnet" Copyright © 1994 David Langford. Originally published in *Irrational Numbers*. Reprinted by permission of the author.

"To See the Sea" Copyright © 1994 Michael Marshall Smith.

"Dagon's Bell" Copyright © 1988 Brian Lumley. Originally published in *Weirdbook* No.
23/24, 1988. Reprinted by permission of the author and the author's agent.

"Only the End of the World Again" Copyright © 1994 Neil Gaiman.

"Afterwords: Contributors' Notes" Copyright © 1994, 2001 Stephen Jones.

www.delreydigital.com

Library of Congress Catalog Card Number: 2001089846
ISBN 0-345-44407-8

This edition published by arrangement with Fedogan & Bremer.

Cover illustration by John Jude Palencar
Cover design by Min Choi

Text design by Holly Johnson
Manufactured in the United States of America

First Ballantine Books Edition: September 2001
10  9  8  7  6  5  4  3  2  1

*For*
*Jim, Dave and Martin,*
*who give form to our dreams,*
*and substance to our nightmares*

# Contents

# Acknowledgments

Special thanks to Jo Fletcher, Bob Garcia and James Turner for their help, all the authors for their patience, and to Philip J. Rahman and Dwayne H. Olson, whose enthusiasm and support made this book possible.

# Introduction:
# Spawn of the Deep Ones

Howard Phillips Lovecraft is probably the most important and influential author of modern supernatural fiction. Lovecraft was born in 1890 and a life-long resident of Providence, Rhode Island, until his untimely death in 1937. Lovecraft's poems, essays and infrequent fiction received popular acclaim in the amateur press and through such pulp magazines as *Weird Tales* and *Astounding Stories.*

Many of his tales are set in the cosmic vistas that exist beyond time and space or in the fear-haunted towns of an imaginary area of Massachusetts. "The Shadow over Innsmouth" is indicative of the latter.

An integral part of several loosely connected stories that have since become identified as the Cthulhu Mythos (named after one of the gods of Lovecraft's eldritch pantheon), "The Shadow over Innsmouth" was written in 1931 and, at some 26,000 words, is one of the author's longest works.

The story re-introduces the reader to the decaying coastal town of Innsmouth (first mentioned in Lovecraft's early short tale "Celephais"), founded by merchant captain Obed Marsh who, in the 1840s, brought back a strange wife from the South Seas with a peculiarly fishy look. It is revealed that the Marshes intermarried with an ocean-dwelling race of humanoid beings called the Deep Ones, creating a species of batrachian hybrids, and the once-prosperous New England seaport has been gradually undermined by a decadent cult called The Esoteric Order of Dagon, committed to the service and ultimate resurrection of Great Cthulhu and other dark gods.

Lovecraft wasn't particularly pleased with the finished story, and in his usual self-deprecatory manner described it as "my own verbose and doubtful swan-song . . . as a sort of grand finale to my present prose period."

Despite the enthusiasm of his literary prodigy, August Derleth, who considered the tale "a dark, brooding story, typical of Lovecraft at his best," other correspondents were more critical, and the despondent author put the manuscript away and turned to other projects.

The typescript remained unpublished until 1936, when Lovecraft gave it to William L. Crawford, a friend of his from the United Amateur Press, who was starting his own publishing imprint. Crawford produced four hundred copies of *The Shadow over Innsmouth* and had half of these bound as a slim book illustrated by Frank Utpatel. Initially this volume was sold for $1.00 apiece, but Crawford managed to distribute only about 150 copies before he ran out of money and had to end his short publishing career. Nowadays it's not surprising that this book is a great rarity amongst collectors of Lovecraftania and commands high prices whenever a copy is occasionally offered for sale.

The story eventually reached a wider readership in *Weird Tales* for January 1942. Since then it has been published extensively and is today justly regarded as one of Lovecraft's finest tales of the macabre.

During his lifetime, Lovecraft strenuously encouraged other

writers to develop themes from the Cthulhu Mythos in their own work, and over the years such authors as Robert Bloch, Ramsey Campbell, August Derleth, Robert E. Howard, Stephen King, Frank Belknap Long, Brian Lumley, Clark Ashton Smith and Colin Wilson, to name only a few, have explored and enhanced his original concepts.

Many diverse hands have individualized ideas to be found in Lovecraft's fiction, and although a number of these stories have used the Deep Ones and their marvel-shadowed dwelling place, there has never before been an attempt to relate a fictional history of Innsmouth and its ichthyoid denizens.

Using H. P. Lovecraft's original novella as inspiration, the all-British contributors to this volume—including established masters of the genre and newer names—depict the dreadful decline of the Massachusetts seaport since the late 1920s: through the war years, the rock 'n' roll era, and the recent political upheavals in eastern Europe, into the modern scientific age and beyond.

In these stories, as the decades pass, Dagon's spawn spreads out from the American east coast to cast its shadow over the British Isles and European mainland, while Innsmouth itself undergoes a metamorphosis both startling and unexpected.

*Iä-R'lyeh! Cthulhu fhtagn! Iä! Iä!*

Stephen Jones,
London, England

# The Shadow over Innsmouth

## H. P. Lovecraft

## I

During the winter of 1927–28, officials of the Federal government made a strange and secret investigation of certain conditions in the ancient Massachusetts seaport of Innsmouth. The public first learned of it in February, when a vast series of raids and arrests occurred, followed by the deliberate burning and dynamiting—under suitable precautions—of an enormous number of crumbling, worm-eaten, and supposedly empty houses along the abandoned waterfront. Uninquiring souls let this occurrence pass as one of the major clashes in a spasmodic war on liquor.

Keener news-followers, however, wondered at the prodigious number of arrests, the abnormally large force of men used in making them, and the secrecy surrounding the disposal of the prisoners. No trials, or even definite charges, were reported; nor were any of the captives seen thereafter in the regular gaols of the nation. There were vague statements about disease and concentration camps, and later about dispersal in various naval and military prisons, but nothing positive ever developed. Innsmouth itself was left almost depopulated, and is even now only beginning to show signs of a sluggishly revived existence.

Complaints from many liberal organisations were met with long confidential discussions, and representatives were taken on trips to certain camps and prisons. As a result, these societies became surprisingly passive and reticent. Newspaper men were harder to manage, but seemed largely to cooperate with the government in the end. Only one paper—a tabloid always discounted because of its wild policy—mentioned the deep-diving submarine that discharged torpedoes downward in the marine abyss just beyond Devil Reef. That item, gathered by chance in a haunt of sailors, seemed indeed rather far-fetched; since the low, black reef lies a full mile and a half out from Innsmouth Harbour.

People around the county and in the nearby towns muttered a great deal among themselves, but said very little to the outer world. They had talked about dying and half-deserted Innsmouth for nearly a century, and nothing new could be wilder or more hideous than what they had whispered and hinted years before. Many things had taught them secretiveness, and there was now no need to exert pressure on them. Besides, they really knew very little; for wide salt marshes, desolate and unpeopled, keep neighbours off from Innsmouth on the landward side.

But at last I am going to defy the ban on speech about this thing. Results, I am certain, are so thorough that no public harm save a shock of repulsion could ever accrue from a hinting of what was found by those horrified raiders at Innsmouth. Besides, what was found might possibly have more than one explanation. I do not know just how much of the whole tale has been told even to me, and I have many reasons for not wishing to probe deeper. For my contact with this affair has been closer than that of any other layman, and I have carried away impressions which are yet to drive me to drastic measures.

It was I who fled frantically out of Innsmouth in the early morning hours of July 16, 1927, and whose frightened appeals for government inquiry and action brought on the whole reported episode. I was willing enough to stay mute while the affair was fresh and uncertain; but now that it is an old story, with public interest and curiosity gone, I have an odd craving to whisper about those few frightful hours in that ill-rumoured and evilly shadowed seaport of death and blasphemous abnormality. The mere telling helps me to restore confidence in my own faculties; to reassure myself that I was not simply the first to succumb to a contagious nightmare hallucination. It helps me, too, in making up my mind regarding a certain terrible step which lies ahead of me.

I never heard of Innsmouth till the day before I saw it for the first and—so far—last time. I was celebrating my coming of age by a tour of New England—sightseeing, antiquarian, and genealogical—and had planned to go directly from ancient Newburyport to Arkham, whence my mother's family was derived. I had no car, but was travelling by train, trolley, and motor-coach, always seeking the cheapest possible route. In Newburyport they told me that the steam train was the thing to take to Arkham; and it was only at the station ticket-office, when I demurred at the high fare, that I learned about Innsmouth. The stout, shrewd-faced agent, whose speech showed him to be no local man, seemed sympathetic toward my efforts at economy, and made a suggestion that none of my other informants had offered.

"You could take that old bus, I suppose," he said with a certain hesitation, "but it ain't thought much of hereabouts. It goes through Innsmouth—you may have heard about that—and so the people don't like it. Run by an Innsmouth fellow—Joe Sargent—but never gets any custom from here, or Arkham either, I guess. Wonder it keeps running at all. I s'pose it's cheap enough, but I never see more'n two or three people in it—nobody but those Innsmouth folks. Leaves the Square—front of Hammond's Drug Store—at 10 a.m. and 7 p.m. unless they've changed lately. Looks like a terrible rattletrap—I've never ben on it."

That was the first I ever heard of shadowed Innsmouth. Any reference to a town not shown on common maps or listed in recent guide-books would have interested me, and the agent's odd manner of allusion roused something like real curiosity. A town able to inspire such dislike in its neighbours, I thought, must be at least rather unusual, and worthy of a tourist's attention. If it came before Arkham I would stop off there—and so I asked the agent to tell me something about it. He was very deliberate, and spoke with an air of feeling slightly superior to what he said.

"Innsmouth? Well, it's a queer kind of a town down at the mouth of the Manuxet. Used to be almost a city—quite a port before the War of 1812—but all gone to pieces in the last hundred years or so. No railroad now—B. & M. never went through, and the branch line from Rowley was given up years ago.

"More empty houses than there are people, I guess, and no business to speak of except fishing and lobstering. Everybody trades mostly either here or in Arkham or Ipswich. Once they had quite a few mills, but nothing's left now except one gold refinery running on the leanest kind of part-time.

"That refinery, though, used to be a big thing, and Old Man Marsh, who owns it, must be richer'n Croesus. Queer old duck, though, and sticks mighty close in his home. He's supposed to have developed some skin disease or deformity late in life that makes him keep out of sight. Grandson of Captain Obed Marsh, who founded the business. His mother seems to've ben some kind of foreigner— they say a South Sea islander—so everybody raised Cain when he married an Ipswich girl fifty years ago. They always do that about Innsmouth people, and folks here and hereabouts always try to cover up any Innsmouth blood they have in 'em. But Marsh's children and grandchildren look just like anyone else so far's I can see. I've had 'em pointed out to me here—though, come to think of it, the elder children don't seem to be around lately. Never saw the old man.

"And why is everybody so down on Innsmouth? Well, young fellow, you mustn't take too much stock in what people around here say. They're hard to get started, but once they do get started they never let up. They've ben telling things about Innsmouth—whispering 'em, mostly—for the last hundred years, I guess, and I gather they're more scared than anything else. Some of the stories would make you laugh—about old Captain Marsh driving bargains with the devil and bringing imps out of hell to live in Innsmouth, or about some kind of devil-worship and awful sacrifices in some place near the wharves that people stumbled on around 1845 or thereabouts—but I come from Panton, Vermont, and that kind of story don't go down with me.

"You ought to hear, though, what some of the old-timers tell about the black reef off the coast—Devil Reef, they call it. It's well above water a good part of the time, and never much below it, but at that you could hardly call it an island. The story is that there's a whole legion of devils seen sometimes on that reef—sprawled about, or darting in and out of some kind of caves near the top. It's a rugged, uneven thing, a good bit over a mile out, and toward the end of shipping days sailors used to make big detours just to avoid it.

"That is, sailors that didn't hail from Innsmouth. One of the things they had against old Captain Marsh was that he was supposed to land on it sometimes at night when the tide was right. Maybe he did, for I dare say the rock formation was interesting, and it's just barely possible he was looking for pirate loot and maybe finding it; but there was talk of his dealing with demons there. Fact is, I guess on the whole it was really the Captain that gave the bad reputation to the reef.

"That was before the big epidemic of 1846, when over half the folks in Innsmouth was carried off. They never did quite figure out what the trouble was, but it was probably some foreign kind of disease brought from China or somewhere by the shipping. It surely was bad enough—there was riots over it, and all sorts of ghastly doings that I don't believe ever got outside of town—and it left the place in awful shape. Never came back—there can't be more'n 300 or 400 people living there now.

"But the real thing behind the way folks feel is simply race prejudice—and I don't say I'm blaming those that hold it. I hate those Innsmouth folks myself, and I wouldn't care to go to their town. I s'pose you know—though I can see you're a Westerner by your talk—what a lot our New England ships used to have to do with queer ports in Africa, Asia, the South Seas, and everywhere else, and what queer kinds of people they sometimes brought back with 'em. You've probably heard about the Salem man that came home with a Chinese wife, and maybe you know there's still a bunch of Fiji Islanders somewhere around Cape Cod.

"Well, there must be something like that back of the Innsmouth people. The place always was badly cut off from the rest of the country by marshes and creeks, and we can't be sure about the ins and outs of the matter; but it's pretty clear that old Captain Marsh must have brought home some odd specimens when he had all three of his ships in commission back in the twenties and thirties. There certainly is a strange kind of streak in the Innsmouth folks today—I don't know how to explain it, but it sort of makes you crawl. You'll notice a little in Sargent if you take his bus. Some of 'em have queer narrow heads with flat noses and bulgy, stary eyes that never seem to shut, and their skin ain't quite right. Rough and scabby, and the sides of their necks are all shrivelled or creased up. Get bald, too, very young. The older fellows look the worst—fact is, I don't believe I've ever seen a very old chap of that kind. Guess they must die of looking in the glass! Animals hate 'em—they used to have lots of horse trouble before autos came in.

"Nobody around here or in Arkham or Ipswich will have anything to do with 'em, and they act kind of offish themselves when they come to town or when anyone tries to fish on their grounds. Queer how fish are always thick off Innsmouth Harbour when there ain't any anywhere else around—but just try to fish there yourself and see how the folks chase you off! Those people used to come here on the railroad—walking and taking the train at Rowley after the branch was dropped—but now they use that bus.

"Yes, there's a hotel in Innsmouth—called the Gilman House—but I don't believe it can amount to much. I wouldn't advise you to try it. Better stay over here and take the ten o'clock bus tomorrow morning; then you can get an evening bus there for Arkham at eight o'clock. There was a factory inspector who stopped at the Gilman couple of years ago, and he had a lot of unpleasant hints about the place. Seems they get a queer crowd there, for this fellow heard voices in other rooms—though most of 'em was empty—that gave him the shivers. It was foreign talk, he thought, but he said the bad thing about it was the kind of voice that sometimes spoke. It sounded so unnatural—slopping-like, he said—that he didn't dare undress and go to sleep. Just waited up and lit out the first thing in the morning. The talk went on most all night.

"This fellow—Casey, his name was—had a lot to say about how the Innsmouth folks watched him and seemed kind of on guard. He found the Marsh refinery a queer place—it's in an old mill on the lower falls of the Manuxet. What he said tallied up with what I'd heard. Books in bad shape, and no clear account of any kind of dealings. You know it's always ben a kind of mystery where the Marshes get the gold they refine. They've never seemed to do much buying in that line, but years ago they shipped out an enormous lot of ingots.

"Used to be talk of a queer foreign kind of jewellery that the sailors and refinery men sometimes sold on the sly, or that was seen once or twice on some of the Marsh womenfolks. People allowed maybe old Captain Obed traded for it in some heathen port, especially since he was always ordering stacks of glass beads and trinkets such as seafaring men used to get for native trade. Others thought and still think he'd found an old pirate cache out on Devil Reef. But here's a funny thing. The old Captain's ben dead these sixty years, and there ain't ben a good-sized ship out of the place since the Civil War; but just the same the Marshes still keep on buying a few of those native trade things—mostly glass and rubber gewgaws, they tell me. Maybe the Innsmouth folks like 'em to look at themselves—Gawd knows they've gotten to be about as bad as South Sea cannibals and Guinea savages.

"That plague of '46 must have taken off the best blood in the place. Anyway, they're a doubtful lot now, and the Marshes and other rich folks are as bad as any. As I told you, there probably ain't more'n

400 people in the whole town in spite of all the streets they say there are. I guess they're what they call 'white trash' down South—lawless and sly, and full of secret doings. They get a lot of fish and lobsters and do exporting by truck. Queer how the fish swarm right there and nowhere else.

"Nobody can ever keep track of these people, and state school officials and census men have a devil of a time. You can bet that prying strangers ain't welcome around Innsmouth. I've heard personally of more'n one business or government man that's disappeared there, and there's loose talk of one who went crazy and is out at Danvers now. They must have fixed up some awful scare for that fellow.

"That's why I wouldn't go at night if I was you. I've never ben there and have no wish to go, but I guess a daytime trip couldn't hurt you—even though the people hereabouts will advise you not to make it. If you're just sightseeing, and looking for old-time stuff, Innsmouth ought to be quite a place for you."

And so I spent part of that evening at the Newburyport Public Library looking up data about Innsmouth. When I had tried to question the natives in the shops, the lunch room, the garages, and the fire station, I had found them even harder to get started than the ticket-agent had predicted; and realized that I could not spare the time to overcome their first instinctive reticences. They had a kind of obscure suspiciousness, as if there were something amiss with anyone too much interested in Innsmouth. At the Y.M.C.A., where I was stopping, the clerk merely discouraged my going to such a dismal, decadent place; and the people at the library showed much the same attitude. Clearly, in the eyes of the educated, Innsmouth was merely an exaggerated case of civic degeneration.

The Essex County histories on the library shelves had very little to say, except that the town was founded in 1643, noted for ship-building before the Revolution, a seat of great marine prosperity in the early nineteenth century, and later a minor factory centre using the Manuxet as power. The epidemic and riots of 1846 were very sparsely treated, as if they formed a discredit to the county.

References to decline were few, though the significance of the later record was unmistakable. After the Civil War all industrial life was confined to the Marsh Refining Company, and the marketing of gold ingots formed the only remaining bit of major commerce aside from the eternal fishing. That fishing paid less and less as the price of the commodity fell and large-scale corporations offered competition, but there was never a dearth of fish around Innsmouth Harbour. Foreigners seldom settled there, and there was some discreetly veiled evidence that a number of Poles and Portuguese who had tried it had been scattered in a peculiarly drastic fashion.

Most interesting of all was a glancing reference to the strange jewellery vaguely associated with Innsmouth. It had evidently impressed the whole countryside more than a little, for mention was made of specimens in the museum of Miskatonic University at Arkham, and in the display room of the Newburyport Historical Society. The fragmentary descriptions of these things were bald and prosaic, but they hinted to me an undercurrent of persistent strangeness. Something about them seemed so odd and provocative that I could not put them out of my mind, and despite the relative lateness of the hour I resolved to see the local sample—said to be a large, queerly proportioned thing evidently meant for a tiara—if it could possibly be arranged.

The librarian gave me a note of introduction to the curator of the Society, a Miss Anna Tilton, who lived nearby, and after a brief explanation that ancient gentlewoman was kind enough to pilot me into the closed building, since the hour was not outrageously late. The collection was a notable one indeed, but in my present mood I had eyes for nothing but the bizarre object which glistened in a corner cupboard under the electric lights.

It took no excessive sensitiveness to beauty to make me literally gasp at the strange, unearthly splendour of the alien, opulent phantasy that rested there on a purple velvet cushion. Even now I can hardly describe what I saw, though it was clearly enough a sort of tiara, as the description had said. It was tall in front, and with a very large and curiously irregular periphery, as if designed for a head of almost freakishly elliptical outline. The material seemed to be predominantly gold, though a weird, lighter lustrousness hinted at some strange alloy with an equally beautiful and scarcely identifiable metal. Its condition was almost perfect, and one could have spent hours in studying the striking and puzzlingly untraditional designs—some simply geometrical, and some plainly marine—chased or moulded in high relief on its surface with a craftsmanship of incredible skill and grace.

The longer I looked, the more the thing fascinated me; and in this fascination there was a curiously disturbing element hardly to be classified or accounted for. At first I decided that it was the queer other-worldly quality of the art which made me uneasy. All other art objects I had ever seen either belonged to some known racial or national stream, or else were consciously modernistic defiances of every recognised stream. This tiara was neither. It clearly belonged to some settled technique of infinite maturity and perfection, yet that technique was utterly remote from any—Eastern or Western, ancient or modern—which I had ever heard of or seen exemplified. It was as if the workmanship were that of another planet.

However, I soon saw that my uneasiness had a second and perhaps equally potent source residing in the pictorial and mathematical suggestions of the strange designs. The patterns all hinted of remote secrets and unimaginable abysses in time and space, and the monotonously aquatic nature of the reliefs became almost sinister. Among these reliefs were fabulous monsters of abhorrent grotesqueness and malignity—half ichthyic and half batrachian in suggestion—which one could not dissociate from a certain haunting and uncomfortable sense of pseudomemory, as if they called up some image from deep cells and tissues whose retentive functions are wholly primal and awesomely ancestral. At times I fancied that every contour of these blasphemous fish-frogs was overflowing with the ultimate quintessence of unknown and inhuman evil.

In odd contrast to the tiara's aspect was its brief and prosy history as related by Miss Tilton. It had been pawned for a ridiculous sum at a shop in State Street in 1873, by a drunken Innsmouth man, shortly afterward killed in a brawl. The Society had acquired it directly from the pawnbroker, at once giving it a display worthy of its quality. It was labelled as of probable East-Indian or Indo-Chinese provenance, though the attribution was frankly tentative.

Miss Tilton, comparing all possible hypotheses regarding its origin and its presence in New England, was inclined to believe that it formed part of some exotic pirate hoard discovered by old Captain Obed Marsh. This view was surely not weakened by the insistent offers of purchase at a high price which the Marshes began to make as soon as they knew of its presence, and which they repeated to this day despite the Society's unvarying determination not to sell.

As the good lady showed me out of the building she made it clear that the pirate theory of the Marsh fortune was a popular one among the intelligent people of the region. Her own attitude toward shadowed Innsmouth—which she had never seen—was one of disgust at a community slipping far down the cultural scale, and she assured me that the rumours of devil-worship were partly justified by a peculiar secret cult which had gained force there and engulfed all the orthodox churches.

It was called, she said, "The Esoteric Order of Dagon," and was undoubtedly a debased, quasi-pagan thing imported from the East a century before, at a time when the Innsmouth fisheries seemed to be going barren. Its persistence among a simple people was quite natural in view of the sudden and permanent return of abundantly fine fishing, and it soon came to be the greatest influence on the town, replacing Freemasonry altogether and taking up headquarters in the old Masonic Hall on New Church Green.

All this, to the pious Miss Tilton, formed an excellent reason for shunning the ancient town of decay and desolation; but to me it was merely a fresh incentive. To my architectural and historical anticipations was now added an acute anthropological zeal, and I could scarcely sleep in my small room at the "Y" as the night wore away.

## II

Shortly before ten the next morning I stood with one small valise in front of Hammond's Drug Store in old Market Square waiting for the Innsmouth bus. As the hour for its arrival drew near I noticed a general drift of the loungers to other places up the street, or to the Ideal Lunch across the square. Evidently the ticket-agent had not exaggerated the dislike which local people bore toward Innsmouth and its denizens. In a few moments a small motor-coach of extreme decrepitude and dirty grey colour rattled down State Street, made a turn, and drew up at the curb beside me. I felt immediately that it was the right one; a guess which the half-illegible sign on the windshield—"Arkham-Innsmouth-Newb'port"—soon verified.

There were only three passengers—dark, unkempt men of sullen visage and somewhat youthful cast—and when the vehicle stopped they clumsily shambled out and began walking up State Street in a silent, almost furtive fashion. The driver also alighted, and I watched him as he went into the drug store to make some purchase. This, I reflected, must be the Joe Sargent mentioned by the ticket-agent; and even before I noticed any details there spread over me a wave of spontaneous aversion which could be neither checked nor explained. It suddenly struck me as very natural that the local people should not wish to ride on a bus owned and driven by this man, or to visit any oftener than possible the habitat of such a man and his kinsfolk.

When the driver came out of the store I looked at him more carefully and tried to determine the source of my evil impression. He was a thin, stoop-shouldered man not much under six feet tall, dressed in shabby blue civilian clothes and wearing a frayed grey golf cap. His age was perhaps thirty-five, but the odd, deep creases in the sides of his neck made him seem older when one did not study his dull, expressionless face. He had a narrow head, bulging, watery blue eyes that seemed never to wink, a flat nose, a receding forehead and chin, and singularly undeveloped ears. His long, thick lip and coarse-pored, greyish cheeks seemed almost beardless except for some sparse yellow hairs that straggled and curled in irregular patches; and in places the surface seemed queerly irregular, as if peeling from some cutaneous disease. His hands were large and heavily veined, and had a very unusual greyish-blue tinge. The fingers were strikingly short in proportion to the rest of the structure, and seemed to have a tendency to curl closely into the huge palm. As he walked toward the bus I observed his peculiarly shambling gait and saw that his feet were inordinately immense. The more I studied them the more I wondered how he could buy any shoes to fit them.

A certain greasiness about the fellow increased my dislike. He was evidently given to working or lounging around the fish docks, and carried with him much of their characteristic smell. Just what foreign blood was in him I could not even guess. His oddities certainly did not look Asiatic, Polynesian, Levantine, or Negroid, yet I could see why the people found him alien. I myself would have thought of biological degeneration rather than alienage.

I was sorry when I saw that there would be no other passengers on the bus. Somehow I did not like the idea of riding alone with this driver. But as leaving time obviously approached I conquered my qualms and followed the man aboard, extending him a dollar bill and murmuring the single word "Innsmouth." He looked curiously at me for a second as he returned forty cents change without speaking. I took a seat far behind him, but on the same side of the bus, since I wished to watch the shore during the journey.

At length the decrepit vehicle started with a jerk, and rattled noisily past the old brick buildings of State Street amidst a cloud of vapour from the exhaust. Glancing at the people on the sidewalks, I thought I detected in them a curious wish to avoid looking at the bus—or at least a wish to avoid seeming to look at it. Then we turned to the left into High Street, where the going was smoother; flying by stately old mansions of the early republic and still older colonial farmhouses, passing the Lower Green and Parker River, and finally emerging into a long, monotonous stretch of open shore country.

The day was warm and sunny, but the landscape of sand, sedge-grass, and stunted shrubbery became more and more desolate as we proceeded. Out the window I could see the blue water and the sandy line of Plum Island, and we presently drew very near the beach as our narrow road veered off from the main highway to Rowley and Ipswich. There were no visible houses, and I could tell by the state of the road that traffic was very light hereabouts. The small, weather-worn telephone poles carried only two wires. Now and then we crossed crude wooden bridges over tidal creeks that wound far inland and promoted the general isolation of the region.

Once in a while I noticed dead stumps and crumbling foundation-walls above the drifting sand, and recalled the old tradition quoted in one of the histories I had read, that this was once a fertile and thickly settled countryside. The change, it was said, came simultaneously with the Innsmouth epidemic of 1846, and was thought by simple folk to have a dark connection with hidden forces of evil. Actually, it was caused by the unwise cutting of woodlands near the shore, which robbed the soil of its best protection and opened the way for waves of wind-blown sand.

At last we lost sight of Plum Island and saw the vast expanse of the open Atlantic on our left. Our narrow course began to climb steeply, and I felt a singular sense of disquiet in looking at the lonely crest ahead where the rutted roadway met the sky. It was as if the bus were about to keep on in its ascent, leaving the sane earth altogether and merging with the unknown arcana of upper air and cryptical sky. The smell of the sea took on ominous implications, and the silent driver's bent, rigid back and narrow head became more and more hateful. As I looked at him I saw that the back of his head was almost as hairless as his face, having only a few straggling yellow strands upon a grey scabrous surface.

Then we reached the crest and beheld the outspread valley beyond, where the Manuxet joins the sea just north of the long line of cliffs that culminate in Kingsport Head and veer off toward Cape Ann. On the far, misty horizon I could just make out the dizzy profile of the Head, topped by the queer ancient house of which so many legends are told; but for the moment all my attention was captured by the nearer panorama just below me. I had, I realized, come face to face with rumour-shadowed Innsmouth.

It was a town of wide extent and dense construction, yet one with a portentous dearth of visible life. From the tangle of chimney-pots scarcely a wisp of smoke came, and the three tall steeples loomed stark and unpainted against the seaward horizon. One of them was crumbling down at the top, and in that and another there were only black gaping holes where clock-dials should have been. The vast huddle of sagging gambrel roofs and peaked gables conveyed with offensive clearness the idea of wormy decay, and as we approached along the now descending road I could see that many roofs had wholly caved in. There were some large square Georgian houses, too, with hipped roofs, cupolas, and railed "widow's walks." These were mostly well back from the water, and one or two seemed to be in moderately sound condition. Stretching inland from among them I saw the rusted, grass-grown line of the abandoned railway, with leaning telegraph-poles now devoid of wires, and the half-obscured lines of the old carriage roads to Rowley and Ipswich.

The decay was worst close to the waterfront, though in its very midst I could spy the white belfry of a fairly well-preserved brick structure which looked like a small factory. The harbour, long clogged with sand, was enclosed by an ancient stone breakwater; on which I could begin to discern the minute forms of a few seated fishermen, and at whose end were what looked like the foundations of a bygone lighthouse. A sandy tongue had formed inside this barrier, and upon it I saw a few decrepit cabins, moored dories, and scattered lobster-pots. The only deep water seemed to be where the river poured out past the belfried structure and turned southward to join the ocean at the breakwater's end.

Here and there the ruins of wharves jutted out from the shore to end in indeterminate rottenness, those farthest south seeming the most decayed. And far out at sea, despite a high tide, I glimpsed a long, black line scarcely rising above the water yet carrying a suggestion of odd latent malignancy. This, I knew, must be Devil Reef. As I looked, a subtle, curious sense of beckoning seemed super-added to the grim repulsion; and oddly enough, I found this overtone more disturbing than the primary impression.

We met no one on the road, but presently began to pass deserted farms in varying stages of ruin. Then I noticed a few inhabited houses with rags stuffed in the broken windows and shells and dead fish lying about the littered yards. Once or twice I saw listless-looking people working in barren gardens or digging clams on the fishy-smelling beach below, and groups of dirty, simian-visaged children playing around weed-grown doorsteps. Somehow these people seemed more disquieting than the dismal buildings, for almost every one had certain peculiarities of face and motions which I instinctively disliked without being able to define or comprehend them. For a second I thought this typical physique suggested some picture I had seen, perhaps in a book, under circumstances of particular horror or melancholy; but this pseudo-recollection passed very quickly.

As the bus reached a lower level I began to catch the steady note of a waterfall through the unnatural stillness. The leaning, unpainted houses grew thicker, lined both sides of the road, and displayed more urban tendencies than did those we were leaving behind. The panorama ahead had contracted to a street scene, and in spots I could see where a cobblestone pavement and stretches of brick sidewalk had formerly existed. All the houses were apparently deserted, and there were occasional gaps where tumbledown chimneys and cellar walls told of buildings that had collapsed. Pervading everything was the most nauseous fishy odour imaginable.

Soon cross streets and junctions began to appear; those on the left leading to shoreward realms of unpaved squalor and decay, while those on the right showed vistas of departed grandeur. So far I had seen no people in the town, but there now came signs of a sparse habitation—curtained windows here and there, and an occasional battered motorcar at the curb. Pavement and sidewalks were increasingly well defined, and though most of the houses were quite old— wood and brick structures of the early nineteenth century—they were obviously kept fit for habitation. As an amateur antiquarian I almost lost my olfactory disgust and my feeling of menace and repulsion amidst this rich, unaltered survival from the past.

But I was not to reach my destination without one very strong impression of poignantly disagreeable quality. The bus had come to a sort of open concourse or radial point with churches on two sides and the bedraggled remains of a circular green in the centre, and I was looking at a large pillared hall on the right-hand junction ahead. The structure's once white paint was now grey and peeling, and the black and gold sign on the pediment was so faded that I could only with difficulty make out the words "Esoteric Order of Dagon." This, then, was the former Masonic Hall now given over to a degraded cult. As I strained to decipher this inscription my notice was distracted by the raucous tones of a cracked bell across the street, and I quickly turned to look out the window on my own side of the coach.

The sound came from a squat-towered stone church of manifestly later date than most of the houses, built in a clumsy Gothic fashion and having a disproportionately high basement with shuttered windows. Though the hands of its clock were missing on the side I glimpsed, I knew that those hoarse strokes were telling the hour of eleven. Then suddenly all thoughts of time were blotted out by an onrushing image of sharp intensity and unaccountable horror which had seized me before I knew what it really was. The door of the church basement was open, revealing a rectangle of blackness inside. And as I looked, a certain object crossed or seemed to cross that dark rectangle; burning into my brain a momentary conception of nightmare which was all the more maddening because analysis could not show a single nightmarish quality in it.

It was a living object—the first except the driver that I had seen since entering the compact part of the town—and had I been in a steadier mood I would have found nothing whatever of terror in it. Clearly, as I realized a moment later, it was the pastor; clad in some peculiar vestments doubtless introduced since the Order of Dagon had modified the ritual of the local churches. The thing which had probably caught my first subconscious glance and supplied the touch of bizarre horror was the tall tiara he wore; an almost exact duplicate of the one Miss Tilton had shown me the previous evening. This, acting on my imagination, had supplied namelessly sinister qualities to the indeterminate face and robed, shambling form beneath it. There was not, I soon decided, any reason why I should have felt that shuddering touch of evil pseudo-memory. Was it not natural that a local mystery cult should adopt among its regimentals a unique type of head-dress made familiar to the community in some strange way—perhaps as treasure-trove?

A very thin sprinkling of repellent-looking youngish people now became visible on the sidewalks—lone individuals, and silent knots of two or three. The lower floors of the crumbling houses sometimes harboured small shops with dingy signs, and I noticed a parked truck or two as we rattled along. The sound of waterfalls became more and more distinct, and presently I saw a fairly deep river-gorge ahead, spanned by a wide, iron-railed highway bridge beyond which a large square opened out. As we clanked over the bridge I looked out on both sides and observed some factory buildings on the edge of the grassy bluff or part way down. The water far below was very abundant, and I could see two vigorous sets of falls upstream on my right and at least one downstream on my left. From this point the noise was quite deafening. Then we rolled into the large semicircular square across the river and drew up on the right-hand side in front of a tall, cupola-crowned building with remnants of yellow paint and with a half-effaced sign proclaiming it to be the Gilman House.

I was glad to get out of that bus, and at once proceeded to check my valise in the shabby hotel lobby. There was only one person in sight—an elderly man without what I had come to call the "Innsmouth look"—and I decided not to ask him any of the questions which bothered me; remembering that odd things had been noticed in this hotel. Instead, I strolled out on the square, from which the bus had already gone, and studied the scene minutely and appraisingly.

One side of the cobblestoned open space was the straight line of the river; the other was a semicircle of slant-roofed brick buildings of about the 1800 period, from which several streets radiated away to the southeast, south, and southwest. Lamps were depressingly few and small—all low-powered incandescents—and I was glad that my plans called for departure before dark, even though I knew the moon would be bright. The buildings were all in fair condition, and included perhaps a dozen shops in current operation; of which one was a grocery of the First National chain, others a dismal restaurant, a drug store, and a wholesale fish-dealer's office, and still another, at the eastern extremity of the square near the river, an office of the town's only industry—the Marsh Refining Company. There were perhaps ten people visible, and four or five automobiles and motor trucks stood scattered about. I did not need to be told that this was the civic centre of Innsmouth. Eastward I could catch blue glimpses of the harbour, against which rose the decaying remains of three once beautiful Georgian steeples. And toward the shore on the opposite bank of the river I saw the white belfry surmounting what I took to be the Marsh refinery.

For some reason or other I chose to make my first inquiries at the chain grocery, whose personnel was not likely to be native to Innsmouth. I found a solitary boy of about seventeen in charge, and was pleased to note the brightness and affability which promised cheerful information. He seemed exceptionally eager to talk, and I soon gathered that he did not like the place, its fishy smell, or its furtive people. A word with any outsider was a relief to him. He hailed from Arkham, boarded with a family who came from Ipswich, and went back home whenever he got a moment off. His family did not like him to work in Innsmouth, but the chain had transferred him there and he did not wish to give up his job.

There was, he said, no public library or chamber of commerce in Innsmouth, but I could probably find my way about. The street I had come down was Federal. West of that were the fine old residence streets—Broad, Washington, Lafayette, and Adams—and east of it were the shoreward slums. It was in these slums—along Main Street—that I would find the old Georgian churches, but they were all long abandoned. It would be well not to make oneself too conspicuous in such neighbourhoods—especially north of the river— since the people were sullen and hostile. Some strangers had even disappeared.

Certain spots were almost forbidden territory, as he had learned at considerable cost. One must not, for example, linger much around the Marsh refinery, or around any of the still used churches, or around the pillared Order of Dagon Hall at New Church Green. Those churches were very odd—all violently disavowed by their respective denominations elsewhere, and apparently using the queerest kind of ceremonials and clerical vestments. Their creeds were heterodox and mysterious, involving hints of certain marvelous transformations leading to bodily immortality—of a sort—on this earth. The youth's own pastor—Dr. Wallace of the Asbury M. E. Church in Arkham—had gravely urged him not to join any church in Innsmouth.

As for the Innsmouth people—the youth hardly knew what to make of them. They were as furtive and seldom seen as animals that live in burrows, and one could hardly imagine how they passed the time apart from their desultory fishing. Perhaps—judging from the quantities of bootleg liquor they consumed—they lay for most of the daylight hours in an alcoholic stupor. They seemed sullenly banded together in some sort of fellowship and understanding—despising the world as if they had access to other and preferable spheres of entity. Their appearance—especially those staring, unwinking eyes which one never saw shut—was certainly shocking enough; and their voices were disgusting. It was awful to hear them chanting in their churches at night, and especially during their main festivals or revivals, which fell twice a year on April 30th and October 31st.

They were very fond of the water, and swam a great deal in both river and harbour. Swimming races out to Devil Reef were very common, and everyone in sight seemed well able to share in this arduous sport. When one came to think of it, it was generally only rather young people who were seen about in public, and of these the oldest were apt to be the most tainted-looking. When exceptions did occur, they were mostly persons with no trace of aberrancy, like the old clerk at the hotel. One wondered what became of the bulk of the older folk, and whether the "Innsmouth look" were not a strange and insidious disease-phenomenon which increased its hold as years advanced.

Only a very rare affliction, of course, could bring about such vast and radical anatomical changes in a single individual after maturity—changes involving osseous factors as basic as the shape of the skull—but then, even this aspect was no more baffling and unheard-of than the visible features of the malady as a whole. It would be hard, the youth implied, to form any real conclusions regarding such a matter; since one never came to know the natives personally no matter how long one might live in Innsmouth.

The youth was certain that many specimens even worse than the worst visible ones were kept locked indoors in some places. People sometimes heard the queerest kind of sounds. The tottering waterfront hovels north of the river were reputedly connected by hidden tunnels, being thus a veritable warren of unseen abnormalities. What kind of foreign blood—if any—these beings had, it was impossible to tell. They sometimes kept certain especially repulsive characters out of sight when government agents and others from the outside world came to town.

It would be of no use, my informant said, to ask the natives anything about the place. The only one who would talk was a very aged but normal-looking man who lived at the poorhouse on the north rim of the town and spent his time walking about or lounging around the fire station. This hoary character, Zadok Allen, was ninety-six years old and somewhat touched in the head, besides being the town drunkard. He was a strange, furtive creature who constantly looked over his shoulder as if afraid of something, and when sober could not be persuaded to talk at all with strangers. He was, however, unable to resist any offer of his favourite poison; and once drunk would furnish the most astonishing fragments of whispered reminiscence.

After all, though, little useful data could be gained from him; since his stories were all insane, incomplete hints of impossible marvels and horrors which could have no source save in his own disordered fancy. Nobody ever believed him, but the natives did not like him to drink and talk with strangers; and it was not always safe to be seen questioning him. It was probably from him that some of the wildest popular whispers and delusions were derived.

Several non-native residents had reported monstrous glimpses from time to time, but between old Zadok's tales and the malformed denizens it was no wonder such illusions were current. None of the non-natives ever stayed out late at night, there being a widespread impression that it was not wise to do so. Besides, the streets were loathsomely dark.

As for business—the abundance of fish was certainly almost uncanny, but the natives were taking less and less advantage of it. Moreover, prices were falling and competition was growing. Of course the town's real business was the refinery, whose commercial office was on the square only a few doors east of where we stood. Old Man Marsh was never seen, but sometimes went to the works in a closed, curtained car.

There were all sorts of rumours about how Marsh had come to look. He had once been a great dandy, and people said he still wore the frock-coated finery of the Edwardian age, curiously adapted to certain deformities. His sons had formerly conducted the office in the square, but latterly they had been keeping out of sight a good deal and leaving the brunt of affairs to the younger generation. The sons and their sisters had come to look very queer, especially the elder ones; and it was said that their health was failing.

One of the Marsh daughters was a repellent, reptilian-looking woman who wore an excess of weird jewellery clearly of the same exotic tradition as that to which the strange tiara belonged. My informant had noticed it many times, and had heard it spoken of as coming from some secret hoard, either of pirates or of demons. The clergymen—or priests, or whatever they were called nowadays—also wore this kind of ornament as a head-dress; but one seldom caught glimpses of them. Other specimens the youth had not seen, though many were rumoured to exist around Innsmouth.

The Marshes, together with the other three gently bred families of the town—the Waites, the Gilmans, and the Eliots—were all very retiring. They lived in immense houses along Washington Street, and several were reputed to harbour in concealment certain living kinsfolk whose personal aspect forbade public view, and whose deaths had been reported and recorded.

Warning me that many of the street signs were down, the youth drew for my benefit a rough but ample and painstaking sketch map of the town's salient features. After a moment's study I felt sure that it would be of great help, and pocketed it with profuse thanks. Disliking the dinginess of the single restaurant I had seen, I bought a fair supply of cheese crackers and ginger wafers to serve as a lunch later on. My programme, I decided, would be to thread the principal streets, talk with any non-native I might encounter, and catch the eight o'clock coach for Arkham. The town, I could see, formed a significant and exaggerated example of communal decay; but being no sociologist I would limit my serious observations to the field of architecture.

Thus I began my systematic though half-bewildered tour of Innsmouth's narrow, shadow-blighted ways. Crossing the bridge and turning toward the roar of the lower falls, I passed close to the Marsh refinery, which seemed oddly free from the noise of industry. This building stood on the steep river bluff near a bridge and an open confluence of streets which I took to be the earliest civic centre, displaced after the Revolution by the present Town Square.

Re-crossing the gorge on the Main Street bridge, I struck a region of utter desertion which somehow made me shudder. Collapsing huddles of gambrel roofs formed a jagged and fantastic skyline above which rose the ghoulish, decapitated steeple of an ancient church. Some houses along Main Street were tenanted, but most were tightly boarded up. Down unpaved side streets I saw the black, gaping windows of deserted hovels, many of which leaned at perilous and incredible angles through the sinking of part of the foundations. Those windows stared so spectrally that it took courage to turn eastward toward the waterfront. Certainly, the terror of a deserted house swells in geometrical rather than arithmetical progression as houses multiply to form a city of stark desolation. The sight of such endless avenues of fishy-eyed vacancy and death, and the thought of such linked infinities of black, brooding compartments given over to cobwebs and memories and the conqueror worm, start up vestigial fears and aversions that not even the stoutest philosophy can disperse.

Fish Street was as deserted as Main, though it differed in having many brick and stone warehouses still in excellent shape. Water Street was almost its duplicate, save that there were great seaward gaps where wharves had been. Not a living thing did I see, except for the scattered fishermen on the distant breakwater, and not a sound did I hear save the lapping of the harbour tides and the roar of the falls in the Manuxet. The town was getting more and more on my nerves, and I looked behind me furtively as I picked my way back over the tottering Water Street bridge. The Fish Street bridge, according to the sketch, was in ruins.

North of the river there were traces of squalid life—active fish-packing houses in Water Street, smoking chimneys and patched roofs here and there, occasional sounds from indeterminate sources, and infrequent shambling forms in the dismal streets and unpaved lanes—but I seemed to find this even more oppressive than the southerly desertion. For one thing, the people were more hideous and abnormal than those near the centre of the town; so that I was several times evilly reminded of something utterly fantastic which I could not quite place. Undoubtedly the alien strain in the Innsmouth folk was stronger here than farther inland—unless, indeed, the "Innsmouth look" were a disease rather than a blood strain, in which case this district might be held to harbour the more advanced cases.

One detail that annoyed me was the distribution of the few faint sounds I heard. They ought naturally to have come wholly from the visibly inhabited houses, yet in reality were often strongest inside the most rigidly boarded-up façades. There were creakings, scurryings, and hoarse doubtful noises; and I thought uncomfortably about the hidden tunnels suggested by the grocery boy. Suddenly I found myself wondering what the voices of those denizens would be like. I had heard no speech so far in this quarter, and was unaccountably anxious not to do so.

Pausing only long enough to look at two fine but ruinous old churches at Main and Church Streets, I hastened out of that vile waterfront slum. My next logical goal was New Church Green, but somehow or other I could not bear to repass the church in whose basement I had glimpsed the inexplicably frightening form of that strangely diademed priest or pastor. Besides, the grocery youth had told me that the churches, as well as the Order of Dagon Hall, were not advisable neighbourhoods for strangers.

Accordingly I kept north along Main to Martin, then turning inland, crossing Federal Street safely north of the Green, and entering the decayed patrician neighbourhood of northern Broad, Washington, Lafayette, and Adams Streets. Though these stately old avenues were ill-surfaced and unkempt, their elm-shaded dignity had not entirely departed. Mansion after mansion claimed my gaze, most of them decrepit and boarded up amidst neglected grounds, but one or two in each street showing signs of occupancy. In Washington Street there was a row of four or five in excellent repair and with finely tended lawns and gardens. The most sumptuous of these— with wide terraced parterres extending back the whole way to Lafayette Street—I took to be the home of Old Man Marsh, the afflicted refinery owner.

In all these streets no living thing was visible, and I wondered at the complete absence of cats and dogs from Innsmouth. Another thing which puzzled and disturbed me, even in some of the best-preserved mansions, was the tightly shuttered condition of many third-story and attic windows. Furtiveness and secretiveness seemed universal in this hushed city of alienage and death, and I could not escape the sensation of being watched from ambush on every hand by sly, staring eyes that never shut.

I shivered as the cracked stroke of three sounded from a belfry on my left. Too well did I recall the squat church from which those notes came. Following Washington Street toward the river, I now faced a new zone of former industry and commerce; noting the ruins of a factory ahead, and seeing others, with the traces of an old railway station and covered railway bridge beyond, up the gorge on my right.

The uncertain bridge now before me was posted with a warning sign, but I took the risk and crossed again to the south bank where traces of life reappeared. Furtive, shambling creatures stared cryptically in my direction, and more normal faces eyed me coldly and curiously. Innsmouth was rapidly becoming intolerable, and I turned down Paine Street toward the Square in the hope of getting some vehicle to take me to Arkham before the still-distant starting-time of that sinister bus.

It was then that I saw the tumbledown fire station on my left, and noticed the red-faced, bushy-bearded, watery-eyed old man in nondescript rags who sat on a bench in front of it talking with a pair of unkempt but not abnormal-looking firemen. This, of course, must be Zadok Allen, the half-crazed, liquorish nonagenarian whose tales of old Innsmouth and its shadow were so hideous and incredible.

## III

It must have been some imp of the perverse—or some sardonic pull from dark, hidden sources—which made me change my plans as I did. I had long before resolved to limit my observations to architecture alone, and I was even then hurrying toward the Square in an effort to get quick transportation out of this festering city of death and decay; but the sight of old Zadok Allen set up new currents in my mind and made me slacken my pace uncertainly.

I had been assured that the old man could do nothing but hint at wild, disjointed, and incredible legends, and I had been warned that the natives made it unsafe to be seen talking with him; yet the thought of this aged witness to the town's decay, with memories going back to the early days of ships and factories, was a lure that no amount of reason could make me resist. After all, the strangest and maddest of myths are often merely symbols or allegories based upon truth—and old Zadok must have seen everything which went on around Innsmouth for the last ninety years. Curiosity flared up beyond sense and caution, and in my youthful egotism I fancied I might be able to sift a nucleus of real history from the confused, extravagant outpouring I would probably extract with the aid of raw whiskey.

I knew that I could not accost him then and there, for the firemen would surely notice and object. Instead, I reflected, I would prepare by getting some bootleg liquor at a place where the grocery boy had told me it was plentiful. Then I would loaf near the fire station in apparent casualness, and fall in with old Zadok after he had started on one of his frequent rambles. The youth had said that he was very restless, seldom sitting around the station for more than an hour or two at a time.

A quart bottle of whiskey was easily, though not cheaply, obtained in the rear of a dingy variety-store just off the Square in Eliot

Street. The dirty-looking fellow who waited on me had a touch of the staring "Innsmouth look," but was quite civil in his way; being perhaps used to the custom of such convivial strangers—truckmen, gold-buyers, and the like—as were occasionally in town.

Reentering the Square I saw that luck was with me; for—shuffling out of Paine Street around the corner of the Gilman House—I glimpsed nothing less than the tall, lean, tattered form of old Zadok Allen himself. In accordance with my plan, I attracted his attention by brandishing my newly purchased bottle; and soon realised that he had begun to shuffle wistfully after me as I turned into Waite Street on my way to the most deserted region I could think of.

I was steering my course by the map the grocery boy had prepared, and was aiming for the wholly abandoned stretch of southern waterfront which I had previously visited. The only people in sight there had been the fishermen on the distant breakwater; and by going a few squares south I could get beyond the range of these, finding a pair of seats on some abandoned wharf and being free to question old Zadok unobserved for an indefinite time. Before I reached Main Street I could hear a faint and wheezy "Hey, Mister!" behind me, and I presently allowed the old man to catch up and take copious pulls from the quart bottle.

I began putting out feelers as we walked along to Water Street and turned southward amidst the omnipresent desolation and crazily tilted ruins, but found that the aged tongue did not loosen as quickly as I had expected. At length I saw a grass-grown opening toward the sea between crumbling brick walls, with the weedy length of an earth-and-masonry wharf projecting beyond. Piles of moss-covered stones near the water promised tolerable seats, and the scene was sheltered from all possible view by a ruined warehouse on the north. Here, I thought, was the ideal place for a long secret colloquy; so I guided my companion down the lane and picked out spots to sit in among the mossy stones. The air of death and desertion was ghoulish, and the smell of fish almost insufferable; but I was resolved to let nothing deter me.

About four hours remained for conversation if I were to catch the eight o'clock coach for Arkham, and I began to dole out more liquor to the ancient tippler; meanwhile eating my own frugal lunch. In my donations I was careful not to overshoot the mark, for I did not wish Zadok's vinous garrulousness to pass into a stupor. After an hour his furtive taciturnity showed signs of disappearing, but much to my disappointment he still sidetracked my questions about Innsmouth and its shadow-haunted past. He would babble of current topics, revealing a wide acquaintance with newspapers and a great tendency to philosophise in a sententious village fashion.

Toward the end of the second hour I feared my quart of whiskey would not be enough to produce results, and was wondering whether I had better leave old Zadok and go back for more. Just then, however, chance made the opening which my questions had been unable to make; and the wheezing ancient's rambling took a turn that caused me to lean forward and listen alertly. My back was toward the fishy-smelling sea, but he was facing it, and something or other had caused his wandering gaze to light on the low, distant line of Devil Reef, then showing plainly and almost fascinatingly above the waves. The sight seemed to displease him, for he began a series of weak curses which ended in a confidential whisper and a knowing leer. He bent toward me, took hold of my coat lapel, and hissed out some hints that could not be mistaken.

"That's whar it all begun—that cursed place of all wickedness whar the deep water starts. Gate o' hell—sheer drop daown to a bottom no saoundin'-line kin tech. Ol' Cap'n Obed done it—him that faound aout more'n was good fer him in the Saouth Sea islands.

"Everybody was in a bad way them days. Trade fallin' off, mills losin' business—even the new ones—an' the best of our menfolks kilt a-privateerin' in the War of 1812 or lost with the *Elizy* brig an' the *Ranger* scow—both on 'em Gilman venters. Obed Marsh he had three ships afloat—brigantine *Columby*, brig *Hetty*, an' barque *Sumatry Queen*. He was the only one as kep' on with the East-Injy an' Pacific trade, though Esdras Martin's barkentine *Malay Pride* made a venter as late as 'twenty-eight.

"Never was nobody like Cap'n Obed—old limb o' Satan! Heh,

heh! I kin mind him a-tellin' abaout furren parts, an' callin' all the folks stupid fer goin' to Christian meetin' an' bearin' their burdens meek an' lowly. Says they'd orter git better gods like some o' the folks in the Injies—gods as ud bring 'em good fishin' in return for their sacrifices, an' ud reely answer folks's prayers.

"Matt Eliot, his fust mate, talked a lot, too, only he was agin' folks's doin' any heathen things. Told abaout an island east of Otha-heite whar they was a lot o' stone ruins older'n anybody knew any-thing abaout, kind o' like them on Ponape, in the Carolines, but with carvin's of faces that looked like the big statues on Easter Island. They was a little volcanic island near thar, too, whar they was other ruins with diff'rent carvin's—ruins all wore away like they'd ben under the sea onct, an' with picters of awful monsters all over 'em.

"Wal, Sir, Matt he says the natives araound thar had all the fish they cud ketch, an' sported bracelets an' armlets an' head rigs made aout of a queer kind o' gold an' covered with picters o' monsters jest like the ones carved over the ruins on the little island—sorter fish-like frogs or frog-like fishes that was drawed in all kinds o' positions like they was human bein's. Nobody cud git aout o' them whar they got all the stuff, an' all the other natives wondered haow they managed to find fish in plenty even when the very next islands had lean pickin's. Matt he got to wonderin' too, an' so did Cap'n Obed. Obed he notices, besides, that lots of the han'some young folks ud drop aout o' sight fer good from year to year, an' that they wa'n't many old folks araound. Also, he thinks some of the folks looks durned queer even fer Kanakys.

"It took Obed to git the truth aout o' them heathen. I dun't know haow he done it, but he begun by tradin' fer the gold-like things they wore. Ast 'em whar they come from, an' ef they cud git more, an' fi-nally wormed the story aout o' the old chief—Walakea, they called him. Nobody but Obed ud ever a believed the old yeller devil, but the Cap'n cud read folks like they was books. Heh, heh! Nobody never believes me naow when I tell 'em, an' I dun't s'pose you will, young feller—though come to look at ye, ye hev kind o' got them sharp-readin' eyes like Obed had."

The old man's whisper grew fainter, and I found myself shuddering at the terrible and sincere portentousness of his intonation, even though I knew his tale could be nothing but drunken phantasy.

"Wal, Sir, Obed he larnt that they's things on this arth as most folks never heerd abaout—an' wouldn't believe ef they did hear. It seems these Kanakys was sacrificin' heaps o' their young men an' maidens to some kind o' god-things that lived under the sea, an' gittin' all kinds o' favour in return. They met the things on the little islet with the queer ruins, an' it seems them awful picters o' frog-fish monsters was supposed to be picters o' these things. Mebbe they was the kind o' critters as got all the mermaid stories an' sech started. They had all kinds o' cities on the sea-bottom, an' this island was heaved up from thar. Seems they was some of the things alive in the stone buildin's when the island come up sudden to the surface. That's haow the Kanakys got wind they was daown thar. Made sign-talk as soon as they got over bein' skeert, an' pieced up a bargain afore long.

"Them things liked human sacrifices. Had had 'em ages afore, but lost track o' the upper world arter a time. What they done to the victims it ain't fer me to say, an' I guess Obed wa'n't none too sharp abaout askin'. But it was all right with the heathens, because they'd ben havin' a hard time an' was desp'rate abaout everything. They give a sarten number o' young folks to the sea-things twict every year— May-Eve an' Hallowe'en—reg'lar as cud be. Also give some o' the carved knick-knacks they made. What the things agreed to give in return was plenty o' fish—they druv 'em in from all over the sea—an' a few gold-like things naow an' then.

"Wal, as I says, the natives met the things on the little volcanic islet—goin' thar in canoes with the sacrifices et cet'ry, and bringin' back any of the gold-like jools as was comin' to 'em. At fust the things didn't never go onto the main island, but arter a time they come to want to. Seems they hankered arter mixin' with the folks, an' havin' j'int ceremonies on the big days—May-Eve an' Hallowe'en. Ye see, they was able to live both in an' aout o' water—what they call amphibians, I guess. The Kanakys told 'em as haow folks from the other islands might wanta wipe 'em aout ef they got wind o' their bein' thar, but they says they dun't keer much, because they cud wipe aout the hull brood o' humans ef they was willin' to bother—that is, any as didn't hev sarten signs sech as was used onct by the lost Old Ones, whoever they was. But not wantin' to bother, they'd lay low when anybody visited the island.

"When it come to matin' with them toad-lookin' fishes, the Kanakys kind o' balked, but finally they larnt something as put a new face on the matter. Seems that human folks has got a kind o' relation to sech water-beasts—that everything alive come aout o' the water onct, an' only needs a little change to go back agin. Them things told the Kanakys that ef they mixed bloods there'd be children as ud look human at fust, but later turn more'n more like the things, till finally they'd take to the water an' jine the main lot o' things daown thar. An' this is the important part, young feller—them as turned into fish things an' went into the water *wouldn't never die.* Them things never died excep' they was kilt violent.

"Wal, Sir, it seems by the time Obed knowed them islanders they was all full o' fish blood from them deep-water things. When they got old an' begun to show it, they was kep' hid until they felt like takin' to the water an' quittin' the place. Some was more teched than others, an' some never did change quite enough to take to the water; but mostly they turned aout jest the way them things said. Them as was born more like the things changed arly, but them as was nearly human sometimes stayed on the island till they was past seventy, though they'd usually go daown under fer trial trips afore that. Folks as had took to the water gen'rally come back a good deal to visit, so's a man ud often be a-talkin' to his own five-times-great-grandfather, who'd left the dry land a couple o' hundred years or so afore.

"Everybody got aout o' the idee o' dyin'—excep' in canoe wars with the other islanders, or as sacrifices to the sea-gods daown below, or from snake-bite or plague or sharp gallopin' ailments or somethin' afore they cud take to the water—but simply looked forrad to a kind o' change that wa'n't a bit horrible arter a while. They thought what they'd got was well wuth all they'd had to give up—an' I guess Obed kind o' come to think the same hisself when he'd chewed over old Walakea's story a bit. Walakea, though, was one of the few as hadn't got none of the fish blood—bein' of a royal line that intermarried with royal lines on other islands.

"Walakea he showed Obed a lot o' rites an' incantations as had to do with the sea-things, an' let him see some o' the folks in the village as had changed a lot from human shape. Somehaow or other, though, he never would let him see one of the reg'lar things from right aout o' the water. In the end he give him a funny kind o' thingumajig made aout o' lead or something, that he said ud bring up the fish things from any place in the water whar they might be a nest of 'em. The idee was to drop it daown with the right kind o' prayers an' sech. Walakea allaowed as the things was scattered all over the world, so's anybody that looked abaout cud find a nest an' bring 'em up ef they was wanted.

"Matt he didn't like this business at all, an' wanted Obed shud keep away from the island; but the Cap'n was sharp fer gain, an' faound he cud git them gold-like things so cheap it ud pay him to make a specialty of 'em. Things went on that way fer years, an' Obed got enough o' that gold-like stuff to make him start the refinery in Waite's old run-daown fullin' mill. He didn't dass sell the pieces like they was, fer folks ud be all the time askin' questions. All the same his crews ud git a piece an' dispose of it naow and then, even though they was swore to keep quiet; an' he let his women-folks wear some o' the pieces as was more human-like than most.

"Wal, come abaout 'thutty-eight—when I was seven year' old— Obed he faound the island people all wiped aout between v'yages. Seems the other islanders had got wind o' what was goin' on, an' had took matters into their own hands. S'pose they musta had, arter all, them old magic signs as the sea-things says was the only things they was afeard of. No tellin' what any o' them Kanakys will chance to git a holt of when the sea-bottom throws up some island with ruins old-er'n the deluge. Pious cusses, these was—they didn't leave nothin' standin' on either the main island or the little volcanic islet excep' what parts of the ruins was too big to knock daown. In some places they was little stones strewed abaout—like charms—with somethin' on 'em like what ye call a swastika naowadays. Prob'ly them was the Old Ones' signs. Folks all wiped aout, no trace o' no gold-like things, an' none o' the nearby Kanakys ud breathe a word abaout the matter. Wouldn't even admit they'd ever ben any people on that island.

"That naturally hit Obed pretty hard, seein' as his normal trade was doin' very poor. It hit the whole of Innsmouth, too, because in seafarin' days what profited the master of a ship gen'lly profited the crew proportionate. Most o' the folks araound the taown took the hard times kind o' sheep-like an' resigned, but they was in bad shape because the fishin' was peterin' aout an' the mills wa'n't doin' none too well.

"Then's the time Obed he begun a-cursin' at the folks fer bein' dull sheep an' prayin' to a Christian heaven as didn't help 'em none. He told 'em he'd knowed of folks as prayed to gods that give somethin' ye reely need, an' says ef a good bunch o' men ud stand by him, he cud mebbe git a holt o' sarten paowers as ud bring plenty o' fish an' quite a bit o' gold. O' course them as sarved on the *Sumatry Queen* an' seed the island knowed what he meant, an' wa'n't none too anxious to git clost to sea-things like they'd heerd tell on, but them as didn't know what 'twas all abaout got kind o' swayed by what Obed had to say, an' begun to ast him what he cud do to set 'em on the way to the faith as ud bring 'em results."

Here the old man faltered, mumbled, and lapsed into a moody and apprehensive silence; glancing nervously over his shoulder and then turning back to stare fascinatedly at the distant black reef. When I spoke to him he did not answer, so I knew I would have to let him finish the bottle. The insane yarn I was hearing interested me profoundly, for I fancied there was contained within it a sort of crude allegory based upon the strangenesses of Innsmouth and elaborated by an imagination at once creative and full of scraps of exotic legend. Not for a moment did I believe that the tale had any really substantial foundation; but none the less the account held a hint of genuine terror, if only because it brought in references to strange jewels clearly akin to the malign tiara I had seen at Newburyport. Perhaps the ornaments had, after all, come from some strange island; and possibly the wild stories were lies of the bygone Obed himself rather than of this antique toper.

I handed Zadok the bottle, and he drained it to the last drop. It was curious how he could stand so much whiskey, for not even a trace of thickness had come into his high, wheezy voice. He licked the nose of the bottle and slipped it into his pocket, then beginning to nod and whisper softly to himself. I bent close to catch any articulate words he might utter, and thought I saw a sardonic smile behind the stained, bushy whiskers. Yes—he was really forming words, and I could grasp a fair proportion of them.

"Poor Matt—Matt he allus was agin' it—tried to line up the folks on his side, an' had long talks with the preachers—no use—they run the Congregational parson aout o' taown, an' the Methodist feller quit—never did see Resolved Babcock, the Baptist parson, agin— Wrath o' Jehovy—I was a mightly little critter, but I heerd what I heerd an' seen what I seen—Dagon an' Ashtoreth—Belial an' Beelzebub—Golden Caff an' the idols o' Canaan an' the Philistines—Babylonish abominations—*Mene, mene, tekel, upharsin*—"

He stopped again, and from the look in his watery blue eyes I feared he was close to a stupor after all. But when I gently shook his shoulder he turned on me with astonishing alertness and snapped out some more obscure phrases.

"Dun't believe me, hey? Heh, heh, heh—then jest tell me, young feller, why Cap'n Obed an' twenty odd other folks used to row aout to Devil Reef in the dead o' night an' chant things so laoud ye cud hear 'em all over taown when the wind was right? Tell me that, hey? An tell me why Obed was allus droppin' heavy things daown into the deep water t'other side o' the reef whar the bottom shoots daown like a cliff lower'n ye kin saound? Tell me what he done with that funny-shaped lead thingumajig as Walakea give him? Hey, boy? An' what did they all haowl on May-Eve, an' agin the next Hallowe'en? An' why'd the new church parsons—fellers as used to be sailors— wear them queer robes an' cover theirselves with them gold-like things Obed brung? Hey?"

The watery blue eyes were almost savage and maniacal now, and the dirty white beard bristled electrically. Old Zadok probably saw me shrink back, for he began to cackle evilly.

"Heh, heh, heh, heh! Beginnin' to see, hey? Mebbe ye'd like to a ben me in them days, when I seed things at night aout to sea from the cupalo top o' my haouse. Oh, I kin tell ye, little pitchers hev big ears, an' I wa'n't missin' nothin' o' what was gossiped abaout Cap'n Obed an' the folks aout to the reef! Heh, heh, heh! Haow abaout the night I took my pa's ship's glass up to the cupalo an' seed the reef a-bristlin' thick with shapes that dove off quick soon's the moon riz? Obed an' the folks was in a dory, but them shapes dove off the far side into the deep water an' never come up . . . Haow'd ye like to be a little shaver alone up in a cupalo a-watchin' shapes *as wa'n't human shapes?* . . . Hey? . . . Heh, heh, heh, heh . . ."

The old man was getting hysterical, and I began to shiver with a nameless alarm. He laid a gnarled claw on my shoulder, and it seemed to me that its shaking was not altogether that of mirth.

"S'pose one night ye seed somethin' heavy heaved offen Obed's dory beyond the reef, an' then larned nex' day a young feller was missin' from home? Hey? Did anybody ever see hide or hair o' Hiram Gilman agin? Did they? An' Nick Pierce, an' Luelly Waite, an' Adoniram Saouthwick, an' Henry Garrison? Hey? Heh, heh, heh, heh . . . Shapes talkin' sign language with their hands . . . them as had reel hands . . .

"Wal, Sir, that was the time Obed begun to git on his feet agin. Folks see his three darters a-wearin' gold-like things as no-body'd never see on 'em afore, an' smoke started comin' aout o' the refin'ry chimbly. Other folks was prosp'rin', too—fish begun to swarm into the harbour fit to kill, an' heaven knows what sized cargoes we begun to ship aout to Newb'ryport, Arkham, an' Boston. 'Twas then Obed got the ol' branch railrud put through. Some Kingsport fishermen heerd abaout the ketch an' come up in sloops, but they was all lost. Nobody never see 'em agin. An' jest then our folks organised the Esoteric Order o' Dagon, an' bought Masonic Hall offen Calvary Commandery for it . . . heh, heh, heh! Matt Eliot was a Mason an' agin' the sellin', but he dropped aout o' sight jest then.

"Remember, I ain't sayin' Obed was set on hevin' things jest like they was on that Kanaky isle. I dun't think he aimed at fust to do no mixin', nor raise no younguns to take to the water an' turn into fishes with eternal life. He wanted them gold things, an' was willin' to pay heavy, an' I guess the *others* was satisfied fer a while . . .

"Come in 'forty-six the taown done some lookin' an' thinkin' fer itself. Too many folks missin'—too much wild preachin' at meetin' of a Sunday—too much talk abaout that reef. I guess I done a bit by tellin' Selectman Mowry what I see from the cupalo. They was a party one night as follered Obed's craowd aout to the reef, an' I heerd shots betwixt the dories. Nex' day Obed an' thutty-two others was in gaol, with everybody a-wonderin' jest what was afoot an' jest what charge agin' 'em cud be got to holt. God, ef anybody'd looked ahead . . . a couple o' weeks later, when nothin' had ben throwed into the sea fer that long . . ."

Zadok was showing signs of fright and exhaustion, and I let him keep silence for a while, though glancing apprehensively at my watch. The tide had turned and was coming in now, and the sound of the waves seemed to arouse him. I was glad of that tide, for at high water the fishy smell might not be so bad. Again I strained to catch his whispers.

"That awful night . . . I seed 'em . . . I was up in the cupalo . . . hordes of 'em . . . swarms of 'em . . . all over the reef an' swimmin' up the harbour into the Manuxet . . . God, what happened in the streets of Innsmouth that night . . . they rattled our door, but pa wouldn't open . . . then he clumb aout the kitchen winder with his musket to find Selectman Mowry an' see what he cud do . . . Maounds o' the dead an' the dyin' . . . shots an' screams . . . shaoutin' in Ol' Squar an' Taown Squar an' New Church Green . . . gaol throwed open . . . proclamation . . . treason . . . called it the plague when folks come in an' faound haff our people missin' . . . nobody left but them as ud jine in with Obed an' them things or else keep quiet . . . never heerd o' my pa no more . . ."

The old man was panting, and perspiring profusely. His grip on my shoulder tightened.

"Everything cleaned up in the mornin'—but they was *traces* . . . Obed he kinder takes charge an' says things is goin' to be changed . . . *others'll* worship with us at meetin'-time, an' sarten haouses hez got to entertain *guests . . . they* wanted to mix like they done with the Kanakys, an' he fer one didn't feel baound to stop 'em. Far gone, was Obed . . . jest like a crazy man on the subjeck. He says they brung us fish an' treasure, an' shud hev what they hankered arter . . .

"Nothin' was to be diff'runt on the aoutside, only we was to keep shy o' strangers ef we knowed what was good fer us. We all hed to take the Oath o' Dagon, an' later on they was secon' an' third Oaths that some on us took. Them as ud help special, ud git special rewards—gold an' sech—no use balkin', fer they was millions of 'em daown thar. They'd ruther not start risin' an' wipin' aout humankind, but ef they was gave away an' forced to, they cud do a lot toward jest that. We didn't hev them old charms to cut 'em off like folks in the Saouth Sea did, an' them Kanakys wudn't never give away their secrets.

"Yield up enough sacrifices an' savage knick-knacks an' harbourage in the taown when they wanted it, an' they'd let well enough alone. Wudn't bother no strangers as might bear tales aoutside—that is, withaout they got pryin'. All in the band of the faithful—Order o' Dagon—an' the children shud never die, but go back to the Mother Hydra an' Father Dagon what we all come from onct—*Iä! Iä! Cthulhu fhtagn! Ph'nglui mglw'nafh Cthulhu R'lyeh, wgah-nagl fhtagn*—"

Old Zadok was fast lapsing into stark raving, and I held my breath. Poor old soul—to what pitiful depths of hallucination had his liquor, plus his hatred of the decay, alienage, and disease around him, brought that fertile, imaginative brain! He began to moan now, and tears were coursing down his channelled cheeks into the depths of his beard.

"God, what I seen senct I was fifteen year' old—*Mene, mene, tekel, upharsin!*—the folks as was missin', an' them as kilt theirselves—them as told things in Arkham or Ipswich or sech places was all called crazy, like you're a-callin' me right naow—but God what I seen—They'd a kilt me long ago fer what I know, only I'd took the fust an' secon' Oaths o' Dagon offen Obed, so was pertected unlessen a jury of 'em proved I told things knowin' an' delib'rit . . . but I wudn't take the third Oath—I'd a died ruther'n take that—

"It got wuss araound Civil War time, *when children born senct 'forty-six begun to grow up*—some of 'em, that is. I was afeard—never did no pryin' arter that awful night, an' never see one o'—*them*—clost to in all my life. That is, never no full-blooded one. I went to the war, an' ef I'd a had any guts or sense I'd a never come back, but settled away from here. But folks wrote me things wa'n't so bad. That, I s'pose, was because gov'munt draft men was in taown arter 'sixty-three. Arter the war it was jest as bad agin. People begun to fall off—mills an' shops shet daown—shippin stopped an' the harbour choked up—railrud give up—but they . . . they never stopped swimmin' in an' aout o' the river from that cursed reef o' Satan—an' more an' more attic winders got a-boarded up, an' more an' more noises was heerd in haouses as wa'n't s'posed to hev nobody in 'em . . .

"Folks aoutside hev their stories abaout us—s'pose you've heerd a plenty on 'em, seein' what questions ye ast—stories abaout things they've seed naow an' then, an' abaout that queer joolry as still comes in from somewhars an' ain't quite all melted up—but nothin' never gits def'nite. Nobody'll believe nothin'. They call them gold-like things pirate loot, an' allaow the Innsmouth folks hez furren blood or is distempered or somethin'. Besides, them that lives here shoo off as many strangers as they kin, an' encourage the rest not to git very cur'ous, specially raound night time. Beasts balk at the critters—hosses wuss'n mules—but when they got autos that was all right.

"In 'forty-six Cap'n Obed took a second wife that nobody in the taown never see—some says he didn't want to, but was made to by them as he'd called in—had three children by her—two as disappeared young, but one gal as looked like anybody else an' was eddicated in Europe. Obed finally got her married off by a trick to an Arkham feller as didn't suspect nothin'. But nobody aoutside'll hev nothin' to do with Innsmouth folks naow. Barnabas Marsh that runs the refin'ry naow is Obed's grandson by his fust wife—son of Onesiphorus, his eldest son, but his mother was another o' them as wa'n't never seed aoutdoors.

"Right naow Barnabas is abaout changed. Can't shet his eyes no more, an' is all aout o' shape. They say he still wears clothes, but he'll take to the water soon. Mebbe he's tried it already—they do sometimes go daown fer little spells afore they go fer good. Ain't ben seed abaout in public fer nigh on ten year'. Dun't know haow his poor wife kin feel—she come from Ipswich, an' they nigh lynched Barnabas when he courted her fifty odd year' ago. Obed he died in 'seventy-eight, an' all the next gen'ration is gone naow—the fust wife's children dead, an' the rest . . . God knows . . ."

The sound of the incoming tide was now very insistent, and little by little it seemed to change the old man's mood from maudlin tearfulness to watchful fear. He would pause now and then to renew those nervous glances over his shoulder or out toward the reef, and despite the wild absurdity of his tale, I could not help beginning to share his vague apprehensiveness. Zadok now grew shriller, and seemed to be trying to whip up his courage with louder speech.

"Hey, yew, why dun't ye say somethin'? Haow'd ye like to be livin' in a taown like this, with everything a-rottin' an' a-dyin', an' boarded-up monsters crawlin' an' bleatin' an' barkin' an' hoppin' araoun' black cellars an' attics every way ye turn? Hey? Haow'd ye like to hear the haowlin' night arter night from the churches an' Order o' Dagon Hall, *an' know what's doin' part o' the haowlin'?* Haow'd ye like to hear what comes from that awful reef every May-Eve an' Hallowmass? Hey? Think the old man's crazy, eh? Wal, Sir, *let me tell ye that ain't the wust!*"

Zadok was really screaming now, and the mad frenzy of his voice disturbed me more than I care to own.

"Curse ye, dun't set that a-starin' at me with them eyes—I tell Obed Marsh he's in hell, an' hez got to stay thar! Heh, heh . . . in hell, I says! Can't git me—I hain't done nothin' nor told nobody nothin'—

"Oh, you, young feller? Wal, even ef I hain't told nobody nothin' yet, I'm a-goin' to naow! You jest set still an' listen to me, boy—this is what I ain't never told nobody . . . I says I didn't do no pryin' arter that night—*but I faound things aout jest the same!*

"Yew want to know what the reel horror is, hey? Wal, it's this—it ain't what them fish devils *hez done, but what they're a-goin' to do!* They're a-bringin' things up aout o' whar they come from into the taown—ben doin' it fer years, an' slackenin' up lately. Them haouses north o' the river betwixt Water an' Main Streets is full of 'em—them devils *an' what they brung*—an' when they git ready . . . I say, when they git ready . . . ever hear tell of a *shoggoth?* . . .

"Hey, d'ye hear me? I tell ye *I know what them things be*—I seen 'em one night when . . . eh-ahhhh-ah! e'yaahhhh . . ."

The hideous suddenness and inhuman frightfulness of the old man's shriek almost made me faint. His eyes, looking past me toward the malodorous sea, were positively starting from his head; while his face was a mask of fear worthy of Greek tragedy. His bony claw dug monstrously into my shoulder, and he made no motion as I turned my head to look at whatever he had glimpsed.

There was nothing that I could see. Only the incoming tide, with perhaps one set of ripples more local than the long-flung line of breakers. But now Zadok was shaking me, and I turned back to watch the melting of that fear-frozen face into a chaos of twitching eyelids and mumbling gums. Presently his voice came back—albeit as a trembling whisper.

*"Git aout o' here!* Git aout o' here! *They seen us*—git aout fer your life! Dun't wait fer nothin'—*they know naow*—Run fer it—quick— *aout o' this taown*—"

Another heavy wave dashed against the loosening masonry of the bygone wharf, and changed the mad ancient's whisper to another inhuman and bloodcurdling scream. "E-yaahhhh! . . . yhaaaaaaa! . . ."

Before I could recover my scattered wits he had relaxed his clutch on my shoulder and dashed wildly inland toward the street, reeling northward around the ruined warehouse wall.

I glanced back at the sea, but there was nothing there. And when I reached Water Street and looked along it toward the north there was no remaining trace of Zadok Allen.

## IV

I can hardly describe the mood in which I was left by this harrowing episode—an episode at once mad and pitiful, grotesque and terrifying. The grocery boy had prepared me for it, yet the reality left me none the less bewildered and disturbed. Puerile though the story was, old Zadok's insane earnestness and horror had communicated to me a mounting unrest which joined with my earlier sense of loathing for the town and its blight of intangible shadow.

Later I might sift the tale and extract some nucleus of historic allegory; just now I wished to put it out of my head. The hour had grown perilously late—my watch said 7:15, and the Arkham bus left Town Square at eight—so I tried to give my thoughts as neutral and practical a cast as possible, meanwhile walking rapidly through the deserted streets of gaping roofs and leaning houses toward the hotel where I had checked my valise and would find my bus.

Though the golden light of late afternoon gave the ancient roofs and decrepit chimneys an air of mystic loveliness and peace, I could not help glancing over my shoulder now and then. I would surely be very glad to get out of malodorous and fear-shadowed Innsmouth, and wished there were some other vehicle than the bus driven by that sinister-looking fellow Sargent. Yet I did not hurry too precipitately, for there were architectural details worth viewing at every silent corner; and I could easily, I calculated, cover the necessary distance in a half-hour.

Studying the grocery youth's map and seeking a route I had not traversed before, I chose Marsh Street instead of State for my approach to Town Square. Near the corner of Fall Street I began to see scattered groups of furtive whisperers, and when I finally reached the Square I saw that almost all the loiterers were congregated around the door of the Gilman House. It seemed as if many bulging, watery, unwinking eyes looked oddly at me as I claimed my valise in the lobby, and I hoped that none of these unpleasant creatures would be my fellow-passengers on the coach.

The bus, rather early, rattled in with three passengers somewhat before eight, and an evil-looking fellow on the sidewalk muttered a few indistinguishable words to the driver. Sargent threw out a mailbag and a roll of newspapers, and entered the hotel; while the passengers—the same men whom I had seen arriving in Newburyport that morning—shambled to the sidewalk and exchanged some faint guttural words with a loafer in a language I could have sworn was not

English. I boarded the empty coach and took the same seat I had taken before, but was hardly settled before Sargent reappeared and began mumbling in a throaty voice of peculiar repulsiveness.

I was, it appeared, in very bad luck. There had been something wrong with the engine, despite the excellent time made from Newburyport, and the bus could not complete the journey to Arkham. No, it could not possibly be repaired that night, nor was there any other way of getting transportation out of Innsmouth, either to Arkham or elsewhere. Sargent was sorry, but I would have to stop over at the Gilman. Probably the clerk would make the price easy for me, but there was nothing else to do. Almost dazed by this sudden obstacle, and violently dreading the fall of night in this decaying and half-unlighted town, I left the bus and reentered the hotel lobby; where the sullen, queer-looking night clerk told me I could have Room 428 on next the top floor—large, but without running water—for a dollar.

Despite what I had heard of this hotel in Newburyport, I signed the register, paid my dollar, let the clerk take my valise, and followed that sour, solitary attendant up three creaking flights of stairs past dusty corridors which seemed wholly devoid of life. My room, a dismal rear one with two windows and bare, cheap furnishings, overlooked a dingy courtyard otherwise hemmed in by low, deserted brick blocks, and commanded a view of decrepit westward-stretching roofs with a marshy countryside beyond. At the end of the corridor was a bathroom—a discouraging relique with ancient marble bowl, tin tub, faint electric light, and musty wooden panelling around all the plumbing fixtures.

It being still daylight, I descended to the Square and looked around for a dinner of some sort; noticing as I did so the strange glances I received from the unwholesome loafers. Since the grocery was closed, I was forced to patronise the restaurant I had shunned before; a stooped, narrow-headed man with staring, unwinking eyes, and a flat-nosed wench with unbelievably thick, clumsy hands being in attendance. The service was all of the counter type, and it relieved me to find that much was evidently served from cans and packages.

A bowl of vegetable soup with crackers was enough for me, and I soon headed back for my cheerless room at the Gilman; getting an evening paper and a flyspecked magazine from the evil-visaged clerk at the rickety stand beside his desk.

As twilight deepened I turned on the one feeble electric bulb over the cheap, iron-framed bed, and tried as best I could to continue the reading I had begun. I felt it advisable to keep my mind wholesomely occupied, for it would not do to brood over the abnormalities of this ancient, blight-shadowed town while I was still within its borders. The insane yarn I had heard from the aged drunkard did not promise very pleasant dreams, and I felt I must keep the image of his wild, watery eyes as far as possible from my imagination.

Also, I must not dwell on what that factory inspector had told the Newburyport ticket-agent about the Gilman House and the voices of its nocturnal tenants—not on that, nor on the face beneath the tiara in the black church doorway; the face for whose horror my conscious mind could not account. It would perhaps have been easier to keep my thoughts from disturbing topics had the room not been so gruesomely musty. As it was, the lethal mustiness blended hideously with the town's general fishy odour and persistently focused on death and decay.

Another thing that disturbed me was the absence of a bolt on the door of my room. One had been there, as marks clearly showed, but there were signs of recent removal. No doubt it had become out of order, like so many other things in this decrepit edifice. In my nervousness I looked around and discovered a bolt on the clothes-press which seemed to be of the same size, judging from the marks, as the one formerly on the door. To gain a partial relief from the general tension I busied myself by transferring this hardware to the vacant place with the aid of a handy three-in-one device including a screwdriver which I kept on my key-ring. The bolt fitted perfectly, and I was somewhat relieved when I knew that I could shoot it firmly upon retiring. Not that I had any real apprehension of its need, but that any symbol of security was welcome in an environment of this kind. There were adequate bolts on the two lateral doors to connecting rooms, and these I proceeded to fasten.

I did not undress, but decided to read till I was sleepy and then lie down with only my coat, collar, and shoes off. Taking a pocket flashlight from my valise, I placed it in my trousers, so that I could read my watch if I woke up later in the dark. Drowsiness, however, did not come; and when I stopped to analyse my thoughts I found to my disquiet that I was really unconsciously listening for something— listening for something which I dreaded but could not name. That in- spector's story must have worked on my imagination more deeply than I had suspected. Again I tried to read, but found that I made no progress.

After a time I seemed to hear the stairs and corridors creak at intervals as if with footsteps, and wondered if the other rooms were beginning to fill up. There were no voices, however, and it struck me that there was something subtly furtive about the creaking. I did not like it, and debated whether I had better try to sleep at all. This town had some queer people, and there had undoubtedly been several disappearances. Was this one of those inns where travellers were slain for their money? Surely I had no look of excessive prosperity. Or were the townsfolk really so resentful about curious visitors? Had my obvious sightseeing, with its frequent map-consultations, aroused unfavourable notice? It occurred to me that I must be in a highly nervous state to let a few random creakings set me off spec- ulating in this fashion—but I regretted none the less that I was un- armed.

At length, feeling a fatigue which had nothing of drowsiness in it, I bolted the newly outfitted hall door, turned off the light, and threw myself down on the hard, uneven bed—coat, collar, shoes, and all. In the darkness every faint noise of the night seemed magnified, and a flood of doubly unpleasant thoughts swept over me. I was sorry I had put out the light, yet was too tired to rise and turn it on again. Then, after a long, dreary interval, and prefaced by a fresh creaking of stairs and corridor, there came that soft, damnably unmistakable sound which seemed like a malign fulfillment of all my apprehensions. Without the least shadow of a doubt, the lock on my hall door was being tried—cautiously, furtively, tentatively—with a key.

My sensations upon recognising this sign of actual peril were perhaps less rather than more tumultuous because of my previous vague fears. I had been, albeit without definite reason, instinctively on my guard—and that was to my advantage in the new and real crisis, whatever it might turn out to be. Nevertheless the change in the menace from vague premonition to immediate reality was a profound shock, and fell upon me with the force of a genuine blow. It never once occurred to me that the fumbling might be a mere mistake. Malign purpose was all I could think of, and I kept deathly quiet, awaiting the would-be intruder's next move.

After a time the cautious rattling ceased, and I heard the room to the north entered with a pass-key. Then the lock of the connecting door to my room was softly tried. The bolt held, of course, and I heard the floor creak as the prowler left the room. After a moment there came another soft rattling, and I knew that the room to the south of me was being entered. Again a furtive trying of a bolted connecting door, and again a receding creaking. This time the creaking went along the hall and down the stairs, so I knew that the prowler had realised the bolted condition of my doors and was giving up his attempt for a greater or lesser time, as the future would show.

The readiness with which I fell into a plan of action proves that I must have been subconsciously fearing some menace and considering possible avenues of escape for hours. From the first I felt that the unseen fumbler meant a danger not to be met or dealt with, but only to be fled from as precipitately as possible. The one thing to do was to get out of that hotel alive as quickly as I could, and through some channel other than the front stairs and lobby.

Rising softly and throwing my flashlight on the switch, I sought to light the bulb over my bed in order to choose and pocket some belongings for a swift, valiseless flight. Nothing, however, happened; and I saw that the power had been cut off. Clearly, some cryptic, evil movement was afoot on a large scale—just what, I could not say. As I stood pondering with my hand on the now useless switch I heard a muffled creaking on the floor below, and thought I could barely distinguish voices in conversation. A moment later I felt less sure that the deeper sounds were voices, since the apparent hoarse barkings and loose-syllabled croakings bore so little resemblance to recognised human speech. Then I thought with renewed force of what the factory inspector had heard in the night in this mouldering and pestilential building.

Having filled my pockets with the flashlight's aid, I put on my hat and tiptoed to the windows to consider chances of descent. Despite the state's safety regulations there was no fire escape on this side of the hotel, and I saw that my windows commanded only a sheer three-story drop to the cobbled courtyard. On the right and left, however, some ancient brick business blocks abutted on the hotel; their slant-roofs coming up to a reasonable jumping distance from my fourth-story level. To reach either of these lines of buildings I would have to be in a room two doors from my own—in one case on the north and in the other case on the south—and my mind instantly set to work calculating what chances I had of making the transfer.

I could not, I decided, risk an emergence into the corridor; where my footsteps would surely be heard, and where the difficulties of entering the desired room would be insuperable. My progress, if it was to be made at all, would have to be through the less solidly built connecting doors of the rooms; the locks and bolts of which I would have to force violently, using my shoulder as a battering-ram whenever they were set against me. This, I thought, would be possible owing to the rickety nature of the house and its fixtures; but I realised I could not do it noiselessly. I would have to count on sheer speed, and the chance of getting to a window before any hostile forces became coordinated enough to open the right door toward me with a pass-key. My own outer door I reinforced by pushing the bureau against it—little by little, in order to make a minimum of sound.

I perceived that my chances were very slender, and was fully prepared for any calamity. Even getting to another roof would not solve the problem, for there would then remain the task of reaching the ground and escaping from the town. One thing in my favour was the deserted and ruinous state of the abutting buildings, and the number of skylights gaping blackly open in each row.

Gathering from the grocery boy's map that the best route out of town was southward, I glanced first at the connecting door on the south side of the room. It was designed to open in my direction, hence I saw—after drawing the bolt and finding other fastenings in place—it was not a favourable one for forcing. Accordingly abandoning it as a route, I cautiously moved the bedstead against it to hamper any attack which might be made on it later from the next room. The door on the north was hung to open away from me, and this—though a test proved it to be locked or bolted from the other side—I knew must be my route. If I could gain the roofs of the buildings in Paine Street and descend successfully to the ground level, I might perhaps dart through the courtyard and the adjacent or opposite buildings to Washington or Bates—or else emerge in Paine and edge around southward into Washington. In any case, I would aim to strike Washington somehow and get quickly out of the Town Square region. My preference would be to avoid Paine, since the fire station there might be open all night.

As I thought of these things I looked out over the squalid sea of decaying roofs below me, now brightened by the beams of a moon not much past full. On the right the black gash of the river-gorge clove the panorama; abandoned factories and railway station clinging barnacle-like to its sides. Beyond it the rusted railway and the Rowley road led off through a flat, marshy terrain dotted with islets of higher and dryer scrub-grown land. On the left the creek-threaded countryside was nearer, the narrow road to Ipswich gleaming white in the moonlight. I could not see from my side of the hotel the southward route toward Arkham which I had determined to take.

I was irresolutely speculating on when I had better attack the northward door, and on how I could least audibly manage it, when I noticed that the vague noises underfoot had given place to a fresh and heavier creaking of the stairs. A wavering flicker of light showed through my transom, and the boards of the corridor began to groan with a ponderous load. Muffled sounds of possible vocal origin approached, and at length a firm knock came at my outer door.

For a moment I simply held my breath and waited. Eternities seemed to elapse, and the nauseous fishy odour of my environment seemed to mount suddenly and spectacularly. Then the knocking was repeated—continuously, and with growing insistence. I knew that the time for action had come, and forthwith drew the bolt of the northward connecting door, bracing myself for the task of battering it open. The knocking waxed louder, and I hoped that its volume would cover the sound of my efforts. At last beginning my attempt, I lunged again and again at the thin panelling with my left shoulder, heedless of shock or pain. The door resisted even more than I had expected, but I did not give in. And all the while the clamour at the outer door increased.

Finally the connecting door gave, but with such a crash that I knew those outside must have heard. Instantly the outside knocking became a violent battering, while keys sounded ominously in the hall doors of the rooms on both sides of me. Rushing through the newly opened connection, I succeeded in bolting the northerly hall door before the lock could be turned; but even as I did so I heard the hall door of the third room—the one from whose window I had hoped to reach the roof below—being tried with a pass-key.

For an instant I felt absolute despair, since my trapping in a chamber with no window egress seemed complete. A wave of almost abnormal horror swept over me and, invested with a terrible but unexplainable singularity, the flashlight-glimpsed dust prints made by the intruder who had lately tried my door from this room. Then, with a dazed automatism which persisted despite hopelessness, I made for the next connecting door and performed the blind motion of pushing at it in an effort to get through and—granting that fastenings might be as providentially intact as in this second room—bolt the hall door beyond before the lock could be turned from outside.

Sheer fortunate chance gave me my reprieve—for the connecting door before me was not only unlocked but actually ajar. In a second I was through, and had my right knee and shoulder against a hall door which was visibly opening inward. My pressure took the opener off guard, for the thing shut as I pushed, so that I could slip the well-conditioned bolt as I had done with the other door. As I gained this respite I heard the battering at the two other doors abate, while a confused clatter came from the connecting door I had shielded with the bedstead. Evidently the bulk of my assailants had entered the southerly room and were massing in a lateral attack. But at the same moment a pass-key sounded in the next door to the north, and I knew that a nearer peril was at hand.

The northward connecting door was wide open, but there was no time to think about checking the already turning lock in the hall. All I could do was to shut and bolt the open connecting door, as well as its mate on the opposite side—pushing a bedstead against the one and a bureau against the other, and moving a washstand in front of the hall door. I must, I saw, trust to such makeshift barriers to shield me till I could get out the window and on the roof of the Paine Street block. But even in this acute moment my chief horror was something apart from the immediate weakness of my defences. I was shuddering because not one of my pursuers, despite some hideous pantings, gruntings, and subdued barkings at odd intervals, was uttering an unmuffled or intelligible vocal sound.

As I moved the furniture and rushed toward the windows I heard a frightful scurrying along the corridor toward the room north of me, and perceived that the southward battering had ceased. Plainly, most of my opponents were about to concentrate against the feeble connecting door which they knew must open directly on me. Outside, the moon played on the ridgepole of the block below, and I saw that the jump would be desperately hazardous because of the steep surface on which I must land.

Surveying the conditions, I chose the more southerly of the two windows as my avenue of escape; planning to land on the inner slope of the roof and make for the nearest skylight. Once inside one of the decrepit brick structures I would have to reckon with pursuit; but I hoped to descend and dodge in and out of yawning doorways along the shadowed courtyard, eventually getting to Washington Street and slipping out of town toward the south.

The clatter at the northerly connection door was now terrific, and I saw that the weak panelling was beginning to splinter. Obviously, the besiegers had brought some ponderous object into play as a battering-ram. The bedstead, however, still held firm; so that I had at least a faint chance of making good my escape. As I opened the window I noticed that it was flanked by heavy velour draperies suspended from a pole by brass rings, and also that there was a large projecting catch for the shutters on the exterior. Seeing a possible means of avoiding the dangerous jump, I yanked at the hangings and brought them down, pole and all; then quickly hooking two of the rings in the shutter catch and flinging the drapery outside. The heavy folds reached fully to the abutting roof, and I saw that the rings and catch would be likely to bear my weight. So, climbing out of the window and down the improvised rope ladder, I left behind me forever the morbid and horror-infested fabric of the Gilman House.

I landed safely on the loose slates of the steep roof, and succeeded in gaining the gaping black skylight without a slip. Glancing up at the window I had left, I observed it was still dark, though far across the crumbling chimneys to the north I could see lights ominously blazing in the Order of Dagon Hall, the Baptist church, and the Congregational church which I recalled so shiveringly. There had seemed to be no one in the courtyard below, and I hoped there would be a chance to get away before the spreading of a general alarm. Flashing my pocket lamp into the skylight, I saw that there were no steps down. The distance was slight, however, so I clambered over the brink and dropped; striking a dusty floor littered with crumbling boxes and barrels.

The place was ghoulish-looking, but I was past minding such impressions and made at once for the staircase revealed by my flashlight—after a hasty glance at my watch, which showed the hour to be 2 a.m. The steps creaked, but seemed tolerably sound, and I raced down past a barn-like second story to the ground floor. The desolation was complete, and only echoes answered my footfalls. At length I reached the lower hall, at one end of which I saw a faint luminous rectangle marking the ruined Paine Street doorway. Heading the other way, I found the back door also open, and darted out and down five stone steps to the grass-grown cobblestones of the courtyard.

The moonbeams did not reach down here, but I could just see my way about without using the flashlight. Some of the windows on the Gilman House side were faintly glowing, and I thought I heard confused sounds within. Walking softly over to the Washington Street side I perceived several open doorways, and chose the nearest as my route out. The hallway inside was black, and when I reached the opposite end I saw that the street door was wedged immovably shut. Resolved to try another building, I groped my way back toward the courtyard, but stopped short when close to the doorway.

For out of an opened door in the Gilman House a large crowd of doubtful shapes was pouring—lanterns bobbing in the darkness, and horrible croaking voices exchanging low cries in what was certainly not English. The figures moved uncertainly, and I realised to my relief that they did not know where I had gone; but for all that they sent a shiver of horror through my frame. Their features were indistinguishable, but their crouching, shambling gait was abominably repellent. And worst of all, I perceived that one figure was strangely robed, and unmistakably surmounted by a tall tiara of a design altogether too familiar. As the figures spread throughout the courtyard, I felt my fears increase. Suppose I could find no egress from this building on the street side? The fishy odour was detestable, and I wondered I could stand it without fainting. Again groping toward the street, I opened a door off the hall and came upon an empty room with closely shuttered but sashless windows. Fumbling in the rays of my flashlight, I found I could open the shutters; and in another moment had climbed outside and was carefully closing the aperture in its original manner.

I was now in Washington Street, and for the moment saw no living thing nor any light save that of the moon. From several directions in the distance, however, I could hear the sound of hoarse voices, of footsteps, and of a curious kind of pattering which did not sound quite like footsteps. Plainly I had no time to lose. The points of the compass were clear to me, and I was glad that all the streetlights were turned off, as is often the custom on strongly moonlit nights in unprosperous rural regions. Some of the sounds came from the south, yet I retained my design of escaping in that direction. There would, I knew, be plenty of deserted doorways to shelter me in case I met any person or group who looked like pursuers.

I walked rapidly, softly, and close to the ruined houses. While hatless and dishevelled after my arduous climb, I did not look especially noticeable; and stood a good chance of passing unheeded if forced to encounter any casual wayfarer. At Bates Street I drew into a yawning vestibule while two shambling figures crossed in front of me, but was soon on my way again and approaching the open space where Eliot Street obliquely crosses Washington at the intersection of South. Though I had never seen this space, it had looked dangerous to me on the grocery youth's map; since the moonlight would have free play there. There was no use trying to evade it, for any alternative course would involve detours of possibly disastrous visibility and delaying effect. The only thing to do was to cross it boldly and openly; imitating the typical shamble of the Innsmouth folk as best I could, and trusting that no one—or at least no pursuer of mine—would be there.

Just how fully the pursuit was organized—and indeed, just what its purpose might be—I could form no idea. There seemed to be unusual activity in the town, but I judged that the news of my escape from the Gilman had not yet spread. I would, of course soon have to shift from Washington to some other southward street; for that party from the hotel would doubtless be after me. I must have left dust prints in that last old building, revealing how I had gained the street.

The open space was, as I had expected, strongly moonlit; and I saw the remains of a park-like, iron-railed green in its centre. Fortunately no one was about, though a curious sort of buzz or roar seemed to be increasing in the direction of Town Square. South Street was very wide, leading directly down a slight declivity to the waterfront and commanding a long view out at sea; and I hoped that no one would be glancing up it from afar as I crossed in the bright moonlight.

My progress was unimpeded, and no fresh sound arose to hint that I had been spied. Glancing about me, I involuntarily let my pace slacken for a second to take in the sight of the sea, gorgeous in the burning moonlight at the street's end. Far out beyond the breakwater was the dim, dark line of Devil Reef, and as I glimpsed it I could not help thinking of all the hideous legends I had heard in the last thirty-four hours—legends which portrayed this ragged rock as a veritable gateway to realms of unfathomed horror and inconceivable abnormality.

Then, without warning, I saw the intermittent flashes of light on the distant reef. They were definite and unmistakable, and awaked in my mind a blind horror beyond all rational proportion. My muscles tightened for panic flight, held in only by a certain unconscious caution and half-hypnotic fascination. And to make matters worse, there now flashed forth from the lofty cupola of the Gilman House, which loomed up to the northeast behind me, a series of analogous though differently spaced gleams which could be nothing less than an answering signal.

Controlling my muscles, and realising afresh how plainly visible I was, I resumed my brisker and feignedly shambling pace; though keeping my eyes on that hellish and ominous reef as long as the opening of South Street gave me a seaward view. What the whole proceeding meant, I could not imagine; unless it involved some strange rite connected with Devil Reef, or unless some party had landed from a ship on that sinister rock. I now bent to the left around the ruinous green; still gazing toward the ocean as it blazed in the spectral summer moonlight, and watching the cryptical flashing of those nameless, unexplainable beacons.

It was then that the most horrible impression of all was borne in upon me—the impression which destroyed my last vestige of self-control and sent me running frantically southward past the yawning black doorways and fishily staring windows of that deserted nightmare street. For at a closer glance I saw that the moonlit waters between the reef and the shore were far from empty. They were alive with a teeming horde of shapes swimming inward toward the town; and even at my vast distance and in my single moment of perception I could tell that the bobbing heads and flailing arms were alien and aberrant in a way scarcely to be expressed or consciously formulated.

My frantic running ceased before I had covered a block, for at my left I began to hear something like the hue and cry of organized pursuit. There were footsteps and guttural sounds, and a rattling motor wheezed south along Federal Street. In a second all my plans were utterly changed—for if the southward highway were blocked ahead of me, I must clearly find another egress from Innsmouth. I paused and drew into a gaping doorway, reflecting how lucky I was to have left the moonlit open space before these pursuers came down the parallel street.

A second reflection was less comforting. Since the pursuit was down another street, it was plain that the party was not following me directly. It had not seen me, but was simply obeying a general plan of cutting off my escape. This, however, implied that all roads leading out of Innsmouth were similarly patrolled; for the denizens could not have known what route I intended to take. If this were so, I would have to make my retreat across country away from any road; but how could I do that in view of the marshy and creek-riddled nature of all the surrounding region? For a moment my brain reeled—both from sheer hopelessness and from a rapid increase in the omnipresent fishy odour.

Then I thought of the abandoned railway to Rowley, whose solid line of ballasted, weed-grown earth still stretched off to the northwest from the crumbling station on the edge of the river-gorge. There was just a chance that the townsfolk would not think of that; since its brier-choked desertion made it half-impassable, and the unlikeliest of all avenues for a fugitive to choose. I had seen it clearly from my hotel window, and knew about how it lay. Most of its earlier length was uncomfortably visible from the Rowley road, and from high places in the town itself; but one could perhaps crawl inconspicuously through the undergrowth. At any rate, it would form my only chance of deliverance, and there was nothing to do but try it.

Drawing inside the hall of my deserted shelter, I once more consulted the grocery boy's map with the aid of the flashlight. The immediate problem was how to reach the ancient railway; and I now saw that the safest course was ahead to Babson Street, then west to Lafayette—there edging around but not crossing an open space homologous to the one I had traversed—and subsequently back northward and westward in a zigzagging line through Lafayette, Bates, Adams, and Bank Streets—the latter skirting the river-gorge—to the abandoned and dilapidated station I had seen from my window. My reason for going ahead to Babson was that I wished neither to re-cross the earlier open space nor to begin my westward course along a cross street as broad as South.

Starting once more, I crossed the street to the right-hand side in order to edge around into Babson as inconspicuously as possible. Noises still continued in Federal Street, and as I glanced behind me I thought I saw a gleam of light near the building through which I had escaped. Anxious to leave Washington Street, I broke into a quiet dog-trot, trusting to luck not to encounter any observing eye. Next on the corner of Babson Street I saw to my alarm that one of the houses was still inhabited, as attested by curtains at the window; but there were no lights within, and I passed it without disaster.

In Babson Street, which crossed Federal and might thus reveal me to the searchers, I clung as closely as possible to the sagging, un-even buildings; twice pausing in a doorway as the noises behind me momentarily increased. The open space ahead shone wide and deso-late under the moon, but my route would not force me to cross it. During my second pause I began to detect a fresh distribution of the vague sounds; and upon looking cautiously out from cover beheld a motorcar darting across the open space, bound outward along Eliot Street, which there intersects both Babson and Lafayette.

As I watched—choked by a sudden rise in the fishy odour after a short abatement—I saw a band of uncouth, crouching shapes loping and shambling in the same direction; and knew that this must be the party guarding the Ipswich road, since that highway forms an exten-sion of Eliot Street. Two of the figures I glimpsed were in voluminous robes, and one wore a peaked diadem which glistened whitely in the moonlight. The gait of this figure was so odd that it sent a chill through me—for it seemed to me the creature was almost *hopping*.

When the last of the band was out of sight I resumed my progress; darting around the corner into Lafayette Street, and cross-ing Eliot very hurriedly lest stragglers of the party be still advancing along that thoroughfare. I did hear some croaking and clattering sounds far off toward Town Square, but accomplished the passage without disaster. My greatest dread was in re-crossing broad and moonlit South Street—with its seaward view—and I had to nerve myself for the ordeal. Someone might easily be looking, and possible Eliot Street stragglers could not fail to glimpse me from either of two points. At the last moment I decided I had better slacken my trot and make the crossing as before in the shambling gait of an average Innsmouth native.

When the view of the water again opened out—this time on my right—I was half-determined not to look at it at all. I could not, however, resist; but cast a sidelong glance as I carefully and imitatively shambled toward the protecting shadows ahead. There was no ship visible, as I had half expected there would be. Instead, the first thing which caught my eye was a small rowboat pulling in toward the abandoned wharves and laden with some bulky, tarpaulin-covered object. Its rowers, though distantly and indistinctly seen, were of an especially repellent aspect. Several swimmers were still discernible; while on the far black reef I could see a faint, steady glow unlike the winking beacon visible before, and of a curious colour which I could not precisely identify. Above the slant-roofs ahead and to the right there loomed the tall cupola of the Gilman House, but it was completely dark. The fishy odour, dispelled for a moment by some merciful breeze, now closed in again with maddening intensity.

I had not quite crossed the street when I heard a muttering band advancing along Washington from the north. As they reached the broad open space where I had had my first disquieting glimpse of the moonlit water I could see them plainly only a block away—and was horrified by the bestial abnormality of their faces and the dog-like subhumanness of their crouching gait. One man moved in a positively simian way, with long arms frequently touching the ground; while another figure—robed and tiaraed—seemed to progress in an almost hopping fashion. I judged this party to be the one I had seen in the Gilmans' courtyard—the one, therefore, most closely on my trail. As some of the figures turned to look in my direction I was transfixed with fright, yet managed to preserve the casual, shambling gait I had assumed. To this day I do not know whether they saw me or not. If they did, my stratagem must have deceived them, for they passed on across the moonlit space without varying their course—meanwhile croaking and jabbering in some hateful guttural patois I could not identify.

Once more in shadow, I resumed my former dog-trot past the leaning and decrepit houses that stared blankly into the night. Having crossed to the western sidewalk I rounded the nearest corner into Bates Street, where I kept close to the buildings on the southern side. I passed two houses showing signs of habitation, one of which had faint lights in upper rooms, yet met with no obstacle. As I turned into Adams Street I felt measurably safer, but received a shock when a man reeled out of a black doorway directly in front of me. He proved, however, too hopelessly drunk to be a menace; so that I reached the dismal ruins of the Bank Street warehouses in safety.

No one was stirring in that dead street beside the river-gorge, and the roar of the waterfalls quite drowned my footsteps. It was a long dog-trot to the ruined station, and the great brick warehouse walls around me seemed somehow more terrifying than the fronts of private houses. At last I saw the ancient arcaded station—or what was left of it—and made directly for the tracks that started from its farther end.

The rails were rusty but mainly intact, and not more than half the ties had rotted away. Walking or running on such a surface was very difficult; but I did my best, and on the whole made very fair time. For some distance the line kept on along the gorge's brink, but at length I reached the long covered bridge where it crossed the chasm at a dizzy height. The condition of this bridge would determine my next step. If humanly possible, I would use it; if not, I would have to risk more street wandering and take the nearest intact highway bridge.

The vast, barn-like length of the old bridge gleamed spectrally in the moonlight, and I saw that the ties were safe for at least a few feet within. Entering, I began to use my flashlight, and was almost knocked down by the cloud of bats that flapped past me. About halfway across there was a perilous gap in the ties which I feared for a moment would halt me; but in the end I risked a desperate jump which fortunately succeeded.

I was glad to see the moonlight again when I emerged from that macabre tunnel. The old tracks crossed River Street at a grade, and at once veered off into a region increasingly rural and with less and less of Innsmouth's abhorrent fishy odour. Here the dense growth of weeds and briers hindered me and cruelly tore my clothes, but I was none the less glad that they were there to give me concealment in case of peril. I knew that much of my route must be visible from the Rowley road.

The marshy region began very shortly, with the single track on a low, grassy embankment where the weedy growth was somewhat thinner. Then came a sort of island of higher ground, where the line passed through a shallow open cut choked with bushes and brambles. I was very glad of this partial shelter, since at this point the Rowley road was uncomfortably near according to my window view. At the end of the cut it would cross the track and swerve off to a safer distance; but meanwhile I must be exceedingly careful. I was by this time thankfully certain that the railway itself was not patrolled.

Just before entering the cut I glanced behind me, but saw no pursuer. The ancient spires and roofs of decaying Innsmouth gleamed lovely and ethereal in the magic yellow moonlight, and I thought of how they must have looked in the old days before the shadow fell. Then, as my gaze circled inland from the town, something less tranquil arrested my notice and held me immobile for a second.

What I saw—or fancied I saw—was a disturbing suggestion of undulant motion far to the south; a suggestion which made me conclude that a very large horde must be pouring out of the city along the level Ipswich road. The distance was great, and I could distinguish nothing in detail; but I did not at all like the look of that moving column. It undulated too much, and glistened too brightly in the rays of the now westering moon. There was a suggestion of sound, too, though the wind was blowing the other way—a suggestion of bestial scraping and bellowing even worse than the muttering of the parties I had lately overheard.

All sorts of unpleasant conjectures crossed my mind. I thought of those very extreme Innsmouth types said to be hidden in crumbling, centuried warrens near the waterfront. I thought, too, of those nameless swimmers I had seen. Counting the parties so far glimpsed, as well as those presumably covering other roads, the number of my pursuers must be strangely large for a town as depopulated as Innsmouth.

Whence could come the dense personnel of such a column as I now beheld? Did those ancient, unplumbed warrens teem with a twisted, uncatalogued, and unsuspected life? Or had some unseen ship indeed landed a legion of unknown outsiders on that hellish reef? Who were they? Why were they there? And if such a column of them was scouring the Ipswich road, would the patrols on the other roads be likewise augmented?

I had entered the brush-grown cut and was struggling along at a very slow pace when that damnable fishy odour again waxed dominant. Had the wind suddenly changed eastward, so that it blew in from the sea and over the town? It must have, I concluded, since I now began to hear shocking guttural murmurs from that hitherto silent direction. There was another sound, too—a kind of wholesale, colossal flopping or pattering which somehow called up images of the most detestable sort. It made me think illogically of that unpleasantly undulating column on the far-off Ipswich road.

And then both stench and sounds grew stronger, so that I paused shivering and grateful for the cut's protection. It was here, I recalled, that the Rowley road drew so close to the old railway before crossing westward and diverging. Something was coming along that road, and I must lie low till its passage and vanishment in the distance. Thank heaven these creatures employed no dogs for tracking—though perhaps that would have been impossible amidst the omnipresent regional odour. Crouched in the bushes of that sandy cleft I felt reasonably safe, even though I knew the searchers would have to cross the track in front of me not much more than a hundred yards away. I would be able to see them, but they could not, except by a malign miracle, see me.

All at once I began dreading to look at them as they passed. I saw the close moonlit space where they would surge by, and had curious thoughts about the irredeemable pollution of that space. They would perhaps be the worst of all Innsmouth types—something one would not care to remember.

The stench waxed overpowering, and the noises swelled to a bestial babel of croaking, baying, and barking without the least suggestion of human speech. Were these indeed the voices of my pursuers? Did they have dogs after all? So far I had seen none of the lower animals in Innsmouth. That flopping or pattering was monstrous—I could not look upon the degenerate creatures responsible for it. I would keep my eyes shut till the sounds receded toward the west. The horde was very close now—the air foul with their hoarse snarlings, and the ground almost shaking with their alien-rhythmed footfalls. My breath nearly ceased to come, and I put every ounce of will power into the task of holding my eyelids down.

I am not even yet willing to say whether what followed was a hideous actuality or only a nightmare hallucination. The later action of the government, after my frantic appeals, would tend to confirm it as a monstrous truth; but could not an hallucination have been repeated under the quasi-hypnotic spell of that ancient, haunted, and shadowed town? Such places have strange properties, and the legacy of insane legend might well have acted on more than one human imagination amidst those dead, stench-cursed streets and huddles of rotting roofs and crumbling steeples. Is it not possible that the germ of an actual contagious madness lurks in the depths of that shadow over Innsmouth? Who can be sure of reality after hearing things like the tale of old Zadok Allen? The government men never found poor Zadok, and have no conjectures to make as to what became of him. Where does madness leave off and reality begin? Is it possible that even my latest fear is sheer delusion?

But I must try to tell what I thought I saw that night under the mocking yellow moon—saw surging and hopping down the Rowley road in plain sight in front of me as I crouched among the wild brambles of that desolate railway cut. Of course my resolution to keep my eyes shut had failed. It was foredoomed to failure—for who could crouch blindly while a legion of croaking, baying entities of unknown source flopped noisomely past, scarcely more than a hundred yards away?

I thought I was prepared for the worst, and I really ought to have been prepared considering what I had seen before. My other pursuers had been accursedly abnormal—so should I not have been ready to face a strengthening of the abnormal element; to look upon forms in which there was no mixture of the normal at all? I did not open my eyes until the raucous clamour came loudly from a point obviously straight ahead. Then I knew that a long section of them must be plainly in sight where the sides of the cut flattened out and the road crossed the track—and I could no longer keep myself from sampling whatever horror that leering yellow moon might have to show.

It was the end, for whatever remains to me of life on the surface of this earth, of every vestige of mental peace and confidence in the integrity of nature and of the human mind. Nothing that I could have imagined—nothing, even, that I could have gathered had I credited old Zadok's crazy tale in the most literal way—would be in any way comparable to the demoniac, blasphemous reality that I saw—or believe I saw. I have tried to hint what it was in order to postpone the horror of writing it down baldly. Can it be possible that this planet has actually spawned such things; that human eyes have truly seen, as objective flesh, what man has hitherto known only in febrile phantasy and tenuous legend?

And yet I saw them in a limitless stream—flopping, hopping, croaking, bleating—surging inhumanly through the spectral moonlight in a grotesque, malignant saraband of fantastic nightmare. And some of them had tall tiaras of that nameless whitish-gold metal . . . and some were strangely robed . . . and one, who led the way, was clad in a ghoulishly humped black coat and striped trousers, and had a man's felt hat perched on the shapeless thing that answered for a head . . .

I think their predominant colour was a greyish-green, though they had white bellies. They were mostly shiny and slippery, but the ridges of their backs were scaly. Their forms vaguely suggested the anthropoid, while their heads were the heads of fish, with prodigious bulging eyes that never closed. At the sides of their necks were palpitating gills, and their long paws were webbed. They hopped irregularly, sometimes on two legs and sometimes on four. I was somehow glad that they had no more than four limbs. Their croaking, baying voices, clearly used for articulate speech, held all the dark shades of expression which their staring faces lacked.

But for all of their monstrousness they were not unfamiliar to me. I knew too well what they must be—for was not the memory of that evil tiara at Newburyport still fresh? They were the blasphemous fish-frogs of the nameless design—living and horrible—and as I saw them I knew also of what that humped, tiaraed priest in the black church basement had so fearsomely reminded me. Their number was past guessing. It seemed to me that there were limitless swarms of them—and certainly my momentary glimpse could have shown only the least fraction. In another instant everything was blotted out by a merciful fit of fainting; the first I had ever had.

## V

It was a gentle daylight rain that awakened me from my stupor in the brushgrown railway cut, and when I staggered out to the roadway ahead I saw no trace of any prints in the fresh mud. Innsmouth's ruined roofs and toppling steeples loomed up greyly toward the southeast, but not a living creature did I spy in all the desolate salt marshes around. My watch was still going, and told me that the hour was past noon.

The reality of what I had been through was highly uncertain in my mind, but I felt that something hideous lay in the background. I must get away from evil-shadowed Innsmouth—and accordingly I began to test my cramped, wearied powers of locomotion. Despite weakness, hunger, horror, and bewilderment I found myself, after a time, able to walk; so started slowly along the muddy road to Rowley.

Before evening I was in the village, getting a meal and providing myself with presentable clothes. I caught the night train to Arkham, and the next day talked long and earnestly with government officials there; a process I later repeated in Boston. With the main result of these colloquies the public is now familiar—and I wish, for normality's sake, there were nothing more to tell. Perhaps it is madness that is overtaking me—yet perhaps a greater horror—or a greater marvel—is reaching out.

As may well be imagined, I gave up most of the foreplanned features of the rest of my tour—the scenic, architectural, and antiquarian diversions on which I had counted so heavily. Nor did I dare look for that piece of strange jewellery said to be in the Miskatonic University Museum. I did, however, improve my stay in Arkham by collecting some genealogical notes I had long wished to possess; very rough and hasty data, it is true, but capable of good use later on when I might have time to collate and codify them. The curator of the historical society there—Mr. E. Lapham Peabody— was very courteous about assisting me, and expressed unusual interest when I told him I was a grandson of Eliza Orne of Arkham, who was born in 1867 and had married James Williamson of Ohio at the age of seventeen.

It seemed that a maternal uncle of mine had been there many years before on a quest much like my own; and that my grandmother's family was a topic of some local curiosity. There had, Mr. Peabody said, been considerable discussion about the marriage of her father, Benjamin Orne, just after the Civil War; since the ancestry of the bride was peculiarly puzzling. That bride was understood to have been an orphaned Marsh of New Hampshire—a cousin of the Essex County Marshes—but her education had been in France and she knew very little of her family. A guardian had deposited funds in a Boston bank to maintain her and her French governess; but that guardian's name was unfamiliar to Arkham people, and in time he dropped out of sight, so that the governess assumed his role by court appointment. The Frenchwoman—now long dead—was very taciturn, and there were those who said she could have told more than she did.

But the most baffling thing was the inability of anyone to place the recorded parents of the young woman—Enoch and Lydia (Meserve) Marsh—among the known families of New Hampshire. Possibly, many suggested, she was the natural daughter of some Marsh of prominence—she certainly had the true Marsh eyes. Most of the puzzling was done after her early death, which took place at the birth of my grandmother—her only child. Having formed some disagreeable impressions connected with the name of Marsh, I did not welcome the news that it belonged on my own ancestral tree; nor was I pleased by Mr. Peabody's suggestion that I had the true Marsh eyes myself. However, I was grateful for data which I knew would prove valuable; and took copious notes and lists of book references regarding the well-documented Orne family.

I went directly home to Toledo from Boston, and later spent a month at Maumee recuperating from my ordeal. In September I entered Oberlin for my final year, and from then till the next June was busy with studies and other wholesome activities—reminded of the bygone terror only by occasional official visits from government men in connection with the campaign which my pleas and evidence had started. Around the middle of July—just a year after the Innsmouth experience—I spent a week with my late mother's family in Cleveland; checking some of my new genealogical data with the various notes, traditions, and bits of heirloom material in existence there, and seeing what kind of a connected chart I could construct.

I did not exactly relish this task, for the atmosphere of the Williamson home had always depressed me. There was a strain of morbidity there, and my mother had never encouraged my visiting her parents as a child, although she always welcomed her father when he came to Toledo. My Arkham-born grandmother had seemed strange and almost terrifying to me, and I do not think I grieved when she disappeared. I was eight years old then, and it was said that she had wandered off in grief after the suicide of my uncle Douglas, her eldest son. He had shot himself after a trip to New England—the same trip, no doubt, which had caused him to be recalled at the Arkham Historical Society.

This uncle had resembled her, and I had never liked him either.

Something about the staring, unwinking expression of both of them had given me a vague, unaccountable uneasiness. My mother and uncle Walter had not looked like that. They were like their father, though poor little cousin Lawrence—Walter's son—had been an almost perfect duplicate of his grandmother before his condition took him to the permanent seclusion of a sanitarium at Canton. I had not seen him in four years, but my uncle once implied that his state, both mental and physical, was very bad. This worry had probably been a major cause of his mother's death two years before.

My grandfather and his widowed son Walter now comprised the Cleveland household, but the memory of older times hung thickly over it. I still disliked the place, and tried to get my researches done as quickly as possible. Williamson records and traditions were supplied in abundance by my grandfather; though for Orne material I had to depend on my uncle Walter, who put at my disposal the contents of all his files, including notes, letters, cuttings, heirlooms, photographs, and miniatures.

It was in going over the letters and pictures on the Orne side that I began to acquire a kind of terror of my own ancestry. As I have said, my grandmother and uncle Douglas had always disturbed me. Now, years after their passing, I gazed at their pictured faces with a measurably heightened feeling of repulsion and alienation. I could not at first understand the change, but gradually a horrible sort of comparison began to obtrude itself on my unconscious mind despite the steady refusal of my consciousness to admit even the least suspicion of it. It was clear that the typical expression of these faces now suggested something it had not suggested before—something which would bring stark panic if too openly thought of.

But the worst shock came when my uncle showed me the Orne jewellery in a downtown safe-deposit vault. Some of the items were delicate and inspiring enough, but there was one box of strange old pieces descended from my mysterious great-grandmother which my uncle was almost reluctant to produce. They were, he said, of very grotesque and almost repulsive design, and had never to his knowledge been publicly worn; though my grandmother used to enjoy looking at them. Vague legends of bad luck clustered around them, and my great-grandmother's French governess had said they ought not to be worn in New England, though it would be quite safe to wear them in Europe.

As my uncle began slowly and grudgingly to unwrap the things he urged me not to be shocked by the strangeness and frequent hideousness of the designs. Artists and archaeologists who had seen them pronounced their workmanship superlatively and exotically exquisite, though no one seemed able to define their exact material or assign them to any specific art tradition. There were two armlets, a tiara, and a kind of pectoral; the latter having in high relief certain figures of almost unbearable extravagance.

During this description I had kept a tight rein on my emotions, but my face must have betrayed my mounting fears. My uncle looked concerned, and paused in his unwrapping to study my countenance. I motioned to him to continue, which he did with renewed signs of reluctance. He seemed to expect some demonstration when the first piece—the tiara—became visible, but I doubt if he expected quite what actually happened. I did not expect it, either, for I thought I was thoroughly forewarned regarding what the jewellery would turn out to be. What I did was to faint silently away, just as I had done in that brier-choked railway cut a year before.

From that day on my life has been a nightmare of brooding and apprehension, nor do I know how much is hideous truth and how much madness. My great-grandmother had been a Marsh of unknown source whose husband lived in Arkham—and did not old Zadok say that the daughter of Obed Marsh by a monstrous mother was married to an Arkham man through a trick? What was it the ancient toper had muttered about the likeness of my eyes to Captain Obed's? In Arkham, too, the curator had told me I had the true Marsh eyes. Was Obed Marsh my own great-great-grandfather? Who—or what—then, was my great-great-grandmother? But perhaps this was all madness. Those whitish-gold ornaments might easily have been bought from some Innsmouth sailor by the father of my great-grandmother, whoever he was. And that look in the staring-eyed faces of my grandmother and self-slain uncle might be sheer fancy on my part—sheer fancy, bolstered up by the Innsmouth shadow which had so darkly coloured my imagination. But why had my uncle killed himself after an ancestral quest in New England?

For more than two years I fought off these reflections with partial success. My father secured me a place in an insurance office, and I buried myself in routine as deeply as possible. In the winter of 1930–31, however, the dreams began. They were very sparse and insidious at first, but increased in frequency and vividness as the weeks went by. Great watery spaces opened out before me, and I seemed to wander through titanic sunken porticos and labyrinths of weedy Cyclopean walls with grotesque fishes as my companions. Then the *other shapes* began to appear, filling me with nameless horror the moment I awoke. But during the dreams they did not horrify me at all— I was one with them; wearing their unhuman trappings, treading their aqueous ways, and praying monstrously at their evil sea-bottom temples.

There was much more than I could remember, but even what I did remember each morning would be enough to stamp me as a madman or a genius if ever I dared write it down. Some frightful influence, I felt, was seeking gradually to drag me out of the sane world of wholesome life into unnameable abysses of blackness and alienage; and the process told heavily on me. My health and appearance grew steadily worse, till finally I was forced to give up my position and adopt the static, secluded life of an invalid. Some odd nervous affliction had me in its grip, and I found myself at times almost unable to shut my eyes.

It was then that I began to study the mirror with mounting alarm. The slow ravages of disease are not pleasant to watch, but in my case there was something subtler and more puzzling in the background. My father seemed to notice it, too, for he began looking at me curiously and almost affrightedly. What was taking place in me? Could it be that I was coming to resemble my grandmother and uncle Douglas?

One night I had a frightful dream in which I met my grandmother under the sea. She lived in a phosphorescent palace of many terraces, with gardens of strange leprous corals and grotesque brachiate efflorescences, and welcomed me with a warmth that may have been sardonic. She had changed—as those who take to the water change—and told me she had never died. Instead, she had gone to a spot her dead son had learned about, and had leaped to a realm whose wonders—destined for him as well—he had spurned with a smoking pistol. This was to be my realm, too—I could not escape it. I would never die, but would live with those who had lived since before man ever walked the earth.

I met also that which had been her grandmother. For eighty thousand years Pth'thya-l'yi had lived in Y'ha-nthlei, and thither she had gone back after Obed Marsh was dead. Y'ha-nthlei was not destroyed when the upper-earth men shot death into the sea. It was hurt, but not destroyed. The Deep Ones could never be destroyed, even though the palaeogean magic of the forgotten Old Ones might sometimes check them. For the present they would rest; but some day, if they remembered, they would rise again for the tribute Great Cthulhu craved. It would be a city greater than Innsmouth next time. They had planned to spread, and had brought up that which would help them, but now they must wait once more. For bringing the upper-earth men's death I must do a penance, but that would not be heavy. This was the dream in which I saw a *shoggoth* for the first time, and the sight set me awake in a frenzy of screaming. That morning the mirror definitely told me I had acquired *the Innsmouth look.*

So far I have not shot myself as my uncle Douglas did. I bought an automatic and almost took the step, but certain dreams deterred me. The tense extremes of horror are lessening, and I feel queerly drawn toward the unknown sea-deeps instead of fearing them. I hear and do strange things in sleep, and awake with a kind of exaltation instead of terror. I do not believe I need to wait for the full change as most have waited. If I did, my father would probably shut me up in a sanitarium as my poor little cousin is shut up. Stupendous and unheard-of splendours await me below, and I shall seek them soon. *Iä-R'lyeh! Cthulhu fhtagn! Iä! Iä!* No, I shall not shoot myself—I cannot be made to shoot myself!

I shall plan my cousin's escape from that Canton madhouse,

and together we shall go to marvel-shadowed Innsmouth. We shall swim out to that brooding reef in the sea and dive down through black abysses to Cyclopean and many-columned Y'ha-nthlei, and in that lair of the Deep Ones we shall dwell amidst wonder and glory forever.

# Beyond the Reef

## Basil Copper

### I

Come in, gentlemen, come in. Make yourselves at home. The place, as you see, is in something of a mess, so I hope you'll forgive the untidiness. Can I offer you gentlemen coffee? It's a cold day. No? Well, just as you please. You must excuse my rudeness if I re-seat myself and finish off my own. I'm a great coffee addict, truth to tell.

"Some cookies, perhaps? Well, there's no accounting for taste. You'll have come about the happenings, surely? It's a long story and I have to collect my thoughts. But I'll get to it, gentlemen, I'll get to it. The Great Storm began it, of course. It disturbed a great many things, a great many lives, as you know. Took a great many lives too. Who would have thought that a mere few weeks could have wrought so great a havoc, have destroyed so many hopes and dreams?

"Ah, I see Captain of Detectives Oates among you. All the way from the County Seat. Well, that proves the importance of what I'm saying. Truth to tell, I've been expecting you these past hours. But then there must have been many facts to collate, many blind alleys, many avenues to explore, if you'll forgive the cliches. The facts themselves are so weird and bizarre I can hardly believe them myself.

"And the tunnels, gentlemen! Have you yet explored their full possibilities? You must take care, you know. They are extremely dangerous. And who knows what lower depths those vast caverns conceal. I see you nod your heads. Even Mr. Oates looks pale. As well you might be, sir. As well you might be. The black abyss and the unnameable.

"No, I am not mad, gentlemen, though I have seen and heard things enough to unhinge the strongest mind these past weeks. A savant and a scholar . . . a qualified scientist too. Where to begin? That is the problem. The State Asylum must be full of people who will seem more sane than I once my story is told. I see you have your secretary and a stenographer present, sir. Well, we shall need them both in due course.

"Oh, you are taking notes already? Well, it makes no matter. I have nothing to conceal, nothing to fear in this world, at least. As to the other, that is an entirely different matter . . . My introductory remarks will perhaps help to convince people that I am as sane as they are. Perhaps better to exist in a constant dream than a living nightmare. The oblivion of insanity would blot out images one would rather forget.

"Please do not be impatient, sir. Mine is a story that will take up a good deal of time in the telling, I can assure you. Man's tragedy is that wonderful machine we call the brain; memory is the curse that makes life a burden. What a disaster that memory makes us savour vain hopes and regrets to their bitterest dregs. What is it Shakespeare says? Makes tragedy of so long life . . . or something to that effect? Well, gentlemen, I have supped from this cup of bitterness to its very last drop.

"Life holds nothing more. Yes, by all means keep on with your shorthand notes. I am getting to the point, I can assure you. This, then, is the sworn statement of Jefferson Holroyd, scholar and scientist, aged forty-five years, and in whole mind and body. It all began, then . . ."

## II

The great storm of January of the year 1932, which struck the town of Innsmouth so cruelly, was completely unexpected, though there had been out of the way happenings which those trained to read the symptoms might have forecast had they read them aright.

But many disparate facts needed to be taken in their entirety; the disconnected fragments, completely inexplicable at the time, could not have been seen as part of a connected whole and it is only with hindsight that meteorologists, scientists and other experts who converged on the area have been able to put something of the truth together.

There had been tremors of things to come much earlier than that. Newspaper reports in the autumn of 1930 described a great tidal bore which swept up the Manuxet, accompanied by a curious phenomenon the locals spoke of as "white lightning." A number of isolated farms on the fringe of the salt marshes were flooded and several people drowned while the town of Rowley was isolated for a time, though no damage was reported from there.

Even inland Arkham was affected by something which the reports described as a "miniature whirlwind" which ripped tiles from the rafters of business premises and completely stripped the shingles from the entire roofs of the more ancient buildings. Scientists put the disturbances down to a seismic tremor or a sort of underwater earthquake far down beyond the Innsmouth reef, which was responsible for the tidal bore while meteorologists ascribed the whirlwind damage and the stormy currents and curious lightning bolts as the effect of masses of cold and warm air meeting. Then, as nothing further happened for some weeks the affair, as is usually the case, was fairly rapidly forgotten by the majority of people, except by those to whom damage or tragedy had actually happened.

Massachusetts is a strange and ancient place, with isolated pockets and scattered communities among the gnarled hills, on the fringes of the marshes and among belts of forest so old that only archaeologists and experts in such matters are able to make an assessment of their age; a state whose remoter areas are regions which time seems to have forgotten, even in these latter days. In 1930 these aspects were even more pronounced and old books in the great library at Miskatonic University spoke of even stranger things so that the Chief Librarian, Jethro Staveley, kept such rare and esoteric works in a remote and locked section, far removed from the public bookstacks, where access was granted only to bona fide scholars or authorized researchers and academics.

This was nominally because of the rarity and value of such arcane volumes but there were those who said that the forbidden knowledge contained within the musty leaves was the real reason why Staveley kept them under such close guard. And more astute observers put the disturbances of 1930 which culminated in the awful happenings of 1932 down to much earlier incidents, such as the burglary at the University Library as far back as the early spring of 1929, when a remote side door was forced, the locked section entered and a chained and particularly obscure tome was stolen; the solid steel links of the chain securing it to the oak shelving being melted as though they had been made of butter.

The University authorities put this effect down to the use of some kind of welding apparatus, their surmises being reinforced by charring of the adjacent shelving and the great heat which had cracked nearby panes of glass. But Staveley turned deathly pale when the news was brought to him and his demeanour was greatly changed after that. Fortunately, he had several typed copies of the missing volume—as indeed was the practice for all the rare documents in the sealed section which were secreted in a steel, vault-like chamber adjoining his office.

When he had consulted these he seemed more troubled than ever and the change in his formerly bluff and friendly, not to say outgoing manner, dated from that moment, according to his closest friends in academic circles. He was closeted with the Dean for most of the following day and that gentleman, Dr. Darrow, seemed equally disturbed.

No news of the burglary was allowed to reach the ears of the press and the incident was made light of within the University itself. But inquiries by friends and fellow academics as to the title of the missing volume and its contents were met with tight-lipped silence on the part of both men and requests to see the copies held in the Librarian's office were answered with polite refusals.

The incident, which had briefly rippled the normally placid life of this great university, was eventually forgotten until other, even more dramatic events impinged upon the public consciousness. Perhaps the term dramatic is a misnomer, for though taken as a chain of circumstances they partook of drama, they were perhaps rather more humdrum when viewed as isolated incidents. The first had nothing to do with the University and occurred only a few weeks after the events previously described. This was a disastrous fire that destroyed priceless seventeenth and eighteenth century records at Arkham Public Library.

So far as the theft was concerned, though inquiries were made on campus itself, the thief who had so desecrated the Library was never found and as nothing was ever given out beyond the immediate circle of the academic staff involved it never reached the ears of the State Police either.

The Library episode faded from the general consciousness, to be supplanted by more subtle and esoteric manifestations. This time the occurrences were in both women student and men student dormitory wings. They consisted merely of subtle movements in the night; windows and doors which, originally fastened and secured, remained obstinately open until the daylight hours; faint footsteps echoing along corridors; taps in communal washrooms that turned on by themselves; and electric lights that inexplicably switched themselves on or off, according to the position in which the switches had been left.

Many were the theories advanced by the students but the consensus was that a sort of war was being waged by young men from other faculties on campus and a period of faintly amused hostility prevailed for a time until two more incidents, the most serious to date, supplanted the earlier ones in the collective consciousness.

The first, which passed at the time for an accident, though it later assumed its true proportions, concerned the Dean himself. There had been a night of particularly high winds and as the Miskatonic University stands on rising ground a number of small trees had fallen victim to the storm. The wind continued fresh at dawn but it had dropped considerably when an extraordinary thing happened.

There was an enormous stone cross standing in the northwestern corner of the Jefferson Campus which commemorated some of the University's dead from the War of Independence and the Great War. It was made of granite and time had evidently made no inroads into its fabric, even though some 200 years had passed since it was first erected, originally as a purely religious symbol; only later did it fulfil a double use as a Christian motif and as a war memorial. Dr. Darrow was passing on his way to deliver a lecture at about ten a.m., when there was a sudden gust of wind. To the horror of nearby undergraduates passing and re-passing, the vast stone cross suddenly split from top to bottom.

Two alert students dragged the horrified doctor from the path of danger, at some risk to themselves, and while Darrow was slightly injured by being hurled to the ground, their prompt and heroic action certainly saved his life. Covered in dust and shaking with fear Dr. Darrow presented a pitiable sight and his amazement at the unexplained collapse of the memorial was mirrored by all those students and members of faculty who had witnessed the incident.

Even more extraordinary was the fact that the inside of the column was "wet and sticky," as one observer termed it. The University's scientific brains were called into play and to their astonishment they found that the interior of the column had "rotted away." The thing was a manifest impossibility as granite cannot rot and is one of the most impermeable of materials. Nevertheless some thing or some agent had worked on the column's interior until it was a mess of friable, gelatinous matter.

The second and more ghastly incident occurred a short time later. In a remote area of the University grounds was a stand of thick woodland, favoured by students in the summer months for various amorous activities. In a small, rocky glen was a miniature pond; no more than a hundred yards long and about forty feet wide, which was believed to be fed by some sort of underground spring. Its black water reflected back the sky sullenly, even in summer, and its brackish contents gave off a faint odour that was somehow repellent. Consequently this was a corner shunned in general; certainly at times of dusk or darkness and one which it was far pleasanter to stroll by on summer days rather than to linger at.

The earlier incidents were certainly eclipsed by the sight of one of the Miskatonic janitors, Jeb Conley, an elderly man who had been absent from duty for some days, floating face downward in those black waters early one February morning. A female student first gave the alarm and, prudently as it turned out, refrained from turning over the body. It was fairly obvious that the man was dead so she very courageously seized a dead branch lying on the bank and gently guided the pool's sombre burden to the shore.

Dr. Nathan Kelly, a medical man on the staff of the University, was hastily summoned and his practised eye saw at once that life was extinct. He was alone at the pond at the time, though knots of students were gathering beneath the trees that fringed the area. He found, as he turned the corpse over, that though the body could not have been in the pool for more than twenty-four hours—as was later established by the autopsy—the man's face had been erased as though it had never existed.

The features were all squashed and flattened by some unknown and hitherto unique agency, so that they were unidentifiable and the whole was coated with a film of nauseous grey slime that no amount of cleansing in the dissecting room could alter or remove. Dr. Kelly did not know it then but it was the beginning of a time of terror.

## III

Dr. Darrow was in his office collating college records one afternoon some days later when his secretary told him that the surveyor in charge of renovation of the memorial cross had called to speak to him. The two men had long been friends but when Andrew Bellows entered the inner office the Dean was at once struck by the changed demeanour of the former. He looked ill at ease and rather furtive, if that were not too strong a word; quite unlike his normal, cheerful self, and the academic was at first puzzled and then concerned as he motioned Bellows to a comfortable leather chair. He ordered two cups of strong coffee from Miss Blomberg and the two men fell into an uneasy silence until the secretary had left the big, panelled room.

Bellows had been engaged to supervise the restoration of the memorial cross, if that were technically possible, and at first the Dean had thought the other's demeanour had something to do with a further disaster, or perhaps a greatly increased estimate of the cost involved. But it was nothing like that, as his visitor soon made clear. He put his cup down meticulously, wiping a small bead of coffee from the rim of the vessel with his handkerchief before coming to the point.

"We had a little accident this morning," he said. "There was a fall of earth in one corner of the roped-off area. It was quite unexpected. In fact, one of the contractor's men would have gone with the earthspill if I hadn't grabbed him by the arm."

The Dean looked surprised.

"Oh," he began hesitantly. "I hope he does not intend to sue the University . . ."

Bellows shook his head. He gave the other a wry grin.

"Nothing like that. But there's something queer about all this. Quite beyond my experience. I have all the plans for the buildings and grounds, covering every foot of University property. I could have sworn there were no crypts or catacombs near there; at least any other than those already built by the founders."

Darrow shook his head impatiently.

"I'm not sure I follow you."

Bellows leaned back in his deep chair and took another long sip of the coffee, choosing his words with particular care.

"That earth-fall didn't seem natural to me," he said. "I know the terrain and there was no normal reason for any such subsidence. We put some planks round the area, of course, and warned people off. I could see a dark hole opening up where the soil had collapsed. This was about fifteen feet from the base of the memorial. One of the reasons, obviously, which led to the near accident you had. But it wasn't the entire reason for the collapse of the cross. Merely a contributory factor."

He could see small signs of impatience on the Dean's face and hurried on before his companion could interrupt. "When the men broke for lunch I got a torch and a rope," he explained. "I went down there. I found something quite extraordinary. So extraordinary, in fact, that I'd like you to take a look at it."

The Dean sniffed. He disliked extravagant language or superlatives as the surveyor knew.

Darrow raised his eyebrows.

"Extraordinary? Isn't that rather a strong term?"

Bellows shook his head.

"It might seem so sitting here. When you've taken a look . . ."

The Dean put down his coffee cup rather abruptly, making a sharp cracking noise in the quiet room.

"But what interest should I find in a hole in the ground, Andrew?"

"You don't understand," Bellows went on. "I got a rope and a torch, as I said. I lowered myself down, taking great care, as you might imagine, as I had no wish to be suffocated by any further earth falls. But as I got down there I could see that the opening widened out considerably. And what's more, a draught of cold air was coming up."

Again Darrow raised his eyebrows.

"I fail to see . . ."

He fell silent as his visitor made a derisive clicking noise with his tongue.

"If you'd just let me finish. The draught of air denoted that I was not descending into a hole or even some sort of well. It told me there must be a passage, perhaps with another entrance, because a draught would not emanate from below otherwise."

He paused a moment and took another reflective gulp at his coffee.

"There was a passage," he said simply. "Or rather, a series of passages. I found myself in a large circular chamber, obviously manmade, because there were tool-marks on the rocky walls. The centre of the roof had supported the cross, now fallen, which had caused the subsidiary collapse. I went carefully round the circle, noting there were strange marks in the dusty floor."

A tremor passed through his frame as he went on.

"It looked as though someone had been dragging heavy sacks along. The marks converged in the central area beneath the cross."

"Curious," Dr. Darrow broke in, his sombre eyes gazing unseeingly across at the rows of ledgers set against the far wall.

"You may well say so," said Bellows. "And that's not all. There were other dark passages leading off at intervals, in a semi-circle, facing west. They seemed long and as I penetrated into the largest I found it appeared to go on for an immense distance. The wind blew steadily down this and brought with it a nauseating smell."

His voice trembled briefly.

"Like decaying vegetable matter. I did not investigate further, as you may imagine, as I had no wish to get lost on my own. There were seven tunnels or passages in all—three each side of the larger, central one. And round the walls of the circular chamber there were incised inscriptions I couldn't make out. I regained the surface without delay and made a series of sketches while the details were clear in my memory. Then I had a heavy wooden trap made, sealing off the entrance to the chamber, and my men placed wheelbarrows filled with rubble upon it to prevent anyone else going there."

The Dean gave him a crooked smile, licking suddenly dry lips.

"It sounds rather as though you were trying to prevent something coming out," he said in a would-be jocular voice. The attempt to lighten the atmosphere was lost on Bellows.

"You are the only other person who knows about this. I felt we two should make some further preliminary investigation before giving this wider circulation."

The other's eyes never left his visitor's face.

"What are you trying to say, Andrew?"

Bellows shrugged.

"I'd like an independent witness of your standing. And I don't care to go down there alone again."

There was a long silence between the two.

"You must have good reason."

"I have. While I was down there I heard sounds. Coming from far off down the passages."

The Dean made a dismal attempt at a laugh, which trailed off into an awkward silence.

"Traffic, perhaps? Drains? Sounds percolating through grilles from the college buildings above?"

"Perhaps," said Bellows slowly. "But I think not. That was the reason I went back to my office and got this."

He tapped the capacious right-hand pocket of the shooting jacket he always wore when visiting building sites.

"My old service revolver. Are you ready?"

The Dean rose reluctantly.

"Very well," he said grimly. "This business must be investigated thoroughly."

# IV

It was late afternoon when the Dean and Bellows arrived at the site of the collapsed column; it had been winched aside and was now covered with tarpaulin, the workmen having finished for the day. The Dean pursed his lips and looked ominously at the scene of his near-fatal accident; the earth was torn up for yards around where the column and the plinth had been removed and the gaping hole of the tunnel, now covered with the rough board trapdoor of which the surveyor had spoken; the rope enclosure and the plank barriers made the whole place look like a building project rather than the campus of a great university.

It was a quiet time of the day; most of the faculty and students were at the early evening meal or engaged in preparing for their next lecture sessions, and only an occasional passing figure emerged and disappeared in the far distance. The Dean's figure was well-known on campus and the respect in which he was held ensured the two men's privacy.

"Shall we begin?" the academic asked.

Something in his companion's stiff attitude arrested him and the words died on his lips. Bellows had turned a little white beneath his tan and his lips trembled slightly. He was in so rapt an attitude of listening that Darrow had to take him by the arm before his companion realised he had spoken.

"What is it?" the Dean asked.

The surveyor shook his arm off.

"Nothing," he said abruptly. "I thought I heard something, that's all. Like a distant rumbling."

The Dean shrugged.

"Passing traffic outside the University grounds," he suggested.

Bellows deferred to him reluctantly.

"Perhaps," he said stiffly. "Well, we'd better get below."

He moved swiftly over to the rough trapdoor, as though shaking off a trance. His movements seemed stiff and mechanical to Darrow, but he said nothing, merely followed, watching carefully, as the large black hole, fringed with fallen earth and small pebbles, lay revealed.

Bellows had equipped himself with a large electric lantern and the Dean had also brought along a hand torch and his leather driving gloves, so that they were reasonably well equipped for their brief expedition, for neither man intended to stay below more than a few minutes. When it would be time to properly explore the passageways below, it would be with a large party, much more comprehensively equipped, for if one was to believe the surveyor's story, the cave system might be quite extensive.

Neither man made any move to descend, merely standing as though hypnotised at the brink of the dark hole in the troubled earth.

"By the way," said the Dean, as though to break a spell. "You have not shown me those drawings you spoke of earlier."

Bellows gave him a relieved look. He fumbled in an inner pocket of his jacket.

"I have them here. Look at this rough copy of one of the inscriptions. What do you make of it?"

The Dean drew in his breath with a loud implosion. Though he did not know the crude symbols his companion had so accurately depicted—nor could he understand their import—he had seen their counterparts before. He had studied many similar things in some of the ancient books in the locked section of the University library. But he merely nodded, as he bent closer to examine the sheafs of ruled paper Bellows had pressed into his hand, oblivious of the keen wind that was now blowing steadily across the dusky campus.

He grunted at last and handed the sheets back.

"Interesting," was the only comment he allowed himself. "Had we not better get on? I have a lecture to deliver later."

Bellows mumbled his apologies and then stooped to the slope of loose shale which descended into the inky blackness below. The Dean now saw that the opening was about four feet square and he hesitated, waiting until his companion had switched on the powerful electric lantern, edging gingerly down the steep incline. Darrow noticed that there was a considerable expanse of the rough concourse below, ending in the dusty, uneven stone floor of which the surveyor had already spoken.

He waited until the latter had gained firm ground below and then descended hesitantly in his turn, glad of the brightness of the lantern which showed him increasingly better detail of the surroundings as the daylight faded out above.

"There's no need to worry," Bellows said, as though he could read the Dean's thoughts. "We're not going far in and I've brought a ball of twine with me in case we decide to explore the passages."

It was indeed a remarkable sight which the surveyor's torch revealed. The Dean gazed round intently at the large circular chamber, licking his lips, his professional instincts gradually erasing the slight fear he had felt on coming below. The fear, he realised, almost entirely engendered by the content of some of the ancient books in the University library; only those in Latin, French and Old English, of course, for some of the works had so far defied the ablest translators of Runic scripts.

The faint sounds of traffic and those slight noises endemic to every great seat of human activity were now completely erased for the two men and an oppressive silence reigned in the vault-like chamber.

Bellows walked slowly round the circular concourse, holding the lantern high so that his companion could make out the strange hieroglyphs which ran in an irregular banded frieze, following the curve of the walls in one unbroken sequence. There were the seven dark tunnels set into the western side of the concourse, facing them like so many black eye-sockets. Each passage was surmounted by larger inscriptions of the banded sequence, as though they had titles or particular functions and Darrow was so absorbed that, after a few minutes, he was completely oblivious of the presence of his companion.

But the latter had been looking round at his feet in the dimmer glow cast by the torch and now he stopped abruptly.

"Hullo!" he said sharply. "These weren't here before."

The Dean followed the dancing lantern beam and saw at first only smudged outlines of something in the dust at his feet.

"They weren't here before," Bellows repeated stubbornly.

Darrow bent forward.

"They do look as though someone has been dragging sacks across the floor," he said dubiously. "But I fail to see . . ."

He broke off as his companion interrupted him.

"You don't understand. There were a few disturbances of the dust as I said earlier."

Here he glanced swiftly at his wrist watch.

"But these further marks have been made only within the last hour."

There was an uneasy silence between the two men.

"Perhaps the workmen have been down here to have a look around," Darrow said unconvincingly.

Bellows shook his head.

"They had their instructions. Besides, there are only my own footprints coming and going in the spillage leading down here. Something has come from one of these tunnels."

The pale gleam of the lantern glanced over the great black entrances ahead.

"See! These tracks in the dust go back into the central one. We'd better have a look at this."

The Dean gave a dry cough.

"Do you think it wise, Andrew?"

The surveyor shook his head.

"Perhaps not. But I'm damned curious. Besides, there are two of us. And we have the lantern and my revolver. I can't see that there's likely to be any danger. And I can't see any harm in our going a little way down the central tunnel."

The Dean shrugged, though he felt far from easy. He glanced again round the central chamber, before acquiescing.

"As you wish. If you think it's safe."

The surveyor looked concerned at the academic's obvious nervousness. He led the way quickly across the concourse, before the other could change his mind. The pale circle of light danced before them. Now that they were in its mouth the tunnel looked bigger than they had imagined and their footsteps echoed unnaturally loud, seeming to reverberate far longer than they should have done. Indeed, the effect was so strange that the two men stopped as of one accord, listening to the distant ripple of sound that took such a long time to die out. But neither said anything and Bellows avoided the other's eyes, feeling a strange heaviness fall across his own heart, though he would not have admitted such a thing to his companion.

Then they walked on again, both men noting the smoothly chiselled walls of the tunnel and the evenness of the floor. The Dean cleared his throat.

"These are obviously man-made, as you earlier observed, Andrew. But the excellence of the workmanship, the antiquity of these workings and their extent . . ."

He broke off, a marvelling quality coming into his voice.

"All this through solid granite. You realise what it means?"

Bellows smiled thinly.

"I ought to. I'm a surveyor by profession. Or hadn't you remembered?"

The Dean shook his head.

"I'm sorry. I didn't mean to sound patronising. But I now realise why you were so worked up about this discovery. We must certainly explore a little. You are unravelling that twine, are you not?"

"Certainly. But this passage is absolutely straight. We have only to retrace our steps."

The Dean shrugged.

"That's as may be. But if we come to a side passage . . ."

Andrew Bellows had his head on one side now, his face taut and strained in the yellow cone of the torchlight, his hand still playing out the thick twine as they slowly advanced. He spoke as though musing to himself.

"There will be no side passages, unless they give direct cross-access to the others. Have you forgotten the subsidiaries? They all lead toward Innsmouth and the sea. And they slightly diverge, as I had earlier observed."

There was a dreamy quality in his voice now.

"Like the setting sun."

The Dean looked at him sharply, all his earlier fears forgotten.

"What are you trying to say?"

"I don't know, really. But there is a greater mystery here than even I had earlier contemplated."

The two men were silent now for five minutes or so as they made steady progress in the warm, still air, the only sound their faint breathing and the sharp, brittle echoes of their onward march. The earlier draught they had felt in the concourse seemed to have died out. They had gone something like a quarter of a mile, the surveyor judged, and the great ball of twine he was unreeling had perceptibly diminished.

Then, he was aware of an almost imperceptible curve in the tunnel, that he knew from his professional experience must bring it eventually to the sea if it ran so far, directly to the ancient seaport of Innsmouth. At the same time there was a faint inrush of air on the two men's faces and an indefinable odour; it had in it a stale, musty smell, mingled with another, stronger aroma; almost as if they were approaching a fish market. The two men, as though seized by a single thought, increased their pace.

Almost at once they were arrested by a strange sight in that mathematically precise world where every surface and plane of the circular walls of the tunnel and its footing beneath, seemed to have been meticulously incised as though with a ruler, so straight and orderly was everything.

Ahead was chaos, depicted in the wavering yellow torchlight; great blocks of stone, smooth as if carved with some gigantic knife, lay tumbled and awry, from floor to ceiling. Yet to the surveyor's expert eye it did not look as though there had been a rock fall. For one thing, the blocks were of a different material to that of the granite from which the passages were hewn. These rocks were dark brown, basaltic and incredibly old; it was as though they had been brought there from a distance. Bellows' lip trembled slightly and his voice also as he whispered to his companion.

"It's almost as though some beings had brought these blocks here . . . for the sole purpose of blocking the tunnel."

Darrow did not speak and the two men stood immobile, their souls weighed down with the secret thoughts within them. The dust marks had long died out, which was bizarre in itself, so it was obvious that no-one had preceded them there, along the tunnel floor. Therefore, the prodigious power that had erected this mighty barrier had come from the other side; that which lay toward the sea and the great reef of Innsmouth.

"This is beyond belief," Bellows muttered at last.

The only answer he got was a strangled gargling noise from his companion. It was so unexpected and horrible in that place that the surveyor almost dropped the torch. He had the revolver out now and moved it in a steady arc but nothing stirred in the smooth expanse of tunnel except for the wavering torchlight. He became aware that Darrow had dropped to his knees. His face was ghastly in the dim light.

"Did you see them?" he asked in a strangled voice.

Bellows felt a sudden chill and he kept his voice steady with an effort.

"No, I saw nothing."

The Dean leaned against him for support.

"Terrible squirming things, with flat heads like snakes. They seemed to go through the wall."

Bellows' voice was trembling as he replied.

"Let us get out of here," he muttered in a low voice, not far from panic himself.

He half-dragged his companion away from the rock wall and they set off at a tottering run, the ball of twine abandoned now, the torchlight dancing on the roof of the passage.

They were both near collapse when they reached the circular chamber and Bellows had to support his companion. Behind them the echoes of their mad progress were prolonged for a far greater interval of time than they should have been.

## V

"I am going to show you something few people have ever seen," said Darrow.

It was almost dusk now and the two men were back in the Dean's study.

"I have had a de-code done of some of the books in the sealed section of the library here. By one of my most brilliant colleagues, Jefferson Holroyd. He spent time on the staff some years ago and now lectures here regularly. Perhaps you've heard of him?"

Bellows glanced at the half-empty whiskey bottle on the desk between them and re-filled his glass. He felt ashamed of his earlier panic now but it was evident that his companion had suffered a far more severe shock; he had had to cancel his lecture and the two men had gone straight to his quarters, after re-sealing the tunnel workings behind them. They seemed to have been talking for hours.

"Vaguely," Bellows said. "What's this business of de-coding? Are these the famous secret books of which I've heard so often?"

The Dean nodded. His face had lost something of its pallor and he appeared more at ease, though he occasionally shot worried glances about the comfortable panelled room. Lights were beginning to prick the distant campus and he moved somewhat unsteadily to draw the thick velvet drapes across the windows. Then he returned to the desk.

"About this hallucination," the surveyor went on, as his companion resumed his seat. "I would suggest . . ."

Darrow shook his head.

"That was no hallucination, Andrew. Those things were as real as you and I, though I glimpsed them only for a few seconds."

Bellows persisted.

"The strange atmosphere, the wavering torchlight, the tension of the moment . . ." he suggested.

Again the vehement shaking of the head.

"Nothing like that. Listen, Andrew, I'm going to tell you something. Something that I shouldn't because the knowledge is restricted to a mere handful of people. Above all, we don't want a panic on campus here."

He lowered his voice as though somebody or something might be listening.

"Peculiar things have been happening over the past two years or so. Strange, unexplainable things, of which this latest is but one manifestation. That's why I asked the help of Holroyd. He's one of the most brilliant cryptographers in the States. He's also a scholar with a mastery of ancient languages. I set him to work on some of the typed copies of the rare volumes here. He's starting to get results. That was why some of the material was stolen from the locked section."

Bellows looked at him sombrely.

"How can you possibly know that?"

Darrow shook his head.

"I just know, Andrew. Deep in my bones."

He smiled thinly, pouring himself more whiskey, with a dash of soda-water this time.

"Fortunately, I'd had everything in those books copied. There are three typescripts of each, all safely under lock and key in areas only two people know about. One of these persons is myself; the other is the University Librarian."

"I don't really know what you're trying to tell me," Bellows said after a long interval of silence. "There doesn't seem to be any point in all these strange happenings . . ."

Darrow leaned forward across the desk, his face a strained, taut mask, bisected by the white line of his straggly mustache.

"There is a point, Andrew. A terrible pattern here. That is why I have such faith in Holroyd. If anyone can find the key to these awful mysteries it is he. I have taken the liberty of sending for him. He should be here within the next ten minutes. He is a man of unimpeachable integrity and he has iron nerve. You and he would be ideally suited to lead the exploration of these passages together. I'm afraid I could not descend there again. My nerves have been too badly shaken. And now there are the problems of the police investigation . . ."

"You surprise me," Bellows said. "I have heard strange rumors about the campus, of course. Gossip about odd happenings over a long period of time. Lights that switch on and off in the students' halls of residence. The discovery of the body of Conley in that pond; the thefts of the books. But I did not know until today that you were so involved or that you had discerned a pattern in all this."

The Dean smiled rather wearily.

"I have learned to conceal my true feelings over the years, my dear Andrew," he said gently. "It is an invaluable attribute when one is dealing with academics, many of them powerful personalities who are sometimes at war with one another."

Bellows smiled too.

"That is not confined merely to the academic world. We all have our crosses to bear."

He stood up as there came a firm, confident rapping at the study door. He waited with interest as the Dean hurried to let the newcomer in.

Holroyd was a good-looking man of about forty-five, lean but powerfully built, with a thick shock of curly hair, just starting to turn grey and a heavy black mustache which made a startling contrast with his strong white teeth when he smiled, which was a frequent occurrence with him. Steady brown eyes surveyed the two men as he stood framed in the doorway before being led over to the desk to be introduced to Bellows, whom he already knew by sight.

"I'd like you to come to the Library, Dr. Darrow," he said without preamble. "I have worked out a mechanical method of assessing the data, using mathematical formulae. The results should be quite interesting. The method could be useful to Miskatonic in the future."

He smiled at the Dean's rising excitement.

"Please don't get your hopes up too high, gentlemen. But it's a start."

The Dean wrinkled up his face.

"Do you mean to say that you actually have some results?"

Holroyd hovered uncertainly between the desk and the door.

"I dislike making too high a claim, Dean, as you know. But things are interesting. These writings are some sort of code, without doubt. And I have managed to reduce a few sentences to English."

The Dean's excitement seemed to have passed to Bellows also because he rose impetuously.

"This we must see."

The three men were talking animatedly, almost as though they had been friends for years as they passed through the Dean's private apartments and ascended the great gloomy staircase which led to the architecturally splendid but somewhat forbidding Central Library of the University. A slight trace of the sunset still lingered and the oriel windows in the arcade leading to the bookstacks themselves stained the parquet blood-red and cast brooding shadows before them as the trio hurried on. But none of them had any thought for their surroundings and presently they found themselves in a vast, shadowy area where green-shaded lamps burned.

It was an L-shaped reference section, set out with long deal tables, many of them weighted down with massive leather-bound volumes; it adjoined the locked and sealed section of the Library to which access was barred to everyone but the Chief Librarian and the

Dean himself. Bellows wondered why that gentleman had himself not been consulted but was told by the Dean that he was currently on leave from his post to visit a sick relative in Maine.

Holroyd had brought the typed symbols of the volume on which he had been working down to the Dean's study with him but his working notes and other material were still scattered about the table as he had left them. There had been an unusual scuttling noise as the men entered and Holroyd looked sharply round the great shadowy place, where the rays of the setting sun competed with the green-shaded lamps.

"Was there anyone in here when you came down?" the Dean asked, unnecessarily sharply, the surveyor thought.

"Not that I know of," Holroyd replied. "The main library is usually left open, is it not, for students' evening study?"

"Of course," the Dean assented hastily. "That was not my meaning . . ."

He broke off, following the direction in which Holroyd was looking. Bellows stared too, noting for the first time the jumbled mass of metal that was lying beneath the far table.

Holroyd swore and went arrow-swift to scrabble among the wreckage. He rose white-faced and incredulous.

"Your deciphering machine?" said the Dean in a tremulous voice.

Holroyd nodded.

"Almost seventeen months' work, gentlemen. Destroyed in a few seconds."

The Dean's voice rose.

"By God, if this is students' work . . ."

Holroyd shook his head.

"You know that is not so."

"But how can you tell?" said Bellows, puzzled. "If there is no-one in here . . ."

Holroyd's handsome face was regaining its normal complexion now.

"The Dean knows what I'm talking about, Mr. Bellows. If you'll forgive me . . ."

He went over quickly, ignoring the wreckage of the shining metal machine on the floor.

"Could it have fallen by itself?" asked Bellows helplessly.

Neither man answered, both absorbed by the cryptographer's frantic scrabbling among the tangled sheets of paper on the desk. Presently Holroyd straightened, his breath coming fast and shallow.

"Nothing?" said the Dean heavily.

Holroyd sank into a chair, looking at his two companions unseeingly. The three men started as a shadow swept across the doorway through which they had just entered. But it was only a college servant hovering uncertainly in the shadowy space.

"It is all right, Tibbs," said the Dean in his normal voice. "A slight accident. I will call if I need you."

The man withdrew with a muffled apology.

"Merely sheets of blank paper," said Holroyd, answering the Dean's previous question, which now seemed to the three men as though it had been spoken at a period remote in time.

"You mentioned something about English phrases," said Darrow when another long interval had elapsed. "Can you remember what it was you were going to tell us?"

An astonishing change had taken place in Holroyd since the Dean had begun speaking. He passed his hand across his forehead.

"They seem to have slipped my mind temporarily," he said apologetically.

"Perhaps the typed notes will refresh your memory," Bellows suggested.

He had not finished speaking when the folder, which Holroyd had placed on a corner of the table, suddenly fluttered to the floor, as though a strong but unseen, unfelt wind had rippled through the vast library. The papers were scattered all about the floor and as the two men went to help their companion sort and collate them they saw that they were nothing more than blank sheets of paper too.

# VI

"It is impossible," the Dean agreed, "and yet it has happened."

The air in this corner of the library was thick with tobacco smoke and Tibbs still hovered, keeping students away from the section, though light and the low murmur of conversation came reassuringly from beyond the far bookstacks.

"The contents of that book have vanished; you cannot remember anything of the de-code; and the machine on which you spent so much time has been destroyed," said Bellows. "This is all of a piece with what happened to the Dean in the tunnel today. It makes a thorough exploration of all the underground passages even more urgent in my opinion."

"Perhaps," said Holroyd heavily. "But it behooves us to go carefully. My research has been put back, it is true. But it is only a delay, not an impasse. A copy of the machine can soon be reconstructed from my working drawings; we have the original of the volume on which I was working under lock and key; and I shall not need anything so fallible as my memory once we begin. And the notes Mr. Bellows has given me are invaluable. The inscriptions in that concourse are similar to those on which I have been working."

Bellows looked skeptical.

"Perhaps that is all these people needed," he suggested. "Time."

"What people?" said the Dean, startled.

Bellows turned to give him a grim glance. "All right, then. Perhaps not people. What would you prefer? Things?"

The Dean's lips were trembling now. There was no doubt about it, Bellows thought.

"You feel there is some connection between what happened tonight and what I saw in that passage?"

Bellows shrugged.

"It could be possible. Many strange incidents have been happening at Miskatonic, from what you tell me. What is your opinion, Mr. Holroyd?"

"I am inclined to agree. I have been shaken tonight, I will admit."
Holroyd glanced at his watch.

"It's almost ten o'clock. Time to eat, surely. There's nothing else
we can do tonight, anyway. And Tibbs is waiting to lock up."

The three men walked back down the great staircase in a sombre
silence.

## VII

Captain of Detectives Cornelius Oates eased his way out of the stifling atmosphere of the green-painted room and gulped in moist air
with gratitude. From the height of Oak Point police station, where
the body had been brought, he had a wide sweep of distant Innsmouth to the left; far out, beyond the reef, there was a band of gauzy
mist in which a flock of birds were diving and soaring in a strange
tangle, as they fought over some booty on the sullen surface of the sea
beneath them; a sea which, inexplicably, did not seem to give back
much light from the almost obscenely overripe orange moon that
hung low in the sky; overripe too were the almost jungle smells that
seemed to come from the rotting wharves of the old downtown dock
area of Innsmouth and the melancholy croaking of frogs served only
to emphasise the outlandishness of the place to which grim duty had
brought him a few short days ago.

Oates sighed. He was a big man, dressed in city clothes and used
to city ways; but he was the best there was in that corner of the nation and he had been brought in from the county seat to lead investigations into the series of events that had puzzled and horrified some
of the more backward and outlandish denizens of the Arkham-Innsmouth area.

Oates turned with relief as the door behind him opened and the
narrow, sandy head of Dr. Ewart Lancaster, the local police surgeon,
appeared in the opening.

"Ever seen anything like it, doc?"

The medic shrugged.

"You were right, Captain. I've been in practice in these parts more'n forty years and it's outside my experience, I don't mind admitting."

Oates looked at him shrewdly in the bright light that sliced the warm darkness from the open door. Even the weather was strange in this benighted place. The doctor lit the stump of a cigar he took from his waistcoat pocket, handed a pack of Havanas to his companion. The police officer selected one fastidiously with the air of a connoisseur, thanked the doctor gruffly and the two men smoked in silence, the gracious aroma expelling the charnel atmosphere of the dissecting room they had just left behind them.

"Yes, Captain," said Dr. Lancaster grimly. "As you remarked on the phone. The facial features removed as though with some sort of obscene sponge. Everything fused together, obliterated. What am I going to put in my report?"

Oates shrugged, his thoughts far away, back in the relatively sane and mundane atmosphere of the city streets he had so recently left.

"Fish, perhaps," he began awkwardly.

Lancaster looked at him incredulously.

"In that pond?" he said mildly. "I've never seen any form of animal life that could do that to a man."

"You misunderstand me, doc," the police officer went on. "For the record, I mean. We've got to put something. The guy fell in, maybe; the shock of the cold water induced a heart attack; the nibbling of fish and the action of the water over a few days?"

The doctor gave a twisted smile.

"You might buy it, Captain. I might buy it. But will the city authorities? They're the ones we have to watch."

He looked at the big detective shrewdly.

"What's your real opinion?"

If he expected an enlightening answer he was disappointed.

Oates scratched his chin, his eyes still fixed on the shimmering mass of mist beyond the reef.

"We have to put something in the report, doc. That's all I'm saying. It may not satisfy us but it has to stop all these silly questions and square the hicks until we can get back to the bottom of things."

Dr. Lancaster had his eyes fixed on Oates' face. He spoke reluctantly.

"You say the Arkham newspaper files you want are away for binding. Go to Innsmouth and poke around incognito. Look at the newspaper reports of a couple of years ago in the library there."

He paused.

"There's all sorts of old tales about creatures that live in the sea beyond the reef. Some people believe they're trying to take over human beings, maybe the entire populations of Innsmouth and Arkham. Nonsense, of course, but it's a starting point."

Oates kept his gaze concentrated far out, conscious of the increasing odour of the swamplands that pressed close to Oak Point on the landward side.

"All I can say is, I admire your fortitude, Dr. Lancaster. You've been here forty years. I've had enough in forty hours."

The doctor smiled grimly, pulling appreciatively on his cigar.

"You get used to anything," he observed.

"Maybe," said Oates. "But the Arkham-Innsmouth area is the damnedest, queerest place I ever struck. With a little more persuading it could sure enough scare the hell out of me."


# VIII


Holroyd woke with a start. At first he did not know where he was. Then he remembered that he had told the Dean and Bellows that he would not return to his house that night. He had quarters on campus where he sometimes slept when he was working late. Now he guessed the moonlight stealing through the window shutters had fallen across his face and wakened him. The sonorous booming of clocks began then; a nightly symphony that combined the steeple timepieces of many of Arkham's crumbling old churches; mingled among those of the much younger but more melodious of the University's public clocks in halls of residence; in chapels; and on the façades of the three great University churches. Although the concert could not have lasted more than a minute or so—such was the discrepancy between the ancient clockwork, often slow by two minutes or more and the more modern, often in advance—he eventually made out that it was somewhere around three a.m. When the wind was right he could sometimes make out the faint echo of Innsmouth's own public timepieces.

Holroyd was about to turn over when he became aware, for the first time, that something unusual was taking place in the room. He guessed, subconsciously, that it was this which had first alerted him from deep sleep. A furtive, insidious noise such as might be made by a child, or perhaps a very old person, rubbing pieces of dry paper together. The mental image was an innocuous one, perhaps, but so incongruous in that time and place that Holroyd began to perspire.

The sound seemed to emanate from somewhere near the wall at his head, pass slowly across the room to a point near the window, only to return once more, becoming a little louder each time. Holroyd closed his eyes but that did no good; the sound did not go away neither did it diminish. Instead, it merely increased his anxiety, for as the furtive noise came closer to him it seemed that something terrible might happen if he did not keep his eyes open. By so doing, he felt, he would hold the thing—whatever it was—at bay by the mere act of being awake, alert and in full possession of his faculties.

At the third passage of the presence Holroyd felt impelled to get up; he could still see nothing, but the light switch was at the far side of the room and to gain it he would have to pass the entire length of the wall from which the sounds were coming. This, understandably enough, he was reluctant to do. Instead, he put on his trousers over his pajamas, began to insinuate his feet into his slippers, by the shimmering half-light of the moon spilling into the room.

To his dismay, however, his right foot seemed to plunge immediately into cold, swampy water, instead of the familiar confines of the slipper. He withdrew his foot as though stung and then he saw the long, grey serpent-thing with the blind white eyes, moving with incredible speed across the carpet, writhing and fibrillating as though it contained a thousand different entities. He let out shriek after shriek as the grey monstrosity darted up his trouser-leg. A nauseous stench was in his nostrils and there was burning pain as he lost consciousness.

When he came to himself he was lying on his bed and there was nothing but the usual muffled night sounds that came faintly to the sleeping campus of Miskatonic University. He felt as though he had been running and his pajamas were saturated with sweat. Somehow, he dragged himself to the light-switch and the blinding light brought reality and the release from nightmare. His slippers were warm and dry, marshalled in their usual place at the side of the bed. It was obvious from their position on the bedside chair that he had never put on his trousers the night before. Relief flooded through him. The whole thing was nightmare then.

But as he turned there came again that nauseous stench. Blood was in his throat; his vocal organs had been so constricted with terror in the dream that he must have bitten his tongue. But why did that awful smell persist? It was then that he saw the trails of dreadful grey slime on the legs of his pajama trousers. He came near to fainting then.

# IX

The following day Oates drove out to Innsmouth in an official police car which he had converted to a civilian vehicle by the simple expedient of affixing masking tape over the police department insignia on the door panels. He wanted to be discreet and he felt oppressed by the abnormality of the events that were beginning to enmesh him. Especially after the doctor's remarks the night before.

It was a dark, sullen day and the old turnpike route, mostly deserted except for the odd farm cart, led him through steep gorges within which the Manuxet ran in raging whiteness; the black rocks which lined the gorges and the white threads of water, combined with the coldness of the air and the loneliness of the situation—for there were few habitations that he could see—inducing a chill of the soul rather than that of the bone; the babbling of the river had a strange, ethereal effect, like the insistent whispering of voices in his ear and twice he almost ran off the road due to the distraction this caused him. He stopped at last and lit a cigarette, glancing down at the gorge at his left side. He was a big, confident man, who had seen death in many forms during his long years as a senior detective, but he was out of his depth here.

Not only in Arkham but physically here on this lonely road, where none of the official police formulas would work, and certainly not in Innsmouth, his destination; a rundown, degraded city, he had heard; a place of sullen silences; of in-breeding; and curious folk who made their furtive livings in ways that he suspected the law would disapprove of. He remembered the words of a fellow officer who had done three years' duty as a young constable in that degenerate place and some of the more vivid phrases came back to him now.

He buttoned up his thick overcoat round his neck, for the car was an open tourer that he had borrowed from the Arkham authorities, and took a pull at the thermos flask of hot coffee he had thoughtfully provided himself with. The roaring of the water in his ears was having a hypnotic effect and the stark black and white, the contrast of the foaming water against the jet-black of the rocks, reminded him uncomfortably of death; perhaps because the juxtaposition recalled the skeletal effect of stripped bone against the blackness of the gorge. He shook off these fanciful thoughts, re-corked the thermos and drove on a few miles more, the comforting feel of his police revolver in its webbing harness reassuring against his breastbone.

He was almost at his destination and the Manuxet gorges opened out to an estuary proper where the sullen pound of the river, yellowish brown now, started to mingle with the green of the outer sea. He stopped the car again and picked up his binoculars from the passenger seat. For a long while he studied the dark reef off the shore of Innsmouth, where the Atlantic surf boomed relentlessly, oblivious of the dark sea birds which flapped and soared above the wavetops; studying the large caves half-seen amid the spray, glimpsing the dark tumbling forms that appeared and disappeared amid the foam; seals, perhaps, or possibly larger sea birds dipping in the boiling welter.

It was turned midday when he at last put the nose of the car into the crumbling suburbs of the old seaport and working from an out-of-date map—for the few passersby huddled in their overcoats did not seem inclined to stop or talk—eventually found the public library, a surprisingly massive brownstone edifice with a pseudo-Greek portico. Oates walked up a dusty marble staircase, his footsteps raising echoes, and eventually made out a faded gilt sign which directed him to the reference section. He had, of course, already been to the main library in Arkham but, as he had told the doctor, had been surprised to find that all their major newspaper files for the past few years had been sent to the County Library Depot for re-binding.

Rather than drive over half Massachusetts he had thought it more convenient to first sample the facilities at Innsmouth, while heeding the advice of Arkham's police chief not to advertise his presence there. He had already decided on the latter course in any event and now, as he tramped the dusty corridors, he was already regretting his errand for it seemed an unlikely quest in such unprepossessing surroundings.

But soft electric lights bloomed ahead and a few moments later he found himself in the presence of an elderly spinster lady, named Miss Thatcher, the reference librarian, who gave him the freedom of the shelves. It was obvious that her duties were not onerous and Oates' brisk personality a marked contrast to those of the few silent, hunched figures at the reading desks in the section behind her.

Oates asked for the relevant newspaper files, which were speedily produced, and he was directed to a side-table beneath a reading lamp, where the bound volumes of the Innsmouth *Recorder* and other regional journals were spread out close to hand. Oates had cleverly asked for several years, including those which had nothing to do with his researches and he busied himself firstly with the pretence of going through these volumes and making pencilled notes which had no connection with his quest.

He was uneasily aware that some of the huddled figures had frozen unnaturally at his entrance and that their pallid, seemingly-uncomprehending faces were turned moon-like toward him; the blank, unformed features reminding the Captain of Detectives of nothing so much as those unfortunates he had occasionally seen incarcerated in lunatic asylums in the great cities of the East. But he flicked the pages unconcernedly, all the while making innocuous noises to Miss Thatcher, who had hovered solicitously at his elbow.

# Father Dagon

But she was soon called away to her desk and Oates was free to pursue his real researches. These concerned the disturbances which had shattered the relative calm of Innsmouth some years earlier. As he read on through the yellowing pages Oates gradually recalled some of the salient features which had sent ripples through the wider world. The catalyst had been a young man, a descendant of Obed Marsh, who had fled the city and had alerted the Federal authorities, who had in turn carried out a series of raids during the years 1928 and 1929.

This had led to the dynamiting of a large number of derelict waterfront properties and, even more strangely, the U. S. Navy had sent vessels which had directed torpedoes downward to caverns deep beneath the great reef which lay a mile or two off the Innsmouth shore. As Oates read on his bewilderment increased but, intrigued, he persisted, and within an hour he had a set of disconnected facts which were as strange as anything he had ever been called upon to investigate. Almost as strange as the present set of circumstances which were the subject of his current investigation, he thought wryly.

If he remembered rightly, the young man involved in the affair and whose precipitate flight from the city had first alerted the authorities, had later been incarcerated in an asylum in upstate New York and to the best of Oates' knowledge, there he remained. The detective's thoughts were disturbed by an irritating rustling and he noticed that one of the derelicts at the adjoining table was making for the door, rolling up a crumpled newspaper as he went. Oates then became aware that the librarian was on the telephone; in the yellow light which silhouetted her in her cubicle, he could see that she was half-turned toward him and seemed to be arguing with someone at the other end of the line.

It was at this point that Oates made a strange discovery. The stories in which he was so interested were headlined on the front pages of the journals and were followed by the first paragraphs of the stories in heavy black type. But on every occasion when he consulted the turn-page which should have continued the narratives, it was to be confronted with other stories, with never a follow-up headline or the remainder of the story.

Miss Thatcher was approaching him now, her lips set in a thin, rigid line.

"We are closing shortly, sir. May I have the volumes?"

Oates was about to expostulate because he assumed from the printed notices elsewhere in the building that it was hours from closing time. But something kept his mouth closed. Similarly, he had been about to point out the curious factor of the missing stories but again he remained silent. There was a curious rigidity; a sense of expectancy in the figures about him that impelled him to silence. He was a very cautious man and he had been in many tight corners. There was nothing sinister about the library; on the surface at any rate; but a sixth sense which every police officer must have told him that silence was the most prudent course at the present stage.

So he smiled pleasantly at the woman and helped her to carry the heavy volumes back to the racks from which they had been extracted. Obviously Miss Thatcher had telephoned some higher authority; or some higher authority had telephoned her. Oates was inclined to discount the latter because no-one could know he was here. Or did they? He re-seated himself at the table, stroking his heavy chin. Someone in police headquarters at Arkham, perhaps? Or possibly Miss Thatcher, alarmed for some reason at a stranger's questioning, had contacted her immediate superior in the same building and asked for instructions. That was more likely and he again began to relax, though aware more than ever of the curious, even alien eyes regarding him from the silent tables in the yellow dusk.

Miss Thatcher paused in front of the table.

"Ten minutes, sir," she said in a clear, precise voice. "Then we close."

Oates nodded.

"Thank you for your help, madam."

The woman drew herself up as though startled. Then she recollected herself.

"Glad to have been of service, sir."

She glanced at the big clock on the far wall.

"It is early closing today, you see."

Oates nodded. The woman might well be right, in which case there was nothing sinister in her attitude. He would check from the notices on the way out. He waited until she had gone back to her desk and then produced a notebook from his pocket. He tore off a sheet from the top and started scribbling in pencil with a strong, steady hand.

Beneath FACTS he began to make notations under number headings.

1. A number of strange occurrences at Miskatonic University, Arkham, in the spring of 1932. Doors opening and shutting of their own volition; lights switching on and off without cause; taps ditto.

2. Great storm of 1932, which caused tremendous damage at Innsmouth, also affected Arkham. A corollary to the great tidal bore of the Manuxet in the autumn of 1930 which caused floods, drowning, and curious effects of "white lightning."

3. Whirlwind which stripped roofs and caused much damage in Innsmouth and Arkham on the same night.

4. Thefts of numbers of arcane and esoteric books at the Library of the University of Miskatonic, Arkham, in a locked section kept by the Chief Librarian, Jethro Staveley. Great heat cracked window glass and shelves were charred. Thief never found.

5. Recently. Large stone cross on campus at the University suddenly collapsed, almost killing the Dean, Dr. Darrow. Inside of column seemed to be "rotted away," though this was a manifest impossibility.

6. Large concourse and number of underground tunnels discovered beneath cross area by surveyor, Andrew Bellows.

7. He and Darrow descend to the catacombs. Darrow badly frightened by something he has seen, which he describes as "being like serpents." Conversely, Bellows sees noth-

ing. Most of these events are kept from press and authorities. My subsequent interview with Darrow elicits
all these facts at third-hand.

8. Holroyd's cryptological investigations into the typed
copies of books from the sealed section of the library
brought to an end by the smashing of his de-coding machine and the theft or mislaying of the decoded papers.
Holroyd reluctant to let the authorities know the nature
of his discoveries lest the police think him "fanciful."
Memory now affected.

9. MOST IMPORTANT OF ALL, the thing which brought
the matter to our attention in the first place; the mysterious death of the college janitor, Jeb Conley, who was
found floating in a pool fed by an underground spring,
after being missing for some days. His features had been
erased in a manner quite outside my experience and that
of the Medical Examiner, Dr. Lancaster.

10. Another curious feature is that when Darrow and Bellows investigated the caverns, there were marks in the
dust, obviously made by the passage of some heavy
person or persons. Later, the marks were found to be
completely erased and a perfectly engineered passage,
leading in the direction of Innsmouth and the sea, incidentally, was found to be blocked by a fall of rock; the
passages appear to be made of granite and the thing
sounds like a manifest impossibility.

11. Are any or all of these events connected? If so, how?

12. Where do we go from here?

13. Obvious conclusion: fairly urgent that we should organ-
ise a thorough search of these tunnels without further
delay.

Oates' scribblings were interrupted by a loud creaking noise. He
rose from the table to find himself alone, except for the old lady librarian, who was hovering by her desk with her hat and coat on. Al-

ready, she had extinguished most of the lights, and the detective found himself in semi-darkness.

He picked up the sheet of paper and walked briskly down toward the entrance to the reference section, his footsteps echoing loudly beneath the vaulted ceiling.

"Good afternoon, Ma'am."

Miss Thatcher gave him a courteous little half-bobbing bow.

"Goodbye, sir," she said primly.

Oates went on to the stairhead, hearing the grating of the lock behind him as she closed the big main door. The light above her desk was extinguished by an external switch in the corridor, he noted, before the angle of the passage hid her from view. As he paused at the top of the stairs he was startled by a sudden draught on the nape of his neck. It was icy and he was so taken aback he staggered for a moment.

The next instant, the sheet of notations pencilled on both sides of the large piece of notepaper went sailing down the shadowy staircase. But Oates was an astute officer and he had his wits about him. He was light on his toes for such a big man and he pounded downward, aware that the strange blast of air was keeping pace, holding the dancing sheet just out of his reach. As Oates reached the main doors of the library the ruled sheet was still whirling as though it had a life of its own; almost as if it were controlled by a string.

It was flapping desperately against the big double doors, as if it were trying to gain the street beyond. A thin man with a scar on his face was outside, struggling to get in. But Oates was on familiar ground now. He had the sheet firmly between thumb and forefinger, put his shoulder firmly to the door. It flew back, smashing the thin man across the side of his jaw. He gave a sharp yelp of pain and fell back, making a hissing noise between jagged teeth.

"I'm so sorry," said Oates pleasantly. "I didn't see anyone there."

He put a match to the sheet of notepaper, used it as a spill to light a cigarette. He stood there savouring the expression on the thin man's face as he watched the sheet turn to ash, while he nursed his jaw with a filthy handkerchief.

"I hope I didn't hurt you."

The thin man hissed something incomprehensible from beneath the handkerchief and slid through the door like a snake. He ascended the steps two at a time while Oates was left with the impression of hatred in the dead-insect eyes. He glanced back over his shoulder, making sure the ash he ground beneath his feet would not leave any information for anyone who might pass that way, glimpsed a notice in the vestibule. Miss Thatcher was right. Today was early closing day for the library.

He went back to his car, parked in a side street. His trained eye immediately noted two things wrong. Someone had pulled at the tape on the door panels which hid its identity as a police vehicle. The second came after he had got into the driving seat, conscious of prying eyes behind shaded windows round about. He tested the brakes carefully; after a few pumping motions he found they faded suspiciously. He remembered the dark and twisting road that led through the gorges back to Arkham.

He sought out a garage in the same street, showed the sullen, reluctant man there his badge of authority; he had his vehicle towed to the workshop and stood over the man until he had made good the repair. When he had tested the linkage and was satisfied that it was secure he put a ten dollar bill on the counter of the grimy office. He deliberately showed the man the butt of his revolver as he re-buttoned his overcoat.

"Take this as a warning," he said. "And remember it. The state authorities know I'm here. So no more tricks."

The man kept his eyes on the floor.

"I don't know what you mean," he mumbled.

"I think you do," Oates said curtly.

He drove quickly out of Innsmouth, through the growing dusk. He watched the rear mirror all the way but there was no sign of anything or anyone following. Nevertheless he did not relax his precautions all the way through the miles of gorges, the sound of the Manuxet making a menacing roar in his ears. It was only when he gained the fresh air of the uplands that he relaxed his guard. He had much to think about as he reached the outskirts of Arkham.

# X

Dr. Darrow slept badly that night. Such dreams as he had were troubled. When he awoke he found it was only two a.m. and he lay for a long time watching the moonlight at the window bars, his mind confused and distrait. Was he really losing his mental faculties? His confusion stemmed from the fact of an interview he had had with Captain Oates as soon as that officer had returned from Innsmouth late that afternoon.

Strangely, the air had then been hot and stormy and just after the two men met in the Dean's study the tempest had broken; a wind like a roaring furnace followed by thunder, lightning and such a tornado of rain that the good doctor hadn't seen in all his long years. Perhaps that was why the interview between the two men had partaken of melodrama.

The Dean had been on difficult ground, of course. Though he had been too polite to say so the former had been certain that the big detective had strongly disapproved of the University's earlier actions; or rather lack of actions. That they had not reported the strange incidents to the police; and that they had tried to hush up even the discovery of the body of Jeb Conley. That had been a primary mistake, the Dean felt, and had not disposed the police favourably toward them. But Oates had been fair, he had to give him that.

The detective had read from his earlier notes of their first conversation, soon after the body had been discovered and the County had decided to send over one of its most efficient and high-ranking officers to take charge. All had gone well until the matter of the collapse of the memorial cross had come up. Tired of the great display of lightning at the windows the two men had drawn the drapes and retired to the Dean's desk where they could talk and make notes in comparative comfort in an area where the storm was merely a distant disturbance.

"I'd just like to run through your earlier statements," Oates had said.

The Dean nodded, listening half-impatiently, blinking violently from time to time at each clap of thunder, as though the unseen lightning troubled his eyes.

"You say you saw these strange creatures come out of the tunnel walls?"

"Eigh? What's that," Darrow interrupted sharply. "There must be some mistake. I really don't understand."

"I have it verbatim here," Oates said shortly. "That's what you told me. I have a complete description. Let me repeat what you first said. Perhaps that will refresh your memory."

He had not read more than two sentences before Darrow interrupted again.

"That's not what I said at all," he commented irritably. "You must have got things wrong. That's what happened to Bellows. He saw these things. Or so he told me. He was in such a state of collapse I had to help him out of the tunnel."

There were spots of red on Oates' cheeks now.

"Come now, Dr. Darrow," he said sternly. "All this was said in the presence of a stenographer. She took notes separately and I'm sure she will corroborate what I've got down here. Apart from Bellows' own statement, of course."

It was the Dean's turn to look bewildered. He licked his lips nervously.

"I'm sure I don't understand, Captain. To the best of my recollection I saw nothing. It was Bellows who spoke of seeing these weird creatures."

Oates paused and made another note in his book.

"And you're prepared to swear to that," he said heavily.

The Dean hesitated again.

"Well, I don't quite know. What does Bellows say?"

Oates let out a heavy sigh, his brow clouded with anger.

"He says exactly what he's always said, doctor," he retorted crisply. "I think you'd really best re-consider your position. This is a very serious matter. And revoking a sworn testimony isn't something a man in your public position ought to enter into lightly."

There was a heavy silence between the two, while the thunder rumbled and rattled at the window panes of the curtained room. Presently the Dean made a nervous drumming noise with his fingers on the desk surface. He looked lost and miserable; out of his depth. Oates felt a stirring of pity for him, even amid his irritation.

"Perhaps you'd better sleep on it, doctor," he said gently. "These events seem to have upset a great many people. And I shall have to prepare a party to descend into those vaults tomorrow. A number of State troopers will be here first thing. Do you feel fit enough to accompany us?"

The Dean flushed as though his integrity had been brought into question.

"Of course," he said firmly.

It was Oates' turn to look staggered.

"But you said categorically earlier that you were so nervous and shattered that nothing would induce you to go down there again!"

Red spots were standing out on Darrow's cheeks as well now.

"Oh, did I?" he said vaguely. "If you say so, Mr. Oates."

The big detective laid down his notebook as though it were about to explode and passed a hand over his face, his mind racing furiously over the booming concussion of the storm raging outside. He had just remembered something. Details that tied up with the Dean's current mental lapse. Blank sheets of paper where there had been notes before. He would question Holroyd again about his own lapse of memory. And only this morning his own carefully prepared notes had almost been lost due to a malign breeze which had sprung up in an enclosed building. Was someone—or something—working in a way beyond his comprehension to obliterate knowledge of events taking place in Arkham and Innsmouth? Something connected with the cataclysms of two years earlier?

Something inimical to life as normal people knew it? Oates was a man of immense experience in his profession and intensely pragmatic. He bit his lip. Even he felt deep undercurrents into which he would rather not venture at the moment. So he stifled all his inner misgivings and merely dismissed the Dean as gently as possible. He would talk the thing over with the medical examiner later. The two men saw eye to eye and the doctor's coldly professional expertise would give much-needed ballast to his own thoughts.

There was also the matter of the person who had tampered with the brakes of his car. That was of definite human agency. So much for the more fanciful imaginings of the Dean and Holroyd. Oates' nostrils twitched with slight amusement at his recollection of Arkham's police chief when the city detective had mentioned the matter of his expenses regarding the garage bill. He had fulminated about the difference between city and rural budgets. The recollection had lightened the tension slightly as Oates proceeded further into the dark morass into which he was becoming entrapped.

His musings had been interrupted by an urgent telephone call from the doctor. It was quite dark when Oates arrived at Oak Point police station on the outskirts of the city and fireflies made a faint green miasma over the marshes that fringed the shore. Again, the croaking of frogs sounded loud and menacing in this God-forsaken spot. Oates wondered, not for the first time, why the city authorities had chosen to erect a substantial police building out here, with not only cells but a mortuary and post-mortem facilities.

But his questionings had been met with shrugs. Arkham had been expanding as a city at that time and there had been a railroad wreck in the area, which had badly strained both police and medical resources. Also, the city fathers had hoped to enlarge the urban boundaries by expanding housing facilities which had never materialised. Now, the station was manned by a sergeant and two other officers while the mortuary facilities were seldom used. Dr. Lancaster had his own theories, of course, but so far he had kept them to himself. He was more forthcoming on the autopsy findings, however. The mortuary had been currently re-opened at this remote spot halfway between Arkham and Innsmouth to avoid further press speculation. Not that there had been much; merely the odd paragraph or two.

The authorities had played down the death of Conley and the corpse had been removed here with such promptitude that no pressmen had been able to view the body before it left the area of the pond. A police car driven by the bored sergeant drove away as Oates arrived and he acknowledged the uniformed officer's languid wave with a similar gesture of his own. He wondered what had been so urgent that Lancaster's call could not have waited until morning.

He walked up the narrow concrete path to the front door of the reception office where a lanky, red-haired officer was speaking in low tones into the old-fashioned sit-up-and-beg type telephone. Oates lifted up the counter flap and went on in back, down a green-painted corridor where filing cabinets were glimpsed behind half-frosted panel doors, and where dim bulbs in stark metal fittings merely emphasised the bleakness of this lonely outpost of law and order.

Dr. Lancaster was waiting just inside the mortuary door, a serious expression on his face. He wore ordinary street clothes and he began without preamble.

"I came over to clean up and finish off my report about an hour ago," he said. "The place is locked, because the mortuary is outside Halloran's jurisdiction."

Halloran was the uniform sergeant in charge of the Oak Point station.

"Well?" Oates queried, watching the doctor's face intently. There was a pallor about the cheeks and a deep seriousness in back of the eyes that hadn't been there before.

"I'd just like you to look at this," Lancaster said.

He led the way down between the mortuary tables to a more secluded area where a tap dripped into a white porcelain sink with a melancholy sound in the silence.

The back door was hanging askew on its hinges and there was the smell of burning in the air. Oates gave a small exclamation as he knelt and looked at the half-melted and buckled metal of the hinges and door-lock.

"Curious, eh?" said the doctor solemnly. "Who'd want to rob this place?"

Oates stood up, dusting the knee of his trousers.

"There's been a robbery, then?"

"Oh, yes. Police evidence."

Oates followed the other's eyes to where drag-marks went across the concrete path to a woodland area fringing the swamp. He followed them down, keeping in the light spilling past the wrecked door, conscious now of a bitter pungency. He noticed slime then, on the edge of the concrete path, and again caught a nauseous stench. The doctor had joined him.

"It won't be any use following," he said wearily. "That way leads only to the swamp. That's where they've taken Conley."

The detective looked at him, momentarily struck dumb.

"The corpse?" he said wonderingly. "But who'd want a corpse?"

Lancaster shrugged, edging back toward the lit sanity of the police station.

"No-one in their senses. But we aren't dealing with the normal. That body represented evidence. Evidence of something abnormal. Now it's disappeared."

Oates said nothing. He glanced at a piece of paper the doctor held out to him. It had crude lettering scribbled on it in an illiterate hand; Oates made out the roughly formed sentence: DONT MEDDLE WITH THINGS THAT DONT CONCERN YOU.

He reached out for the paper to examine it more closely when a sudden wind sprang up that took the two men by surprise. The note was whirled from their grasp, halfway between doctor and police officer. Then it was gone toward the dark wood and they saw it no more. Oates clamped his lips tight shut, opened them again to speak of the incident in the library. He had a quick mental image of the man with the scar.

Then he decided to keep his own counsel. After all, what was the use?

All he said was, "We'd better sort out something sensible for your report," as he led the way back inside the station.

The doctor lingered, listening to the croaking of the frogs, watching the distant points of green light over the swamp.

He gave a short laugh.

"Does it matter what we put, Captain? No-one's going to believe us, anyway."

# XI

Bellows was first down the dark opening beneath the fallen cross, confident and professional as he guided the cohorts of strong, uniformed State troopers into the large concourse so that the whole place was soon a humming mass of activity.

Despite the Dean's eagerness to descend, Oates had again glimpsed a strangeness in the academic's demeanour and had pressed him to remain above. Several of the biggest and strongest officers remained above ground level, for such activity on campus could not pass unnoticed, but the stationing of police vehicles and wooden planking barriers were sufficient to keep the general public at a distance.

Powerful electric torches were being distributed and many of these would be stationed at intervals along the tunnels in order to provide permanent lighting while the searches went on. By their light Oates had more than once glimpsed strange expressions on Holroyd's face. He was a changed man from the previous day and more than once the Captain of Detectives had asked the cryptologist if he was all right.

"Of course," he had replied, somewhat irritably, Oates thought. "Why should I not be?"

Now Oates shook his head.

"You don't look well," he commented. "That was quite a jolt you had yesterday."

Holroyd shrugged. He had his face turned away from the other but Oates could still see muscles working in the lean throat. Holroyd did not look too reliable for the work they might have to do and Oates resolved to stick close to him.

Now he called a short conference in the centre of the concourse, briefing the State troopers again as to the plan of action. Each man had been issued with a whistle and a pre-arranged code would bring reinforcements and help as required. When he was certain that all the officers had a clear idea of what they should do, he asked them to remain in the concourse while a small party again reconnoitred the central tunnel. Both Holroyd and Bellows had told him it was completely blocked by fallen masonry but he wanted to make sure.

A uniformed police captain and six State troopers accompanied Bellows, Oates and Holroyd into the central tunnel. The place was as light as day as three of the police deployed their torches and the party set out with brisk, confident steps. Unlike Bellows' original exploration with the Dean, this morning's excursion was brief; in a very few minutes, it seemed, they came up against the blockage in the tunnel but a sudden exclamation of astonishment from the surveyor brought the party to a halt.

"What's wrong?" Oates asked sharply, taking in the barrier ahead.

Bellows turned amazed features to him.

"This is impossible."

"I don't understand."

Bellows ignored him, ran forward and passed his fingers over the wall before them.

"A broken fall of jagged stone blocks completely sealed this tunnel. Today there's a smooth, unbroken masonry wall that looks as though it has been here for years. The thing is impossible . . ."

He sounded stunned.

Oates could not suppress a slight prickling of the scalp but he seemed quite normal as he questioned the surveyor.

"You're sure about this? Might you not have been mistaken? You had only low-powered torches, if I recall . . ."

Bellows shook his head fiercely.

The police captain caught Oates' eyes. Both men could sense the growing unease among the uniformed personnel; Holroyd's face was a mass of perspiration.

"Let's get on with the search, Mr. Oates," said the uniformed captain, his face a granite mask. "We can sort this out later."

"Surely," said Oates with relief and the party then turned abruptly and marched back down the tunnel, those present keeping their thoughts to themselves. But Oates knew that Bellows' self-confidence was crumbling and Holroyd was close to cracking even

118

before they had started. He might get the latter to stay with the rearguard while they explored the other six tunnels.

The next two hours were ones of unceasing activity. Large contingents of police, split into four parties, explored the remaining passages. Oates led one, the police captain the second and Bellows and Holroyd the third and fourth, though Oates made sure another senior police officer was close to Holroyd throughout. Three of the parties had returned within the two hours; they had tramped through miles of smooth, man-made passages without seeing anything untoward.

Strangely, all three passages had petered out, coming to precisely engineered points; the vee-shapes accurately and smoothly hewn until they met. No-one had seen anything like it. While they waited, Oates saw the Dean's anxious face hovering halfway up the slope beyond the trapdoor and joined him for some fresh air, at the same time giving him the latest news on the day's activities.

The two men's conversation was interrupted by the arrival of a big State trooper from the sixth smaller tunnel—that on the extreme left of the concourse—in a condition of barely suppressed excitement. They had found an extremely long and obviously travelled tunnel, wide and slightly curving, which was now leading downward at the point they had reached, some two miles in. The Captain of State troopers had wisely called a halt there and had sent Strang, the trooper, to report the discovery to Oates and the others.

There were twenty officers in the party, including Holroyd, and the trooper did not anticipate any particular danger at the time he had left to make his way back. Oates had some reservations, however, and conferred aside with Bellows, while the State troopers split themselves into two parties. The bulk would remain behind in the concourse as a reserve and guard the tunnel entrances, until the main party returned.

A few minutes later the relief party set off to rejoin the others in the most westerly of the tunnels and Oates soon saw that the passage was indeed different from the others. Though the entrance was insignificant it soon widened out and the roof was so high it was almost beyond the range of their torches. It curved slightly in places and was soon going downhill, though always in a westerly direction.

Bellows had a compass with him and the needle, though it swung a little, always bore to the west. Now there was a breeze blowing in their faces and with it came the faint musty smell Oates had already noted at Oak Point.

"What do you make of the direction?" Oates asked, after he had estimated they must be more than halfway to the rendezvous point.

The surveyor shrugged.

"Toward Innsmouth and the sea," he replied shortly. "But I find the engineering talents employed absolutely stupefying. All this is unique in my experience."

Oates nodded.

"It's also a little too convenient for my liking."

Bellows looked at him, his face strained in the light of the torches the two men carried. They were alone, the trooper who had come to fetch them remaining in the concourse with the rear party.

"I don't quite understand."

"All the other passages blocked or sealed. As though something wanted us to take this one. The most westerly route. The one that leads to Innsmouth and the sea."

Bellows shook his head.

"Beyond the reef," he said in almost dreamy tones. "I'd come to much the same conclusion myself."

The two men quickened their pace. They were going round a gentle curve, ever more subtly downward when they came to a dark section of tunnel. The way had been lit by torches placed on the passage floor before, but now there was no sign of light in the jet-blackness ahead. Then Oates' torch caught a flash in the gloom and at the same moment his foot kicked against something. Bellows was before him. The remains of the metal torch was oddly buckled, the metal seemingly melted. The surveyor almost dropped it as he straightened.

"Still warm," he whispered.

At the same time there came a faint warning whistle from far ahead, a sharp fusillade of gun shots and a strange bleating noise that reverberated against the dark, smooth walls ahead. The two men were already pounding toward the source of the sounds, Oates' revolver out, throats constricted with fear, minds clouded with thoughts of the unknown.

# XII

Oates stopped their headlong rush in a few moments, putting his hand on his companion's arm.

"We're not thinking straight."

He put the whistle to his lips, blew with all his might. Bellows joined him. Then they stood, torches burning steadily in the darkness, listening with straining ears. Ten seconds passed, then twenty; moments long as eternity. Then, the silvery answering notes that spelt out: We are on our way. They seemed to pierce the darkness like rays of shining light. Oates and Bellows ran on, conscious that there were no sounds ahead of them. Their torches showed nothing but the tunnel, leading steadily downward; a salt wind now, blowing on their faces, bearing with it the strange smell of subterranean depths. The passage was becoming smaller as it went downhill.

At last they came to a curve more extreme than the others, the way ahead more precipitate. The dancing torch beams picked out shapeless pieces of metal on the floor of the tunnel. Oates recognised with a tightening of the throat the distorted, half-melted remnants of what had once been police revolvers. There were no signs of a struggle but something that looked like scorch marks on the passage walls ahead. That and vestiges of the grey slime that Oates had seen out at Oak Point. He came to a full stop, held the wrist of the other man.

"But aren't we going on?" Bellows said. "The others may be hurt or in great danger."

Oates shook his head.

"That's what they want us to do," he said, his voice betraying a slight tremor. "The whole thing has been made too simple. The Captain should have waited. Instead, it's my bet he went on down that slope. It looks a bad place."

Bellows directed his torch downward, conscious of a faint humming sound about them.

"For an ambush?"

Oates shrugged.

"For anything. Anything bad, that is. We stay here until the others come up. The Captain's party may be beyond all help by now, anyway."

Bellows' face was grey.

"You can't mean that. Holroyd too . . . ?"

"I do mean it. There are things around here inimical to man. They come from the Innsmouth area. These tunnels were probably their chief outlets to the outside world. They've established a firm foothold in Innsmouth, and now in Arkham, probably with the aid of local people. Two years ago they almost succeeded. Now they're trying again. And they don't intend to fail."

Bellows' face was glazed with perspiration.

"This all sounds insane . . ." he began hoarsely.

"You'll just have to trust me," Oates told him. "I've got some of the pieces. But there are still a lot missing. Maybe we'll never know the whole truth. And we can't yet tell friend from foe. Someone in Arkham blew the whistle on me yesterday when I went to Innsmouth. My visit was expected. Measures were taken. I'm lucky to be here."

Bellows laughed cynically.

"Lucky, did you say?"

He turned as they caught the welcome sound of running feet behind them. At the same time the slithering noise ahead began once more, mingled with the bleating they had heard earlier. The dancing torch beams caught flickering shapes, snake-like heads that hissed and darted fire. An insidious music began in their ears, mingled with obscene whisperings that seemed to penetrate their brains. Oates gritted his teeth, started to fire blindly into the mass of squamous serpent-beings that advanced up the tunnel toward them.

His nerves steadied; this was something he could see. The bullets would probably make little impression but the deafening explosions beneath the vaulted roof blotted out the inroads that were being made into his mind. Something tore ahead of him and he saw one of the things slither to a halt; it seemed to flicker and disappear into the wall. The awful stink was in their nostrils. Then there came the reassuring sound of heavy boots on the tunnel floor and the space was filled with a great mass of State troopers.

The tunnel was wreathed in smoke as they knelt and started to fire steadily into the packed mass of rope-like beings that blocked the passage ahead. They wavered and broke and seemed to trickle away like water. Oates felt his legs buckle beneath him and then there were strong hands under his arms and he was being dragged clear, together with the surveyor. As by some unspoken command the band of men that blocked the tunnel stepped slowly backward, keeping ranks unbroken, torches held steadily, going upward to the sanity of the concourse and the open air far above.

"Explosives are the only answer," Bellows whispered brokenly.

"Maybe," said Oates shortly, sheathing his revolver, his nerve restored. "Though the things that were able to drill all this might find them but an ineffective deterrent."

"Have you any better suggestions? We must block these tunnels somehow."

His voice broke into a rasping shudder.

"Did you see those creatures' eyes?"

Oates nodded grimly.

"I'm not likely to forget."

The strange march continued, the whole party walking backward, weapons raised.

They did not regain normality until they could hear answering whistles from the concourse. Then the babble of voices surrounded them and amid the tumult Bellows suddenly felt his legs going from under him and he lapsed unconscious to the ground.

# XIII

In submitting the attached report I would like to make a few general observations which would not normally come within the purview of the Department.

1. In the event of anything happening to me I would like you to contact and rely upon the testimony of Dr. Ewart Lancaster, police surgeon of Arkham, who has seen many strange things in his career, but none stranger, I think, than the happenings at Arkham and Innsmouth these past few months.

2. Please also contact those people mentioned in my report; i.e. Dr. Darrow, Dean of the Faculty at Miskatonic; the cryptologist Jefferson Holroyd; and the surveyor Andrew Bellows, all of whom have experienced a number of the events detailed in the report.

3. Dr. Lancaster's original autopsy findings on the man Jeb Conley (and which must now supersede those he prepared for public consumption) can be absolutely relied upon and I corroborate them in every detail. Please see paragraph 34 (c) for my own preliminary findings and for my corroboration of Dr. Lancaster's experiences at Oak Point police station two nights ago. Conley's death was undoubtedly murder, and the disappearance of the corpse and the bizarre and unexplained manner of death should not obscure that.

4. Thorough investigation should be made among senior personnel of the Arkham Police Department and also among citizens of both Arkham and Innsmouth, for it was obvious that my trip to Innsmouth was leaked in advance and this could have led to my death

when the brakes of the police vehicle I was using were tampered with. Local people are obviously working in with these creatures though for what reasons; e.g. profit, coercion, fear etc., my investigations have not yet revealed.

5. As strange and inexplicable as you may find my official report I urge you not to ignore it and ask you to remember our twenty-year friendship and whether you have ever had occasion to doubt the veracity of the material I have previously placed before you.

> With every regard, I am, sir,
> Your obedient servant,
> Cornelius Oates
> Captain of Detectives, County Force.

# XIV

Holroyd was running. The insidious voices were still in his ears and the weirdness and wildness of what he had seen was so recent and so strong that it seemed to have completely burned itself into his consciousness. He appeared to have been running for hours, because it was now dark; his clothing was torn and dishevelled; his face and hands scratched and bleeding; and the perspiration streamed from every pore.

He had left the University area and as though by some atavistic instinct was making for his own house off campus, as the neighborhood seemed familiar to him. He remembered, as he went up the zigzag concrete path that led to the front door, that his housekeeper was not due there today. He usually dined in college that evening. That would be good. No-one must see him in this condition.

He slackened his pace, realising he was near collapse. As he put his key in the front door-lock his head swam and he almost fell. He clung to the bunch of keys, willed himself not to faint. Not that he had any idea as to why he should have fainted. His memory had been erased as though some unknown force had insidiously eroded the patterns from his brain. All he could recollect was that he had been deadly afraid; that he had taken flight; and that he was now home.

He let himself into the deserted house, switched on the entrance light and carefully avoiding his image in a silver-gilt mirror, somehow got upstairs, almost on his hands and knees. He avoided switching on the bedroom light, undressed quickly by the glow of a street lamp spilling in through the window and ran a shower. The sting of the cold water, rapidly effaced by the hot, seemed to revive him and a quarter of an hour later, dressed in clean clothes and with a glass of whiskey in his hand he felt almost restored to normal.

He was aware of hunger then and pausing only to put his mud-stained clothing into the laundry basket for the housekeeper to attend to next day, he padded downstairs, finding some legs of chicken and a blueberry pie in the kitchen icebox. He sat down at the small pine table in the kitchen, consuming the makeshift meal, his mind suspended in a state of neutrality. A blank opaqueness obtruded between himself and reality, as though a veil of mist had descended over his perceptions. It was not unpleasant and he tried to prolong the feeling, almost revelling in the animal comfort of the food and the drink and his clean clothes after the terrors of the past hours.

Presently he remembered the library and his de-coding machine. He got up then and went to his study, searching for some scribbled notes he had made the previous week. He returned with them and a blank scratch-pad to the kitchen, first drawing the blinds furtively as though someone might be crouching on the walk outside. He busied himself with some abstruse calculations, checking and re-checking his figures against his original notes.

A faint scratching noise against the outer walls of the house escaped his attention; or if it did not he paid it no heed, for it was like nothing more than a light wind that agitated vines that clothed the trellis on the façade. He was absorbed now and an hour must have passed while his pen passed busily over the paper. Later he was conscious that he was cold and his attention was then drawn to the whiskey glass, which was empty.

He went back to the living room and crossed to the bar to replenish his drink, oblivious of the strange shadows that were dancing across the windows outside. It was quite still now, only the faint hum of a passing automobile intruding into the deathly silence. He resumed his seat in the kitchen, went back to his notes; after a few minutes more the contents of his glass remained untasted at his elbow, so concentrated was his attention. The deep chime of an old cased clock on the landing at last brought him to realise that it was past nine o'clock.

Then he went round checking doors and windows, dropping the automatic catch on the front door, making sure the kitchen was secure too. It was a long-standing routine when he was sleeping at home and though he knew that Mrs. Karswell would have secured everything before she left, it was a habit so ingrained that he felt compelled to go through the gestures, even though he would have been shocked to find she had been lax in some respect. He paused near the back door, again checking the time from his watch, as though it were of supreme importance.

The telephone rang then and he went out into the hall to answer it. A deep, glutinous voice he did not recognise was on the other end of the line. At first he could not make out the words. The fog seemed to have descended on his brain once more. The voice was vaguely familiar but still he could not place it. The unknown caller appeared to be giving him some sort of instructions. He listened more intently, tried to concentrate on the words, which poured like smoke through his brain and out again without having any apparent effect. The voice ended at last and Holroyd thanked the dead instrument before replacing it in the cradle. He stumbled back to the kitchen, his hands over his ears, more confused than ever. He checked his watch, was shocked to see that a whole half-hour had passed. Then he picked up his glass and took a few tentative sips. The spirit seemed to rouse his sluggish spirit and he turned to his notes, conscious now of a great weariness of soul and body that had settled on him.

Even the scratching of the pen filled him with disgust and he threw it from him with a little gesture of petulance. The ink made a long blob across the whiteness of the paper which reminded him of something. But he could not make it out. He was tired. That was it. Presently he would remember. It was about this time he heard the furtive footsteps. They seemed to come down the front path and pause at the main door.

Holroyd sat as though frozen, his ears alert to the slightest sound. But there was no expected knock or ring at the doorbell.

Instead, the slouching steps were circling the house by way of the little paved path that went all the circumference of the building. The furtive noise was cut off by the angle of the house and Holroyd, still hunched agonisingly at the kitchen table, waited an age until the sound again became audible, this time on the kitchen side. Then there was a pause and a sudden brittle drumming of fingers on the kitchen window pane. It was a tiny, almost jaunty sound as though the unseen visitor had decided to have his little joke but to the listener in the kitchen it denoted obscene horror. He sat shrivelled in his chair, waiting for a repetition but the footsteps passed on until the kitchen door was quietly tried. Holroyd almost screamed then but somehow he suppressed the sounds.

Another age passed and the footsteps moved away. Still Holroyd sat on in the paralysis of dream. When the front door bell sounded it was like an explosion of the system. Scalding waves of acid washed across the cryptologist's nerves. He raised himself from the table, sweat beading his forehead. He drained the last of the whiskey in the glass and set off at a shambling run upstairs. From the bathroom window he could overlook the front porch. He cautiously twitched back the gauze curtain.

A dark, reassuring figure was standing in the porch light, looking bewilderedly about him. Relief flooded through Holroyd. He thought he knew who the visitor was now. But why had the man not announced himself at the beginning, instead of all that furtive circling of the building? Holroyd went over to the bathroom mirror, switched on the light and looked at himself properly for the first time. Apart from dark rings beneath the eyes and a certain pallor of complexion he looked quite normal. He paused a moment longer, adjusting his tie as the imperious pealing of the bell went on.

The visitor had evidently seen the bathroom light come on and realised he was at home. Holroyd switched it off, straightened himself up and walked slowly back down the stairs. The bell sounded again as he crossed the hall. He opened the door cautiously on the chain, unable at first to see his visitor's face as he was standing immediately beneath the lamp, his hat shading his features.

"Come along, Holroyd," said an irritable voice. "I have some important matters to discuss."

"Oh, it's you," said Holroyd in a relieved tone. "Come in." The guest looked about him suspiciously as he crossed the threshold. The cryptologist led the way back into the living room, drawing the heavy velvet drapes before ushering his visitor into a chair.

His mind was more alert now, thoughts beginning to crystallise.

He knew what he had to do as he crossed to the bar to offer his guest a drink.

## XV

Dr. Lancaster was on a lonely stretch of highway halfway between Innsmouth and Arkham when he ran out of gasoline. He had been called urgently to a lonely farmhouse but when he arrived the people there, who did not even own a telephone, knew nothing of any medical emergency. Lancaster had sworn in a genteel sort of way, driving back the lonely miles, so preoccupied with his thoughts and his own and Oates' problem that he had quite forgotten to look at the gauge.

Fortunately, he had left the gorges far behind and in any event he always carried a spare can in the trunk of the vehicle. It would take only a few minutes to put another two gallons in the tank. Strangely enough, he was certain the tank had been more than half full earlier in the day. There had been a strong smell of gasoline, it was true, when he regained the car at the farmhouse and it might be that there was some leak in the tank. He would have his own garage in Arkham look at it tomorrow.

He left the headlights of the vehicle on and went around in back to unlock the trunk. He was preoccupied with the present problem and the other thoughts that oppressed him but even so he thought he saw a faint shadow at the corner of his eye, just beyond the yellow cones cast by the headlamps. He was on an S-bend where the heavy trees and foliage came down almost to the road's edge. It was a sombre place, even in daylight, yet he felt no particular sense of danger. With the expertise of long practice he quickly unscrewed the cap of the can, got the funnel from the floor of the trunk and carefully started to re-fill the tank.

He had got about halfway through this operation when he heard the faint rustling in the bushes. He stopped the pouring, screwed back the cap on the gasoline tank and put down the half-full can, all his senses alert. His mind was now directed toward the telephone call; the lateness of the hour; the loneliness of the terrain; and the fact that the people at the farm had no phone.

It all began to add up. Humming quietly to himself, though in fact his nerves were on edge, Lancaster stepped round the rear of the car, carrying the open can in his left hand while with his right he leaned into the driving seat and re-started the engine.

It made a satisfying sound in the silence of the night and simultaneously he noticed something like a flickering, snake-like undulation that came along the roadside verge. And again the stealthy crackling in the bushes. All fear dropped away from Lancaster; he was a man with very steady nerves, as he needed to be in his profession, and he knew exactly what he was going to do. He eased his cigarette lighter from his vest pocket and waited expectantly, hearing only the faint soughing of the night wind over the steady drone of the motor.

"Is there anyone there?"

Even to himself his voice sounded a little unsteady but his pulse beat evenly enough. He moved around to the rear of the car again, facing the roadside verge, strongly illuminated by the beams of the headlights. He repeated the question and again came the crackle. This time the doctor saw a bush to his right move gently, as though someone were standing there, in the shadow where the headlights' illumination began to die away.

Then the branches parted and alien eyes, glaucous and triangular, stared out at the tense form of the doctor. There was a brittle rattling that sent fingers of fear brushing up his spine for the first time. Incredulously, he glimpsed the snake-head surmounting a semi-transparent, slug-like body; the rest of it mercifully hidden by the thick undergrowth which encroached on to the road at that point. The thing lunged at him, the long body flowing like a reptile's from out the bushes, while the rest of it was hidden.

The horrified doctor noted the vestiges of a humanoid face beneath the layers of grey-green reptilian skin and a shrill mewling cry broke from the thing as it slithered toward him with incredible speed. Lancaster screamed then but he did not lose his nerve. With a dexterity born of sheer terror he directed a stream of gasoline over the advancing monstrosity, which halted in its headlong progress. The doctor ran back, having the presence of mind to lay a trail of gasoline leading away from the car. The thing hesitated, the mewling replaced by the thin, brittle rattling he had heard before.

Then Lancaster ripped the prescription form from off the pad in his pocket, stroked the lighter with trembling fingers and lit the paper. He threw it toward the obscenity that hesitated fatally at the roadside. There was a roar as the gasoline caught and then the doctor hurled the can full at the creature while he ran to the front of the automobile with a speed that astonished him. He let off the brake and pushed the car clear of the advancing line of fire that moved with tremendous momentum.

The thing emitted a high-pitched shriek as fire licked at it, caught the bushes beyond. There was a soft explosion, presumably when the gasoline can went up, and yellow fire blossomed. Then a writhing, blazing, dying creature that yet moved and functioned with a sentient consciousness went flaming away into the darkness of the undergrowth as Lancaster, mentally expunging these horrors from his mind, let in the clutch and the car hurtled on into the merciful darkness leading back to the sanity of Arkham.

Presently even the orange glow in the rear mirror faded to blackness and Lancaster was aware that he was alive and free, albeit drenched with perspiration and shaking from his ordeal. He could hardly control the car or handle the gear-changes and when he reached the outskirts of Arkham, he parked briefly, reaching for the flask of brandy in his medical bag.

When he was sufficiently master of himself he drove home, finding the time was still only ten p.m. Then he hurled himself at the telephone.

# XVI

Oates was having a ham sandwich in the police canteen when the call came. At first he could not make out who was on the line but when the doctor was a little more coherent the big detective's own excitement rapidly mounted to a state approaching that of the older man.

"What things?" he said, asking Lancaster to repeat himself for the third time.

"These obscenities," the doctor said in a trembling voice. "They have distinct human attributes. I believe they are able to change their form at will. Innsmouth, Oates . . . The degenerate species of which we have spoken from time to time. I believe with all my soul that wherever they come from, they are able to physically ingest human beings."

Oates was stunned but he went on automatically making notes.

"The old reports said things came from out the sea; from around the reef that lies off Innsmouth," he observed slowly. "It's all too fantastic for words."

"Fantastic, yes," the doctor went on, "but a reality we have to deal with. There's a deadly danger there. But we have the answer. Gasoline!"

"Gasoline?" said Oates uncomprehendingly.

"Gasoline, man! Gasoline!" the doctor repeated. "That's the one area they're vulnerable. They can destroy people, yes. And they seem capable of generating great heat themselves, so powerful it can buckle metal, as we have seen. But they can't abide fire themselves. That may be our salvation. I've been studying the reports for years. That's why they wanted me out of the way. That's why they tampered with your brakes. We were both getting too near the truth."

"We shall both be candidates for the county asylum if this becomes public," Oates growled.

Lancaster drummed with trembling fingers on the edge of the telephone mouthpiece.

"It's our only salvation, man! You know I'm speaking the truth. You've seen those passages. And you know the left-hand one leads toward Innsmouth and the sea. Now they're ready to take over Arkham. It all ties in. The destruction of Holroyd's machine . . ."

He went on in a semi-incoherent fashion but Oates was already won over. Not that he needed winning over. He had come to much the same conclusions himself, long before tonight's conversation.

"Those things are ready to move," Lancaster went on. "We've no time to lose. Will you make the arrangements?"

"It will take a day or two," Oates said dubiously. "We've got to do it right. And my superiors . . ."

"Leave them out of it," Lancaster said crisply.

He sounded much calmer now.

"It may be too late if we go through official channels. You already have those squads of State troopers. That should be enough."

"What do you propose?"

"We'd better meet tonight," the doctor said. "I'll come over to Police H.Q. I feel too vulnerable here after what happened. We have much to talk about. We'll need thousands of gallons of gasoline. As well as explosives."

Oates swore.

"You know what you're asking?"

Lancaster clicked his teeth impatiently. He seemed to have completely recovered his nerve.

"When you've heard my full story you'll want to take action tonight!"

"All right," Oates said finally. "I'll see you in an hour. I'll have the coffee pot on in case you need sobering up."

The doctor gave a hollow laugh.

"I've taken one short slug of brandy all evening, Captain. I'm sober all right. I wish I were not."

Oates modified his manner. His voice was gentle when he replied.

"All right, doc. I believe you. Come on in and we'll get this thing organised."

# XVII

"It may not have been entirely my fault, gentlemen. The Captain there knows that I was well enough when he first got to know me. But events in the Library of Miskatonic and what I eventually deduced from the decodes began to have their effect upon me. I knew that you had noted this yourself, Captain, when we spoke in the concourse when we and the State Police began to explore the passages. I knew then what the end would be but I dared not say anything.

"Those things out there know; yes, I tell you, they know even what we are thinking; even as we sit here in my quiet house beings are regarding us with alien eyes. As the Captain has so cleverly deduced, together with the good doctor, they come from beyond the reef. That is the storm-centre which has plagued Innsmouth and, to a certain extent, Arkham, for a long, long time. I see Captain Oates, at least, believes me. He is a very wise man. Perhaps he may be the saving of us. Who knows. Dr. Lancaster too. But these things are diabolically cunning and they seem to be everywhere.

"Why do you think I ran headlong through the darkness tonight? Not only to escape their physical presence but their infiltration. Oh, yes, gentlemen. They have learned how to infiltrate the brains of human beings and to assume their personalities even, these Old Ones. That is why I had to do what I did tonight. I could see the reptilian trait in his eyes. It was him or me. I had to do it, gentlemen, I'm sure you see that. These things are everywhere.

"I see some of the officers present tonight remain skeptical. Well, that is only to be expected. You wonder, perhaps, why I keep my hands hidden beneath these thick gloves, even indoors. It is because I fear the taint myself. And when I saw the webbing between his fingers as he rang the bell, I knew there was only one way of it. You will say, of course, that I obeyed the promptings of these things from the reef, who have learned to assume human identity. I tell you that my character and will-power have been able to rise above all that.

"It was rather the opposite, gentlemen. I knew he meant me great harm even from the furtive way he went around the house before announcing himself by means of the door bell. Ah, if only you knew how I suffered during those minutes which seemed like hours! But you will want the proof. Please come to the kitchen, gentlemen. There is a trap-door beneath the table, let into the parquet. Yes, if those two strong officers would move it, we shall be able to open the hatch.

"There, gentlemen, there! Weltering in his own blood! Is it not a hideous spectacle! Yet, what was I to do? It must be obvious to the meanest intelligence here that the metamorphosis was upon it. I struck just in time, did I not?

"Be careful of that ladder, gentlemen. The treads are slippery, as you can see . . . Not blood, though it may look red to you. Greenish ichor, rather. And the stench! It is something I shall carry with me to the grave.

"What a hideous sight! I should have burned him, of course, but it was impossible here in the house; or in this closely-knit urban atmosphere. I see you shake your heads; I sense the disbelief in your eyes. Fools! I tell you it is but the facsimile of the man you knew, the hideous masquerade of a devilish thing from beyond. Gentlemen! Gentlemen! Please believe me! Why do you advance to pinion me? I am not mad! I beg you to believe me . . ."

# XVIII

Report from Captain of Detectives Oates to Chief of Bureau, State Police:

1. My plan of action, as outlined in the main report enclosed herewith, is of my own origination and I bear the entire responsibility, except in respect of the medical conclusions drawn up by Dr. Lancaster. As you will realise from radio and newspapers long before you get this, the plan will have been carried out.

2. The purpose of this appendix is merely to assure you of the logic of my actions and the inescapable conclusions to which I have been led since my arrival in

Arkham. I refer you to my earlier missives, particularly Nos. 1, 2 and 3 and the attached material provided by Dr. Lancaster.

3. As you will learn in due course, Jefferson Holroyd, eminent scholar of Miskatonic University, has been transported to the County Asylum, on the medical advice of Dr. Lancaster, who signed the certificate of committal, and by my orders also. He committed murder while insane and a preliminary medical examination has revealed startling changes not only in his personality but in certain degenerative and repellent physical aspects. These are dealt with by Dr. Lancaster in some detail.

4. The remains of one of the strange creatures glimpsed in the areas of Arkham and Innsmouth, three-quarters incinerated by fire, as the result of Dr. Lancaster's timely action, have been refrigerated in the city mortuary in Arkham and are available for further medical inspection. From the physical characteristics exhibited you will see why my actions tomorrow night are so necessary.

5. As detailed in my main report, the body of Dr. Darrow, Dean of the Faculty of Miskatonic University, hideously mangled and hacked about with a kitchen knife, was found in a cellar beneath the house of Jefferson Holroyd. He has already confessed to the murder and there is no doubt he was responsible for the unfortunate man's death. Please see specific details in my main report.

6. None of these facts have yet been made known to the press or the general public and if I do not return from the action we have proposed to take, please understand that I have acted from the best of all possible motives.

7. All the matters briefly glanced over in Headings 1 to 6 above are fully expanded upon in the main reports

by myself and Dr. Lancaster and bizarre as you may think them, I can assure you they are well attested by reliable witnesses. The missing State troopers under the command of Captain Uriah Dale must be presumed dead; there is no doubt of that and I would be grateful if you would have the next of kin informed.

8. The names and ranks of those officers who fell in the line of duty in the passages leading in the Innsmouth direction are detailed in the attached list, compiled by colleagues from the State Police.

I recommend that Sergeant John P. Ellermann be advanced to the rank of Captain for the distinguished service in these matters he has rendered over the past few days.

I am, sir, your obedient servant
Cornelius Oates
Captain of Detectives, County Force.

# XIX

Dr. Lancaster's face was corpse-like and strained in the weird bluish lighting of the tunnels. They were in the fifth and largest of the passages, the one that sloped steeply away toward Innsmouth and the sea. There were dozens of State troopers, heavily armed, standing on guard but nothing had been seen or heard for the past two days.

Bellows was hurrying down the sloping tunnel toward them. He too had changed over the past forty-eight hours, Oates thought.

"A message from Ellermann on the surface," the surveyor said. "Telephone message just came in from the army officer commanding the operations at Innsmouth. The town has been entirely evacuated. All civilians and animals have been removed from the area, the nearest being some five miles back."

"House to house clearance?" said Oates.

Bellows nodded.

"House to house. Ambulances removed a number of invalids to district hospitals."

Lancaster expressed his approval.

"It seems to have been a pretty thorough operation," he said.

Oates turned back to Bellows.

"What time?"

"The message came through at eight o'clock. It's taken me half an hour to get down here. The cordon of State Police and Army personnel were withdrawing by truck then. They should be back in position now, sealing off all roads leading to Innsmouth and the sea."

Oates again glanced at his wrist watch. He had himself, together with the civic authorities, checked the placing of the blasting powder the previous night. The caves along the Innsmouth shore had been thoroughly checked and nothing had been found; but subterranean caverns still led off a large pit on shore descending steeply beneath the surface of the sea, out toward the reef.

Here Bellows' expertise had proved invaluable. All involved had agreed that it would be far too dangerous to try to explore out there. But the configurations of the monstrous tunnels had helped in that respect. A number of rubber-wheeled trolleys had been constructed, the explosive carefully loaded aboard them, and each individual load had been winched with infinite care down the precipitous slopes into incredible depths.

Bellows had devised an ingenious arrangement to account for any curves in the tunnels. There was a circular rail running around each trolley, within which the individual loads of blasting powder had been carefully packed, protected by padding; the trolley wheels were made to swivel in any direction, so that as soon as one of the vehicles came in contact with a wall or other obstacle, it would immediately set off at another tangent, impelled by its own weight.

The winches were equipped with measuring devices and before they came to a halt they had registered in excess of five thousand feet. Engineering works on the beach, where the tunnels came out, had consisted of cutting a deep trench on the sea-shore leading to the vast pit on the beach which led sloping away toward and under the sea.

A silence had fallen between the three men most involved in the work of the past days, though in reality there was tremendous noise down here, not only from the hundreds of men engaged, but from the heavy throbbing of the pumps. For many hours thousands of gallons of gasoline had been delivered from those pumps, the fuel sluicing down, eventually debouching into the deep trench on the beach and thence to the huge tunnel that led beneath the sea. The air was heavy with the stink of gasoline. This was a dangerous task and everyone involved had been relieved of matches or anything which might cause a spark and all personnel wore rubber-soled boots.

"There will be a tremendous explosion," Bellows said reflectively. "Even if the reef is not destroyed the surface of the sea will show visible signs. It will be like a miniature volcano."

Oates nodded, his mind heavy with thought. Intercut with the images of the past weeks; the horrors of the sudden deaths; the snake-like creatures glimpsed in the tunnel and by Lancaster; the whole brooding atmosphere of the Innsmouth-Arkham axis; was the impending climax to the long drama. He had had his figures and whole scheme submitted to the most rigorous examination by engineers and mathematicians of the Miskatonic faculty and they had been adamant in their objections; not at its feasibility but at the inherent dangers.

Oates was having all the State troopers and other personnel cleared from the tunnels, of course; that was only common sense. All that gasoline had been pumped down; the telephone link had reported back that the liquid flow had reached the beach, had followed the deep ditch exactly and had disappeared into the great borehole. It must have reached the area of the blasting powder long ago. It needed only for him to ignite the chain which would detonate one of the greatest man-made explosions of modern history.

No human being would suffer; he was convinced of that. But would the resulting holocaust rid the world of something so monstrous as to be almost beyond belief? And if he failed there was an awesome responsibility on his shoulders. But he must not fail. His only regret was that he might die before learning the result of all these painstaking operations.

The scientists had warned him there would be a danger of a monstrous blowback when the gasoline ignited; in which case the passage leading to the beach would act like the barrel of a gun and send a blast of searing heat back up the shaft, roasting everything in its path.

They had urged that the pumping operation should begin at the borehole on the beach; this would have been the solution in the normal event but there were insuperable problems, in that the black basaltic cliffs dropped almost precipitously to the shore at that point, rugged boulders and chasms preventing vehicular access from the top. Similarly the main tunnel narrowed as it descended and when it debouched on to the beach the passage was only about four feet across, making it impossible for personnel and the pumps to descend that way. Any other solution would have taken months and there was no time for that.

"How are you going to do it?" the doctor asked Oates.

Real silence had fallen at last; the pumps had been switched off and the vehicles and troops and police were withdrawing up the passage, giving the three men curious looks.

"Electrical spark," Oates said shortly. "Worked out by Bellows here. A clockwork motor on a ratchet will start operating in about twenty minutes after switch-on. We've worked out that's how long it will take the trolley bearing the mechanism to reach the lower tunnel. That will set a circuit going; generating a series of sparks that should trigger off the gasoline in a further ten minutes. The theory is that a wall of fire will descend from the beach and in turn set off the blasting powder far below."

Lancaster gave him a twisted smile.

"That's the theory, Captain."

Oates nodded abstractedly, looking across at the curious circular trolley with its rubber wheels.

"No sense hanging about," he said. "I'm going to set the mechanism. I'll join you later. You start off up now. And that's an order."

His two companions glanced at one another in silence.

"As long as you know what you're doing," Bellows said. "You sure you don't want me to stay? I set this thing up, remember."

Oates shook his head.

"I can manage. We'll all meet up top."

"So long as we don't all meet up in the sky," said the doctor lugubriously.

The three men exchanged strained smiles. Then the other two went, walking carefully, the stench of gasoline emphasising the volatile vaporous mixture in the air. Oates felt perspiration cold on his face. The insidious whispering inside his head had begun again. He had no time to lose.

He walked foreward to where the precipitous slope leaned down into the primeval darkness beyond the reach of the specially sealed hand lamps. He pulled the trolley out gently from the wall, set the calibrating dial as Bellows had shown him, not once but a dozen times. His heart was pumping uncomfortably, even drowning out the ticking of the clockwork mechanism. He checked his watch again. He had just twenty minutes.

Oates was not a religious man but he prayed now.

"God protect us from the powers of darkness," he said.

Then he was launching the rubber-sided trolley down the steep slope into the blackness and into the ultimate horror of the pulsating things that writhed and ululated beyond the reef that lay off the dark and blasphemous Innsmouth shore.

# The Big Fish

## Jack Yeovil

The Bay City cops were rousting enemy aliens. As I drove through the nasty coast town, uniforms hauled an old couple out of a grocery store. The Taraki family's neighbours huddled in thin rain howling asthmatically for bloody revenge. Pearl Harbour had struck a lot of people that way. With the Tarakis on the bus for Manzanar, neighbours descended on the store like bedraggled vultures. Produce vanished instantly, then destruction started. Caught at a sleepy stop light, I got a good look. The Tarakis had lived over the store; now, their furniture was thrown out of the second-storey window. Fine china shattered on the sidewalk, spilling white chips like teeth into the gutter. It was inspirational, the forces of democracy rallying round to protect the United States from vicious oriental grocers, fiendishly intent on selling eggplant to a hapless civilian population.

Meanwhile my appointment was with a gent who kept three pictures on his mantelpiece, grouped in a triangle around a statue of the Virgin Mary. At the apex was his white-haired mama, to the left Charles Luciano, and to the right, Benito Mussolini. The Tarakis, American-born and registered Democrats, were headed to a dust-bowl concentration camp for the duration, while Gianni Pastore, Sicilian-born and highly unregistered capo of the Family Business, would spend his war in a marble-fronted mansion paid for by nickels and dimes dropped on the numbers game, into slot machines, or exchanged for the favours of nice girls from the old country. I'd seen his mansion before and so far been able to resist the temptation to bean one of his twelve muse statues with a bourbon bottle.

Money can buy you love but can't even put down a deposit on good taste.

The palace was up in the hills, a little way down the boulevard from Tyrone Power. But now, Pastore was hanging his mink-banded fedora in a Bay City beachfront motel complex, which was a real estate agent's term for a bunch of horrible shacks shoved together for the convenience of people who like sand on their carpets.

I always take a lungful of fresh air before entering a confined space with someone in Pastore's business, so I parked the Chrysler a few blocks from the Seaview Inn and walked the rest of the way, sucking on a Camel to keep warm in the wet. They say it doesn't rain in Southern California, but they also say the U.S. Navy could never be taken by surprise. This February, three months into a war the rest of the world had been fighting since 1936 or 1939 depending on whether you were Chinese or Polish, it was raining almost constantly, varying between a light fall of misty drizzle in the dreary daytimes to spectacular storms, complete with DeMille lighting effects, in our fear-filled nights. Those trusty Boy Scouts scanning the horizons for Jap subs and Nazi U-Boats were filling up influenza wards, and manufacturers of raincoats and umbrellas who'd not yet converted their plants to defense production were making a killing. I didn't mind the rain. At least rainwater is clean, unlike most other things in Bay City.

A small boy with a wooden gun leaped out of a bush and sprayed me with sound effects, interrupting his onomatopoeic chirruping with a shout of "Die, you slant-eyed Jap!" I clutched my heart, staggered back, and he finished me off with a quick burst. I died for the Emperor and tipped the kid a dime to go away. If this went on long enough, maybe little Johnny would get a chance to march off and do real killing, then maybe come home in a box or with the shakes or a taste for blood. Meanwhile, especially since someone spotted a Jap submarine off Santa Barbara, California was gearing up for the War Effort. Aside from interning grocers, our best brains were writing songs like "To Be Specific, It's Our Pacific," "So Long Momma, I'm Off to Yokohama," "We're Gonna Slap the Jap Right Off the Map" and "When Those Little Yellow Bellies Meet the Cohens and the Kellys." Zanuck had donated his string of Argentine polo ponies to West Point and got himself measured for a comic opera Colonel's uniform so he could join the Signal Corps and defeat the Axis by posing for publicity photographs.

I'd tried to join up two days after Pearl Harbour but they kicked me back onto the streets. Too many concussions. Apparently, I get hit on the head too often and have a tendency to black out. When they came to mention it, they were right.

The Seaview Inn was shuttered, one of the first casualties of war. It had its own jetty, and by it were a few canvas-covered motor launches shifting with the waves. In late afternoon gloom, I saw the silhouette of the *Montecito,* anchored strategically outside the three-mile limit. That was one good thing about the Japanese; on the downside, they might have sunk most of the U.S. fleet, but on the up, they'd put Laird Brunette's gambling ship out of business. Nobody was enthusiastic about losing their shirt-buttons on a rigged roulette wheel if they imagined they were going to be torpedoed any moment. I'd have thought that would add an extra thrill to the whole gay, delirious business of giving Brunette money, but I'm just a poor, twenty-five-dollars-a-day detective.

The Seaview Inn was supposed to be a stopping-off point on the way to the *Monty* and now its trade was stopped off. The main building was sculpted out of dusty ice cream and looked like a three-storey radiogram with wave-scallop friezes. I pushed through double-doors and entered the lobby. The floor was decorated with a mosaic in which Neptune, looking like an angry Santa Claus in a swimsuit, was sticking it to a sea-nymph who shared a hairdresser with Hedy Lamarr. The nymph was naked except for some strategic shells. It was very artistic.

There was nobody at the desk and thumping the bell didn't improve matters. Water ran down the outside of the green-tinted windows. There were a few steady drips somewhere. I lit up another Camel and went exploring. The office was locked and the desk register didn't have any entries after December 7, 1941. My raincoat dripped and began to dry out, sticking my jacket and shirt to my shoulders. I shrugged, trying to get some air into my clothes. I noticed Neptune's face quivering. A thin layer of water had pooled over the mosaic and various anemone-like fronds attached to the sea god were apparently getting excited. Looking at the nymph, I could understand that. Actually, I realised, only the hair was from Hedy. The face and the body were strictly Janey Wilde.

I go to the movies a lot but I'd missed most of Janey's credits: *She-Strangler of Shanghai, Tarzan and the Tiger Girl, The Perils of Jungle Jillian.* I'd seen her in the newspapers though, often in unnervingly close proximity with Pastore or Brunette. She'd started as an Olympic swimmer, picking up medals in Berlin, then followed Weissmuller and Crabbe to Hollywood. She would never get an Academy Award but her legs were in a lot of cheesecake stills publicising no particular movie. Air-brushed and made-up like a good-looking corpse, she was a fine commercial for sex. In person she was as bubbly as domestic champagne, though now running to flat. Things were slow in the detecting business, since people were more worried about imminent invasion than missing daughters or misplaced love letters. So when Janey Wilde called on me in my office in the Cahuenga Building and asked me to look up one of her ill-chosen men friends, I checked the pile of old envelopes I use as a desk diary and informed her that I was available to make inquiries into the current whereabouts of a certain big fish.

Wherever Laird Brunette was, he wasn't here. I was beginning to figure Gianni Pastore, the gambler's partner, wasn't here either. Which meant I'd wasted an afternoon. Outside it rained harder, driving against the walls with a drumlike tattoo. Either there were hailstones mixed in with the water or the Jap air force was hurling fistfuls of pebbles at Bay City to demoralise the population. I don't know why they bothered. All Hirohito had to do was slip a thick envelope to the Bay City cops and the city's finest would hand over the whole community to the Japanese Empire with a ribbon around it and a bow on top.

There were more puddles in the lobby, little streams running from one to the other. I was reminded of the episode of *The Perils of Jungle Jillian* I had seen while tailing a child molester to a Saturday matinee. At the end, Janey Wilde had been caught by the Panther Princess and trapped in a room which slowly filled with water. That room had been a lot smaller than the lobby of the Seaview Inn and the water had come in a lot faster.

Behind the desk were framed photographs of pretty people in pretty clothes having a pretty time. Pastore was there, and Brunette, grinning like tiger cats, mingling with showfolk: Xavier Cugat, Janey Wilde, Charles Coburn. Janice Marsh, the pop-eyed beauty rumoured to have replaced Jungle Jillian in Brunette's affections, was well represented in artistic poses.

On the phone, Pastore had promised faithfully to be here. He hadn't wanted to bother with a small-timer like me but Janey Wilde's name opened a door. I had a feeling Papa Pastore was relieved to be shaken down about Brunette, as if he wanted to talk about something. He must be busy because there were several wars on. The big one overseas and a few little ones at home. Maxie Rothko, bar owner and junior partner in the *Monty,* had been found drifting in the seaweed around the Santa Monica pier without much of a head to speak of. And Phil Isinglass, man-about-town lawyer and Brunette frontman, had turned up in the storm drains, lungs full of sandy mud. Disappearing was the latest craze in Brunette's organisation. That didn't sound good for Janey Wilde, though Pastore had talked about the Laird as if he knew Brunette was alive. But now Papa wasn't around. I was getting annoyed with someone it wasn't sensible to be annoyed with.

Pastore wouldn't be in any of the beach shacks but there should be an apartment for his convenience in the main building. I decided to explore further. Jungle Jillian would expect no less. She'd hired me for five days in advance, a good thing since I'm unduly reliant on eating and drinking and other expensive diversions of the monied and idle.

The corridor that led past the office ended in a walk-up staircase. As soon as I put my size nines on the first step, it squelched. I realised something was more than usually wrong. The steps were a quiet little waterfall, seeping rather than cascading. It wasn't just water, there was unpleasant, slimy stuff mixed in. Someone had left the bath running. My first thought was that Pastore had been distracted by a bullet. I was wrong. In the long run, he might have been happier if I'd been right.

I climbed the soggy stairs and found the apartment door unlocked but shut. Bracing myself, I pushed the door in. It encountered resistance but then sliced open, allowing a gush of water to shoot around my ankles, soaking my dark blue socks. Along with water was a three-weeks-dead-in-the-water-with-rotten-fish smell that wrapped around me like a blanket. Holding my breath, I stepped into the room. The waterfall flowed faster now. I heard a faucet running. A radio played, with funny little gurgles mixed in. A crooner was doing his best with "Life is Just a Bowl of Cherries," but he sounded as if he were drowned full fathom five. I followed the music and found the bathroom.

Pastore was face down in the overflowing tub, the song coming from under him. He wore a silk lounging robe that had been pulled away from his back, his wrists tied behind him with the robe's cord. In the end he'd been drowned. But before that hands had been laid on him, either in anger or with cold, professional skill. I'm not a coroner, so I couldn't tell how long the Family Man had been in the water. The radio still playing and the water still running suggested Gianni had met his end recently but the stench felt older than sin.

I have a bad habit of finding bodies in Bay City and the most profit-minded police force in the country have a bad habit of trying to make connections between me and a wide variety of deceased persons. The obvious solution in this case was to make a friendly phone call, absent-mindedly forgetting to mention my name while giving the flatfeet directions to the late Mr. Pastore. Who knows, I might accidentally talk to someone honest.

That is exactly what I would have done if, just then, the man with the gun hadn't come through the door . . .

I had Janey Wilde to blame. She'd arrived without an appointment, having picked me on a recommendation. Oddly, Laird Brunette had once said something not entirely uncomplimentary about me. We'd met. We hadn't seriously tried to kill each other in a while. That was as good a basis for a relationship as any.

Out of her sarong, Jungle Jillian favoured sharp shoulders and a veiled pill-box. The kiddies at the matinee had liked her fine, especially when she was wrestling stuffed snakes, and dutiful Daddies took no exception to her either, especially when she was tied down and her sarong rode up a few inches. Her lips were four red grapes plumped together. When she crossed her legs you saw a swimmer's smooth muscle under her hose.

"He's very sweet, really," she explained, meaning Mr. Brunette never killed anyone within ten miles of her without apologising afterwards, "not at all like they say in those dreadful scandal sheets."

The gambler had been strange recently, especially since the war shut him down. Actually the *Montecito* had been out of commission for nearly a year, supposedly for a refit although as far as Janey Wilde knew no workmen had been sent out to the ship. At about the time Brunette suspended his crooked wheels, he came down with a common California complaint, a dose of crackpot religion. He'd been tangentially mixed up a few years ago with a psychic racket run by a bird named Amthor, but had apparently shifted from the mostly harmless bunco cults onto the hard stuff. Spiritualism, orgiastic rites, chanting, incense, the whole deal.

Janey blamed this sudden interest in matters occult on Janice Marsh, who had coincidentally made her name as the Panther Princess in *The Perils of Jungle Jillian,* a role which required her to torture Janey Wilde at least once every chapter. My employer didn't mention that her own career had hardly soared between *Jungle Jillian* and *She-Strangler of Shanghai,* while the erstwhile Panther Princess had gone from Republic to Metro and was being built up as an exotic in the Dietrich-Garbo vein. Say what you like about Janice Marsh's *Nefertiti,* she still looked like Peter Lorre to me. And according to Janey, the star had more peculiar tastes than a seafood buffet.

Brunette had apparently joined a series of fringe organisations and become quite involved, to the extent of neglecting his business and thereby irking his long-time partner, Gianni Pastore. Perhaps that was why person or persons unknown had decided the Laird wouldn't mind if his associates died one by one. I couldn't figure it out. The cults I'd come across mostly stayed in business by selling sex, drugs, power or reassurance to rich, stupid people. The Laird hardly fell into the category. He was too big a fish for that particular bowl.

The man with the gun was English, with a Ronald Colman accent and a white aviator's scarf. He was not alone. The quiet, truck-sized bruiser I made as a fed went through my wallet while the dapper foreigner kept his automatic pointed casually at my middle.

"Peeper," the fed snarled, showing the photostat of my license and my supposedly impressive deputy's badge.

"Interesting," said the Britisher, slipping his gun into the pocket of his camel coat. Immaculate, he must have been umbrella-protected between car and building because there wasn't a spot of rain on him. "I'm Winthrop. Edwin Winthrop."

We shook hands. His other companion, the interesting one, was going through the deceased's papers. She looked up, smiled with sharp white teeth, and got back to work.

"This is Mademoiselle Dieudonne."

"Geneviève," she said. She pronounced it "Zhe-ne-vyev," suggesting Paris, France. She was wearing something white with silver in it and had quantities of pale blonde hair.

"And the gentleman from your Federal Bureau of Investigation is Finlay."

The fed grunted. He looked as if he'd been brought to life by Willis H. O'Brien.

"You are interested in a Mr. Brunette," Winthrop said. It was not a question, so there was no point in answering him. "So are we."

"Call in a Russian and we could be the Allies," I said.

Winthrop laughed. He was sharp. "True. I am here at the request of my government and working with the full co-operation of yours."

One of the small detective-type details I noticed was that no one even suggested informing the police about Gianni Pastore was a good idea.

"Have you ever heard of a place called Innsmouth, Massachu-setts?"

It didn't mean anything to me and I said so.

"Count yourself lucky. Special Agent Finlay's associates were called upon to dynamite certain unsafe structures in the sea off Inns-mouth back in the twenties. It was a bad business."

Geneviève said something sharp in French that sounded like swearing. She held up a photograph of Brunette dancing cheek to cheek with Janice Marsh.

"Do you know the lady?" Winthrop asked.

"Only in the movies. Some go for her in a big way but I think she looks like Mr. Moto."

"Very true. Does the Esoteric Order of Dagon mean anything to you?"

"Sounds like a Church-of-the-Month alternate. Otherwise, no."

"Captain Obed Marsh?"

"Uh-uh."

"The Deep Ones."

"Are they those coloured singers?"

"What about Cthulhu, Y'ha-nthlei, R'lyeh?"

"*Gesundheit.*"

Winthrop grinned, sharp moustache pointing. "No, not easy to say at all. Hard to fit into human mouths, you know."

"He's just a bedroom creeper," Finlay said, "he don't know noth-ing."

"His grammar could be better. Doesn't J. Edgar pay for elocution lessons?"

Finlay's big hands opened and closed as if he would rather there were a throat in them.

"Gene?" Winthrop said.

The woman looked up, red tongue absently flicking across her red lips, and thought a moment. She said something in a foreign language that I didn't understand.

"There's no need to kill him," she said in French. Thank you very much, I thought.

Winthrop shrugged and said "Fine by me." Finlay looked disappointed.

"You're free to go," the Britisher told me. "We shall take care of everything. I see no point in your continuing your current line of inquiry. Send in a chit to this address," he handed me a card, "and you'll be reimbursed for your expenses so far. Don't worry. We'll carry on until this is seen through. By the way, you might care not to discuss with anyone what you've seen here or anything I may have said. There's a War on, you know. Loose lips sink ships."

I had a few clever answers but I swallowed them and left. Anyone who thought there was no need to kill me was all right in my book and I wasn't using my razored tongue on them. As I walked to the Chrysler, several ostentatiously unofficial cars cruised past me, headed for the Seaview Inn.

It was getting dark and lightning was striking down out at sea. A flash lit up the *Montecito* and I counted five seconds before the thunder boomed. I had the feeling there was something out there beyond the three-mile limit besides the floating former casino, and that it was angry.

I slipped into the Chrysler and drove away from Bay City, feeling better the further inland I got.


I take *Black Mask*. It's a long time since Hammett and the fellow who wrote the Ted Carmady stories were in it, but you occasionally get a good Cornell Woolrich or Erle Stanley Gardner. Back at my office, I saw the newsboy had been by and dropped off the *Times* and next month's pulp. But there'd been a mix-up. Instead of the *Mask,* there was something inside the folded newspaper called *Weird Tales.* On the cover, a man was being attacked by two green demons and a stereotype vampire with a widow's peak. " 'Hell on Earth,' a Novelette of Satan in a Tuxedo by Robert Bloch" was blazed above the title. Also promised were "A new Lovecraft series, 'Herbert West—Re-Animator' " and " 'The Rat Master' by Greye la Spina." All for fifteen cents, kids. If I were a different type of detective, the brand who said *nom de* something and waxed a moustache whenever he found a mutilated corpse, I might have thought the substitution an omen.

In my office, I've always had five filing cabinets, three empty. I also had two bottles, only one empty. In a few hours, the situation would have changed by one bottle.

I found a glass without too much dust and wiped it with my clean handkerchief. I poured myself a generous slug and hit the back of my throat with it.

The radio didn't work but I could hear Glenn Miller from somewhere. I found my glass empty and dealt with that. Sitting behind my desk, I looked at the patterns in rain on the window. If I craned I could see traffic on Hollywood Boulevard. People who didn't spend their working days finding bodies in bathtubs were going home not to spend their evenings emptying a bottle.

After a day, I'd had some excitement but I hadn't done much for Janey Wilde. I was no nearer being able to explain the absence of Mr. Brunette from his usual haunts than I had been when she left my office, leaving behind a tantalising whiff of *essence de chine.*

She'd given me some literature pertaining to Brunette's cult involvement. Now, the third slug warming me up inside, I looked over it, waiting for inspiration to strike. Interesting echoes came up in relation to Winthrop's shopping list of subjects of peculiar interest. I had no luck with the alphabet soup syllables he'd spat at me, mainly because "Cthulhu" sounds more like a cough than a word. But the Esoteric Order of Dagon was a group Brunette had joined, and Innsmouth, Massachusetts, was the East Coast town where the organisation was registered. The Esoteric Order had a temple on the beach front in Venice, and its mumbo-jumbo handouts promised

"ancient and intriguing rites to probe the mysteries of the Deep."
Slipped in with the recruitment bills was a studio biography of Janice
Marsh, which helpfully revealed the movie star's place of birth as
Innsmouth, Massachusetts, and that she could trace her family back
to Captain Obed Marsh, the famous early 19th century explorer of
whom I'd never heard. Obviously Winthrop, Geneviève and the FBI
were well ahead of me in making connections. And I didn't really
know who the Englishman and the French girl were.

I wondered if I wouldn't have been better off reading *Weird Tales.*
I liked the sound of "Satan in a Tuxedo." It wasn't Ted Carmady with
an automatic and a dame, but it would do. There was a lot more
thunder and lightning and I finished the bottle. I suppose I could
have gone home to sleep but the chair was no more uncomfortable
than my Murphy bed.

The empty bottle rolled and I settled down, tie loose, to forget
the cares of the day.


Thanks to the War, Pastore only made page 3 of the *Times.* Apparently the noted gambler-entrepreneur had been shot to death. If that
was true, it had happened after I'd left. Then, he'd only been tortured
and drowned. Police Chief John Wax dished out his usual "over by
Christmas" quote about the investigation. There was no mention of
the FBI, or of our allies, John Bull in a tux and Mademoiselle la Guil-
lotine. In prison, you get papers with neat oblongs cut out to remove
articles the censor feels provocative. They don't make any difference:
all newspapers have invisible oblongs. Pastore's sterling work with
underprivileged kids was mentioned but someone forgot to write
about the junk he sold them when they grew into underprivileged
adults. The obit photograph found him with Janey Wilde and Janice
Marsh at the premiere of a George Raft movie. The phantom Jap sub
off Santa Barbara got more column inches. General John L. DeWitt,
head of the Western Defense Command, called for more troops to
guard the coastline, prophesying "death and destruction are likely to
come at any moment." Everyone in California was looking out to sea.

After my regular morning conference with Mr. Huggins and Mr.

Young, I placed a call to Janey Wilde's Malibu residence. Most screen idols are either at the studio or asleep if you telephone before ten o'clock in the morning, but Janey, with weeks to go before shooting started on *Bowery to Bataan,* was at home and awake, having done her thirty lengths. Unlike almost everyone else in the industry, she thought a swimming pool was for swimming in rather than lounging beside.

She remembered instantly who I was and asked for news. I gave her a précis.

"I've been politely asked to refrain from further investigations," I explained. "By some heavy hitters."

"So you're quitting?"

I should have said yes, but "Miss Wilde, only you can require me to quit. I thought you should know how the federal government feels."

There was a pause.

"There's something I didn't tell you," she told me. It was an expression common among my clients. "Something important."

I let dead air hang on the line.

"It's not so much Laird that I'm concerned about. It's that he has Franklin."

"Franklin?"

"The baby," she said. "Our baby. My baby."

"Laird Brunette has disappeared, taking a baby with him?"

"Yes."

"Kidnapping is a crime. You might consider calling the cops."

"A lot of things are crimes. Laird has done many of them and never spent a day in prison."

That was true, which was why this development was strange. Kidnapping, whether personal or for profit, is the riskiest of crimes. As a rule, it's the province only of the stupidest criminals. Laird Brunette was not a stupid criminal.

"I can't afford bad publicity. Not when I'm so near to the roles I need."

*Bowery to Bataan* was going to put her among the screen immortals.

"Franklin is supposed to be Esther's boy. In a few years, I'll adopt him legally. Esther is my house-keeper. It'll work out. But I must have him back."

"Laird is the father. He will have some rights."

"He said he wasn't interested. He . . . um, moved on . . . to Janice Marsh while I was . . . before Franklin was born."

"He's had a sudden attack of fatherhood and you're not convinced?"

"I'm worried to distraction. It's not Laird, it's *her*. Janice Marsh wants my baby for something vile. I want you to get Franklin back."

"As I mentioned, kidnapping is a crime."

"If there's a danger to the child, surely . . ."

"Do you have any proof that there is danger?"

"Well, no."

"Have Laird Brunette or Janice Marsh ever given you reason to believe they have ill-will for the baby?"

"Not exactly."

I considered things.

"I'll continue with the job you hired me for, but you understand that's all I can do. If I find Brunette, I'll pass your worries on. Then it's between the two of you."

She thanked me in a flood and I got off the phone feeling I'd taken a couple of strides further into the LaBrea tar pits and could feel sucking stickiness well above my knees.

I should have stayed out of the rain and concentrated on chess problems but I had another four days' worth of Jungle Jillian's retainer in my pocket and an address for the Esoteric Order of Dagon in a clipping from a lunatic scientific journal. So I drove out to Venice, reminding myself all the way that my wipers needed fixing.

Venice, California, is a fascinating idea that didn't work. Someone named Abbot Kinney had the notion of artificially creating a city like Venice, Italy, with canals and architecture. The canals mostly ran dry and the architecture never really caught on in a town where, in the twenties, Gloria Swanson's bathroom was considered an aesthetic triumph. All that was left was the beach and piles of rotting fish. Venice, Italy, is the Plague Capital of Europe, so Venice, California, got one thing right.

The Esoteric Order was up the coast from Muscle Beach, housed in a discreet yacht club building with its own small marina. From the exterior, I guessed the cult business had seen better days. Seaweed had tracked up the beach, swarmed around the jetty, and was licking the lower edges of the front wall. Everything had gone green: wood, plaster, copper ornaments. And it smelled like Pastore's bathroom, only worse. This kind of place made you wonder why the Japs were so keen on invading.

I looked at myself in the mirror and rolled my eyes. I tried to get that slap-happy, let-me-give-you-all-my-worldly-goods, gimme-some-mysteries-of-the-orient look I imagined typical of a communicant at one of these bughouse congregations. After I'd stopped laughing, I remembered the marks on Pastore and tried to take detecting seriously. Taking in my unshaven, slept-upright-in-his-clothes, two-bottles-a-day lost soul look, I congratulated myself on my foresight in spending fifteen years developing the ideal cover for a job like this.

To get in the building, I had to go down to the marina and come at it from the beach-side. There were green pillars of what looked like fungus-eaten cardboard either side of the impressive front door, which held a stained glass picture in shades of green and blue of a man with the head of a squid in a natty monk's number, waving his eyes for the artist. Dagon, I happened to know, was half-man, half-fish, and God of the Philistines. In this town, I guess a Philistine God blended in well. It's a great country: if you're half-fish, pay most of your taxes, eat babies and aren't Japanese, you have a wonderful future.

I rapped on the squid's head but nothing happened. I looked the squid in several of his eyes and felt squirmy inside. Somehow, up close, cephalopod-face didn't look that silly.

I pushed the door and found myself in a temple's waiting room. It was what I'd expected: subdued lighting, old but bad paintings, a few semi-pornographic statuettes, a strong smell of last night's incense to cover up the fish stink. It had as much religious atmosphere as a two-dollar bordello.

"Yoo-hoo," I said, "Dagon calling . . ."

My voice sounded less funny echoed back at me.

I prowled, sniffing for clues. I tried saying *nom de something* and twiddling a non-existent moustache but nothing came to me. Perhaps I ought to switch to a meerschaum of cocaine and a deerstalker, or maybe a monocle and an interest in incunabula.

Where you'd expect a portrait of George Washington or Jean Harlow's Mother, the Order had hung up an impressively ugly picture of "Our Founder." Capt. Obed Marsh, dressed up like Admiral Butler, stood on the shore of a Polynesian paradise, his good ship painted with no sense of perspective on the horizon as if it were about three feet tall. The Capt., surrounded by adoring if funny-faced native tomatoes, looked about as unhappy as Errol Flynn at a Girl Scout meeting. The painter had taken a lot of trouble with the native nudes. One of the dusky lovelies had hips that would make Lombard green and a face that put me in mind of Janice Marsh. She was probably the Panther Princess's great-great-great grandmother. In the background, just in front of the ship, was something like a squid emerging from the sea. Fumble-fingers with a brush had tripped up again. It looked as if the tentacle-waving creature were about twice the size of Obed's clipper. The most upsetting detail was a robed and masked figure standing on the deck with a baby's ankle in each fist. He had apparently just wrenched the child apart like a wishbone and was emptying blood into the squid's eyes.

"Excuse me," gargled a voice, "can I help you?"

I turned around and got a noseful of the stooped and ancient Guardian of the Cult. His robe matched the ones worn by squid-features on the door and baby-ripper in the portrait. He kept his face shadowed, his voice sounded about as good as the radio in Pastore's bath and his breath smelled worse than Pastore after a week and a half of putrefaction.

"Good morning," I said, letting a bird flutter in the higher ranges of my voice, "my name is, er . . ."

I put together the first things that came to mind.

"My name is Herbert West Lovecraft. Uh, H. W. Lovecraft the Third. I'm simply fascinated by matters Ancient and Esoteric, don't ch'know."

"Don't ch'know" I picked up from the fellow with the monocle and the old books.

"You wouldn't happen to have an entry blank, would you? Or any incunabula?"

"Incunabula?" he wheezed.

"Books. Old books. Print books, published before 1500 anno domini, old sport." See, I have a dictionary too.

"Books . . ."

The man was a monotonous conversationalist. He also moved like Laughton in *The Hunchback of Notre Dame* and the front of his robe, where the squidhead was embroidered, was wet with what I was disgusted to deduce was drool.

"Old books. Arcane mysteries, don't ch'know. Anything cyclopaean and doom-haunted is just up my old alley."

"The *Necronomicon*?" He pronounced it with great respect, and great difficulty.

"Sounds just the ticket."

Quasimodo shook his head under his hood and it lolled. I glimpsed greenish skin and large, moist eyes.

"I was recommended to come here by an old pal," I said. "Spiffing fellow. Laird Brunette. Ever hear of him?"

I'd pushed the wrong button. Quasi straightened out and grew about two feet. Those moist eyes flashed like razors.

"You'll have to see the Cap'n's Daughter."

I didn't like the sound of that and stepped backwards, towards the door. Quasi laid a hand on my shoulder and held it fast. He was wearing mittens and I felt he had too many fingers inside them. His grip was like a gila monster's jaw.

"That will be fine," I said, dropping the flutter.

As if arranged, curtains parted, and I was shoved through a door. Cracking my head on the low lintel, I could see why Quasi spent most of his time hunched over. I had to bend at the neck and knees to go down the corridor. The exterior might be rotten old wood but the

heart of the place was solid stone. The walls were damp, bare and covered in suggestive carvings that gave primitive art a bad name. You'd
have thought I'd be getting used to the smell by now, but nothing doing. I nearly gagged.

Quasi pushed me through another door. I was in a meeting room
no larger than Union Station, with a stage, rows of comfortable arm-
chairs and lots more squid-person statues. The centrepiece was very
like the mosaic at the Seaview Inn, only the nymph had less shells and
Neptune more tentacles.

Quasi vanished, slamming the door behind him. I strolled over
to the stage and looked at a huge book perched on a straining lectern.
The fellow with the monocle would have salivated, because this
looked a lot older than 1500. It wasn't a Bible and didn't smell
healthy. It was open to an illustration of something with tentacles and
slime, facing a page written in several deservedly dead languages.

"The *Necronomicon*," said a throaty female voice, "of the mad
Arab, Abdul Al-Hazred."

"Mad, huh?" I turned to the speaker. "Is he not getting his royal-
ties?"

I recognised Janice Marsh straight away. The Panther Princess
wore a turban and green silk lounging pajamas, with a floorlength
housecoat that cost more than I make in a year. She had on jade earrings, a pearl cluster pendant and a ruby-eyed silver squid brooch.
The lighting made her face look green and her round eyes shone. She
still looked like Peter Lorre, but maybe if Lorre put his face on a body
like Janice Marsh's, he'd be up for sex goddess roles too. Her silk
thighs purred against each other as she walked down the temple aisle.

"Mr. Lovecraft, isn't it?"

"Call me H. W. Everyone does."

"Have I heard of you?"

"I doubt it."

She was close now. A tall girl, she could look me in the eye. I had
the feeling the eye-jewel in her turban was looking me in the brain.
She let her fingers fall on the tentacle picture for a moment, allowed
them to play around like a fun-loving spider, then removed them to
my upper arm, delicately tugging me away from the book. I wasn't

unhappy about that. Maybe I'm allergic to incunabula or perhaps an undiscovered prejudice against tentacled creatures, but I didn't like being near the *Necronomicon* one bit. Certainly the experience didn't compare with being near Janice Marsh.

"You're the Cap'n's Daughter?" I said.

"It's an honorific title. Obed Marsh was my ancestor. In the Esoteric Order, there is always a Cap'n's Daughter. Right now, I am she."

"What exactly is this Dagon business about?"

She smiled, showing a row of little pearls. "It's an alternative form of worship. It's not a racket, honestly."

"I never said it was."

She shrugged.

"Many people get the wrong idea."

Outside, the wind was rising, driving rain against the Temple. The sound effects were weird, like sickening whales calling out in the Bay.

"You were asking about Laird? Did Miss Wilde send you?"

It was my turn to shrug.

"Janey is what they call a sore loser, Mr. Lovecraft. It comes from taking all those bronze medals. Never the gold."

"I don't think she wants him back," I said, "just to know where he is. He seems to have disappeared."

"He's often out of town on business. He likes to be mysterious. I'm sure you understand."

My eyes kept going to the squid-face brooch. As Janice Marsh breathed, it rose and fell and rubies winked at me.

"It's Polynesian," she said, tapping the brooch. "The Cap'n brought it back with him to Innsmouth."

"Ah yes, your home town."

"It's just a place by the sea. Like Los Angeles."

I decided to go fishing, and hooked up some of the bait Winthrop had given me. "Were you there when J. Edgar Hoover staged his fireworks display in the twenties?"

"Yes, I was a child. Something to do with rum-runners, I think. That was during Prohibition."

"Good years for the Laird."

"I suppose so. He's legitimate these days."

"Yes. Although if he were as Scotch as he likes to pretend he is, you can be sure he'd have been deported by now."

Janice Marsh's eyes were sea-green. Round or not, they were fascinating. "Let me put your mind at rest, Mr. Lovecraft or whatever your name is," she said, "the Esoteric Order of Dagon was never a front for boot-legging. In fact it has never been a front for anything. It is not a racket for duping rich widows out of inheritances. It is not an excuse for motion picture executives to gain carnal knowledge of teenage drug addicts. It is exactly what it claims to be, a church."

"Father, Son and Holy Squid, eh?"

"I did not say we were a Christian church."

Janice Marsh had been creeping up on me and was close enough to bite. Her active hands went to the back of my neck and angled my head down like an adjustable lamp. She put her lips on mine and squashed her face into me. I tasted lipstick, salt and caviar. Her fingers writhed up into my hair and pushed my hat off. She shut her eyes. After an hour or two of suffering in the line of duty, I put my hands on her hips and detached her body from mine. I had a fish taste in my mouth.

"That was interesting," I said.

"An experiment," she replied. "Your name has such a ring to it. Love . . . craft. It suggests expertise in a certain direction."

"Disappointed?"

She smiled. I wondered if she had several rows of teeth, like a shark.

"Anything but."

"So do I get an invite to the back-row during your next Dagon hoedown?"

She was businesslike again. "I think you'd better report back to Janey. Tell her I'll have Laird call her when he's in town and put her mind at rest. She should pay you off. What with the War, it's a waste of manpower to have you spend your time looking for someone who isn't missing when you could be defending Lockheed from Fifth Columnists."

"What about Franklin?"

"Franklin the President?"

"Franklin the baby."

Her round eyes tried to widen. She was playing this scene inno-cent. The Panther Princess had been the same when telling the white hunter that Jungle Jillian had left the Tomb of the Jaguar hours ago.

"Miss Wilde seems to think Laird has borrowed a child of hers that she carelessly left in his care. She'd like Franklin back."

"Janey hasn't got a baby. She can't have babies. It's why she's such a psycho-neurotic case. Her analyst is getting rich on her bewildering fantasies. She can't tell reality from the movies. She once accused me of human sacrifice."

"Sounds like a square rap."

"That was in a film, Mr. Lovecraft. Cardboard knives and catsup blood."


Usually at this stage in an investigation, I call my friend Bernie at the District Attorney's office and put out a few fishing lines. This time, he phoned me. When I got into my office, I had the feeling my telephone had been ringing for a long time.

"Don't make waves," Bernie said.

"Pardon," I snapped back, with my usual lightning-fast wit.

"Just don't. It's too cold to go for a swim this time of year."

"Even in a bathtub."

"Especially in a bathtub."

"Does Mr. District Attorney send his regards?"

Bernie laughed. I had been an investigator with the DA's office a few years back, but we'd been forced to part company.

"Forget him. I have some more impressive names on my list."

"Let me guess. Howard Hughes?"

"Close."

"General Stillwell?"

"Getting warmer. Try Mayor Fletcher Bowron, Governor Culbert Olson, and State Attorney General Earl Warren. Oh, and Wax, of course."

I whistled. "All interested in little me. Who'd 'a thunk it?"

"Look, I don't know much about this myself. They just gave me a message to pass on. In the building, they apparently think of me as your keeper."

"Do a British gentleman, a French lady and a fed the size of Mount Rushmore have anything to do with this?"

"I'll take the money I've won so far and you can pass that question on to the next sucker."

"Fine, Bernie. Tell me, just how popular am I?"

"Tojo rates worse than you, and maybe Judas Iscariot."

"Feels comfy. Any idea where Laird Brunette is these days?"

I heard a pause and some rumbling. Bernie was making sure his office was empty of all ears. I imagined him bringing the receiver up close and dropping his voice to a whisper.

"No one's seen him in three months. Confidentially, I don't miss him at all. But there are others . . ." Bernie coughed, a door opened, and he started talking normally or louder. ". . . of course, honey, I'll be home in time for Jack Benny."

"See you later, sweetheart," I said, "your dinner is in the sink and I'm off to Tijuana with a professional pool player."

"Love you," he said, and hung up.

I'd picked up a coating of green slime on the soles of my shoes. I tried scraping them off on the edge of the desk and then used yesterday's *Times* to get the stuff off the desk. The gloop looked damned esoteric to me.

I poured myself a shot from the bottle I had picked up across the street and washed the taste of Janice Marsh off my teeth.

I thought of Polynesia in the early 19th century and of those fisheyed native girls clustering around Capt. Marsh. Somehow, tentacles kept getting in the way of my thoughts. In theory, the Capt. should have been an ideal subject for a Dorothy Lamour movie, perhaps with Janice Marsh in the role of her great-great-great and Jon Hall or Ray Milland as girl-chasing Obed. But I was picking up Bela Lugosi vibrations from the set-up. I couldn't help but think of bisected babies.

So far none of this running around had got me any closer to the Laird and his heir. In my mind, I drew up a list of Brunette's known associates. Then, I mentally crossed off all the ones who were dead. That brought me up short. When people in Brunette's business die, nobody really takes much notice except maybe to join in a few drunken choruses of "Ding-Dong, the Wicked Witch is Dead" before remembering there are plenty of other Wicked Witches in the sea. I'm just like everybody else: I don't keep a score of dead gambler-entrepreneurs. But, thinking of it, there'd been an awful lot recently, up to and including Gianni Pastore. Apart from Rothko and Isinglass, there'd been at least three other closed casket funerals in the profession. Obviously you couldn't blame that on the Japs. I wondered how many of the casualties had met their ends in bathtubs. The whole thing kept coming back to water. I decided I hated the stuff and swore not to let my bourbon get polluted with it.

Back out in the rain, I started hitting the bars. Brunette had a lot of friends. Maybe someone would know something.


By early evening, I'd propped up a succession of bars and leaned on a succession of losers. The only thing I'd come up with was the blatantly obvious information that everyone in town was scared. Most were wet, but all were scared.

Everyone was scared of two or three things at once. The Japs were high on everyone's list. You'd be surprised to discover the number of shaky citizens who'd turned overnight from chisellers who'd barely recognise the flag into true red, white and blue patriots prepared to shed their last drop of alcoholic blood for their country. Everywhere you went, someone sounded off against Hirohito, Tojo, the Mikado, kabuki and origami. The current rash of accidental deaths in the Pastore-Brunette circle were a much less popular subject for discussion and tended to turn loudmouths into closemouths at the drop of a question.

"Something fishy," everyone said, before changing the subject.

I was beginning to wonder whether Janey Wilde wouldn't have done better spending her money on a radio commercial asking the Laird to give her a call. Then I found Curtis the Croupier in Maxie's.

He usually wore the full soup and fish, as if borrowed from Astaire. Now he'd exchanged his carnation, starched shirtfront and pop-up top hat for an outfit in olive drab with bars on the shoulder and a cap under one epaulette.

"Heard the bugle call, Curtis?" I asked, pushing through a crowd of patriotic admirers who had been buying the soldier boy drinks.

Curtis grinned before he recognised me, then produced a supercilious sneer. We'd met before, on the *Montecito*. There was a rumour going around that during Prohibition he'd once got involved in an honest card game, but if pressed he'd energetically refute it.

"Hey cheapie," he said.

I bought myself a drink but didn't offer him one. He had three or four lined up.

"This racket must pay," I said. "How much did the uniform cost? You rent it from Paramount?"

The croupier was offended. "It's real," he said. "I've enlisted. I hope to be sent overseas."

"Yeah, we ought to parachute you into Tokyo to introduce loaded dice and rickety roulette wheels."

"You're cynical, cheapie." He tossed back a drink.

"No, just a realist. How come you quit the *Monty*?"

"Poking around in the Laird's business?"

I raised my shoulders and dropped them again.

"Gambling has fallen off recently, along with leading figures in the industry. The original owner of this place, for instance. I bet paying for wreaths has thinned your bankroll."

Curtis took two more drinks, quickly, and called for more. When I'd come in, there'd been a couple of chippies climbing into his hip pockets. Now he was on his own with me. He didn't appreciate the change of scenery and I can't say I blamed him.

"Look, cheapie," he said, his voice suddenly low, "for your own good, just drop it. There are more important things now."

"Like democracy?"

"You can call it that."

"How far overseas do you want to be sent, Curtis?"

He looked at the door as if expecting five guys with tommy guns to come out of the rain for him. Then he gripped the bar to stop his hands shaking.

"As far as I can get, cheapie. The Philippines, Europe, Australia. I don't care."

"Going to war is a hell of a way to escape."

"Isn't it just? But wouldn't Papa Gianni have been safer on Wake Island than in the tub?"

"You heard the bathtime story, then?"

Curtis nodded and took another gulp. The juke box played "Doodly-Acky-Sacky, Want Some Seafood, Mama" and it was scary. Nonsense, but scary.

"They all die in water. That's what I've heard. Sometimes, on the *Monty*, Laird would go up on deck and just look at the sea for hours. He was crazy, since he took up with that Marsh popsicle."

"The Panther Princess?"

"You saw that one? Yeah, Janice Marsh. Pretty girl if you like clams. Laird claimed there was a sunken town in the bay. He used a lot of weird words, darkie bop or something. Jitterbug stuff. Cthul-whatever, Yog-Gimme-a-Break. He said things were going to come out of the water and sweep over the land, and he didn't mean U-Boats."

Curtis was uncomfortable in his uniform. There were dark patches where the rain had soaked. He'd been drinking like W. C. Fields on a bender but he wasn't getting tight. Whatever was troubling him was too much even for Jack Daniel's.

I thought of the Laird of the *Monty*. And I thought of the painting of Capt. Marsh's clipper, with that out-of-proportion squid surfacing near it.

"He's on the boat, isn't he?"

Curtis didn't say anything.

"Alone," I thought aloud. "He's out there alone."

I pushed my hat to the back of my head and tried to shake booze out of my mind. It was crazy. Nobody bobs up and down in the water with a sign round their neck saying "Hey Tojo, Torpedo Me!" The *Monty* was a floating target.

"No," Curtis said, grabbing my arm, jarring drink out of my glass.

"He's not out there?"

He shook his head.

"No, cheapie. He's not out there *alone*."

All the water taxis were in dock, securely moored and covered until the storms settled. I'd never find a boatman to take me out to the *Montecito* tonight. Why, everyone knew the waters were infested with Japanese subs. But I knew someone who wouldn't care any more whether or not his boats were being treated properly. He was even past bothering if they were borrowed without his permission.

The Seaview Inn was still deserted, although there were police notices warning people away from the scene of the crime. It was dark, cold and wet, and nobody bothered me as I broke into the boathouse to find a ring of keys.

I took my pick of the taxis moored to the Seaview's jetty and gassed her up for a short voyage. I also got my .38 Colt Super Match out from the glove compartment of the Chrysler and slung it under my armpit. During all this, I got a thorough soaking and picked up the beginnings of influenza. I hoped Jungle Jillian would appreciate the effort.

The sea was swelling under the launch and making a lot of noise. I was grateful for the noise when it came to shooting the padlock off the mooring chain but the swell soon had my stomach sloshing about in my lower abdomen. I am not an especially competent seaman.

The *Monty* was out there on the horizon, still visible whenever the lightning lanced. It was hardly difficult to keep the small boat aimed at the bigger one.

Getting out on the water makes you feel small. Especially when the lights of Bay City are just a scatter in the dark behind you. I got the impression of large things moving just beyond my field of perception. The chill soaked through my clothes. My hat was a felt sponge, dripping down my neck. As the launch cut towards the *Monty,* rain and spray needled my face. I saw my hands white and bath-wrinkled on the wheel and wished I'd brought a bottle. Come to that, I wished I was at home in bed with a mug of cocoa and Claudette Colbert. Some things in life don't turn out the way you plan.

Three miles out, I felt the law change in my stomach. Gambling was legal and I emptied my belly over the side into the water. I stared at the remains of my toasted cheese sandwich as they floated off. I thought I saw the moon reflected greenly in the depths, but there was no moon that night.

I killed the engine and let waves wash the taxi against the side of the *Monty*. The small boat scraped along the hull of the gambling ship and I caught hold of a weed-furred rope ladder as it passed. I tethered the taxi and took a deep breath.

The ship sat low in the water, as if its lower cabins were flooded. Too much seaweed climbed up towards the decks. It'd never re-open for business, even if the War were over tomorrow.

I climbed the ladder, fighting the water-weight in my clothes, and heaved myself up on deck. It was good to have something more solid than a tiny boat under me but the deck pitched like an airplane wing. I grabbed a rail and hoped my internal organs would arrange themselves back into their familiar grouping.

"Brunette," I shouted, my voice lost in the wind.

There was nothing. I'd have to go belowdecks.

A sheet flying flags of all nations had come loose, and was whipped around with the storm. Japan, Italy and Germany were still tactlessly represented, along with several European states that weren't really nations any more. The deck was covered in familiar slime.

I made my way around towards the ballroom doors. They'd blown in and rain splattered against the polished wood floors. I got inside and pulled the .38. It felt better in my hand than digging into my ribs.

Lightning struck nearby and I got a flash image of the abandoned ballroom, orchestra stands at one end painted with the name of a disbanded combo.

The casino was one deck down. It should have been dark but I saw a glow under a walkway door. I pushed through and cautiously descended. It wasn't wet here but it was cold. The fish smell was strong.

"Brunette," I shouted again.

I imagined something heavy shuffling nearby and slipped a few steps, banging my hip and arm against a bolted-down table. I kept hold of my gun, but only through superhuman strength.

The ship wasn't deserted. That much was obvious.

I could hear music. It wasn't Cab Calloway or Benny Goodman. There was a Hawaiian guitar in there but mainly it was a crazy choir of keening voices. I wasn't convinced the performers were human and wondered whether Brunette was working up some kind of act with singing seals. I couldn't make out the words but the familiar hawk-and-spit syllables of "Cthulhu" cropped up a couple of times.

I wanted to get out and go back to nasty Bay City and forget all about this. But Jungle Jillian was counting on me.

I made my way along the passage, working towards the music. A hand fell on my shoulder and my heart banged against the backsides of my eyeballs.

A twisted face stared at me out of the gloom, thickly-bearded, crater-cheeked. Laird Brunette was made up as Ben Gunn, skin shrunk onto his skull, eyes large as hen's eggs.

His hand went over my mouth.

"Do Not Disturb," he said, voice high and cracked.

This wasn't the suave criminal I knew, the man with tartan cummerbunds and patent leather hair. This was some other Brunette, in the grips of a tough bout with dope or madness.

"The Deep Ones," he said.

He let me go and I backed away.

"It is the time of the Surfacing."

My case was over. I knew where the Laird was. All I had to do was tell Janey Wilde and give her her refund.

"There's very little time."

The music was louder. I heard a great number of bodies shuffling around in the casino. They couldn't have been very agile, because they kept clumping into things and each other.

"They must be stopped. Dynamite, depth charges, torpedoes . . ."

"Who?" I asked. "The Japs?"

"The Deep Ones. The Dwellers in the Sister City."

He had lost me.

A nasty thought occurred to me. As a detective, I can't avoid making deductions. There were obviously a lot of people aboard the *Monty*, but mine was the only small boat in evidence. How had everyone else got out here? Surely they couldn't have swum?

"It's a war," Brunette ranted, "us and them. It's always been a war."

I made a decision. I'd get the Laird off his boat and turn him over to Jungle Jillian. She could sort things out with the Panther Princess and her Esoteric Order. In his current state, Brunette would hand over any baby if you gave him a blanket.

I took Brunette's thin wrist and tugged him towards the staircase. But a hatch clanged down, and I knew we were stuck.

A door opened and perfume drifted through the fish stink.

"Mr. Lovecraft, wasn't it?" a silk-scaled voice said.


Janice Marsh was wearing pendant squid earrings and a lady-sized gun. And nothing else.

That wasn't quite as nice as it sounds. The Panther Princess had no nipples, no navel and no pubic hair. She was lightly scaled between the legs and her wet skin shone like a shark's. I imagined that if you stroked her, your palm would come away bloody. She was wearing neither the turban she'd affected earlier nor the dark wig of her pictures. Her head was completely bald, skull swelling unnaturally. She didn't even have her eyebrows pencilled in.

"You evidently can't take good advice."

As mermaids go, she was scarier than cute. In the crook of her left arm, she held a bundle from which a white baby face peered with unblinking eyes. Franklin looked more like Janice Marsh than his parents.

"A pity, really," said a tiny ventriloquist voice through Franklin's mouth, "but there are always complications."

Brunette gibbered with fear, chewing his beard and huddling against me.

Janice Marsh set Franklin down and he sat up, an adult struggling with a baby's body.

"The Cap'n has come back," she explained.

"Every generation must have a Cap'n," said the thing in Franklin's mind. Dribble got in the way and he wiped his angel-mouth with a fold of swaddle.

Janice Marsh clucked and pulled Laird away from me, stroking his face.

"Poor dear," she said, flicking his chin with a long tongue. "He got out of his depth."

She put her hands either side of Brunette's head, pressing the butt of her gun into his cheek.

"He was talking about a Sister City," I prompted.

She twisted the gambler's head around and dropped him on the floor. His tongue poked out and his eyes showed only white.

"Of course," the baby said. "The Cap'n founded two settlements. One beyond Devil Reef, off Massachusetts. And one here, under the sands of the Bay."

We both had guns. I'd let her kill Brunette without trying to shoot her. It was the detective's fatal flaw, curiosity. Besides, the Laird was dead inside his head long before Janice snapped his neck.

"You can still join us," she said, hips working like a snake in time to the chanting. "There are raptures in the deeps."

"Sister," I said, "you're not my type."

Her nostrils flared in anger and slits opened in her neck, flashing liverish red lines in her white skin.

Her gun was pointed at me, safety off. Her long nails were lacquered green.

I thought I could shoot her before she shot me. But I didn't. Something about a naked woman, no matter how strange, prevents you from killing them. Her whole body was moving with the music. I'd been wrong. Despite everything, she was beautiful.

I put my gun down and waited for her to murder me. It never happened.

I don't really know the order things worked out. But first there was lightning, then, an instant later, thunder.

Light filled the passageway, hurting my eyes. Then, a rumble of noise which grew in a crescendo. The chanting was drowned.

Through the thunder cut a screech. It was a baby's cry. Franklin's eyes were screwed up, and he was shrieking. I had a sense of the Cap'n drowning in the baby's mind, his purchase on the purloined body relaxing as the child cried out.

The floor beneath me shook and buckled and I heard a great straining of abused metal. A belch of hot wind surrounded me. A hole appeared. Janice Marsh moved fast, and I think she fired her gun, but whether at me on purpose or at random in reflex I couldn't say. Her body sliced towards me and I ducked.

There was another explosion, not of thunder, and thick smoke billowed through a rupture in the floor. I was on the floor, hugging the tilting deck. Franklin slid towards me and bumped, screaming, into my head. A half-ton of water fell on us and I knew the ship was breached. My guess was that the Japs had just saved my life with a torpedo. I was waist deep in saltwater. Janice Marsh darted away in a sinuous fish motion.

Then there were heavy bodies around me, pushing me against a bulkhead. In the darkness, I was scraped by something heavy, cold-skinned and foul-smelling. There were barks and cries, some of which might have come from human throats.

Fires went out and hissed as the water rose. I had Franklin in my hands and tried to hold him above water. I remembered the peril of Jungle Jillian again and found my head floating against the hard ceiling.

The Cap'n cursed in vivid 18th century language, Franklin's little body squirming in my grasp. A toothless mouth tried to get a biter's grip on my chin but slipped off. My feet slid and I was off-balance, pulling the baby briefly underwater. I saw his startled eyes through a wobbling film. When I pulled him out again, the Cap'n was gone and Franklin was screaming on his own. Taking a double gulp of air, I plunged under the water and struggled towards the nearest door, a hand closed over the baby's face to keep water out of his mouth and nose.

The *Montecito* was going down fast enough to suggest there were plenty of holes in it. I had to make it a priority to find one. I jammed my knee at a door and it flew open. I was poured, along with several hundred gallons of water, into a large room full of stored gambling equipment. Red and white chips floated like confetti.

I got my footing and waded towards a ladder. Something large reared out of the water and shambled at me, screeching like a seabird. I didn't get a good look at it. Which was a mercy. Heavy arms lashed me, flopping boneless against my face. With my free hand, I pushed back at the thing, fingers slipping against cold slime. Whatever it was was in a panic and squashed through the door.

There was another explosion and everything shook. Water splashed upwards and I fell over. I got upright and managed to get a one-handed grip on the ladder. Franklin was still struggling and bawling, which I took to be a good sign. Somewhere near, there was a lot of shouting.

I dragged us up rung by rung and slammed my head against a hatch. If it had been battened, I'd have smashed my skull and spilled my brains. It flipped upwards and a push of water from below shoved us through the hole like a ping-pong ball in a fountain.

The *Monty* was on fire and there were things in the water around it. I heard the drone of airplane engines and glimpsed nearby launches. Gunfire fought with the wind. It was a full-scale attack. I made it to the deckrail and saw a boat fifty feet away. Men in yellow slickers angled tommy guns down and sprayed the water with bullets.

The gunfire whipped up the sea into a foam. Kicking things died in the water. Someone brought up his gun and fired at me. I pushed myself aside, arching my body over Franklin as bullets spanged against the deck.

My borrowed taxi must have been dragged under by the bulk of the ship.

There were definitely lights in the sea. And the sky. Over the city, in the distance, I saw firecracker bursts. Something exploded a hundred yards away and a tower of water rose, bursting like a puffball. A depth charge.

The deck was angled down and water was creeping up at us. I held on to a rope webbing, wondering whether the gambling ship still had any lifeboats. Franklin spluttered and bawled.

A white body slid by, heading for the water. I instinctively grabbed at it. Hands took hold of me and I was looking into Janice Marsh's face. Her eyes blinked, membranes coming round from the sides, and she kissed me again. Her long tongue probed my mouth like an eel, then withdrew. She stood up, one leg bent so she was still vertical on the sloping deck. She drew air into her lungs—if she had lungs—and expelled it through her gills with a musical cry. She was slim and white in the darkness, water running off her body. Someone fired in her direction and she dived into the waves, knifing through the surface and disappearing towards the submarine lights. Bullets rippled the spot where she'd gone under.

I let go of the ropes and kicked at the deck, pushing myself away from the sinking ship. I held Franklin above the water and splashed with my legs and elbows. The *Monty* was dragging a lot of things under with it, and I fought against the pull so I wouldn't be one of them. My shoulders ached and my clothes got in the way, but I kicked against the current.

The ship went down screaming, a chorus of bending steel and dying creatures. I had to make for a launch and hope not to be shot. I was lucky. Someone got a polehook into my jacket and landed us like fish. I lay on the deck, water running out of my clothes, swallowing as much air as I could breathe.

I heard Franklin yelling. His lungs were still in working order.

Someone big in a voluminous slicker, a sou'wester tied to his head, knelt by me, and slapped me in the face.

"Peeper," he said.

"They're calling it the Great Los Angeles Air Raid," Winthrop told me as he poured a mug of British tea. "Some time last night a panic started, and everyone in Bay City shot at the sky for hours."

"The Japs?" I said, taking a mouthful of welcome hot liquid.

"In theory. Actually, I doubt it. It'll be recorded as a fiasco, a lot of jumpy characters with guns. While it was all going on, we engaged the enemy and emerged victorious."

He was still dressed up for an embassy ball and didn't look as if he'd been on deck all evening. Geneviève Dieudonne wore a fisherman's sweater and fatigue pants, her hair up in a scarf. She was looking at a lot of sounding equipment and noting down readings.

"You're not fighting the Japs, are you?"

Winthrop pursed his lips. "An older war, my friend. We can't be distracted. After last night's action, our Deep Ones won't poke their scaly noses out for a while. Now I can do something to lick Hitler."

"What really happened?"

"There was something dangerous in the sea, under Mr. Brunette's boat. We have destroyed it and routed the . . . uh, the hostile forces. They wanted the boat as a surface station. That's why Mr. Brunette's associates were eliminated."

Geneviève gave a report in French, so fast that I couldn't follow.

"Total destruction," Winthrop explained, "a dreadful set-back for them. It'll put them in their place for years. Forever would be too much to hope for, but a few years will help."

I lay back on the bunk, feeling my wounds. Already choking on phlegm, I would be lucky to escape pneumonia.

"And the little fellow is a decided dividend."

Finlay glumly poked around, suggesting another dose of depth charges. He was cradling a mercifully sleep-struck Franklin, but didn't look terribly maternal.

"He seems quite unaffected by it all."

"His name is Franklin," I told Winthrop. "On the boat, he was . . ."

"Not himself? I'm familiar with the condition. It's a filthy business, you understand."

"He'll be all right," Geneviève put in.

I wasn't sure whether the rest of the slicker crew were feds or servicemen and I wasn't sure whether I wanted to know. I could tell a Clandestine Operation when I landed in the middle of one.

"Who knows about this?" I asked. "Hoover? Roosevelt?"

Winthrop didn't answer.

"Someone must know," I said.

"Yes," the Englishman said, "someone must. But this is a war the public would never believe exists. In the Bureau, Finlay's outfit are known as 'the Unnameables,' never mentioned by the press, never honoured or censured by the government, victories and defeats never recorded in the official history."

The launch shifted with the waves, and I hugged myself, hoping for some warmth to creep over me. Finlay had promised to break out a bottle later but that made me resolve to stick to tea as a point of honour. I hated to fulfil his expectations.

"And America is a young country," Winthrop explained. "In Europe, we've known things a lot longer."

On shore, I'd have to tell Janey Wilde about Brunette and hand over Franklin. Some flack at Metro would be thinking of an excuse for the Panther Princess's disappearance. Everything else—the depth charges, the sea battle, the sinking ship—would be swallowed up by the War.

All that would be left would be tales. Weird tales.

# Return to Innsmouth

## Guy N. Smith

For two decades I have fought against the urge to return to Innsmouth. I say "return," for although I have never been there I know that diabolical place as well as if I had been born there and lived with its horrors. In my frequent nightmares I have walked its deserted streets, hastened past the former Masonic Hall that is now the Esoteric Order of Dagon, smelled the nauseating fish odours that permeate the early nineteenth century buildings as a reminder that nothing has changed nor ever will.

My great-aunt, Miss Anna Tilton, who dedicated her life to the service of the Newburyport Public Library, wrote her own account of the happenings at Innsmouth, a hundred pages of handscript that came to me via the will of my uncle upon his death. Enclosed with the manuscript was the published account of one Williamson, together with newspaper clippings, dated 1927–28, of the Federal government's attack on that seaport and the subsequent torpedoing of the Devil Reef just off the coastline. Crumbling, supposedly empty, houses were dynamited and many arrests were made although there were no public trials.

I tried to convince myself that those fishlike creatures that had spawned in the sea and inter-bred with the inhabitants of Innsmouth had been annihilated, that Dagon Hall had been blasted off the face of the earth, that the evil had been destroyed forever. My research revealed nothing which would either deny or confirm my worst fears. Innsmouth was just another seaport at the mouth of the Manuxet, cut off from civilization by its salt marshes with their maze of creeks; Arkham, Ipswich and Newburyport might as well have been a thousand miles away.

Truly, the matter should have been no business of mine. I had been born in New York and moved to New Jersey to take up a post in insurance. My life was routine, boring but safe. I had no cause to concern myself with the evil legends of Innsmouth. Far rather that my uncle had forgotten my existence than inflicted upon me those accursed documents which plagued me day and night with their accounts of unspeakable happenings, which most sane people would have dismissed as the ramblings of some amateur writer of weird fiction whose attempts to have her works published had resulted in failure. Such was her bitterness that in her dying hour her demented and senile brain had hit upon the idea of cursing her bloodline, afflicting them with her ramblings so that they would know no peace. It was her twisted way of ensuring that her pathetic attempts at literature would survive after her death.

Only I knew that Anna Tilton was no embittered failure, for Williamson had written commendably of her attempts to help him in his own ill-fated investigation of those awful events. I began wondering how much of Innsmouth still stood, if anybody still lived and fished there now; and if so, were their bodies misshapen, their skins scaly and their eyes unblinking?

The dreams increased with frightening regularity, escalated to terrifying proportions; I was trapped in Innsmouth, a human beast of the chase hounded through those dilapidated streets by hunting packs of amphibious creatures, grunting their lust for me so that they might sacrifice me to some vile deity deep in the watery hell of that abyss off Devil Reef.

It was in the Spring that I finally conceded that I must return to Innsmouth. Unless I pandered to my fears, I would surely end my days in some asylum, screaming my terror aloud during the nocturnal hours when my cell became a room in the dreaded Gilman House, the shouts of my warders becoming the inarticulate cries of my subterranean pursuers as they sought to break through to me.

My long journey took me to Newburyport where I called at the public library and saw with my own eyes that tiara, where the beginning of my worst fears were confirmed. *It existed.* Behind the glass of its case, resting on purple velvet, it was identical in every detail to Miss Tilton's, and Williamson's, description. If only, on leaving that austere building, I had boarded the next train back to New Jersey, then at least I would have spent my declining years in the comparative safety of a mental hospital. Far rather insanity and nightmares than that which befell me as a result of my decision to carry on to Innsmouth.

It was whilst I stood in the sunlit street outside the library, awaiting the arrival of the bus that would take me on the last stage of my journey, that I chanced to glimpse my shadow on the sidewalk. At first I thought that possibly the distortion was caused by some overhead obstruction of the sun's rays, the branches of a tree or the overhang of a building. But there was nothing that could in any way have impinged upon my own shadow, cause that elongation of the skull, the squatness of the figure and the stooping of the shoulders. In panic I crossed the road and consulted my reflection in the window of a shop; I was as I had always been, *yet on glancing again at my shadow I perceived that it was still grotesque.*

Suffice that I arrived in Innsmouth towards evening, my delay caused by the lateness of the bus and the seeming reluctance of its sullen driver to reach our destination. I was the only passenger, another fact that served to disconcert me. Was it still that nobody went to Innsmouth, that the town was shunned because of its history? Or because of its present?

Innsmouth was exactly as I knew it would be. Perhaps the dereliction had been increased by the dynamiting and the passing years since Anna Tilton described it. But, essentially, it was the same place.

Those nineteenth century brick and wooden edifices, crumbling, windows boarded up, deserted streets, not so much as a scavenging dog or cat in sight. With an hour or so of daylight remaining, I wandered down Lafayette Street, crossed over to Adams Street and stood there surveying the shoreward slums that lay to the east. I knew they were inhabited, even though I saw nobody, sensed that *something* lived amidst the sprawling degradation. Yet again I looked for my shadow but the sun had slipped below the western horizon.

I almost expected to encounter old Zadok Allen sitting by the fire station but most certainly he would be dead and gone, years ago. I glimpsed some figures in the distance, staring in my direction, but they hurried away at my approach. Before me lay the circular green, beyond it that pillared building on the junction which had been the Order of Dagon Hall. I found myself shying from it, fearful lest one of its doors might be open and I should be afforded a glimpse of a priestly figure inside, wearing a tiara identical to that which rested in the glass showcase of the Newburyport Public Library. But its portals remained closed, for which I was greatly relieved.

The Gilman House was still standing, its lower windows lighted, the mullioned panes glinting evilly across the street. I hesitated. Would that there had been a means of transportation away from here before nightfall, but the bus had already departed for Arkham and the railway was disused. *I accepted with a sense of trepidation that I was condemned to passing the night hours in Innsmouth.*

The hotel clerk was how I expected to find him, a tall head on a short neck, his skin rough as though he suffered from eczema, his eyes staring unblinkingly at me. There was just one room vacant, he muttered as he consulted a register. I nodded and handed over three dollars.

The room itself had a familiarity about it as though I had stayed there before, the claustrophobic prison of my nightmares, and so aptly described by Williamson in his writings that it may well have been the very same one from which he had fled on that terrible night. I knew that there would be no bolt on the door and that I would find one on the clothespress. It took me several minutes to transfer it to the door.

The north and south intersecting doors had bolts; I shot them firmly. I had not eaten but I preferred to endure the pangs of hunger rather than risk going outside in search of food. Fate had decreed that I come here; whatever the nocturnal hours had in store for me I must accept, for there was nothing that I could do to change the course of events. If I survived, and walked unscathed from here in the morning light, then I knew that I should have peace of mind for the rest of my life.

As an added precaution I pushed the heavy dresser up against the door. I could do no more in the way of self-preservation, so I lay on the bed fully clothed and tried to read by the dim light of the single bulb suspended over me. My concentration lapsed, the printed words became meaningless, and I found myself listening to the noises which came from down below.

Some time later the bulb extinguished as I had half-expected it to and plunged me into Stygian blackness. The darkness increased my sense of smell, it seemed, and I became aware of that strong fishy odour as though the fishermen of Innsmouth had piled their catch up in the street below and left it to decompose.

There were movements outside my door, stealthy steps that made a flopping sound. I tensed when I heard a key inserted in the lock; it rattled but the bolt held, and after a time the key was withdrawn. Now they were trying the other doors, giving up when they found the strong bolts obstructed their entry.

Voices uttered sounds that were neither words nor from human vocal chords, a whispered grunting that embodied their anger and frustration because I had denied them their prey. But surely wooden doors would not withstand a combined assault, sheer strength of numbers would overcome such paltry obstacles.

The stench was overpowering almost to the point of suffocation and I struggled to breathe. I recalled how Williamson had fled that night, run the gauntlet of these creatures of Dagon, but even at the height of my terror I dismissed the idea of bursting through one of the intersecting doors and leaping from a window on to the roof of an adjoining building. I pinned my hopes on my improvised fortifications, and if they succumbed to my enemy, then I accepted that I would face sacrifice in the black depths of that unfathomable abyss off Devil Reef.

I lay there rigid with fright, my fingernails gouging my palms until they bled, hearing the door weakening as those outside brought some kind of battering ram with which to split the stout woodwork. My senses swam. I attempted to scream but no sound came from my trembling lips. The darkness was becoming blacker by the second, now tinged with scarlet, as I hovered on the brink of merciful unconsciousness that would at least spare me the climax of this hideous trauma.

It was as I felt myself slipping gently into a state of blissful unawareness that I heard the door finally begin to yield.


The morning dawned with a dismal greyness, the fingers of daylight creeping in through the single window to stroke me into wakefulness. I sat up with a sense of disbelief, stared uncomprehendingly around me. The door was still bolted, the cumbersome dresser wedged firmly up against it. There was no sign of damage to the oaken panels.

I leaped from the bed, rushed to inspect the other two doors and discovered that neither bore any signs of damage. I was trembling violently. It appeared then that those nocturnal fiends had failed in their attempts to reach me just when it seemed that they had breached my crude defences.

Miraculously, I had survived the night hours unscathed and now, with luck, I might escape from Innsmouth and leave behind all the horrors which even the might of the armed forces had failed to destroy so many years ago.

With no small amount of trepidation I descended the stairs. There was no sign of the staring, sullen clerk, for which I was grateful. I walked out into the street and looked about me. There was not a soul in sight, just that faint marine odour which the morning breeze was beginning to dissipate.

I had no idea what time the bus departed for Arkham, but it would doubtless be hours before it arrived. Perhaps then, my best course was to begin walking along the road that led away from Innsmouth and when that battered conveyance eventually caught me up, I would board it.

I cared not for my dishevelled appearance, nor the fact that I was unwashed, my only desire to be away from here. I had purged myself of the curse handed down to me from Anna Tilton and my uncle. I had seen Innsmouth and survived the attempts of those who sought to drag me down into their hell of everlasting degradation. I would never be able to forget it but at least I was spared.

It was some time before I became aware that I had lost my way, possibly taken the wrong junction at the Green. For I seemed to be heading seawards, before me lay those flat salt marshes, intersected with wide and deep creeks, and that building at the mouth of the Manuxet was undoubtedly the infamous Marsh refinery.

I had to exert a conscious effort to turn around, almost as though the coast held me in a hypnotic grip, dragging my feet as though I had blundered into a sucking mire that was determined to hold me. Eventually, I managed it, forced myself to walk back the way I had come.

I tried to hurry but my efforts were slow, doubtless due to exhaustion after the terror of the past hours. But as I neared Innsmouth I found myself moving more easily. Whatever the effects of my proximity to the coast, I had shaken them off. Ahead of me was the road to Arkham and my step was quicker. I had made an error in my directions but, thankfully, I had rectified it.

By now the sun was up, its rays beginning to warm my chilled body and raise my spirits. It was only then that I recalled the disfiguration of my shadow on the previous day and instinctively I turned to check on it.

In that awful moment cold terror gripped me again and the

faintness that had assailed me during the night returned. I stood aghast, searched the rough surface of the road around me, stared in rising panic, unable to understand.

For where previously the sun had cast a misshapen form on the ground, now there was nothing. *I had no shadow.*

# The Crossing

## Adrian Cole

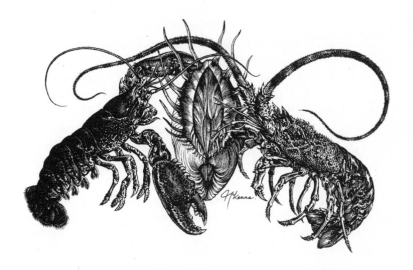

*It is a common belief, particularly among Christians, that it is the Devil, and he alone, who preys on human souls, seeking to suborn or otherwise pervert them away from the light. A common belief, and a fallacy that makes the human soul so vulnerable to other forces that exist. Forces which trawl no less hungrily than Satan and his various minions and whose methods are no less insidious.*

—Ludwig Kreigmann, "The Hungry Stars"

Among my mail was an unexpected postcard. The lurid blue sky, unique only to such postcards, drew my eye. Beneath it clustered the houses of a fishing village that could have been one of dozens in the Southwest of England, probably Cornwall. It was an area I had always meant to visit, but never had.

I flipped the card over, frowning. The writing was so badly penned that I couldn't read a word of it. Yet it had been addressed clearly enough, in archaic, printed letters. I sat at the kitchen table, glancing at the other bills and circulars before returning to the postcard. Again I tried to read the writing, but it continued to defy me.

Later, as I was rinsing the breakfast dishes, the village on the card suddenly brought to mind my odd awakening that morning.

I could smell the sea. Probably that was putting it too simply, but my mind had made the jump as I came out of sleep. If I had tried to analyse it more fully, I would have said it was a mixture of seaweed, fish and salt. But it had been very strong, as strong as it had been brief. Clearly an illusion. After all, I lived almost two hundred miles from the sea and couldn't remember the last time I'd been anywhere near it. As a child, perhaps.

My mother used to take me to the seaside, though it had been more from a sense of duty than from sharing my enthusiasm. Like all boys, I had imagined a trip to the sea as a promise of great adventure, crammed with every conceivable pleasure. It should have been a family event, but for me it had never been that.

I had never known my father. The man, a shadow never clearly focused for me by my mother, had left her when I was no more than a few months old. Ironically he had gone to sea, a wanderer by nature.

My mother had tried to hide her bitterness, but as I grew older, I understood that particular darkness better. She lived with another man, Bob, who had become my surrogate father, and whom she loved possessively. That hadn't made it easy for me to show my own genuine affection for Bob, but it was a better life; some of the gaps were filled, others were lost in the occasional silences of my mother, silences that Bob never sought to disturb.

I left the kitchen. In the living room I looked at the framed photograph of my son, David. The boy was nearly twenty now. He beamed from the picture, his arm around the shoulders of a blonde girl who was so obviously as happy as he was. They'd marry soon. There was no point in my telling them they were too young. What did

I know about it? I grinned to myself. Like father, like son? There was an irony in that. My own marriage had not been a success. David's mother was remarried now.

The split had been mercifully painless, not at all like I had heard divorces were supposed to be. Irene and I had remained friends, and I actually liked Tony, the man she had since married. I had always been thankful that Tony had never made it hard for me where David was concerned. Tony was sensible enough never to try to come between David and his father, and as a result he had won David over very quickly.

It should have made it all so simple, everyone being so considerate and understanding. But it had never been enough for me to see David at weekends, to go away with him for a week's holiday, or to speak to him on the phone whenever I wanted to. I could not help feeling inadequate, cheated, though I never let them see it. Tony was no doubt astute enough to know it.

And now? David would be even less accessible soon. This would be the first year we had not gone away for a week together somewhere. But all kids outgrew holidays with their parents. I suppose I had been damn lucky that David had been amenable to it for so long. But he had his girl now, and skiing in the Alps. The boy had a bright future, undoubtedly a good degree, and a potentially lucrative job in the city.

The prospect of a holiday without David was a grim one. And to spend it here, redecorating possibly, or building the porch I had been promising myself, held little appeal.

I realised I had brought the postcard with me into the room. Again I looked at it. The name of the little port was printed clearly. Appledore. North Devon. I grunted with abrupt realisation. It was somewhere in that part of England where my father was believed to live, when he wasn't at sea, although he would have retired long ago.

Again I tried to read the awful scrawl. The signature was tiny, crabbed. It was hopeless, but within the message I was sure I could make out the word "father." I shook my head. My mind had made the connection, fooling me.

I studied the picture of the village, its rows of fishing boats. Another world. Could my father really be hiding somewhere along that tiny quayside? How old would he be now? Seventy? More? Was the card perhaps the last effort of an old man to ask to be forgiven? I discarded the postcard, but even then I think I must have made the decision to follow it up.

As the coach wound through the low dunes and beyond to the small sea front, I had my first sight of Appledore. On the far side of the wide estuary, tucked under the hills that came down to the water beyond, the fishing village looked as if it had been set on its very shore, more a part of the sea than the land. There were more dunes somewhere beyond the hills, the open sea beyond them, but it was the houses that caught the eye: I could have been gazing back a hundred years or more. They had a changeless look to them, quaint and crowded, perched on the estuary's edge. They must have been about a mile away across the broad river; and the coach would have to travel upriver for another three miles before there was a bridge and a journey back downriver to the village.

Behind the hills, the sun had already started to drop; there was a hint of gold in the sky.

I'd booked a week here by the sea. Already I felt lonely without David. And this place, beautiful though it was, seemed so remote. I'd begun to wonder if the coach would ever get there.

There was a bridge at Bideford. Here I had to disembark and catch another, smaller bus to get to Appledore, but as it threaded the country roads, emerging at last on the quayside, I determined to enjoy my stay. The ghost of my errant father may or may not be here, but I told myself it didn't really matter.

As I found the guest house, I was aware of the village's postcard tranquillity, the stark contrast with the environment I had left. For a moment it was an oddly disjointing calm.

In the distance, far across the ebbing grey tide of the estuary, I saw sunlight flash on a vehicle, my coach perhaps, retreating to a more familiar world.

As I had suspected, the boarding house turned out to be a pub, and after I had eaten my tea in a back room with a handful of other guests (two families on sight-seeing holidays, bound for the north Cornwall coast) I went in to the public bar. I am not a tall man, but I had to duck down to avoid the low beams: I might have been in an old sailing galleon. The impression of looking into the past, even stepping into it, persisted. But it had become somehow reassuring.

There were a few men in the bar; I felt sure they were locals. They had the look of the sea about them, as if their faces belonged on sailing ships, shaped by salt and spray. I'd made a point of reading something about the North Devon coast and its shipping history. There'd been a good few sailing ships built here, and Appledore itself had a real reputation for producing rugged men, Barmen they had been called, after the dangerous sand bars out in the estuary and wide bay beyond it. A hundred years ago and more, they'd voyaged over to the New World, searching out the shoals of cod off New England, or fetching home cargoes of tobacco, their sailing vessels as seaworthy as any others. I'd seen old photographs in the books, children sculling small rowing boats almost as soon as they could walk. If my father had been a seaman, I could understand why this place had been so magnetic.

I watched the men at the bar discreetly. They were enjoying a private joke, not ignoring me, but their manner suggested they would not be as approachable as the people I was used to. But I had already made up my mind to ask a few questions about my father.

"Excuse me?"

One of the men, a thick-set fellow with a tangled beard and eyes that sparkled, as if he found me mildly amusing, nodded affably.

"I don't suppose you'd know where I could find a man called Silas Waite? He lived in Appledore at one time."

The bearded man continued to nod, turning to his companions. "Silas Waite," he repeated in a rich burr. "Your father knew him, didn't he, Dennis?"

The man he addressed put down his empty glass. His hands were huge and callused; I imagined them hauling deep sea nets. "I met 'un when I was a boy. Years ago."

"Has he left?"

The man, Dennis, nodded. "He never settled here. Used to stop off, but never for more'n a few months. Father sailed with 'un. Good trawlerman, Silas Waite. Likely ended up in New England. More'n a few did."

"When was the last time he was here? I'm sorry, I should have said, he was my father. I've been trying to trace him."

The three men eyed me as if judging it strange that I should not know the whereabouts of my own father. None of them seemed to be able to answer my question.

"Did he have any other relations here, or close friends?"

But again they could offer little help. I was tempted to show them the postcard: it was tucked inside my jacket, but I felt no real encouragement to do so. Instead I thanked them, moving away to a table.

Others entered the pub throughout the evening, and although a few nodded to me, none of them seemed ready to begin a casual conversation without being approached. I sipped my beer, thinking that tomorrow I would look into any local libraries I could find and see if I could trace an address. It was beginning to seem like a long shot and I started to feel foolish. I put it down to the long coach journey, and decided on an early night.

Outside, the air was extremely still, and the moonlight washed the narrow streets vividly. The tiny houses crowded me, many of them unlit, though they were not shops but mostly cottages. I could hear the sea, in the middle distance, and as I passed the mouth of a slipway, I caught a strong smell of weed and salt, the precise smell I had thought I detected a few mornings ago when I'd woken up at home. A premonition, I grinned to myself.

The beer and my tiredness had combined with the strong sea air to make me light-headed, and the gloom that had threatened me in the pub dissipated. There was no one about: I might have been the only person alive in the entire village. I walked down the ramp of the slipway, curious to see the sand and its landscape by night.

It was treacherous underfoot: at high tide the sea slopped well up the stone ramp. But I was careful not to fall. At the bottom there was a glistening expanse of muddy sand and rock, black in the moonlight. It humped up across the estuary, pools of trapped water gleaming between its mud banks. The tide had retreated a long way out, leaving the quay and walls of the village exposed, clumps of weed hanging from the stones below the high water mark. Small boats were scattered here and there on the mud, their buoys half submerged.

I walked out on to the sand, testing it, relieved that it was not eager to suck me under; instead it was unexpectedly firm. The tide was so low that it looked almost possible to walk across the estuary to the village on its far shore, but I had no intention of being so foolhardy. Even so, I made my way carefully out on to the sands, aware that I had only the silent boats for company. I had never been in such an open space before, not even in a park. The moonlight was surprisingly brilliant, and north of where I stood, on the far shore where the tidal river turned for the open sea, huge banks of dunes rose up, amassed over the centuries by the Atlantic tide. They formed a bizarre terrain, a desolate, microcosmic world.

My isolation began to make me uneasy. I imagined the tide racing in, trapping me. Turning, I looked back at the village, surprised that I had wandered quite so far across the mud flats. To my right, I heard an odd sound: gurgling, as if water swirled down into the sand. Listening, I was aware of other faint sounds beneath my feet, though I took them to be natural to this place.

As I began to retrace my steps, I felt sure something had shifted. I began to think this whole venture was foolish. Panic breathed close by me. My toe caught on an object under the sand and sent me sprawling. The mud stank of rotting fish; I rolled over to get my face away from its evil exhalations. As I lurched up, I saw something poking out of the mud some yards ahead of me.

At first I thought it must be a branch, swept down here by the river. But as I looked at it, it moved, pushing down at the mud like an exposed arm, trying to thrust the rest of its body up out of the cloying muck.

Something groaned behind me, but I could not bring myself to look back. I lurched across the mud, veering away from the branch: how could it possibly be anything else?

The slipway was no more than forty yards away, but I could see a finger of water sliding across the space between. Dark objects swirled in the water, but they could have been anything. I tried to run, but now the sand did pull at me. Abruptly I trod on something soft and squishy and had to stifle a cry as I looked down and saw a face.

Aghast, I stared at the horror, drawing back my foot. But the moonlight showed me the truth: a jellyfish, large as a dinner plate, helplessly stranded. I struggled away from it, glancing towards the slipway.

Someone stood halfway down it. They were evidently watching me, too hidden in shadow to be clearly discerned. Convinced that something was trying to drag itself free of the sand, I got to the foot of the slope. As I went to mount it, the thin coating of weed on its stones defied me and I crashed to my knees. Gaping up, stupid as a fish, I could see the figure. It had moved on up the slipway, but still watched as if waiting for me. Curiously, I felt a desire to reach it, as if it were vital for me to communicate with it.

I almost called for help, but knew I was being ridiculous. If the men in the pub saw me now, they would snort with laughter. Served me right for being idiotic enough to wander out on to the mud flats.

It was difficult getting back on to the slipway, but I managed it and climbed slowly. By the time I was near the top, the figure had turned away, swallowed by the street above.

I was about to take a last scathing look at the mud banks, when something prevented me. I could hear the sea clearly, but there was something else now, a slithering sound of movement over the sand, from more than one direction. Angry with myself for not having the courage to look, I turned into the street. There was no one about: the village might have died. Then the figure emerged from a doorway a short distance ahead of me. The moon was behind it, so it was cast like a shadow, but I could see that it wore a heavy coat that would have been more suitable for a storm, or an ocean crossing. The collar was turned up, covering the back of the figure's head. It was the coat of a seaman. But why was the fellow waiting for me? I thought of the postcard. Could this be the sender? Then why the irritating mystery?

As I stepped forward, the figure moved on. It was clear that he wanted me to follow, but why the hell didn't the man just approach me? There was no point trying to argue it out: the figure had moved too briskly.

Again I lost him, but discovered that he had turned up another street, even more narrow and confined than the one I was in. And he was waiting for me. Or was all this my imagination?

Was the figure trying to avoid me, justifiably disturbed by my ludicrous antics on the sands?

I entered the cobbled street. The houses were in darkness, the doors locked. Was everyone asleep?

Before I realised it, the figure had slipped into a door or an entry, out of sight. I swore under my breath, but followed, incapable of doing anything else. Stone steps led down into a darkness that was impenetrable. The smell that came up from below was unpleasant, as though it reached down to the sea. This was where I needed a torch, I told myself. But I took a step at a time, very slowly, convinced that I was an utter fool to be doing any of this.

Beyond the steps in the darkness I could hear the sea, and a breeze suddenly caught me, shocking me with its strength, its coldness, as though it had come straight off the open ocean. I had gone down as far as I dared. I had to turn back.

The infuriating figure was above me, beyond the last step. I caught a glimpse of face before it was gone, the face of an old man. A man, perhaps, who had known my father?

"Hey!" I shouted, the sound muffled by the confines of the walls. Quickly I went up to the street, but to my exasperation the man had gone. I ran down towards the wider avenue, coming into it in time to see the shape turning down another street some yards beyond me. I was about to race after him, determined to catch up with him, when something odd about my surroundings struck me. *I didn't recognise them.* It wasn't just a case of being in an unfamiliar place. These houses were not the same ones I'd seen a few minutes earlier. The cold breeze washed over me again, and I had this bizarre idea of fractured time. Frantically I looked about me. These were simply *not* the same houses. Or for that matter, the same streets.

Where the hell was this place?

The figure must have the answer. He had—what, led me here? There would be an explanation, just as there was for the things I had stupidly imagined on the sands. This was the village, but just another street, surely?

There was a sign on one of the crumbling brick walls. "Fish Street." I hadn't noticed it before, nor had I noticed the dark shape that rose up between leaning roofs and clustered chimneys: it was a steeple, but one that looked as though the hand of God had chopped its top third away. I had seen a church from the road when I'd first arrived, but its tower had been intact.

A sudden disgusting stench blew in from the seaward side of the town, so powerful that I gagged, turning to see other figures shambling along the street. They seemed to be stooped, drunk perhaps, heads down. I felt a powerful desire not to be seen by them, so quickly moved on in the direction taken by the figure. Again I felt the acute need to find the man.

The side streets and alleys that ran off from this main thoroughfare were more unusual than I remembered. Decay had positively set in, many roofs collapsed, as if I had returned to the village twenty years on, with no repairs having been made to it. And it seemed far larger, not merely a village. Between two warehouses, neither of which I recalled, I glimpsed the sea.

*The tide was almost full!*

How could it be possible? It had been far out only minutes ago.

Voices drifted toward me from the rear, deep, guttural murmurings, distorted by the angled buildings. I felt cold: there was certain menace in the sounds.

Movement ahead made me jerk with shock. It was the figure. This time it waved me to it. I was almost relieved. Other voices sounded from up the street. It must be the buildings which so distorted them. I was sure these people were converging on me.

The figure had entered a low corridor that led through a rotting gateway to one of the derelict cottages. There were no lights, no curtains. But the smell of decay was even more powerful than that of the sea. Shadows hopped in the street behind me, and moonlight gleamed on something jagged. There was evil purpose in that gathering.

I reached the doorway and went within, closing the thick oak door, glad of its rusting bolt, which I slammed home. The figure waited before a worm-eaten table, the walls festooned with webs. This cottage had not seen proper use for decades. Moonlight seeped in through the smashed panes. Outside it had become as silent as a graveyard.

A match spat as the figure lit a candle. Our twin shadows danced for a moment. The face of the man was ancient, his skin like parchment, his eyes the eyes of the damned.

"You're lookin' fer Silas Waite." It was a statement.

I nodded. I might have been standing before a corpse.

"I am he."

Startled, I peered at the face. "*You?* You sent the card?"

"I'm yore father."

It should have been an emotional jolt, that confrontation with this figure from the myths of my past, but I felt suddenly stupid, throat drying. But how else could this old man know about the postcard?

"I'm Silas Waite. I came to fetch you, boy."

There was no question of relief, no stirring of joy in me. I knew then that he could only be alien to me, as remote as my childhood. I could not even feel the clamminess of guilt. I chose words clumsily. "Are you . . . hiding?" I thought of the clandestine chase, these grim surroundings.

"Not here. I didn't want to be seen in my old place."

"But you do live in Appledore?"

"I haven't been back for many, many years." He spoke with a thick accent, and it was only now that I recognised it. It was American, almost Puritan.

"But you can't live here, in this hovel?"

"This will be my last night here, thanks to you, boy. Tonight I go free. Out to—" But he stopped, listening to something beyond the door. He seemed satisfied that it had been nothing. "I've done my share of trawling. Now I can rest. Earned my keep, my passage."

"Back to America?" I said hesitantly, not understanding.

The old man screwed up his face. "Back? You're already here, boy. You've crossed. I brought you over. Like I promised them I would."

"What the hell are you talking about?" I was angry now, confused by this nonsense. The old man's mind was wandering, lost on one of his many voyages. Why in God's name had I come?

"Innsmouth. You're in Innsmouth."

I had never heard of the place. "Look, can't we go and talk? I'm staying in a pub. We can—"

"I don't have much time. They'll come for me soon enough. I can hear the breakers on the Reef." A look of extraordinary longing crossed his face as he said this. "It's your term now."

Had he said term, or turn? "My turn? To what?"

"You're my son. You'll take my place, as I took my father's. And when it's over for you, when you've trawled your share for them, you can go back. Bring your own offspring. They won't let you swim out to Devil Reef until you've delivered him."

I could make no sense of it at all. The poor fellow had completely lost his mind. Who looked after him? He couldn't possibly live here on his own.

"They'll be here soon. I'll go now." Again he smiled that appalling smile of longing.

"Who? Who's coming?"

"Dagon's children. They'll instruct you."

He didn't after all, know me. I could have been anyone. And yet, the postcard. *How* had he found me? Had someone else put him up to it?

"Who is Dagon?" I asked.

He shuddered, but not with the cold. It was with an almost lascivious delight. Then he began murmuring something so obscure, so twisted, that I must have stared at him dumbly. Was he about to have a fit? His eyes rolled, and as his mouth opened, I saw that his tongue was *forked*.

A clear knock sounded on the door I had bolted. And I realised that I had not shaken off the pursuit after all. There were at least a dozen people out there. And it was me they had come for.

"Serve them well," said Silas Waite. My father? It had become increasingly more unlikely. There could be no ties between us. I could not bring myself to bridge that frightful gap. He reached out for me, but I wanted to shout my rejection.

As he stepped towards me, the moonlight daubed his hands and wrists. *They were scaled.*

I lurched forward, thrusting at his chest, and he tumbled back, taken completely unawares by my sudden turn of mood. I could hear the door being pummelled. Frantically I rushed past the falling Waite; his claws dragged at my legs, but I was beyond his reach and out through a door behind him.

I was in almost total darkness, blundering through another room. Vaguely I made out some stairs, which seemed the only escape from this suddenly nightmarish hovel. I dived upwards. Behind me there was a splintering of rotting wood, the shouts of whoever it was that gave chase. Like hounds scenting blood, the inhabitants of this vile place were unquestionably after mine. I heard Waite scream something, possibly a curse, invoking the name, Dagon. I recalled it partly. An ancient god?

The stairs cracked under me and for a moment I almost lost my footing as a section collapsed. But I clung on to the wormy banister and hauled myself upwards. Below me, shapes writhed, the smell from the ground floor unbelievable. I could hear water, as if the tide had suddenly sloshed in to the rooms there. They tried to follow me, but the stairs wouldn't bear their weight: more of the wood ripped away.

Moonlight again guided me. I crossed a filthy room to a window that had long since rotted out. There was no glass. Fear moved me now. I would do anything to get away from these lunatics. God alone knew what was going on in this place.

I scrambled on to the window sill, reaching up for the gutter outside. It was strong enough to enable me to drag myself up and on to the roof tiles. Carefully I wriggled across them until I was able to cling to the brickwork of the chimney stack. I swung my legs up over the apex of the roof, pausing to get my breath back. The view that greeted me as I looked out over the town (for town it was) almost made me loosen my grip.

This was not Appledore. What had he called this place? Innsmouth? I could make no logical sense of my being here. The tide was full, and I saw its leaping waves reaching for the first of the quayside houses. Beyond them there were others, *already submerged, only their roofs and fallen chimneys visible.*

But worse, there was some kind of reef out in the bay, lit up by an unnatural fire. And by that weird light I could see swarms of—what, seals?—crawling over it. But as I looked more carefully, I could see similar shapes flopping out of the sea on to the quay beyond. They were not seals. If they had once been human, they were no longer.

Slates shattered beside me as something burst up through the roof. I stared in horror, realising that a skylight had been flung open. It crashed down on the roof, ripped from its hinges, and went sliding over the guttering, hitting the courtyard below. A head and shoulders appeared through the hole: it was Silas Waite. But he, too, was animated by something beyond human understanding. His terrible eyes gazed into mine, no more than a few feet away. I lifted my foot, preparing to drive my heel into his face.

Just as something, a shred of guilt, perhaps, stopped me, so a shadow crossed his face, and for an instant I caught a glimpse of the man beneath, Waite as he must once have been. He seemed to struggle with his inner demon, to be what he was. At last I felt a stab of sympathy for him.

But below him there were sounds, deep croaks, and Waite cried as if someone had struck him, urging him on with his grim work. Again his scaled flesh reached out for me.

"Go with them!" he shrieked. "They won't release me until you have taken my place! I can't go to the Reef. Don't let them deny me. Not after all these years! Go with them!"

I pressed myself back against the chimney stack. Some of its bricks were loose, but I clung on. Other people had gathered in the street below us, but mercifully the shadows hid them completely. I could hear them slithering about as though the tide had reached even this far into the town.

"Why must you go to the reef?" I asked him.

He had been trying to get on to the roof, but could only squirm in the narrow vent, caught like a fish on a rock. "Dagon's children are there. They'll welcome me. I've trawled for them all these years. I'll be one of them at last. Don't deny me. Your turn will come."

It made no sense. He could see I wanted to escape him and made an even greater effort to get on to the roof. I pulled a brick loose from the chimney and held it up as a weapon.

"I don't know how you brought me here, but you'd better show me the way back." I reached forward and gripped his wrist, pinning it to the slates. Again our eyes locked. It was all I could do to stare at him, at the torment I saw in his face.

He snarled, clawing at me with his free hand and I smashed at it with the brick. But he clung on tenaciously, immune, it seemed, to physical pain.

The voices below grew in volume, in excitement. I had been seen. They meant to capture me. I had to get clear of this place or God alone knew what these lunatics meant to do.

Waite began to sob, pleading with me to go with them, tears streaming down his face. It only served to anger me. I raised the brick again. "Take me back!" I shouted at him. "Take me back, or I'll—"

It came to me as I released a torrent of the vilest abuse I could dredge up from my fury that it was not the monster I ranted at, not this lunatic old man, but the ghost of the man who had deserted me all those years ago, the father I had never known. His crime. The loneliness of boyhood, the frustration, the sorrow of my mother, these were the things that goaded me now, pouring a livid power into the hand that held the brick. I swung it for a killing blow.

But he must have read murder in my face, and perhaps, at last, understood why. His inhumanity dissolved for a moment: I saw only a bewildered old man, searching for images from his own past. His eyes fastened on my face.

"Son—" he murmured.

"We must get away from this place," I told him, the brick quivering between us. "Do you hear me?"

My fury must have cowed the beast that drove him, at least for a while. Dumbly he nodded. "Help me up."

A change had come over him, yet I didn't trust his moods. But only he could show me the way back to Appledore, through whatever bizarre gate had brought us here.

Slowly I dragged him up on to the roof with me. Something tried to follow, but I beat it back, tossing the brick at it, and others I had dislodged. Waite bent over, more beast than man, but there was for a moment no suggestion of treachery. I gripped his arm.

"Follow the roofs. Find a way down," I told him.

Nodding, he began the dangerous climb across the slate landscape. I followed, turning now and then to try and see if we were followed, but the inhabitants of Innsmouth appeared to have chosen another route to attempt our capture. Waite muttered to himself, and though I couldn't hear the words, they were not the peculiar sounds he had been uttering earlier. He was like a man unable to recover fully from a bad dream. I forced myself to pity him, suppress the murder that had welled up so horribly in me.

The houses were tightly packed and we must have travelled a number of streets before we finally found our way cut off by too wide a gap. We would have to go down. I could hear nothing in the black street below. But as we dropped on to a lower roof, we had to cling to the shadows. Someone was moving beneath us.

I watched in stupefaction as a grotesque procession emerged from a side street, trudging towards the quay and the strange waters beyond it. There were several beings, I can only call them that, leading this procession. They were hunched over, almost hopping, and although I could not see their eyes clearly, they looked uncommonly wide. Moonlight gleamed on flesh that seemed slick, oiled like the scales of fish. These beings were terrible enough, but even more disturbing were the people with them. For they were men and women, presumably of this town, their heads bent in misery, their footsteps sluggish, almost drugged. Twenty or more of them were being herded along, making no attempt to break free. With a start I realised where I had seen a similar procession before.

On faded black and white film. The concentration camps. The victims being led to their grim destinations. And these people below me were in just such a predicament.

I gripped Waite again, and must have ground his thin bones.

"Who are they?" Something he had said earlier came back to me. About *trawling*. For what, people?

"No more," he whispered. "I have done enough. I have bought my place on Devil Reef."

I could not believe the implications of what he was saying. Instead we watched the procession disappear. Silence followed it. So far our pursuers had not found us out.

"You could stay here. Then, in the end, bring your own son when it is time for you to come to the Reef," he murmured.

David? Was he telling me I should *serve* in this horrific place, freeing myself by bringing *David* here?

He looked at me miserably, the agony of years breaking him. "It's the only way. If I am to be free. Would you abandon your father to their eternal revenge?"

I clutched at his collar, wrenching it, almost choking him. "You would buy your life with my *son's*! You want me to act as you did? Betray him?"

I could see the real beast tearing at him. It had nothing to do with this nightmare town. He had nurtured it himself, until it had fastened into him, a remorseless parasite. But I had woken it, that merciless guilt, and I could see it now, eating into his guts. And I needed its fire to keep him moving, guiding me back.

"Take me back," I whispered to it, using it cruelly. He had forced me to choose. How easy it was to be brutal.

Inside him, the beast squirmed. It heard me.

We dropped down to the street, winding our way through stinking alleys, ankle deep in seawater. I recognised none of the places. If anything, they were older and more derelict than those I had seen already.

But eventually we came to a street marked "Fish Street" and I knew it.

As we stood at the mouth of the narrow passage that led off from it to the steps, Waite hung back. "I can't return. Have pity."

"You can't stay here—"

"If I go back," he croaked, "I'll not last. I'm Dagon's. The sea there will wash me back to face them. No matter how long it takes, it'll deliver me to him, alive. You go. And keep away from the sea, boy. It won't forget you."

There were voices coming towards us once more, converging on this street.

"They won't follow," he said. "Only you and I can cross. It's how I was able to serve—" But he stopped, cutting short a confession I did not want to hear. He, too, had come to a decision, and I realised then that he must, after all, have been my father. Otherwise, why would he have abandoned his mad plan to trap me there? Our blood had triumphed over his dark god. "I'll keep them off long enough," he added.

I paused, then ran up the alley, closing my mind to his final revelation. But in the end it tipped the balance against him. He had known I needed a last push. I fled down the steps into the darkness. Behind me I heard the terrible voices of the hunt and the solitary shout of the trawlerman.

And so I went back to my own world. To the fishing village of Appledore, where, for all those years, my father had netted his unwary catch, the human diet for the dark god of his choice.

# Down to the Boots

## D. F. Lewis

The fen stank of fish. The moonlit puddles stretched as far as her eyes could see, as she shuffled ponderously from her shanty house at the sodden side of the sea-strained lands. For years, the waves had not returned to within sight of her leaning roofs and stair-case chimney-stacks, as if they had been mopped up by the persnickety underGod who had more common ground with a housewife washing the public pavements outside her suburban semi than with Madge . . . *she* just stopped and stared, balding broom in her hand, surrendering her heart as well as her hearth to the sluggish entropy of Earth's curds and separates . . .

Madge leaned on the broom handle, just listening to the distant irregular pulse of the sea. The lighthouse, one luminous speck far out amid the other floaters in her eyes, tried in vain to keep rhythm with the natural bloodbeat of the Earth . . . it failed mainly because the beacon's stokers had gone home for their breakfast in far-off Innsmouth Town.

Furthermore, she could just discern the pitiful drone of tuneless foghorns, as if even further out on the plane of her memories there lurked the blackened hulks of her various husbands' fishing steamers, long exhausted of fuel as well as catch. The fishes' flapping tails had in fact ceased their futile puddle-stirrings, ever since the seas withdrew in much panic during the Great Storm of '87: none of the fish had managed to stay the dreadful surge and were merely beached around Madge's shanty, like so many suffocating slimy insects, with salt gill tears.

Tonight, the moon was full: it revealed the herring-bones' clicking as nothing but the fitful wind amid their teetering attempts to become one giant skeleton memorial of the One Fish Soul. Madge could not fathom the foghorns' relentlessness. They made no sense, except, perhaps, the fog drifting with the moving air across the sea proper, was probably due to arrive here any minute, allowing the wind then to blow off to other more seasonable commitments inland.

Her husbands were all dead, except hopefully the latest one. And *he* had trudged off through the puddles even earlier that night. So early, he'd not even bothered to go to bed. He did not want to miss the tide, as so many of his predecessors had done before finally catching it late in their lives . . . and the tide's beginnings were at the end of beach upon beach of hardening ribbed mud. His boots, on first leaving the shanty, had made loud sucking noises, the deep treads reaching even beyond Madge's drowsing ears, into a dream where she could not find the ability to follow. Life's pull was stronger. Waking was the magnetic north, draining her blood in sporadic spurts towards the poles of her death.

None of them come back. It was tantamount to a ritual, a delayed menstrual sacrificer which seemed as pointless as it was self-destructive. Fishing, though, was in her husbands' essence, more in the nature of hooking mouthless cancers from the swamp in the belly than God's critters from the draining creeks of the sea lands.

As she stood at the shanty door, she managed to imagine the propeller-choked steamers upon the craters of churning brine that could still bear their floating hulks: the fly-rods spinning webs from deckrail to deckrail into a vast tangled cat's cradle game she and her sister often fell out over in the olden days: the trailing nets flapping in their wake like so much living weed: the monsters deep down at the bottom of the involuted chimney-cores of dead volcanos, their serrated backfins carving as far up as possible, in foolhardy attempts to return to the universe, to that huge space above the sky where they'd been created out of nothing but the mind-power of the master creature who stood above even God in the hierarchy of dreams . . .

Yes, they were nothing but dreams, Madge insisted. She stomped her foot, but lost it in the process beneath the mulch.

Then she saw them: her husband's thigh boots stood out from the fen like the blackened stumps of Earth's teeth, ill-pulled by a dentist God, Himself with a grin of decaying vampire fangs, each of these two death prongs liable to hurt Him more than his victim . . .

She shook herself. Dreaming again. They could not be his boots. But, if not, what were they?

That previous night, they'd spoken, perhaps for the last time.

"Don't forget to take your lunchbox, Owen . . . and your leggings are hanging up by the latchdoor."

"I don't want the leggings. The boots are quite enough—reaching to the crotch as they do."

"But your most li-able parts will then be open to the soakings . . ."

"Did I ever tell you of my father? He said don't be caught dead in your leggings, son, for people'll think you were a nancy-boy . . ."

"What rubbish!" She bit her tongue.

"No, there's something to that. There's not enough time to be a belt-and-braces man. Life's too thin for moithering . . ."

Unaccountably, tears had filled his eyes. But then she put it down to remembering his dad. Perhaps *he'd* left his own wife, in similar circumstances, to go fishing. There seemed no point in such an occupation, when the fishers themselves never came back . . . nor the fish with them. Only the stale bread would ever have to suffice, with no bony slimy innards to make two slices palatable enough.

She'd kissed him on the salt-stained lips for the first time, before retiring for the night, knowing he would sit up until it was time to go. How could anyone sit and do nothing? Her own thoughts were not sufficient to keep her going, without her hands doing something, like tatting, fishbone knitting, or baking stale bread: like making a start on the growing housework: but even such chores which seemed to multiply even as she slaved over them, could not staunch the fevering of her brain: she needed more: there was no rest inside her: she'd rather be dead than idle.

The dawn was slowly slipping up the side of the sky like a creamy yellow sea with clouds for waves. The moon had nowhere to hide, the land being flattened to the end of sight. Only the two tall boots stood up like sentries, betokening Owen'd become a ghost even before he'd left the catchment area of the shanty and before he got to the edge of the so-called sea: where his craft would still be bobbing at anchor, or beached upon the frozen ripples of the mud . . .

His leatherskin jacket-top smacks were lying beside the boots like a dead monster's hide, its inner body gutted like a fish and gambolling off somewhere to fright another new widow with its kinship to a giant insect.

She whispered to her widowmaker's ghost, in case it could hear: "I told you to take your leggings." But that did not seem to make much sense: so she took the stubbled broom and proceeded to sweep up the endless puddles, as best she could in the circumstances.

# The Church in High Street

## Ramsey Campbell

*. . . the Herd that stand watch at the secret portal each tomb is known to have, and that thrive on that which groweth out of the inhabitants thereof . . .*

—ABDUL ALHAZRED, NECRONOMICON

If I had not been a victim of circumstances, I would never have gone to ancient Temphill. But I had very little money in those days, and when I recalled the invitation of a friend who lived in Temphill to become his secretary, I began to hope that this post—open some months before—might still be available. I knew that my friend would not easily find someone to stay with him long; not many would relish a stay in such a place of ill repute as Temphill.

Thinking thus, I gathered into a trunk what few belongings I had, loaded it into a small sports car which I had borrowed from another friend gone on a sea voyage, and drove out of London at an hour too early for the clamorous traffic of the city to have risen, away from the cell-like room where I had stayed in a tottering, blackened backstreet house.

I had heard much from my friend, Albert Young, about Temphill and the customs of that decaying Cotswold town where he had lived for months during his research into incredibly superstitious beliefs for a chapter in his forthcoming book on witchcraft and witchcraft lore. Not being superstitious myself, I was curious at the way in which apparently sane people seemed to avoid entering Temphill whenever possible—as reported by Young—not so much because they disliked the route, as because they were disturbed by the strange tales which constantly filtered out of the region.

Perhaps because I had been dwelling upon these tales, the country seemed to grow disquieting as I neared my destination. Instead of the gently undulating Cotswold hills, with villages and half-timbered thatched houses, the area was one of grim, brooding plains, sparsely habited, where the only vegetation was a grey, diseased grass and an infrequent bloated oak. A few places filled me with a strong unease— the path the road took beside a sluggish stream, for instance, where the reflection of the passing vehicle was oddly distorted by the green, scum-covered water; the diversion which forced me to take a route straight through the middle of a marsh, where trees closed overhead so that the ooze all around me could barely be seen; and the densely wooded hillside which rose almost vertically above the road at one point, with trees reaching toward the road like myriad gnarled hands, all wearing the aspect of a primeval forest.

Young had written often of certain things he had learned from reading in various antique volumes; he wrote of "a forgotten cycle of superstitious lore which would have been better unknown;" he mentioned strange and alien names, and toward the last of his letters— which had ceased to come some weeks before—he had hinted of actual worship of trans-spatial beings still practiced in such towns as Camside, Brichester, Severnford, Goatswood and Temphill. In his very last letter he had written of a temple of "Yog-Sothoth" which existed conterminously with an actual church in Temphill where monstrous rituals had been performed. This eldritch temple had been, it was thought, the origin of the town's name—a corruption of the original "Temple Hill"—which had been built around the hill-set church, where "gates," if opened by now long-forgotten alien incantations, would gape to let elder demons pass from other spheres. There was a particularly hideous legend, he wrote, concerning the errand on which these demons came, but he forebore to recount this, at least until he had visited the alien temple's earthly location.

On my entrance into the first of Temphill's archaic streets, I began to feel qualms about my impulsive action. If Young had meanwhile found a secretary, I would find it difficult, in my indigence, to return to London. I had hardly enough funds to find lodging here, and the hotel repelled me the moment I saw it in passing—with its leaning porch, the peeling bricks of the walls, and the decayed old men who stood in front of the porch and seemed to stare mindlessly at something beyond me as I drove by. The other sections of the town were not reassuring, either, particularly the steps which rose between green ruins of brick walls to the black steeple of a church among pallid gravestones.

The worst part of Temphill, however, seemed to be the south end. On Wood Street, which entered the town on the northwest side, and on Manor Street, where the forested hillside on the left of the first street ended, the houses were square stone buildings in fairly good repair; but around the blackened hotel at the center of Temphill, the buildings were often greatly dilapidated, and the roof of one three-story building—the lower floor of which was used as a shop, with a sign—*Poole's General Store*—in the mud-spattered windows—had completely collapsed. Across the bridge beyond the central Market Square lay Cloth Street, and beyond the tall, uninhabited buildings of Wool Place at the end of it could be found South Street, where Young lived in a three-story house which he had bought cheaply and been able to renovate.

The state of the buildings across the skeletal river bridge was even more disturbing than that of those on the north side. Bridge Lane's grey warehouses soon gave way to gabled dwellings, often with broken windows and patchily unpainted fronts, but still inhabited. Here scattered unkempt children stared resignedly from dusty front steps or played in pools of orange mud on a patch of waste ground, while the older tenants sat in twilit rooms, and the atmosphere of the place depressed me as might a shade-inhabited city ruin.

I entered into South Street between two gabled three-story houses. Number 11, Young's house, was at the far end of the street. The sight of it, however, filled me with forebodings—for it was shuttered, and the door stood open, laced with cobwebs. I drove the car up the driveway at the side and got out. I crossed the grey, fungus-overgrown lawn and went up the steps. The door swung inward at my touch, opening upon a dimly-lit hall. My knocks and calls brought no answer, and I stood for a few moments undecided, hesitant to enter. There was a total absence of footprints anywhere on the dusty floor of the hall. Remembering that Young had written about conversations he had had with the owner of Number 8, across the road, I decided to apply to him for information about my friend.

I crossed the street to Number 8 and knocked on the door. It was opened almost immediately, though in such silence as to startle me. The owner of Number 8 was a tall man with white hair and luminously dark eyes. He wore a frayed tweed suit. But his most startling attribute was a singular air of antiquity, giving him the impression of having been left behind by some past age. He looked very much like my friend's description of the pedantic John Clothier, a man possessed of an extraordinary amount of ancient knowledge.

When I introduced myself and told him that I was looking for Albert Young, he paled and was briefly hesitant before inviting me to enter his house, muttering that he knew where Albert Young had gone, but that I probably wouldn't believe him. He led me down a dark hall into a large room lit only by an oil lamp in one corner. There he motioned me to a chair beside the fireplace. He got out his pipe, lit it, and sat down opposite me, beginning to talk with an abrupt rush.

"I took an oath to say nothing about this to anyone," he said. "That's why I could only warn Young to leave and keep away from—

that place. He wouldn't listen—and you won't find him now. Don't look so—it's the truth! I'll have to tell you more than I told him, or you'll try to find him and find—*something else. God knows what will happen to me now*—once you've joined *Them,* you must never speak of their place to any outsider. But I can't see another go the way Young went. I should let you go there—according to the oath—but *They'll* take me sooner or later, anyway. You get away before it's too late. Do you know the church in High Street?"

It took me some seconds to regain my composure enough to reply. "If you mean the one near the central square—yes, I know it."

"It isn't used—as a church, now," Clothier went on. "But there were certain rites practiced there long ago. They left their mark. Perhaps Young wrote you about the legend of the temple existing in the same place as the church, but in another dimension? Yes, I see by your expression that he did. But do you know that rites can still be used at the proper season to open the gates and let through *those from the other side?* It's true. I've stood in that church myself and watched the gates open in the center of empty air to show visions that made me shriek in horror. I've taken part in acts of worship that would drive the uninitiated insane. You see, Mr. Dodd, the majority of the people in Temphill still visit the church on the right nights."

More than half convinced that Clothier's mind was affected, I asked impatiently, "What does all this have to do with Young's whereabouts?"

"It has everything to do with it," Clothier continued. "I warned him not to go to the church, but he went one night in the same year when the Yule rite had been consummated, and *They* must have been watching when he got there. He was held in Temphill after that. *They* have a way of turning space back to a point—I can't explain it. He couldn't get away. He waited in that house for days before *They* came. I heard his screams—and saw the color of the sky over the roof. *They* took him. That's why you'll never find him. And that's why you'd better leave town altogether while there's still time."

"Did you look for him at the house?" I asked, incredulous.

"I wouldn't go into that house for any reason whatever," confessed Clothier. "Nor would anyone else. The house has become theirs now. *They* have taken him *Outside*—and who knows what hideous things may still lurk there?"

He got up to indicate that he had no more to say. I got to my feet, too, glad to escape the dimly-lit room and the house itself. Clothier ushered me to the door, and stood briefly at the threshold glancing fearfully up and down the street, as if he expected some dreadful visitation. Then he vanished inside his house without waiting to see where I went.

I crossed to Number 11. As I entered the curiously-shadowed hall, I remembered my friend's account of his life here. It was in the lower part of the house that Young had been wont to peruse certain archaic and terrible volumes, to set down his notes concerning his discoveries, and to pursue sundry other researches. I found the room which had been his study without trouble; the desk covered with sheets of notepaper—the bookcases filled with leather- and skin-bound volumes—the incongruous desk-lamp—all these bespoke the room's onetime use.

I brushed the thick dust from the desk and the chair beside it, and turned on the light. The glow was reassuring. I sat down and took up my friend's papers. The stack which first fell under my eye bore the heading *Corroborative Evidence,* and the very first page was typical of the lot, as I soon discovered. It consisted of what seemed to be unrelated notes referring to the Mayan culture of Central America. The notes, unfortunately, seemed to be random and meaningless. "Rain gods (water elementals?). Trunk-proboscis (ref. Old Ones). Kukulkan (Cthulhu?)"—Such was their general tenor. Nevertheless, I persisted, and presently a hideously suggestive pattern became evident.

It began to appear that Young had been attempting to unify and correlate various cycles of legend with one central cycle, which was, if recurrent references were to be believed, far older than the human race. Whence Young's information had been gathered if not from the antique volumes set around the walls of the room, I did not venture to guess. I pored for hours over Young's synopsis of the monstrous and alien myth-cycle—the legends of how Cthulhu came from an indescribable milieu beyond the furthest bounds of this universe—of the polar civilizations and abominably unhuman races from black Yuggoth on the rim—of hideous Leng and its monastery-prisoned high priest who had to cover what should be its face—and of a multitude of blasphemies only rumored to exist, save in certain forgotten places of the world. I read what Azathoth had resembled *before* that monstrous nuclear chaos had been bereft of mind and will—of many-featured Nyarlathotep—of shapes which the crawling chaos could assume, shapes which men have never before dared to relate—of how one might glimpse a dhole, and what one would see.

I was shocked to think that such hideous beliefs could be thought true in any corner of a sane world. Yet Young's treatment of his material hinted that he, too, was not entirely skeptical concerning them. I pushed aside a bulky stack of papers. In so doing, I dislodged the desk blotter, revealing a thin sheaf of notes headed *On the legend of the High Street Church.* Recalling Clothier's warning, I drew it forth.

Two photographs were stapled to the first page. One was captioned *Section of tesselated Roman pavement, Goatswood,* the other *Reproduction engraving p. 594 "Necronomicon."* The former represented a group of what seemed to be acolytes or hooded priests depositing a body before a squatting monster; the latter a representation of that creature in somewhat greater detail. The being itself was so hysterically alien as to be indescribable; it was a glistening, pallid oval, with no facial features whatsoever, except for a vertical, slit-like mouth, surrounded by a horny ridge. There were no visible members, but there was that which suggested that the creature could shape any organ at will. The creature was certainly only a product of some morbid artist's diseased mind—but the pictures were nevertheless oddly disturbing.

The second page set forth in Young's all too familiar script a local legend to the effect that Romans who had laid the Goatswood pavement had, in fact, practiced decadent worship of some kind, and hinting that certain rites lingered in the customs of the more primitive present-day inhabitants of the area. There followed a paragraph translated from the *Necronomicon.* "The tomb-herd confer no benefits upon their worshippers. Their powers are few, for they can but disarrange space in small regions and make tangible that which cometh forth from the dead in other dimensions. They have power wherever the chants of Yog-Sothoth have been cried out at their seasons, and can draw to them those who will open their gates in the charnel-houses. They have no substance in this dimension, but enter earthly tenants to feed through them while they await the time when the stars become fixed and the gate of infinite sides opens to free That Which Claws at the Barrier." To this Young had appended some cryptic notes of his own—"Cf. legends in Hungary, among aborigines Australia.—Clothier on High Church, Dec. 17," which impelled me to turn to Young's diary, pushed aside in my eagerness to examine Young's papers.

I turned the pages, glancing at entries which seemed to be unrelated to the subject I sought, until I came to the entry for December 17. "More about the High Street Church legend from Clothier. He spoke of past days when it was a meeting-place for worshippers of morbid, alien gods. Subterranean tunnels supposedly burrowed down to onyx temples, etc. Rumors that all who crawled down those tunnels to worship were not human. References to passages to other spheres." So much, no more. This was scarcely illuminating. I pressed on through the diary.

Under date of December 23, I found a further reference: "Christmas brought more legends to Clothier's memory today. He said something about a curious Yule rite practiced in the High Street Church—something to do with evoked beings in the buried necropolis beneath the church. Said it still happened on the eve of Christmas, but he had never actually seen it."

Next evening, according to Young's account, he had gone to the church. "A crowd had gathered on the steps leading off the street. They carried no light, but the scene was illuminated by floating globular objects which gave off a phosphorescence and floated away at my approach. I could not identify them. The crowd presently, realizing I had not come to join them, threatened me and came for me. I fled. I was followed, but I could not be sure *what* followed me."

There was not another pertinent entry for several days. Then, under date of January 13, Young wrote: "Clothier has finally confessed that he has been drawn into certain Temphill rites. He warned me to leave Temphill, said I must not visit the church in High Street after dark or I might awaken *them*, after which I might be *visited*—and not by people! His mind appears to be in the balance."

For nine months thereafter, no pertinent entry had been made. Then, on September 30, Young had written of his intention to visit the church in High Street that night, following which, on October 1, certain jottings, evidently written in great haste. "What abnormalities—what cosmic perversions! Almost too monstrous for sanity! I cannot yet believe what I saw when I went down those onyx steps to the vaults—that herd of horrors! . . . I tried to leave Temphill, but all streets turn back to the church. Is my mind, too, going?" Then, the following day, a desperate scrawl—"I cannot seem to leave Temphill. All roads return to No. 11 today—the power of those from *Outside.* Perhaps Dodd can help." And then, finally, the frantic beginnings of a telegram set down under my name and address and evidently intended to be sent. *Come Temphill immediately. Need your help . . .* There the writing ended in a line of ink running to the edge of the page, as if the writer had allowed his pen to be dragged off the paper.

Thereafter nothing more. Nothing save that Young was gone, vanished, and the only suggestion in his notes seemed to point to the church in High Street. Could he have gone there, found some concealed room, been trapped in it? I might yet then be the instrument of freeing him. Impulsively, I left the room and the house, went out to my car, and started away.

Turning right, I drove up South Street toward Wool Place. There were no other cars on the roads, and I did not notice the usual pavement loafers; curiously, too, the houses I passed were unlit, and the overgrown patch in the center, guarded by its flaking railing and blanched in the light of the moon over the white gables, seemed desolate and disquieting. The decaying quarter of Cloth Street was even less inviting. Once or twice I seemed to see forms starting out of doorways I passed, but they were unclear, like the figments of a distorted imagination. Over all, the feeling of desolation was morbidly strong, particularly in the region of those dark alleys undulating between unlit, boarded houses. In High Street at last, the moon hung over the steeple of the hill-set church like some lunar diadem, and as I moved the car into a depression at the bottom of the steps the orb sank behind the black spire as if the church were dragging the satellite out of the sky.

As I climbed the steps, I saw that the walls around me had iron rails set into them and were made of rough stone, so pitted that beaded spiders' webs glistened in the fissures, while the steps were covered with a slimy green moss which made climbing unpleasant. Denuded trees overhung the passage. The church itself was lit by the gibbous moon which swung high in the gulfs of space, and the tottering gravestones, overgrown with repulsively decaying vegetation, cast curious shadows over the fungus-strewn grass. Strangely, though the church was so manifestly unused, an air of habitation clung to it, and I entered it almost with the expectation of finding someone— caretaker or worshipper—beyond the door.

I had brought a flashlight with me to help me in my search of the nighted church, but a certain glow—a kind of iridescence—lay within its walls, as of moonlight reflected from the mullioned windows. I went down the central aisle, flashing my light into one row of pews after the other, but there was no evidence in the mounded dust that anyone had ever been there. Piles of yellowed hymnals squatted against a pillar like grotesque huddled shapes of crouching beings, long forsaken—here and there the pews were broken with age—and the air in that enclosed place was thick with a kind of charnel musk.

I came at last toward the altar and saw that the first pew on the left before the altar was tilted abnormally in my direction. I had noted earlier that several of the pews were angled with disuse, but now I saw that the floor beneath the first pew was also angled upward, revealing an unlit abyss below. I pushed the pew back all the way—for the second pew had been set at a suitably greater distance—thus exposing the black depths below the rectangular aperture. The flickering yellow glow from my flashlight disclosed a flight of steps, twisting down between dripping walls.

I hesitated at the edge of the abyss, flashing an uneasy glance around the darkened church. Then I began the descent, walking as quietly as possible. The only sound in the core-seeking passage was the dripping of water in the lightless area beyond the beam of my flashlight. Droplets of water gleamed at me from the walls as I spiraled downward, and crawling black things scuttled into crevices as though the light could destroy them. As my quest led me further into the earth, I noticed that the steps were no longer of stone, but of earth itself, out of which grew repulsively bloated, dappled fungi, and saw that the roof of the tunnel was disquietingly supported only by the flimsiest of arches.

How long I slithered under those uncertain arches I could not tell, but at last one of them became a grey tunnel over strangely-colored steps, uneroded by time, the edges of which were still sharp, though the flight was discolored with mud from the passage of feet from above. My flashlight showed that the curve of the descending steps had now become less pronounced, as if its terminus was near, and as I saw this I grew conscious of a mounting wave of uncertainty and disquiet. I paused once more and listened.

There was no sound from beneath, no sound from above. Pushing back the tension I felt, I hastened forward, slipped on a step, and rolled down the last few stairs to come up against a grotesque statue, life-size, leering blindly at me in the glow of my flashlight. It was but one of six in a row, opposite which was an identical, equally repulsive sextet, so wrought by the skill of some unknown sculptor as to seem terrifyingly real. I tore my gaze away, picked myself up, and flashed my light into the darkness before me.

Would that a merciful oblivion could wipe away forever what I saw there!—the rows of grey stone slabs reaching limitlessly away into darkness in claustrophobic aisles, on each of them shrouded corpses staring sightlessly at the ebon roof above. And nearby were archways marking the beginning of black winding staircases leading *downward* into inconceivable depths; sight of them filled me with an inexplicable chill superimposed upon my horror at the charnel vision before me. I shuddered away from the thought of searching among the slabs for Young's remains—if he were there, and I felt intuitively that he lay somewhere among them. I tried to nerve myself to move forward, and was just timidly moving to enter the aisle at the entrance of which I stood, when a sudden sound paralyzed me.

It was a whistling rising slowly out of the darkness before me, augmented presently by explosive sounds which seemed to increase in volume, as if the source of it were approaching. As I stared affrightedly at the point whence the sound seemed to rise, there came a prolonged explosion and the sudden glowing of a pale, sourceless green light, beginning as a circular illumination, hardly larger than a hand. Even as I strained my eyes at it, it vanished. In a few seconds, however, it reappeared, three times its previous diameter—and for one dreadful moment I glimpsed through it a hellish, alien landscape, as if I were looking through a window opening upon another, utterly foreign dimension! It blinked out even as I fell back—then returned with even greater brilliance—and I found myself gazing against my will upon a scene being seared indelibly on my memory.

It was a strange landscape dominated by a trembling star hanging in a sky across which drifted elliptical clouds. The star, which was the source of the green glowing, shed its light upon a landscape where great, black triangular rocks were scattered among vast metal buildings, globular in shape. Most of these seemed to be in ruins, for whole segmentary plates were torn from the lower walls, revealing twisted, peeling girders which had been partially melted by some unimaginable force. Ice glittered greenly in crevices of the girders, and great flakes of vermilion-tinted snow settled towards the ground or slanted through the cracks in the walls, drifting out of the depths of that black sky.

For but a few moments the scene held—then abruptly it sprang to life as horrible white, gelatinous shapes flopped across the landscape toward the forefront of the scene. I counted thirteen of them, and watched them—cold with terror—as they came forward to the edge of the opening—and *across it,* to flop hideously into the vault where I stood!

I backed toward the steps, and as in a dream saw those frightful shapes move upon the statues nearby, and watched the outlines of those statues blur and begin to move. Then, swiftly, one of those dreadful beings rolled and flopped toward me. I felt something cold as ice touch my ankle. I screamed—and a merciful unconsciousness carried me into my own night. . . .

———————

When I woke at last I found myself on the stones between two slabs some distance from the place on the steps where I had fallen—a horrible, bitter, furry taste in my mouth, my face hot with fever. How long I had lain unconscious I could not tell. My light lay where it had fallen, still glowing with enough illumination to permit a dim view of my surroundings. The green light was gone—the nightmarish opening had vanished. Had I but fainted at the nauseating odors, at the terrible suggestiveness of this charnel crypt? But the sight of a singularly frightening fungus in scattered patches on my clothing and on the floor—a fungus I had not seen before, dropped from what source I could not tell and about which I did not want to speculate—filled me with such awful dread that I started up, seized my light, and fled, plunging for the dark archway beyond the steps down which I had come into this eldritch pit.

I ran feverishly upward, frequently colliding with the wall and tripping on the steps and on obstacles which seemed to materialize out of the shadows. Somehow I reached the church. I fled down the central aisle, pushed open the creaking door, and raced down the shadowed steps to the car. I tugged frantically at the door before I remembered that I had locked the car. Then I tore at my pockets—in vain! The key-ring carrying all my keys was gone—lost in that hellish crypt I had so miraculously escaped. The car was useless to me— nothing would have induced me to return, to enter again the haunted church in High Street.

I abandoned it. I ran out into the street, bound for Wood Street and, beyond it, the next town—open country—any place but accursed Temphill. Down High Street, into Market Square, where the wan moonlight shared with one high lamp standard the only illumination, across the Square into Manor Street. In the distance lay the forests about Wood Street, beyond a curve, at the end of which Temphill would be left behind me. I raced down the nightmarish streets, heedless of the mists that began to rise and obscure the wooded country slopes that were my goal, the blurring of the landscape beyond the looming houses.

I ran blindly, wildly—but the hills of the open country came no nearer—and suddenly, horribly, I recognized the unlit intersections and dilapidated gables of Cloth Street—which should have been far behind me, on the other side of the river—and in a moment I found myself again in High Street, and there before me were the worn steps of that repellent church, with the car still before them! I tottered, clung to a roadside tree for a moment, my mind in chaos. Then I turned and started out again, sobbing with terror and dread, racing with pounding heart back to Market Square, back across the river, aware of a horrible vibration, a shocking, muted whistling sound I had come to know only too well, aware of fearful pursuit . . .

I failed to see the approaching car and had time only to throw myself backward so that the full force of its striking me was avoided. Even so, I was flung to the pavement and into blackness.

I woke in the hospital at Camside. A doctor returning to Camside through Temphill had been driving the car that struck me. He had taken me, unconscious and with a contusion and a broken arm, from that accursed city. He listened to my story, as much as I dared tell, and went to Temphill for my car. It could not be found. And he could find no one who had seen me or the car. Nor could he find books, papers, or diary at No. 11 South Street where Albert Young had lived. And of Clothier there was no trace—the owner of the adjacent house said he had been gone for a long time.

Perhaps they were right in telling me I had suffered a progressive hallucination. Perhaps it was an illusion, too, that I heard the doctors whispering when I was coming out of anaesthesia—whispering of the frantic way in which I had burst into the path of the car—and worse, of the strange fungus that clung to my clothes, even to my face at my lips, as if it grew there!

Perhaps. But can they explain how now, months afterward, though the very thought of Temphill fills me with loathing and dread, I feel myself irresistibly drawn to it, as if that accursed, haunted town were the mecca toward which I must make my way? I had begged them to confine me—to prison me—anything—and they only smile

# Cthulhu

and try to soothe me and assure me that everything will "work itself out"—the glib, self-reassuring words that do not deceive me, the words that have a hollow sound against the magnet of Temphill and the ghostly whistling echoes that invade not only my dreams but my waking hours!

I will do what I must. Better death than that unspeakable horror . . .

*Filed with the report of P.C. Villars on the disappearance of Richard Dodd, 9 Gayton Terrace, W.7. Manuscript in Dodd's script, found in his room after his disappearance.*

# Innsmouth Gold

## David Sutton

Talman gave me a sceptical look. It wasn't that he thought I was crazy, but maybe just a little nuts.

"Well, George," he said at last, "I think you've been drinking too much of that sour-mash in the Kentucky sun!" I had been living south of the line for five years, that part was certainly true. As for the whiskey, I didn't touch the stuff. Talman and I had been firm friends for around twenty years, a long relationship established through our mutual love of North American wildlife. We'd completed several expeditions together over the years on mainland America, and also once into the forested wilds of northern Canada. Eventually, my teaching commitments had meant a move of home, but luckily, or unluckily, as things worked out, half a decade on had found me back in my beloved Boston. The downside of that was I had no job and very little money.

We were sitting in the open basement of a bar near Charles Street in the Back Bay area, sipping cold beers. It was October, but the weather was mild and cloudy. The trees lining the sidewalk were beginning to transform themselves into fiery-crowned beacons of the season. I nodded to my companion, smiling. He was beginning to show his mid-forties age now with a greying hair line. Ignoring his quip about the bourbon I said, "Fred, do you remember the old days? We'd take off for the hills at the drop of a hat. At the merest sniff of something rare and interesting, with little more than fourth-hand evidence that we'd ever get to see the critter." I was, to put it mildly, selling my story.

"Agreed," he replied. "We sure would race off in our younger days. But, you know, George, there ain't never been any gluttons seen in New England. North of the Hudson Bay, or Labrador maybe, but not this far south. Those animals are *rare.*"

He used the common name for the animal we had been discussing—the wolverine. And he was right, it was extremely uncommon and certainly not to be seen in Massachusetts. However, I was angling for some excuse to pay a visit to the wooded coast around Newburyport. So I pushed again: "I have it on good authority that wolverines have been seen around the state border with New Hampshire and I'd like to make this field trip if—"

"All right, George." He interrupted, sipping his beer. "I'll loan you the two thousand dollars. That should cover your expenses. You can use my camping gear."

I was secretly overjoyed, but tried not to show too much emotion. "And what about the Toyota?" I knew George was too good a friend to let me down, but pushing like this I was asking for a kick in the ass. However, his 4WD was a second car and I was pretty sure he could spare it for a week or so.

He stared at me for a full minute then; his keen grey eyes—eyes that had sharpened their gaze over years of animal-watching—held me like a rabbit mesmerized by a weasel. My heart lurched and I thought he was going to renege on the whole deal.

He smiled. "And the Jap car. Okay, so I'm a complete fool!"

"You won't regret it, Fred, I really appreciate what you're doing.

The money's just a loan too, you'll get that back, just as soon as I get my life straight." I was beginning to babble and I knew it. "Another beer?" I felt I could now splash out with my last few dollars.

"Sure," he replied. "But I'll get 'em." When he'd ordered from the waitress, he said, "How about a little wager, George? Double or quits. If you see this damned wolverine and take a picture of it I'll stand the loan. If you fail, you owe me four big ones."

I could hardly refuse, even though I knew I was going to lose the bet. No one was going to see a wolverine that was outside a museum anywhere in the New England woods. However, I pretended to mull it over. We had been habitual betting buddies in the old days; fifty here, fifty there as to who'd see this bird or that snake first. My reply matched the role I was playing. "It'll make me search all the harder, but I reckon my sources are unimpeachable. You're on!"

Over the next few days, as I was getting my loan from Talman and equipping myself in his station wagon, the October weather began to worsen. The change was still only a chill in the air, letting everyone know winter was just around the corner. Finally, I set off from Talman's house in the Boston suburbs. Till the end he thought I was on a wild goose chase to find the southernmost sighting of the world's most vicious mammalian carnivore. If only he'd known . . .

In fact, my final destination was the salt marsh that surrounded the deserted town of Innsmouth. And it wasn't any animal I was hunting.

It was gold.

You may think I *was* crazy, but let me fill in the gaps and you'll see I was driven by the lure of gold fever; and maybe a little bit of the call of the wild.

Innsmouth is a coastal town—thriving once I suppose, but now deserted—on the mouth of the Manuxet river, between Ipswich and Newburyport. It is surrounded by a wide salt marsh on the landward side, a desolate and unpeopled place. During the seventeenth century a lot of the ancient woodland in the area was cut down, which allowed wind-blown sand to penetrate inland and this led to the creation of the morass. More recently, global warming has raised the sea level a few inches. It might not sound like much, but it has had the effect of making the wetland all the more permanent. Heavy forestation further inland adds to Innsmouth's isolation, but that doesn't matter: poor fishing over the last eighty-ninety years has left the town without sufficient industries to survive, hence the ghost town it's now become.

I drove north off the Fitzgerald Expressway, along the coast on route 95 into wilder, pleasant country. Small, sleepy New England towns and radiant red and gold autumnal trees conveyed to me a sense of homeliness and safety. There ain't a prettier sight than this State in the Fall. Passing the turn-off for Arkham reminded me of the research I'd done there when first returning home from Middlesboro. That, and the things which an acquaintance had told me—Bill Poynter was a conspiracy buff and liked to delve into government records released through the Freedom of Information Act.

It was Poynter who first introduced me to the reason why I was so desperate to visit Innsmouth's salt marsh. We'd been drinking pals in Middlesboro, since he and I worked for the same educational establishment. Naturally we talked a lot about our respective hobbies. His was digging for dirt and scandal in government papers. He told me one day about a major FBI raid on a little town called Innsmouth in 1927.

"The FBI cover-story was that the raid was to bring the bootleggers to justice," Poynter had said. "Innsmouth was a major center for the production and traffic in illegal liquor. It was prohibition, after all."

"But," I asked him, not really needing the mysterious prompting in his voice, "there was another reason for the raid, wasn't there?"

"You said it, Geo—" he always shortened my name to sound like I was the prefix to some unmentioned earth science "—that raid had other fish to fry, at least for some of the senior Feds involved. It was, no less," he became conspiratorial, "to cream off a roomful of gold that lay for the taking at the town's Obed Marsh Refinery."

Poynter's story didn't sound too loony, although some of the other things I'd heard about Innsmouth did. Poynter went on to say that the Bureau people stashed their cache of gold somewhere in the marsh outside of town. And there it had remained to this day.

"Why hadn't the agents gone back for their loot when the heat was off?" I asked him.

"Apparently there was a lot of fuss and palaver," he replied. "Seems, however, that they just couldn't find where they'd hidden it, especially since agent Mahoney, the guy who knew the backwoods like the back of his hand, had inconveniently gotten himself shot dead in an unconnected raid in Boston a few months later."

There arose in my mind half-a-dozen unanswered questions, so at the time I took Poynter's story with a pinch of salt. However, I had since discovered that there was a gold refining plant in Innsmouth and that it produced some opulent, strange-looking jewellery. Its trademark appeared to be designs based on some south sea island religion or motif. The reality of the gold factory clinched it for me. Innsmouth had died. Nobody lived there anymore. The harvest of the sea had gone, depleted fish stocks turning the trawlermen inland for work; and before that, the gold which was spirited away destroyed Innsmouth's other major industry. Maybe a few crooked FBI agents had used the liquor raid to cover their own illegal interest in Obed Marsh's gold. Maybe that hoard still lay where it had been hidden in 1927. And maybe I could be a millionaire. It was too good a chance to pass up without at least one crack at it.

My drive up the coast was leisurely. I felt relaxed for the first time in months. I glanced in the rear-view mirror, and I saw that my face was looking better than it had for a long time. I'd always looked weather-beaten, you'd expect that, but the last year or so had left me looking fifty rather than forty. But blue eyes were now keen, rather than dull; and the crow-feet around them and the sallow cheeks had almost gone. My blond hair was clean and tidy looking, instead of greasy and unkempt.

On the passenger seat lay the camera I'd bought. What I was searching for didn't need photographing, but there was bound to be wildlife worth shooting in the woods. My destination was about sixty miles from Boston, but I felt so good that I drove slowly, stopping at places here and there, taking a few photos to familiarise myself with the autofocus Canon. A small township provided some typical New England buildings from the turn of the century and it reminded me of Arkham. I had stayed in Arkham for about a week last summer, sleeping rough for the latter half as my dwindling resources ran dangerously low. During researches at the library of the Miskatonic University, I built up a good picture of the annals of Innsmouth. That, in addition to what Poynter had told me, was all I needed to convince me about the bullion.

Innsmouth's had its fair share of history. Besides the all-too-familiar story of the 1927 assault, which must have sounded the death-knell for the place, there were other strange stories. It was easy to see how such yarns began. My English ancestors came from legend-haunted Cornwall, where a dozen books wouldn't be enough to document all the ghost stories of that county. Add the lost sunken city of Lyonesse and the mythic sea serpent, Morgawr, and you have a rich literature of tall tales. Let's face it, any rural place like that has such folk stories. Innsmouth was no exception.

There was much supposition that the FBI foray was unrelated to the illicit distillation of whisky (or gold for that matter), but organised to exterminate a brood of mutant humans living in the town and on Devil Reef, which lay a couple of miles offshore. The federal agents *had* dynamited the skerry, but my guess is that it provided a handy and secluded spot to moor the boats that were used to ship the liquor down the coast. Devil Reef is rarely seen nowadays, what with the rise in the sea level and the blasting, and it remains submerged except on occasional neap tides. Thus there was a blending of truth and fiction, an ideal mix to turn seekers after facts off the scent.

So absorbed was I in my thoughts that I nearly missed the turn-off. The old, run-down road was badly signposted and not often used. In fact, there were so many potholes in the blacktop that I was glad I was in a four-wheel drive. The road looped down, snaking into a wide valley that was all but hidden by a mixed forest. The trees and the undergrowth were making demands on the unkempt highway, encroaching, brooding over me as I drove slowly on. It was quiet, too. Unearthly quiet. All I could hear through the open window was the engine and the exhaust. I was tempted to switch on the radio, but didn't. Finally, the road ran out of asphalt into a dirt track with coppery-leaved silver birches forming a tunnel above me. A few old tyre ruts were impressed into the dried mud, indicating that it had been some time since anyone had ventured this way.

The car bucked as it rode the uneven surface. What I was searching for was a disused railroad that at one time branched to Innsmouth from Rowley. It had been obsolete since before almost anyone could remember, and I surmised that the track, which had been laid on an embankment built across the marsh, was a likely contender as a site for the concealment of gold. My concentration was beginning to lapse, and suddenly the rightside front wheel hit a deep depression in the road. The wagon lurched sideways, coming to a stop and throwing me onto the passenger seat.

I cursed. The engine had cut out and the Toyota was tipped at a steep angle. It might be difficult to drive it out, but, as I surveyed my surroundings I noticed that the woods had become almost impenetrable for vehicles in any case. From now on I would have to move on foot. Heaving the rucksack on my back, I was again aware of the disquieting lack of birdsong. Anyhow, the first job was to scan the rather ancient map I'd bought from a bookstore along the way.

The store owner had said that nothing much had changed in that part of the country since the cartographers last surveyed it. "There's some bad weather 'spected," he continued, as if I'd asked him for the forecast. "Jest on the radio, snow's comin' down aff the Green Mountains."

"No problem," I responded. "I'm an old hand in those sort of conditions."

The old man pulled off his bi-focals resignedly, as though his dissuading tactics had failed, which they had. He stared at me with unfocused eyes before riding another snippet to deter me. "Innsmouth's got . . . *folks* livin' in them run-down houses as wouldn't take kindly to strangers."

"Oh?" I said, my surprise showing. "I thought the town was abandoned some years ago? In any case," I continued, "I'm not interested in the town itself, I'm actually up here checking out the wildlife."

He didn't seem to take my meaning immediately because he said, "Yep, that's right—they're wild folks livin' up there."

"You mean like squatters, or hippies?" I asked.

"Mebbe."

I'd left without really looking too closely at the map, but opening it now I saw that it was detailed, showing the extent of the forest and the few homesteads that were swallowed within it; the marsh and the old rail track. There was a fairly decent plan of Innsmouth as well, the coastline, the Manuxet river and Devil Reef. A cross indicating a church in the town was given the unwieldy title "Esoteric Order of Dagon Church," and I remembered the name from my earlier researches. Apparently Innsmouth had gone over to some weird religion, I surmised something like the holy wailers or Mormons, or somesuch. Either way, it didn't stop the town profiteering from their poteen. I found my route, marked it on the map and checked my bearings. Taking a quick look at a compass, I headed north, directly into the brush. It was hard work, the undergrowth of briars dense, clasping and tearing at my boots with every step. Serried stands of mountain ash, sugar maple and fir inhibited my progress for a while, finally opening up to thickets of mountain holly, chokeberry and cinnamon fern.

As the October daylight began to fade, I arrived at the margins of the marsh. With it went my cheerfulness. Above, grey clouds merged with a condensed, cold mist over the distant flat landscape. Drowned spruces, gaunt, skeletal, rose up out of the water like thin, many-digited, bony limbs. Quite a number of New England's lowland swamps have been filled in with garbage, destroying unique environments, so for me it should have been a real pleasure to see Innsmouth's bog still in existence. However, a chill ran through my body and my light mood became dark. Night was fast approaching and I could go no further that day. Besides, the swamp impeded my progress, the water level was so high. I would have to backtrack into the woods and trace a circuitous route, testing the marsh every now and then to see if there was some semi-solid ground which would carry me to the branch line.

I pitched my tent on terra firma in a clearing nearby and quickly switched on the lamp inside to banish the thickening shadows that surrounded me. After eating a simply-cooked meal and drinking a welcome hot mug of coffee, I took to my sleeping bag. As I lay there, basked by the comforting yellow glow that gaudily lit up my tent, I heard animal sounds for the first time that day. They were the boomings of frogs lurking in the bog laurel and sedges at the water's edge. Aside from the usual croaks, there were some less familiar gruntings, almost like a subdued barking. These low frequency resonances continued for some time and began to get on my nerves. I found it incredible that I, a former great outdoors man, should feel uneasy over a few amphibians.

I shivered, cold air fitting me like a vest inside the sleeping bag. The lamp flickered tentatively and the fabric above me flapped in a breeze. I trembled again, trying to shrug off the sensation I had of being observed. The temptation to scramble clear of my temporary shelter began to gnaw at my thoughts. I waited, listening to the frogs' guttural conversations. I was almost becoming inured to the croaks and clicks when a loud splash nearby startled me. For all the world it was as though a large rock had been thrown into the swamp. There were no alligators in this part of the country that could have accounted for such a disturbance and the only other creature I could think of was a beaver, but they didn't inhabit this district either. And somehow I couldn't envisage a bear jumping into a swamp.

I sat, shivering, the sleeping-bag around my waist, my ears attuned to the slightest auditory clue. I slowly reached out and switched off the lamp. Black night fell upon me and my eyes tried to compensate by sending flares and sparks across my retina. I held my jaw hard shut to stop my teeth from chattering. The frogs had ceased their barking and I didn't want to be the first to break the silence. I could imagine the fog outside sliding through the forest, lying like a heavy gas over the waters of the nearby swamp, hiding whatever had made that splash.

I didn't want my presence to be known. If I sat still long enough, whatever was out there would, I hoped, move on. At that moment I could not imagine what kind of animal was roaming the woods and it left my imagination to run wild. I had never been so scared in all my life. If I didn't believe in intuitive fear before, I certainly believed it that night.

It's funny how terror is easily dissipated. When I woke the next morning, I was surprised that I had actually been able to fall asleep. Like in a dream, my terror of the previous night had faded clean away. Even so, the bizarre fables of Innsmouth's past and the mutant strain of humans said to inhabit the place filled my thoughts as I awoke. Those legends, which I had skimped over in my local history research, lingered only as wild inventions in my mind and I couldn't really remember the precise details. There was something about hideous transformations taking place over time, like a caterpillar into a butterfly, but in this case it would have been from the beautiful to the ugly. And something about Innsmouth's throat-gagging fishy smell. Thinking about ichthyic stenches, I noticed a lingering aroma when I left my tent that morning. The coast was not many miles off, so I guessed that a waft of the seashore was being driven inland from a low tide that had exposed strands of seaweed. Or maybe the reef had been unveiled with its raft of weed and putrefying fish? Either way, the smell was definitely there and not as pleasant as you'd expect from a sea breeze.

I was making good progress and by midday found myself able to walk the boggy sphagnum and mud of the swamp. The locality I was tramping inclined gently upwards, rising out of the lying waters, and my boots gripped firmer ground every few hundred yards. Heading north-east now, I expected to see the railroad any time. Then, through a single file of bristling birches, I found the low embankment designating a straight line across country. My plan was to walk the track, right into Innsmouth if need be, taking it as slowly as necessary, searching for anything that might give a clue to the whereabouts of the stockpile of gold. My guess was, because of the wetland, the FBI men would have had to hide or bury their ill-gotten gains somewhere on solid ground, and the rampart before me was the only safe place that was well above the tidal sweep of the waters.

I started to plod along the weed-choked ties. Old bits of track iron, the clinker of fused ash, and other detritus littered the route. It had been exposed here for many years. There were no Coca-Cola cans or polystyrene fast-food containers like you'd expect. Nobody had walked this way in a long, long time. On either side of me the marshland swept away into methane mists, concealing all distant tracts of land.

A fine rain washed out of featureless grey skies, dampening my spirits, which had lightened for a short time after I'd stumbled across the railroad. I shrugged my rucksack higher on my shoulders, hunching beneath its weight, my eyes forever gazing towards the gravel, gleaming wetly under my boots. The tracks were shedding flakes of corroded metal and here and there brambles clawed across as though determined to hide forever its desolation.

For a time I imagined myself a hobo, one of a few individuals privy to the secret world of disused railroads, time-forgotten highways of steel, branching across country to distant ghost towns where loose-shuttered windows banged a tune to the shivering winds.

Permeating with the low-lying fog across the marshland, the film of rain brought sky down to meet tenuous earth as the swamp and the distant trees were swallowed up behind an opaque canescent shroud. I stopped for a time, and decided it might be useful to erect the tent here and use the location as a base from which to search the area. I could also rest with some shelter over my head until the rain eased a little. By four-thirty the light was fading and the drizzle had not let up. I called it a day and promised myself that tomorrow would see me intent on making significant distance towards the coast. By leaving the rucksack and provisions, I would be able to make better progress, with the knowledge that there would be dry shelter to crawl back into.

The next day I was up at dawn and felt refreshed. There'd been no disturbances in the night to unnerve me. As the sun slid slowly up behind veils of cloud on the eastern horizon, the distant lowlands of the marsh became more visible. The trees were sparser in the distance, giving way to coarse grasses and reeds, and clear, sunlit waterways cut sinuous routes through them. Here and there small islands rose out of the water, hummocks from which a few birches clung. And as the day became brighter, far off I thought I could see darkened buildings—the outskirts of Innsmouth. The railroad ahead of me turned a wide arc towards the right, and east, while on the left, away off, the land began to rise to a craggy headland. I could smell the distant sea, at least I thought it was that brine tang, but it was a strong, decaying odor, like rotting seaweed. Before long I realised the effluvium actually came from the salt-marsh surrounding me. The water, where it could be seen between the reeds, was gummy and weed-choked, almost stagnant. I knew this would be an ideal place to observe waders and other birds whose habitat this was, but I could not concentrate on ornithology and didn't even bother to take the camera with me.

I walked about six miles in bright sunshine, a cool breeze softening its warmth. Even so, the trek was making me sweat. I found no sign of where the gold might be hidden, no soil that looked as though it had been dug up, no markers to indicate a hiding place. I explored the whole area of the ridge on which the rail tracks were built, moving underbrush aside, poking into every hole. It was exhausting work. About two miles distant I saw where the track breached the town. Innsmouth's buildings, those that were visible to me, reminded me of bones, their rotten timber roofs poking skywards like ribs. They looked like warehouses, old wooden structures. It appeared that I was destined to visit the town after all, when unexpectedly I came across a deep pit hollowed out of the side of the ridge. Funny thing was, the soil looked freshly excavated, the way you can tell if an animal's den is still inhabited. I put it down to a washout caused by the recent downpour. Scrambling beneath the slope, mud and stones tumbling with me, I saw that the pit was even larger than it looked from above, and I should have realised that this could not have been the place where the gold was hidden. At the time though, everything else was forgotten. I had found the entrance to a cave which sloped under the railway above, deep into the earth.

Luckily, I had my flashlight with me and so without delay I stooped down and entered the cavern. It was like a burrow and very steep at first as it traced a route below the level of the bog. I marvelled that very little moisture was seeping through, although the stench of dead fish filled the air. The fetor was overpowering and I found it necessary to tie my handkerchief around my nose and mouth, but it hardly helped at all. The reek was so bad that the tunnel had to lead to Innsmouth's beach. I wondered idly whether it filled up at high tide.

I felt the walls surrounding me and was surprised to find them solid, like petrified earth, and that no doubt accounted for the lack of swamp water leaching in. My immediate thoughts were of an undiscovered smuggler's hideaway, but the cavern was too extensive for that and too far from the coast. Nothing about the place gave me a real clue as to its use or its construction. Further thoughts were interrupted when the beam from my flashlight bounced back from a dead end, a blockage of old, rotten-looking timbers. It appeared to be a very temporary and hastily erected structure, an impression that was reinforced by the water trickling between the cracks. Almost before I could consider my next move, a great wash of debris burst through the wooden wall.

I blinked in sudden shock for brief seconds before turning to flee the wall of dirt and water that plunged into the tunnel as if it consciously intended to engulf me. I ran for my life, my legs stretching as far and as fast as they could in the cramped space. I could hear the deadly slosh of water sluicing behind me, still coming at me despite the rising angle of the cave. I turned my head to see what chance I'd have of not drowning and thought I saw something swimming in that torrent, something big, with scaly skin. I screamed, believing a dead body was being washed along behind me. The notion that I was going to be buried with the rotting flesh of a human cadaver was a shock so powerful that it spurred me on; that and the dead white eyes, like bulging, unblinking frog eyes forced unnaturally into human sockets which glared at me out of the rush of water!

By the time I fell out of the entrance, my chest felt like a steam-engine ready to blow, but I didn't stop there; I clawed with my hands and feet for higher ground, tearing at the stumps of grass for purchase. Behind me the noisome flood suddenly gushed out of the opening, swilling rapidly down the lower slope to join the no less rancid waters of the swamp. I looked back, but in all that debris, black water and stench, no dead body came floating out; it must have been lodged in the narrow confines of the cave. Finally the flow stopped. I was sitting, trying to gather my breath with raw gulps of air, my heart tripping, my eyes flooding their own stream down my cheeks as if to imitate the cataract. My hands were raw, ribboned with blood from the wicked barbs of the brambles I had grabbed in my flight. I had to return to my camp as fast as possible to treat the wounds, to dry off, and to let my terror subside.

It was quicker walking back since I plied a straight line. My ardor for the lost gold was unabated, but at that moment I doubted very much whether I would enter any other underground chamber ever again. The shock of seeing that bloated thing—I can only imagine it was a corpse long-pickled in the vile swamp water—was too much. Bad enough merely coming across a dead body, but to have one chasing you through underground floodwaters, that was something far, far more frightening.

I arrived exhausted at the camp as the third day was beginning to fade. Maybe I was too old for this sort of thing now. It was at that moment my heart received another thunderbolt—my tent had been half torn down. There was a series of long gashes in the side which flapped like a canvas claw. When I struggled inside of what was left I found that the lamp was smashed and that the food had been ransacked. As I gathered what equipment was salvageable, I began to feel cold. A flurry of snow was starting to blow across the landscape and with it an icy breeze. The sleeping bag was shredded and unusable. The tent offered no shelter. I only had some food in tins and fresh water that had survived in the backpack. I decided my best option was to make for Innsmouth. Besides the walk keeping me warm, I was bound to find shelter of some sort in one of the old buildings. Tomorrow I would have to retrace my steps to the car if only to re-supply myself with provisions.

As I set out, the snow was easing off, but the wind had picked up and was making an eerie whispering sound as it sighed through the bullrushes in the surrounding darkness. I was grateful that my flashlight was holding out as it allowed me to move fairly briskly along without stumbling. My head down against the wind, I jogged, following the monotony of the rail ties as they appeared one after another in the light's beam. I almost failed to notice the buildings designating the outskirts of Innsmouth. In the near distance were those skeletal warehouses I'd seen earlier in the day, the wooden rafters poking at the sky, blackened, salt-weathered timbers like charred bones.

But it wasn't the sight of the decrepit edifices I noticed so much as the lights which moved inside, stray shafts penetrating cracks in the walls and glowing strangely behind dirt-dark windows. My precipitate pace had slowed almost to a stop as I contemplated the scene before me. The gnarly bookshop man's words, about there being people here, returned to haunt me and I shivered. My watch told me it was near midnight and the air felt very cold, but my gooseflesh was not altogether due to the temperature. It was the bizarre patterns of the lights that unnerved me, as though several people moved about within the otherwise darkened structure, in stealth and silence for some otherworldly reason.

I wiped snow flecks from my face and stood still, finally remembering to switch off the flashlight. In the intervening dark I heard odd sounds wafting up out of the wind's rustling amongst the undergrowth. It was those damned frogs again, and their amphibious croakings and barkings. As my eyes became accustomed to the night, I could see that the nearest building squatted in the margins of the marsh, or maybe the water level had risen to half-drown it. Either way, it sagged into the viscous water as though it were being reclaimed by a slow but omniscient liquid deity. I crouched low, feeling very exposed on the high ground and with those feverish yellow beams of light pointing in my direction. I heard my breathing as a loud rasp, a counterpoint to the incredible croaking of the frogs. The muscle of my heart was crushing, pounding the blood through seemingly inoperable valves and my ears rang with this inner cacophony. My hands were trembling as the two great doors of the warehouse opened slowly outwards, their lower halves submerged, making the movement ponderous.

Within were the waving streams of light, though I was unable to make out their source or their reason, except that they emanated from *beneath* the water that formed an undulating floor within the building. This I noted in one brief moment, before all my attention was focused on the forms which emerged through the water, some of them swimming, some wading in the shallows towards me. I think I screamed then, and I turned to make desperate flight from that unholy spot. But God, those awful moments were like an eon, a time in which my eyes could not block out the sight of the shapes, flopping, wading, barking as they inexorably massed in my direction. I realised that the body in the cave had been neither dead nor human, at least not altogether Homo sapiens. These monsters were some kind of batrachian animal or human deformities of the most terrible kind. Their skin the color of slate or dead seaweed, mottled and coarse; their eyes bulging, dead fish orbs; their stink the most obnoxious, sickening pall of saline decay, which grew more overpowering as the creatures came closer. By the beams of light, my final clear view of them left me with one lasting impression: that these abortions from hell were an insane remnant of the mutants that I had read about and so foolishly disbelieved in. A grim race of Deep Ones, sea beings who had mated with the inhabitants of Innsmouth. As I screamed and ran, the slapping of the demons' feet behind me, and their hideous croaking, kept pace. If I tripped and fell, I'd surely be done for.

Those slimy, crested, amphibious abominations who chased me, they were old, past their time. Their breath at my back smelt of it and the texture of their skins bore the suggestion of the final stages of gangrenous flesh. I shattered the night with the torment of terror from my tortured larynx. But death was not the final revolting consummation I rushed from, trying to find power in the railroad; feeling the stones bite beneath my pounding feet, my torso leaning into the wind, leaning out of arms' reach of the horde at my back.

No, death wasn't the ultimate horror. For, while I had crouched and watched the last living remnants of Innsmouth's abysmal evolution stream out of that shattered portal, I realised with a shock that all of the slippery, sub-human lifeforms—*all of them*—were *fe-male* . . . If I hadn't escaped that God-forsaken swamp . . . oh, Jesus, if those mephitic-ridden hags had ever taken me alive!

I wonder sometimes, worry even, for the next poor fool who will eventually enter that lost, forgotten town. He might not be so lucky as I. And Innsmouth might once more give birth, like a festering wound, like a sampling of hell, and all the slithering forms of night-mare will come out of the fogs and mists to bear witness to a new and darker age. . . .

# Daoine Domhain

## Peter Tremayne

How should I start? Do I have time to finish? Questions pour into my mind and remain unanswered, for they are unanswerable. But I must get something down on paper; at least make some attempt to warn people of the terrible dangers that lurk in the depths for mankind. How foolish and pitifully stupid a species we are, thinking that we are more intelligent than any other species, thinking that we are the "chosen" race. What arrogance—what ignorance! What infantile minds we have compared to . . . But I must begin as it began for me.

My name is Tom Hacket. My home is Rockport, Cape Ann, Massachusetts. My family history is fairly typical of this area of America. My great-grandparents arrived from County Cork, Ireland, to settle in Boston. My grandfather, Daniel, was born in Ireland but had come to America with his parents when only a few years old. Neither my father nor I ever had the desire to visit Ireland. We had no nostalgic yearnings, like some Irish-Americans, to visit the "old country." We felt ourselves to be purely American. But grandfather Daniel . . . well, he is the mystery in our family. And if I were to ascribe a start to these curious events then I would say that the beginning was my grandfather.

Daniel Hacket had joined the United States Navy and served as a lieutenant on a destroyer. Sometime in the early Spring of 1928, he went on leave to Ireland, leaving his wife and baby (my father) behind in Rockport. He never came back; nor did anyone in the family ever hear from him again. My grandmother, according to my father, always believed that he had been forcibly prevented from returning.

The US Navy took a more uncharitable line and posted him as a deserter. After grandmother died, my father expressed the opinion, contrary to his mother's faith in Daniel Hacket's fidelity, that his father had probably settled down with some colleen in Ireland under an assumed name. If the truth were known, he always felt bitter about the mysterious desertion of his father. However, the interesting thing was that my father never sold our house in Rockport; we never moved. And it was only towards the end of my father's life that he revealed the promise he made to grandmother. She had refused to move away or sell up in the belief that one day Daniel Hacket would attempt to get in touch if he were able. She had made my father promise to keep the old house in the family for as long as he was able.

No one asked that promise of me. I inherited the old wooden colonial-style house, which stood on the headland near Cape Ann, when my father died of cancer. My mother had been dead for some years and, as I had no brothers or sisters, the lonely old house was all mine. I was working as a reporter for the *Boston Herald* and the house was no longer of interest to me. So I turned it over to a real estate agent thinking to use the money to get a better apartment in Boston itself.

I can't recall now why I should have driven up to the house that particular week. Of course, I made several journeys to sort through three generations of family bric-a-brac which had to be cleared before any new owner set foot in the place. Maybe that was the reason. I know it was a Tuesday afternoon and I was sifting through a cardboard box of photographs when the door bell buzzed as someone pressed firmly against it.

The man who stood there was tall, lean with a crop of red-gold hair and a broad smile. I had the impression of handsomeness in spite of the fact that I noticed he wore an eye-patch over his right eye and, on closer inspection, his right shoulder seemed somewhat misshapen by a hump. When he spoke, it was obvious he was Irish. That did not make him stand out in itself for Boston is an Irish city. But he possessed a quaint old world charm and courtesy which was unusual. And his one good eye was a sharp, bright orb of green.

"Is this the Hacket house?" he asked.

I affirmed it was.

"My name is Cichol O'Driscoll. I'm from Baltimore."

"That's a long journey, Mr. O'Driscoll," I said politely, wondering what the man wanted. At the same time I was thinking that his first name, he pronounced it "Kik-ol," was an odd one for an Irishman. "Did you fly up this morning?"

He gave a wry chuckle.

"Ah, no. Not Baltimore, Maryland, sir. But the place which gave it its name—Baltimore in County Cork, Ireland."

It would have been churlish of me not to invite him in and offer him coffee, which he accepted.

"You are a Hacket, I presume?" he asked.

I introduced myself.

"Then I'm thinking that Mrs. Sheila Hacket no longer lives?"

"She was my grandmother. No. She has been dead these fifteen years past."

"And what of her son, Johnny?"

I shrugged.

"My father. He died three weeks ago."

"Ah, then I am sorry for your troubles."

"But what is this about?" I frowned.

242

"Little to tell," he said in that curious Irish way of speaking English. "As I said, I am from Baltimore which is a small fishing port in the south west of Ireland. A year ago I purchased an old croft on Inishdriscol, that is one of the islands that lie just off the coast, to the west from Baltimore. I am refurbishing it to make it into a holiday cottage. Well, one of my builders was pulling down a wall when he found some sort of secret cavity and in this cavity he came across an old oilskin pouch. Inside was a letter addressed to Mrs. Sheila Hacket at Rockport, Massachusetts, with a note that if she no longer lived then it should be handed to her son, Johnny. The letter was dated May the First, Nineteen Twenty-Eight."

I stared at the man in fascination.

"And you have come all this way to deliver a letter written sixty-three years ago?"

He chuckled, shaking his head.

"Not exactly. I have business in Boston. I own a small export business in Ireland. And so I thought I would kill two birds with one stone, as they say. It is not a long run up here from Boston. In fact, I had to pass by to get to Newburyport where I also have business. I thought it would be fascinating if I could deliver the letter if Sheila or Johnny Hacket survived after all these years. But I didn't really expect to find them. When the people in the local store told me the Hacket house still stood here, I was fairly surprised."

He hesitated and then drew out the package and deposited it on the table. It was as he said, an old oilskin pouch, not very bulky.

"Well, I guess you have a right to this."

He stood up abruptly, with a glance at his wristwatch.

"I must be off."

I was staring at the package.

"What's in it?" I asked.

"Just a letter," he replied.

"I mean, what's in the letter?"

His face momentarily contorted in anger.

"I haven't opened it. It's not addressed to me," he said in annoyance.

"I didn't mean it like that," I protested. "I didn't mean to sound insulting. It's just . . . well, don't you want to know what it is you have brought?"

He shook his head.

"The letter is clearly addressed. It is not for me to examine the contents."

"Then stay while I examine it," I invited, feeling it was the least I could do to repay the man for bringing it such a distance.

He shook his head.

"I'm on my way to Newburyport. I've a cousin there." He grinned again recovering his good humor. "It's a small world." He paused, then said: "I'll be passing this way next week on my way back to Boston. Purely out of curiosity, I would like to know whether the letter contained something of interest. Maybe it's part of some local history of our island Inishdriscol."

"What does that mean?"

"Driscoll's Island. The O'Driscolls were a powerful ruling clan in the area," he responded proudly.

In fact, I arranged to meet Cichol O'Driscoll the next week in Boston because I had to return there to work on the following Monday morning. I watched him walk off down the drive for presumably he had left his car in the roadway. I remember thinking that it was odd to come across such old world charm and courtesy. The man must have flown a couple of thousand miles and never once attempted to open the letter he had brought with him. I turned to where it lay on the kitchen table, picked it up and turned it over and over in my hands. It was only then that I suddenly realised the identity of the hand which had penned the address.

How stupid of me not to have realised before—but it is curious how slowly the mind can work at times. The date, the handwriting—which I had recently been looking at in the papers I had been sorting out—all pointed to the fact that here was a letter from my grandfather—Daniel Hacket.

With my hands suddenly shaky with excitement, I opened the oilskin and took out the yellowing envelope. Using a kitchen knife, I slit it open. I extracted several sheets of handwriting and laid them carefully on the flat surface of the table.

Inishdriscol,
near Baltimore,
Country Cork,
Ireland.
April 30, 1928.

Dearest Sheila,

If you read these words you may conclude that I am no longer part of this world. Courage, my Sheila, for you will need it if these words reach you for I will require you to make them known so that the world may be warned. You must tell the Navy Department that they were not destroyed, that they still exist, watching, waiting, ready to take over . . . they have been waiting for countless millennia and soon, soon their time will come.

Today is the feast of Beltaine here. Yes, ancient customs still survive in this corner of the world. This is the feast day sacred to Bile, the old god of death, and I must go down into the abyss to face him. I do not think that I shall survive. That is why I am writing to you in the hope that, one day, this will find its way into your hands so that you may know and warn the world. . . .

But first things first. Why did I come here? As you know, it was purely by chance. You will recall the extraordinary events at Innsmouth a few months ago? How agents of the Federal Government, working with the Navy Department, dynamited part of the old harbor? It was supposed to be a secret, but the fact of the destruction of the old seaport could not be kept from those who lived along the Massachusetts coast. In addition to that operation, I can tell you that my ship was one of several which were sent to depth-charge and torpedo the marine abyss just beyond Devil Reef. We were told it was merely some exercise, a war-game, but there was considerable scuttlebutt as to why the old harbor should be destroyed at the same time that the deeps were depth-charged. Some sailors conjured up visions of terrifying monsters which we were supposed to be destroying. There was talk of creatures—or beings who dwelt in the great depths—which had to be annihilated before they wiped out mankind. At the time, we officers treated these rumors and tales with humorous gusto.

When the operation was finished, and we returned to port, the officers and men who took part in the exercise were given an extraordinary four weeks' leave; extraordinary for it was unprecedented to my knowledge of the service. I now realise that it was done for a purpose—to stop the men from talking about that strange exercise. The idea being, I suppose, that when they returned they would have forgotten the event and there would be no further speculation about it.

Well, four weeks' leave was facing me. I had always wanted to see the place where I was born. Do you remember how you insisted that I go alone when it was discovered little Johnny had scarlet fever and, though out of danger, would not be able to make the trip to Ireland and you would not leave him? I was reluctant to go. Ah, would to God I had not done so. Would to God I had never set eyes on the coast of Ireland.

I took passage to Cork, landing at the attractive harbor of Cobh, and set out to Baltimore, where I had been born. The place is a small fishing port set in a wild and desolate country on the edge of the sea. It stands at the end of a remote road and attracts few visitors unless they have specific business there. The village clusters around an excellent harbor and on a rocky eminence above it is the O'Driscoll castle which, I was later told, has been in ruins since 1537. The only way to approach it is by a broad rock-cut stair. Incidentally, practically everyone in the town is called O'Driscoll for this was the heart of their clan lands. When the sun shines, the place has an extraordinary beauty. The harbor is frequently filled with fishing-boats and small sailing ships and there are many islands offshore.

On local advice I went up to the headland which they call the Beacon hereabouts. The road was narrow and passes between grey stone walls through open, stony country. From this headland there is a spectacular view of the islands. The locals call them "Carbery's

Hundred Isles." Opposite is the biggest, Sherkin Island, on which stands the ruins of another O'Driscoll Castle and those of a Franciscan friary, also destroyed in 1537. Beyond is Inis Cleire or Clear Island with its rising headland, Cape Clear, with yet another O'Driscoll castle called Dunanore, and four miles from the farthest tip of Cape Clear is the Fastnet Rock.

Everyone in the area speaks the Irish language, which has put me at a disadvantage and I now wish my parents had passed on their knowledge to me. All I have learnt is that Baltimore is merely an anglicisation of *Baile an Tigh Móir*—the town of the big house—and that some local people also call it Dún na Séad—the fort of jewels.

There was a certain hostility in the place, for it must be remembered that the War of Independence against England is not long past and that was followed with a bitter civil war which ended in 1923, only five years ago. Memories of that terrible time are still fresh in people's minds and color their attitude to strangers until they are able to judge whether the stranger means them harm or no.

Within a few days of arriving in Baltimore I found that I had not been born actually in the village but on one of the nearby islands called Inishdriscol, or Driscoll's Island. I soon persuaded a fisherman to take me there, it being three miles from Baltimore harbor. It is a large enough island with a small village at one end and a schoolhouse at the other with its overall shape resembling the letter "T".

I was able to hire a cottage close by the very one in which I had been born. The owners, Brennan told me, were away to America to seek their fortune. Brennan is the only one who speaks English on the island. He is a curious fellow combining local mayor, entrepreneur, head fisherman, counsellor . . . you name it and Brennan fits the role. Brennan is his first name, at least that is how I pronounce it, for he showed me the proper spelling of it which was written Bráonáin and the English of it is "sorrow." Naturally, he is also an O'Driscoll and, for the first time, I learnt the meaning of the name which is correctly spelt *O hEidersceoil* and means "intermediary." Names mean a great deal in this country. Our own name, Hacket, is—unfortunately—not well respected here for in 1631 two corsair galleys from Algiers sacked

Baltimore, killed many of the inhabitants and carried off two hundred to be sold as slaves in Africa. They were guided through the channels to the town by a man called Hacket, who was eventually caught and hung in the city of Cork. Ah, if only I had knowledge of this language, how interesting these arbitrary signs we use would become.

In lieu of any other companion to converse with I have been much thrown together with Brennan and he has been my guide and escort on the island. Indeed I found no close relatives although most people knew of my family and several claimed distant kinship. After a while I settled down to a life of lazy fishing and walking.

It was after I had been on the island a few days that two more visitors arrived, but only for a few hours stay on the island. Brennan told me that one was some representative of the English Government and the other was an official of the Irish Government. Apparently, during the War of Independence, a number of English soldiers and officials had disappeared, unknown casualties of the conflict. It seems that there had been a small military post on the island. A captain, a sergeant and four men. One night, the captain disappeared. It was assumed that he had been caught by the local guerrillas, taken away and shot. All investigations had proved fruitless in discovering exactly how he had met his end. No one on the island had talked. Nor had the guerrillas, many of whom were now members of the Irish Government, issued any information on the subject. Now, nine years after the disappearance, the English Government, in cooperation with the Irish Free State Government, were attempting to close the case.

I met the English official while out walking one morning and we fell into conversation about the problem.

"Trouble is," he said, "these damned natives are pretty close."

He blandly ignored the fact that I had been born on the island and could, therefore, be classed as one of the "damned natives."

"Nary a word can you get out of them. Damned code of silence, as bad as Sicilians."

"You think the local people killed this Captain . . . ?"

"Pfeiffer," he supplied. "If they didn't, I'm sure they know who did. Maybe it was a guerrilla unit from the mainland. There wasn't much activity on the islands during the war although there was a lot of fighting in West Cork. A lot of bad blood, too. Political differences run deep. Take these people now . . . they don't like the Irish Government official that I'm with."

"Why not?"

"He represents the Free State. This area was solidly Republican during the Civil War. They lost, and they hate the Free State Government. I suppose they won't tell us anything. Damned waste of time coming here."

I nodded in sympathy with his task.

"Well, if you give me your card, perhaps if I hear anything . . . any drop of gossip which might help . . . I could drop you a line. You never know. They might talk to me whereas they would not talk to you."

He smiled enthusiastically.

"That would be pretty sporting of you, lieutenant." (He pronounced it in the curious way that the English do as "left-tenant".)

"When did your man disappear?"

"Nine years ago. Actually, exactly nine years ago on April the Thirtieth." He paused. "You are staying at the pink-wash cottage near the point, aren't you?"

I confirmed I was.

"Curiously, that's where Captain Pfeiffer was billeted when he disappeared."

The officials left the island later that day and I raised the subject with Brennan. I had been a little arrogant in assuming that because I had been born on the island, and was of an old island family, that I would be trusted any more than the officials from Dublin and London. I was an American, a stranger, and they certainly would not divulge the hidden secrets of the island to me. Brennan was diplomatic in answering my questions but the result was the same. No one was going to talk about the fate of the captain.

A few days later, I had almost forgotten Pfeiffer. Brennan and I went out fishing. We were after sea trout, *breac,* as he called it. Brennan took me out in his skiff, at least I describe it as a skiff. He called it a *naomhóg,* a strange very light boat which was made of canvas, spread over a wooden frame and hardened by coatings of pitch and tar. Although frail, the craft was very manoeuvrable in the water and rode heavy seas with amazing dexterity. A mile or two from the island was a weird crooked rock which rose thirty or forty feet out of the sea. Brennan called it *camcarraig* and when I asked the meaning of the name he said it was simply "crooked rock." Brennan reckoned the sea trout ran by here and into Roaring Water Bay, close by. So we rowed to within a few yards of the pounding surf, crashing like slow thunder against the weed-veined rock, and cast our lines.

The fishing went well for some time and we hauled a catch that we could not be ashamed of.

Suddenly, I cannot remember exactly how it happened, a dark shadow seemed to pass over us. I looked up immediately expecting a cloud to have covered the sun. Yet it was still high and shining down, though it was as if there were no light coming from it. Nor were there any clouds in the sky to account for the phenomenon. I turned to Brennan and found him on his knees in the bow of the boat, crouching forward, his eyes staring at the sea. It were then that I observed that the water around us had turned black, the sort of angry green blackness of a brooding sea just before the outbreak of a storm, discolored by angry scudding clouds. Yet the sky was clear.

I felt the air, dank and chill, oppressive and damp against my body.

"What is it?" I demanded, my eyes searching for some explanation to the curious sensation.

Brennan had now grabbed at the oars and started to pull away from the crooked rock, back towards the distant island shore. His English had deserted him and he was rambling away in eloquent Irish and, despite his rowing, would now and then lift his hand to genuflect.

"Brennan," I cried, "calm down. What are you saying?"

After some while, when we were well away from the crooked rock, and the sun was warm again on our bodies and the sea was once more the reflected blue of the sky, Brennan apologised.

"We were too near the rock," he said. "There is an undercurrent there which is too strong for us."

I frowned. That was not how it had seemed to me at all. I told him so but he dismissed me.

"I was only fearful that we would be swept into the current," he said. "I merely offered up a little prayer."

I raised an eyebrow.

"It seemed a powerful long prayer," I observed.

He grinned.

"Long prayers are better heard than short ones."

I chuckled.

"And what was the prayer you said? In case I have need of it."

"I merely said, God between me and the Devil, nine times and nine times nine."

I was puzzled.

"Why nine? Wouldn't seven be a luckier number?"

He looked amazed at what he obviously thought was my appalling ignorance.

"Seven? Seven is an unlucky number in these parts. It is the number nine which is sacred. In ancient times the week consisted of nine nights and nine days. Didn't Cuchulainn have nine weapons, didn't King Loegaire, when setting out to arrest St. Patrick, order nine chariots to be joined together according to the tradition of the gods? Wasn't Queen Medb accompanied by nine chariots and . . ."

I held up my hand in pacification at his excited outburst.

"All right. I believe you." I smiled. "So the number nine is significant."

He paused and his sea-green eyes rested on mine for several seconds and then he shrugged.

That evening I went to Tomás O'Driscoll's croft which served as an inn, or rather a place where you could buy a drink and groceries from the mainland when they came in by the boat. The place is called a *sibin,* or shebeen, as it is pronounced in English, which signifies an unlicensed drinking house. Several of the old men of the island were gathered there and Brennan sat on a three legged stool by the chimney-corner, smoking his pipe. As I have said, everyone looked up to Brennan as the spokesman for the island and the old men were seated around him talking volubly in Irish. I wished I could understand what they were saying.

Two words kept being repeated in this conversation, however. *Daoine Domhain.* To my ears it sounded like "dayn'ya dow'an." Only when they noticed me did a silence fall on the company. I felt a strange uneasiness among them. Brennan was regarding me with a peculiar expression on his face which held a note of . . . well, it took me some time before I reasoned it . . . of sadness in it.

I offered to buy drinks for the company but Brennan shook his head.

"Have a drink on me and welcome," he said. "It's is not for the likes of you to buy drinks for the likes of us."

They seemed to behave strangely to me. I cannot put my finger on it for they were not unfriendly, nor did they stint in hospitality, yet there was something odd—as if they were regarding me as a curiosity, watching and waiting . . . yet for what?

I returned back to the croft early that evening and noted that the wind was blowing up from the south, across *camcarraig* and towards the headland on which the handful of cottages on the island clung precariously. Oddly, above the noise of the blustering wind, stirring the black, angry swells which boomed into Roaring Water Bay and smacked against the granite fortresses of the islands, I heard a whistling sound which seemed less like the noise of the wind and more like the lonely cry of some outcast animal, wailing in its isolation. So strong did the noise seem that I went to the door and stood listening to it just in case it was some animal's distress cry. But eventually the noise was lost in the howl of the wind from the sea.

There is some ancient proverb, I forget how it goes. Something about "out of the mouths of babes and sucklings . . ." I was reminded of that two days later when I happened to be fishing from the high point beyond my cottage, where the seas move restlessly towards the land from the *camcarraig*. It was a lazy day and the fish were not in a mood for taking the bait. Nonetheless I was content, relaxing, almost half asleep.

I was not aware of any presence until I heard a voice close to my ear say something in Irish. I blinked my eyes and turned to see a young girl of about nine years old, with amazing red-gold hair, which tumbled around her shoulders. She was an extraordinarily attractive child, with eyes of such a bright green color they seemed unreal. She was staring at me solemnly. Her feet were bare and her dress was stained and torn, but she had a quiet dignity which sat oddly on the appearance of terrible poverty. Again she repeated her question.

I shook my head and replied in English, feeling stupid.

"Ah, it is a stranger you are."

"Do you speak English?" I asked in amazement, having accepted Brennan as the only English-speaker on the island.

She did not answer my superfluous question for it was obvious she understood the language.

"The sea is brooding today," she said, nodding at the dark seas around *camcarraig*. "Surely the *Daoine Domhain* are angry. Their song was to be heard last night."

"Dayn'ya dow'an?" I asked, trying to approximate the sounds of the words. It was the same expression which had been used in the shebeen a few nights ago. "What is that?"

"Musha, but they are the Fomorii, the dwellers beneath the sea. They were the evil-ones who dwelt in Ireland long before the coming of the Gael. Always they have battled for our souls, sometimes succeeding, sometimes failing. They are the terrible people . . . they have but a single eye and a single hand and a single foot. They are the terrible ones . . . the Deep Ones—the *Daoine Domhain*."

I smiled broadly at this folklore solemnly proclaimed by this young girl.

She caught my smile and frowned. Her face was suddenly serious.

"God between us and all evil, stranger, but it is not good to smile at the name of the Deep Ones."

I assured her that I was not smiling at them. I asked her what her name was but she would not tell me. She turned to me and I saw an abrupt change in her expression. Abruptly a sadness grew in her eyes, and she turned and ran away. That left me disturbed. I wondered who her mother was because I felt I ought to go to the child's parents in case they thought I had deliberately scared her. I should explain that I meant the child no harm in case she was afraid of something I had said or of some expression on my face.

I was packing my rods when Brennan came by. I greeted him, and my first question was about the child. He looked mighty puzzled and said that there was no child on the island who could speak English. When he perceived that I was annoyed because he doubted my word, he tried to placate me by saying that if I had seen such a child, then it must have come from another island or the mainland and was visiting.

He offered to walk back with me to my cottage and on the way I asked him: "Who exactly were the Fomorii?"

For a moment he looked disconcerted.

"My, but you are the one for picking up the ancient tales," was his comment.

"Well?" I prompted, as it seemed he was going to say nothing further on the subject.

He shrugged.

"They are just an ancient legend, that's all."

I was a little exasperated and he saw it for he then continued: "The name means the dwellers under the sea. They were a violent and misshapen people who represented the evil gods in ancient times. They were led by Balor of the Evil Eye and others of their race such as Morc and Cichol but their power on land was broken at the great battle at Magh Tuireadh when they suffered defeat by the Tuatha Dé Danaan, the gods of goodness."

"Is that all?" I asked, disappointed at the tale.

Brennan raised a shoulder in an eloquent gesture.

"Is it not enough?" he asked good humoredly.

"Why are they called the Deep Ones?" I pressed.

A frown passed across his brow.

"Who told you that?" his voice was waspish.

"Were you not talking about the Deep Ones in the shebeen the other night? Dayn'ya Do'wan. Isn't that the Irish for Deep Ones? And why should you be talking of ancient legends?"

He seemed to force a smile.

"You have the right of it," he conceded. "We talk of ancient legends because they are part of us, of our heritage and our culture. And we call the Fomorii by this name because they dwell in the great deeps of the sea. No mystery in that."

I nodded towards *camcarraig.*

"And they are supposed to dwell near that rock?"

He hesitated, then said indifferently, "So legend goes. But a man like yourself does not want to dwell on our ancient tales and legends."

It was as if he had excluded me from my ancestry, ignored the fact that I had been born on the island.

Then he would talk no more either about the girl or the Deep Ones—the Fomorii—or the *Daoine Domhain.*

Two nights later as I was eating my supper in the main room of the tiny two roomed cottage, I felt a draught upon my face and glanced up. I was astonished, for there standing with her back to the door was the little girl. The first thought that filled my mind was how quietly she must have entered not to disturb me. Only the soft draught from the door, supposedly opening and shutting, had alerted me. Then I realised that it was curious for a young child to be out so late and visiting the cottage of a stranger. I knew the islanders were trusting people but this trust bordered on irresponsibility.

She was staring at me with the same sadness that I had seen in her eyes when she had left me on the cliff top.

"What is it?" I demanded. "Why are you here and who are you?"

I recalled Brennan had claimed there was no such girl on the island. But this was no apparition.

"You have been chosen," she whispered softly. "Beware the feast of the Fires of Bíle, god of death. The intermediary will come for you then and take you to them. They are awaiting; nine years will have passed at the next feast. They wait every nine years for reparation. So be warned. You are the next chosen one."

My mouth opened in astonishment, not so much at what the girl was saying but at the words and phraseology which she used, for it was surely well beyond the ability of a nine-year-old to speak thus.

Abruptly as she came she went, turning, opening the door and running out into the dusk of the evening. I hastened to the door and peered into the gloom. There was no one within sight.

I have strong nerves, as well you know, but I felt a curious feeling of apprehension welling in me.

That night I was awakened by an odd wailing sound. At first I thought it was the noise of the wind across the mountain, whistling and calling, rising and falling. But then I realised it was not. It was surely some animal, lonely and outcast. The cry of a wolf, perhaps? But this was a bare rock of an island and surely no wolves could survive here? It went on for some time before it died away and I finally settled back to sleep.

The next morning I called by Tomás O'Driscoll's place and found Brennan, as usual, seated in the little bar-room. Once again he refused to accept a drink from me and instead offered me a glass of whiskey.

"Brennan," I said, my mind filled with the visit of the young child, "you are frugal with the truth because there is a little, red-haired girl living on this island. She can speak English."

His face whitened a little and he shook his head violently and demanded to know why I asked.

I told him and his face was ghastly. He genuflected and muttered something in Irish whereupon Tomás behind the bar replied sharply to him. Brennan seemed to relax and nodded, obviously in agreement at what Tomás had said.

"What's going on here?" I asked harshly. "I insist that you tell me."

Brennan glanced about as if seeking some avenue of escape.

I reached forward and grabbed him angrily by the shoulder.

"No need for hurt," he whined.

"Then tell me," I insisted firmly.

"She's just a tinker girl. She and her family often come to the island to lift the salmon from the rock pool at the north end of the island. They must be there now. I swear I didn't know the truth of it.

But that's who she is. Tinkers are not good people to be knowing. They say all manner of strange things and claim they have the second sight. I wouldn't be trusting them."

He looked down at his glass and would say no more.

All at once I had a firm desire to quit this island and these strange people with their weird superstitions and folk ways. I might have been born on the island but they were no longer my people, no longer part of me. I was an American and in America lay reality.

"Can I get a boat to the mainland, to Baltimore today, Brennan?" I asked.

He raised his eyes to mine and smiled sadly.

"Not today nor tomorrow, Mr. Hacket," he replied softly.

"Why so?"

"Because this evening is May Day Eve. It's one of our four main holidays."

I was a little surprised.

"Do you celebrate Labor Day?"

Brennan shook his head.

"Oh, no. May Day and the evening before it is an ancient feastday in the old Celtic calendar stretching back before the coming of Christianity. We call it Bealtaine—the time of the Fires of Bíle, one of the ancient gods."

I felt suddenly very cold, recalling the words of the tinker child.

"Are you saying that tonight is the feast of the god of death?"

Brennan made an affirmative gesture.

The girl had warned me of the feast of the Fires of Bíle when some intermediary would come for me and take me to . . . to them? Who were "them"? The Deep Ones, of course. The terrible Fomorii who dwelt beneath the seas.

I frowned at my thoughts. What was I doing? Was I accepting their legends and folklore? But I had been born on the island. It was my reality also, my legends and my folklore as much as it was their own. And was I suddenly accepting the girl's second sight without question? Was I believing that she had come to warn me . . . about what? I must be going mad.

I stood there shaking my head in bewilderment.

I *was* going mad, even to credit anything so ridiculous.

"Have a drink, Mr. Hacket," Brennan was saying. "Then you will be as right as ninepence."

I stared at him for a moment. His words, an expression I had frequently heard in the area, triggered off a memory.

"Nine," I said slowly. "Nine."

Brennan frowned at me.

But suddenly I had become like a man possessed. Nine years ago to this day had Captain Pfeiffer disappeared from the very same cottage in which I was staying. The girl had said something about them waiting every nine years for reparation. Nine was the mystical number of the ancient Celts. The week was counted by nine nights and nine days and three weeks, the root number of nine, gave twenty-seven nights which was the unit of the month, related to the twenty-seven constellations of the lunar zodiac. Nine, nine, *nine . . . !* The number hammered into my mind.

Was I going crazy?

What was I saying? That every ninth year these people made some sacrifice to ancient pagan gods whom they believed dwelt in the depths of the sea—the *Daoine Domhain*—the Deep Ones? That the English army captain, Pfeiffer, had been so sacrificed nine years before, nine years ago on this very night?

I found Brennan looking at me sympathetically.

"Don't worry, Mr. Hacket," he said softly. "There is no joy in that. It does no good to question what cannot be understood."

"When can I get a boat to the mainland?"

"After the feast is done." He was apologetic but firm.

I turned and left the shebeen and began to walk towards the point.

Brennan followed me to the door for he called after me.

"There's no fear in it. I'll come along for you tonight. Tonight."

I turned and strode through the village street and made my way to the north end of the island. I was determined to find the tinker child and demand some explanation. It was not a big place and eventually I came across a collection of dirty, rough-patched tents grouped in front of a smouldering turf fire at which a woman of in-discernible age was turning a large fish on a spit. There seemed no one else about.

I climbed down the rocks to get to the encampment which was sited on the beach; a fairly large strip of sand.

The woman, brown faced and weather beaten, clearly someone used to the outdoor life, watched me coming with narrowed eyes. There was suspicion on her features. She greeted me at first in Irish but when I returned the reply in English she smiled, her shoulders relaxed and she returned the greeting in kind.

"A grand day, sir. Are you staying on the island for the fishing then?"

"I am," I replied.

"Ah. By your voice you would be American."

I confirmed that I was. I was looking about for some sign of the girl but there seemed no one but the woman, who, now I came to observe her more closely, resembled the child with her mass of red hair.

"My man is fishing," the woman said, catching my wondering gaze.

"Ah," I said in noncommittal tone. "And do you have a child?"

"My girl, Sheena, sir."

The suspicion was back in her eyes.

"I thought I saw her a while ago," I said.

The woman shrugged.

"That you may."

"Is it right that you have the gift of second sight?" I demanded abruptly.

The woman looked taken aback and studied me for several long seconds before replying.

"Some of us have. Is it a fortune that you are wanting?"

I nodded.

"I'll be charging a shilling."

I reached in my pocket and handed over the coin which the woman took with alacrity.

"Is it your palm you wish read or shall I see what the tea-leaves say?"

I was about to reply when the flap of the tent moved and there stood the child. She regarded me with her large solemn, sad eyes and seemed to let out a sigh.

"He is the chosen one, mother. He has already been warned," she said softly.

The woman stared from me to the child and back again. Her face was suddenly white and she threw the coin back at me as if it had suddenly burnt her hands.

"Away from here, mister." Her voice was sharp.

"But . . ."

"Have you no ears to hear with? Did you not hear what Sheena said? She is gifted with the second sight. She can see beyond the un-seeable. If you value your soul, man, heed her warning. Now be away." She glanced about her, her face showing that she was badly frightened. "Sheena, find your father . . . we must leave this place now."

Slowly I retreated, shaking my head in wonder. At least I had proved to myself that I was not hallucinating. The girl, Sheena, ex-isted. A tinker girl with, supposedly, the gift of second sight, who gave me a warning . . .

I walked up to the point above my cottage and sat myself on a rock gazing out across the dark brooding sea towards *camcarraig*. What nightmare world had I landed in? Was I losing all sense of rea-son? Was I accepting shadows for reality? Did I really believe that the girl had some strange power to foresee evil and warn me about it? I was the chosen one. Chosen for what purpose? And what had really happened to Captain Pfeiffer nine years ago, nine years this very night?

I shivered slightly.

The sea was a mass of restless blackness and far away, as if from the direction of *camcarraig*, I heard the strange cry which had dis-turbed my slumber on the previous night; a soft, whistling wail of a soul in torment.

It was while I sat there listening that I recalled the words of the child.

"You have been chosen. Beware the feast of the Fires of Bíle, god of death. The intermediary will come for you then and take you to them. They are waiting. Nine years will have passed at the next feast. They wait every nine years for reparation. So be warned. You are the next chosen."

Abruptly I heard Brennan calling to me from the doorway of the shebeen.

"There's no fear in it. I'll come along for you tonight."

Brennan O'Driscoll. O'Driscoll who had explained the meaning of the name O hEidersceoil—*intermediary!*

Brennan was the one who would take me to the Deep Ones!

I rose then and began to scour the island in search of a boat, any boat, any form of floating transportation to get me away from this crazy nightmare. But there was none. I was alone, isolated and imprisoned. Even the tinkers had apparently departed. I was left alone with the islanders.

Left alone to my fate.

That was this afternoon, my darling Sheila. Now it is dusk and I am writing this by the light of the storm lantern on the table in the tiny cottage. Soon Brennan O'Driscoll will come for me. Soon I shall know if I am truly crazy or whether there is some reality in this nightmare. It is my intention to take these pages and wrap them in my old oilskin pouch and hide them behind a loose brick in the chimney breast of this cottage. In the hope that, should anything happen to me this evening, then, God willing, this letter will eventually reach your beloved hands or those of young Johnny, who may one day grow to manhood and come seeking word of his unfortunate father. Soon it will be dark and soon Brennan will come . . . The intermediary; intermediary between me and what? What is it waiting out there in the deep? Why do they demand reparation every nine years and reparation for what? God help me in my futility. Daniel Hacket.


Thus was the writing on the browning pages ended as if hurriedly. I sat for a while staring at those strange words and shaking my head in disbelief. What madness had seized my grandfather to write such a curious fantasy?

The wind was getting up and I could hear the seas roaring and crashing at the foot of the point where our house stood, gazing eastward towards the brooding Atlantic. The weather was dark and bleak for a late April day and I turned to switch on the light.

That something had disarranged my grandfather's mind was obvious. Had he remained living on the island? Surely not, for the US Navy's enquiries at the time would have discovered him. But if he had disappeared, why hadn't the natives of this island, Inishdriscol, reported he was missing? Had he thrown himself into the sea while his mind had been so unbalanced and drowned, or what had taken place . . . ? The questions flooded my thoughts.

I suddenly realised that he had written the curious document, which so clearly demonstrated his warped mental condition, exactly sixty-three years ago this very night. It was April 30. A childish voice echoed in my mind, reciting the nine times table—seven nines are sixty-three!

I shivered slightly and went to the window to gaze out at the blackness of the Atlantic spread before me. I could see the winking light from the point further down the coast which marked the passage to Innsmouth, and far out to sea I could just make out the pulsating warning sweep of the lighthouse at Devil Reef beyond which was sited one of the great deeps of the Atlantic. Deeps. The Deep Ones. What nonsense was that?

As I stood there, my mind in a whirl, staring out in the darkness beyond the cliff edge, I heard soft whistling, like a curious wind. It rose and fell with regular resonance like the call of some lonely outcast animal. It whistled and echoed across the sea with an uncanniness which caused me to shiver.

I pulled the curtains to and turned back into the room.

Well, the old world Irishman had surely brought me an intriguing story. No wonder my grandfather had never returned. For some weird reason he had gone insane on that far distant Irish island and perhaps no one now would know the reason why.

I would have much to ask Cichol O'Driscoll when I saw him. Perhaps he could set forth an investigation when he returned to Baltimore in order to find out how my grandfather had died and why no one had notified my grandmother of either his death or his disappearance.

I frowned at some hidden memory and turned back to my grandfather's manuscript.

"They were a violent misshapen people who represented the evil gods in ancient Ireland. They were led by Balor of the Evil Eye and others of the race such as Morc and Cichol. . . ."

*Cichol!* With his one eye and hump-shaped back!

I could not suppress the shiver which tingled against my spine.

I tried to force a smile of cynicism.

Cichol O'Driscoll. O'Driscoll—the intermediary. April 30—the eve of the Bealtaine, the feast of the Fires of Bíle. Seven times nine is sixty-three . . .

*Daoine Domhain.* The Deep Ones. "They wait every nine years for reparation."

Then I knew that I would be seeing Cichol O'Driscoll again. Very soon.

Outside the wind was rising from the mysterious restless Atlantic swell, keening like a soul in torment. And through the wind came the whistling call of some lonely outcast animal.

# A Quarter to Three

## Kim Newman

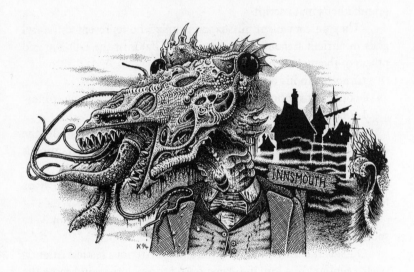

Sometimes the nights get to you, right? When there's no-one pushing coins into it, the juke plays Peggy Lee over and over again. "Fever." The finger-click backing track gets into your skull. Like a heartbeat, you've got it in there for the rest of your life. And in the off-season, which when you're talking about the 'Mouth is—let's face it—all year round, sometimes you go from midnight 'til dawn with no takers at all. Who can blame them: we serve paint stripper *au lait* and reinforced concrete crullers. When I first took the graveyard shift at Cap'n Cod's 24 Hour Diner, I actually liked the idea of being paid (just) to stay up all night with no hassles. Maybe I'd get to finish *Moby Dick* before Professor Whipple could flunk me. Anyway, that's not the way it worked out.

Two o'clock and not a human face in sight. And in late November, the beachfront picture window rattles in the slightest breeze. The waves were shattered noisily on the damn useless shingles. The 'Mouth isn't a tourist spot, it's a town-sized morgue that smells of fish. All I'd got for company was a giant cardboard cutout of the Cap'n, giving a scaly salute and a salty smile. He hasn't got much of a face left, because he used to stand outside and get a good sloshing whenever the surf was up. I don't know who he was in the first place—the current owner is a pop-eyed lardo called Murray Something who pays in smelly cash—but now he's just a cutout ghost. I'd talk to *him* only I'd be worried that some night he'd talk right back.

It's a theme diner, just like all the others up and down the coast. Nets on the ceiling, framed dead fish on the walls, Formica on the tables, and more sand on the floor than along the seashore. And it's got a gurgling coffee machine that spits out the foulest brew you've ever tasted, and an array of food under glass that you'd swear doesn't change from one month to the next. I was stuck in a groove again, like Peggy if I forget to nudge the juke in the middle of that verse about Pocahontas. It's that damn chapter "The Whiteness of the Whale." I always trip over it, and it's supposed to be the heart of the book.

I didn't notice her until the music changed. Debbie Reynolds, singing "It Must Have Been Moonglow." Jesus. She must have come in during one of my twenty-minute "blinks." She was sitting up against the wall, by the juke, examining the counter. Young, maybe pretty, a few strands of blonde hair creeping out from under her scarf, and wearing a coat not designed for a pregnant woman. It had a belt that she probably couldn't fasten. I'm in Eng. Lit. at MU, not pre-med, but I judged that she was just about ready to drop the kid. Maybe quints.

"Can I help you, Ma'am?" I asked. Murray likes me to call the mugs "sir" and "ma'am" not "buddy" and "doll" or "asshole" and "drudge." It's the only instruction he ever dished out.

She looked at me—big hazel eyes with too much red in them—but didn't say anything. She looked tired, which isn't surprising since it was the middle of the night and she was about to give birth to the Incredible Bulk.

"Coffee?" I suggested. "If you're looking for a way to end it all, you could do worse. Cheaper than strychnine. Maybe you want ice cream and pickles?"

"That's crap," she said, and I realised that she really was young. If she weren't pregnant, I'd have accused her of being up after her bedtime. Sixteen or seventeen, I guessed. Cheerleader-pretty, but with a few lines in there to show she had more to worry about than who's dating Buddy-Bob Fullback these days or how she'll get through the Home Ec. quiz next Friday. "About cravings, that's crap. You don't want to eat weird stuff. Me, I don't want to eat at all, ever again. But you gotta, or you disintegrate. It's like having a tapeworm. You eat as much as you can, but you still go hungry. The fo-etus gets all the goodies."

Fo-etus. That was how she pronounced it. I kind of liked the sound of it.

"Well, what does your fo-etus fancy this morning?"

"A cheeseburger."

"This is a fish place, Ma'am. No burgers. I can melt some cheese on a fishcake and give it to you in a bap."

"Sounds like shit. I'll have one, for the mutant . . ."

Julie London was on now, "Cry Me a River." "Cryyyyy me a river, cuhry me a river, I cried a reever over you." That has one of the best rhymes in the English language in it; "plebian" with "through with me an' . . . now you say you're lonely . . ."

I slapped the frozen cake on the hotplate and dug out some not-too-senile cheese. We don't stock the kind that's better if it's got mold on it.

"Have you got liquor?"

"Have you got ID?"

"Shit, how come you can get knocked up five years before you can have a drink in this state?"

The ice in the cake popped and hissed. Julie sounded broken-hearted in the background. It must be a tough life.

"I don't make the rules."

"I won't get drunk. The fo-etus will."

"He's underage too, Ma'am."

"It's an it. They did tests."

"Pardon?"

"Ginger ale . . ."

"Fine."

". . . and put a shot of something in it."

I gave in and dug out the scotch. Not much call for it. The high-lander on the label had faded, a yellowing dribble down his face turning him leprous. I splashed the bottom of a glass, then added a full measure of soft drink. She had it down quickly and ordered another. I saw to it and flipped the cake over. I wish I could say it smelled appetising.

"I'm not married," she said. "I had to leave school. There goes my shot at college. Probably my only chance to get out of the 'Mouth. Oh well, that's another life on the rocks. You must get a lot of that."

"Not really. I don't get much of anyone in here. I think the Cap'n will be dropping the 24 Hour service next year. All his old customers drowned or something. It's entropy. Everything's winding down. You have to expect it."

I melted the cheese and handed her her cheesefish bap. She didn't seem interested in it. I noticed she had a pile of quarters stacked in a little tower on the bar. She was feeding the juke regularly.

"This is my song," she said. Rosemary Clooney, "You Took Advantage of Me." "The bastard certainly did."

She was a talker, I'd spotted that early. After midnight, you only get talkers and brooders. I didn't really have to say anything, but there'd be pauses if I didn't fill in the gaps.

"Your boyfriend?"

"Yeah. Fuckin' amphibian. He's supposed to be here. I'm meeting him."

"What'll happen?"

"Who knows. Some folks ain't human."

She pushed her plate around and prodded the bap. I had to agree with her. I wouldn't have eaten it, either. Murray never asked me if I could cook.

"Look, the lights . . ." She meant the sea lights. It's a localised phenomenon in the 'Mouth. A greenish glow just out beyond the shallows. Everyone freaks first time they see it. "He'll be here soon. Another ginger ale plus."

I gave her one. She took it slower. Captain Ahab looked insanely up from the broken-spined paperback on the counter, obsessed with his white whale. Crazy bastard. I'd love to see him on a talk show with one of those Greenpeace activists.

There was someone coming up from the beach. She shifted on her stool, uncomfortably keeping her pregnancy away from the rim of the counter. She didn't seem interested one way or the other. "It's him."

"He'll be wet."

"Yeah. That he will."

"It don't matter. I don't do the mopping up. That's the kid who gets the daytime haul."

It was Sinatra now. The main man. "It's a quarter to three . . ."

"No-one in the place except you and me," I said, over the Chairman of the Board. Her smile was cracked, lopsided, greenish. She had plaque.

The door was pushed inward, and in he waddled. As you might expect, he didn't look like much. It took him a long time to get across the diner, and he wasn't breathing easily. He moved a bit like Charles Laughton as Quasimodo, dragging wetly. It was easy to see what she had seen in him; it left a thin damp trail between his scuffed footprints. By the time he got to the counter, she had finished her drink.

He got up onto a stool with difficulty, his wet, leather-linked fingers scrabbling for a grip on the edge of the bar. The skin over his cheeks and neck puffed in and out as he tried to smile at her.

". . . could tell you a lot," sung Frankie, "but you've got to be true to your code . . ." She put her glass down, and looked me in the eye, smiling. "Make it one for my baby, and one more for the *toad*."

# The Tomb of Priscus

## Brian Mooney

ather Shea! It's that Professor Calloway!"

My housekeeper, a widow from County Offaly, offered the telephone reluctantly, as if afraid that its touch would taint. Mrs. Byrne is a good soul but she disapproves of Calloway. She believes that he tempts me into bad ways.

"Roderick." Calloway's voice was abrupt. "Come on over. I've something to show you." He hung up before I could answer.

During the course of—and, it must be said, because of—my long friendship with Professor Reuben Calloway, I have been involved in some bizarre and frightening experiences. The end result of this telephone call was to be the fearful tragedy at Lower Benhoe.

The morning was fine and held portent of a good summer. I was at a loose end and the drive to Southdown University would be a pleasant one, so I shrugged at Mrs. Byrne and went to find my jacket.

The roads were fairly clear and the journey did not take long. Leaving my shoddy Land Rover in the visitors' car park, I walked through the main quadrangle, warm in the sunshine and bordered by clumps of daffodils and other spring flowers, into the mellow brick building graced with high-mullioned windows and then along a wood-panelled hall until I came to my friend's study. I gave a brief knock and entered.

As always, the room was a clutter of papers, books and periodicals heaped haphazardly over the furniture and floor. On a time-worn antique side table rested a black Royal typewriter, itself almost a museum piece, with a partly-completed sheet of A4 Bond jutting from its platen. The windows were tightly sealed, the central heating turned high and the place reeked with the stale smell of Turkish tobacco. Calloway glanced up from a notebook and laid aside the fountain pen with which he had been making an entry.

He removed the gold-rimmed half-spectacles which he wore for reading and writing. "Ah, Roderick, there you are," he grunted as if I had only been into the next-door office for a few moments rather than not having seen him for several months. "I thought you might appreciate an odd coincidence."

We have been friends for many years, so I did not take offence at Calloway's manner. Moving a pile of dog-eared essays from a chair, I sat opposite him and waited.

After making several additional notations in his book, he said, "Have a look at that while I pour you a coffee." He flicked a sepia-tinted photograph across his desk to me. "Strong, black, no sugar, right?"

"Fine, thanks." I took one brief look at the photograph and could feel my lip curling with distaste. "It's ... profane," I said, casting it down.

"Yes, yes," muttered Calloway, his tone impatient. "By our Christian standards, perhaps. But suspend prejudice, Roderick, suspend prejudice and take another look." He placed a cup at my elbow.

I retrieved the print and studied it. It was old and creased, over-exposed and badly faded, and yet somehow it remained powerfully disturbing. It showed a crucifixion. But not the holy one.

Calloway handed me a large magnifying glass. "This might help."

The crucifix itself was not the symbolic cross of Christianity but rather the true T-form favored by the Romans. There was a bulky thing hanging from the horizontal bar, gross head slumped upon a barrel chest. I say *thing* deliberately; the age and condition of the photograph made the nature of the victim uncertain, there being both human and non-human aspects to that tortured form. After careful scrutiny of the head, the angle of which almost hid the features, I concluded that it was vaguely amphibian and I said so.

"It's statuary, I take it," was my comment. "Some piece of Satanic impedimenta?"

Calloway shook his head as he lit a Turkish cigarette. "Far from it," he said. "That photograph was taken from the life. Or, to be more accurate, from the death."

"Some unfortunate animal sacrificed at a Black Mass, then?"

"No," replied Calloway. "You see there an Innsmouth hybrid. The photograph came from the archives of the American FBI. I take it that you've never heard of Innsmouth?"

When I shook my head he continued, "Little wonder, really. You won't find it listed in any tourist guide, nor in any atlas. It's neither a place nor a history that the American authorities have any pride in. In fact, they did their best to wipe a chunk of Innsmouth from the map, although they were not entirely successful."

He stubbed out his cigarette and took a sip of coffee. "Innsmouth is a small port in Massachusetts. The story, as slowly pieced together by interested parties, is this: many years ago, certainly long before the American civil war, Innsmouth seafarers began to trade with a peculiar race of Pacific islanders. It transpired that these islanders had been interbreeding with . . . something else, something inhuman, something from the ocean depths."

"It's supposed to be impossible for different species to interbreed," I interrupted.

Calloway held up a big hand to still my protest. "Perhaps in the normal course of nature," he said. "But we are not talking of normality here. Anyway, in time some of the Innsmouth people located an Atlantic colony of these sea things and began to interbreed in their turn. The resulting hybrids, at birth, were human, or near enough to human as to make no difference. However, around about middle life they would begin to change, firstly into what you see in that photograph . . . and then into something much worse."

Calloway hauled himself from his large swivel chair and waddled to the window, to stand staring out across the sunlit campus. "In the past, Roderick, you have heard me allude to the so-called Ancient Ones." He turned, pointing to the photograph. "Beings such as the Innsmouth creatures are worshippers and servants of those terrible old gods. I won't tell you of their rituals other than to say that they are vile beyond imagination."

He returned to his desk, reaching for his cigarette case. "Sometime in the late twenties, the Federal authorities got wind of what was happening at Innsmouth and agents were despatched to deal with the situation. They were ruthless but not quite thorough. Many Innsmouth dwellers escaped.

"A number of them went into the sea, an environment to which the physical change particularly suited them. Others were not fully metamorphosed and the sea was therefore effectively barred to them as sanctuary. Some sought refuge inland. The thing in the picture was caught by a band of farmers, who held a lynching party. The Innsmouth people were not popular with their near neighbors."

"Lynching is wicked in any circumstances," I said. "But crucifixion . . . why, that's even more barbaric than hanging or shooting."

"For all that they were living in the twentieth century, the people in that part of Massachusetts were a very superstitious lot," Calloway said. "The area had been recognised as a hotbed of witchcraft and black magic for very many years. A lot of locals had a peasant wisdom about how to deal with the abnormal. I think that the lynch mob guessed crucifixion would be far more efficacious than hanging. And after the picture was taken, the corpse was incinerated.

"The intention was to ensure complete destruction. There was no attempt to conceal the killing. The farmers were quite open with the federals about what had happened and handed over the photograph without quibble. The press got wind of it, but unlike the authorities they got short shrift from the lynchers. New Englanders tend to be close-mouthed, even today; back then the preponderance of strange events on their homeground tended to reinforce rather than relax their natural reticence.

"That photograph is the sole remaining evidence and it exists only because somebody filched it from the records before they were destroyed as part of a general cover-up. It was sent to me by an American colleague who knows of my interest in such matters."

"I assume that the authorities did nothing about the lynching?" I asked.

Calloway shook his head, fleshy jowls wobbling. "Why should they? The locals had only done what the government was bent on doing—a little more brutally, perhaps, but to the same end. Well, Roderick, you must be wondering what all this is leading to?"

I nodded. "You mentioned a coincidence," I reminded him.

With a smug grin, Calloway pushed three more photographs towards me. This time they were colored Polaroid prints.

The first was of a low stone portal, deep set into what looked like an earthen tunnel. The camera, probably a simple one, had been held some distance from the doorway, and while I could make out that there were vague shapes upon the jambs and indistinct marks upon the lintel, even with the magnifying-glass they were not clear.

The second and third Polaroids showed the opposing jambs. Each had an identical relief carving, depicting a crucifixion very similar to that shown in the American photograph. In both carvings, something undoubtedly batrachian was portrayed. Bulging eyes stared straight forward, great loose mouths twisted in sneering hatred.

"I'm hooked," I said. "Tell me more."

"These creatures, these 'Deep Ones' as they have sometimes been called, are incredibly ancient," said Calloway. "There is evidence that throughout history various races have had some contact with them. Sumerian and first dynasty Egyptian priests certainly knew of them, as did the Chinese of the Hsai and Shang dynasties."

"But you're talking of periods of—what?—between five and six thousand years ago!"

Calloway shrugged. "I have seen artifacts which suggest that our palaeolithic ancestors knew of the Deep Ones. They could well ante-date mankind."

He went to light another cigarette and with a muttered impreca-tion hurled an empty matchbox at an already overflowing waste-bas-ket. There was a pause while he scrabbled through desk drawers. At last he found a fresh box and relaxed. "Generally, Roderick, these be-ings have shunned the human race, not through fear but because they can afford to await the return of their hideous gods. They have a longevity beyond our ken, and they limit their contact with mankind to those who worship them." Calloway rose to refill my coffee cup. As he poured he said, "Those Polaroids were taken a couple of days ago, at an archaeological dig a few miles from Hastings, and I received them first mail today." He set down the fresh coffee and took a sheet of paper from the jumble on his desk. "This letter was with them." The paper was cheap, obviously ripped from a rough jotter pad, but the handwriting was elegant. The letter read:

*My dear Calloway,*

*I'm in luck. After some years of fruitless requests I have been granted permission to excavate a site at Lower Bedhoe in Sussex.*

*The previous landowner, a stubborn old devil called Sir Peter Grensham, would not allow any research into the site but his heir and only living relative is an Australian with flourish-ing business interests in his own country. He does not want to come to England and intends to sell off his UK interests in due course. In the meantime, he granted leave to dig and my team started work there several weeks ago.*

*There is a small stone circle at the site together with a bar-row and I judge both to be contemporary with Stonehenge. Now here is a curious thing, Calloway. We have made our way into the mound and have found the entrance to a sepulchre which I swear is Roman. There is considerable work to be done, for the tomb's entrance is blocked by an enormous stone. I hope to break through in the near future.*

*Apart from the anomaly of there being an apparently Roman tomb in a British barrow, there are some weird carvings at the tomb's entrance. Knowing of your interest in oddities, I enclose photographs.*

*I have not seen their like before and I am hoping that you might be able to shed some light. Why not come over and see them first-hand? I will be grateful for any help you can give.*

*Yours sincerely,*
*Alaric Wayt*

"Wayt was once a member of staff at Southdown," explained Calloway. "Some years ago, though, he inherited a small fortune and is now able to pursue his profession free of any academic institute. Like many academics, Wayt is probably less open-minded than he would pretend—note the way he refers to my occult knowledge as an 'interest in oddities.' They all choose similar euphemisms. Wayt will want me to explain the carvings to him. At this time, I have no intention of doing so."

"Why?"

"Because if I do so, when he publishes his findings about this dig, he will very properly attribute the explanation to me. The ensuing deluge of scorn would pour upon my head and not his. Academics are every bit as bitchy as actors.

"That apart, Roderick, how would you like to take a drive into Sussex to look at an ancient tomb?"

We arrived at the site of Wayt's dig during the early afternoon. The journey along the coast road from Southdown had been a pleasant one and it was only when we at last reached Lower Bedhoe, which was about half-a-mile inland, that we encountered any difficulty. The local people were reluctant to direct us to the dig.

Lower Bedhoe was a very small village, little more than a main street with several short side roads off and some scattered cottages in the countryside about. In common with many English villages of its kind, it had a green and a duckpond, around which stood an early Norman church, a pub and—most unusual these days—a working smithy. There was a village store–cum–post office and an old two-roomed school from which could be heard the chatter of small children.

We asked for directions first at the store. The proprietor, a small man with shrivelled, prune-like cheeks, said, "A bad business that dig, gentlemen. I wouldn't be doing you any favors by telling you how to get there. Good day to you." He turned to serve a customer, obviously dismissing us.

Enquiries of other inhabitants met with varying negative attitudes. At best there was an indifferent shrugging of shoulders coupled with a refusal to answer, at worst there were several instances of open hostility. The blacksmith and the publican were both exceptionally aggressive. Perhaps if I had been readily identifiable as a priest our reception might have been more polite, but I was casually dressed.

At length we drove out of the village and within a mile or so stopped to hail a laborer working in a field. He ambled over with grudging step to see what was wanted. When I asked him where we could find the site his eyes squinted with suspicion.

"You two diggers?" he demanded.

"What?"

"You gonna help them out there with the diggin' up of things best left to rest?"

Calloway leaned across to offer the man a cigarette. "We're with the Department of the Environment," he said. "We want to check the legality of what they are doing there."

The man's demeanor changed. He accepted the cigarette with dirty, stubby fingers, lit it and puffed with enjoyment. "Good for you, mister! You go and slap some kind of order on them if you can. Dunno if what they're doin' is legal or not but it ain't right, that's for sure.

"Drive on the way you're goin', maybe half to three-quarters of a mile, you'll come to a double bend. Round that on the left you'll see a youth hostel set back a few yards. Couple hundred yards more, there's an old track leading off the road. Turn there an' you'll see two hills, a small one in front of a big one. Dad and his Lad, we call them round here. Them diggin' fellers have got a camp in between the two. You get rid of them, mister. Us folks here'll thank you right enough." He touched the peak of his tattered cap and went back to his work.

"Interesting," commented Calloway as I engaged first gear to drive on. "I've heard of digs fermenting bad feeling among primitive peoples but never in a place like this."

The instructions proved accurate and very soon we were approaching a rise which could only be the Lad. It was not so much a hill, more of an intrusive lump on the landscape, perhaps about as high as a two-storey house. Behind that was a far larger hill, one hundred and fifty feet or so, crested by thick woodland. The little valley separating the hills was filled with a colorful miscellany of tents, ranging from the smallest of modern lightweights to a well-worn canvas affair so big as to be almost a marquee. I stopped the Land Rover, applying the handbrake firmly.

"There's Wayt," said Calloway, pointing to where two men stood at a trestle table set up in front of the marquee.

The elder of the two, a broad man of medium height with a mane of white hair, gave a cheery wave and came to greet us. "Calloway! Pleased that you could make it."

"Hello, Wayt," said Calloway. "This is my friend, Father Shea. He's here because his vehicle is more suited to this terrain than is my old Rolls."

"Good to know you, Shea," said Wayt, his handshake firm. He gestured towards the crew-cut younger man, who called out "Hi there!" with a strong American accent. "That's my right-hand, Ken Porter. Ken's a research student from Wisconsin University. You wouldn't believe that he's my fellow countryman, would you?"

"You surprise me," I said. Wayt's own deep tones were very British.

"I was born in the States, Father Shea," the archaeologist explained. "My parents died when I was very young. I was brought to England by a distant cousin of my father's and was raised here."

"Your letter suggests that you're feeling very pleased with yourself," said Calloway.

"Most assuredly," acknowledged Wayt. "I'd almost despaired of ever getting a crack at this place. I'm delighted that the new Sir John was more amenable than the old fellow. The locals seem a tad miffed, though."

"We noticed," was Calloway's dry comment. "Where is the site?"

"Behind the larger hill. There's a small plateau just before you reach the coastal cliffs. I've got about a dozen enthusiastic youngsters up there right now, all beavering away. Ken and I just came down to update our chart. Have a look."

Wayt took us to the trestle table which was covered with a large site diagram picked out on graph paper. "This is the barrow," said Wayt, pointing. "The tomb's entrance is here, facing inland. You'll see that there are a dozen stones making up the circle and here, nearest to the cliff, is a flat stone which was probably a sacrificial altar."

"I thought that all of the stone circles in Britain had been recorded," said Calloway. "But I've never heard of this one."

"No," said Wayt. "Not many outsiders have. Successive landowners have been very tight-lipped about it. It was only after the war that it was discovered. Pure chance, really. An RAF spotter plane was testing some new kind of camera by taking a series of coastal photos. They got some very good shots of the site. There was nothing classified about the pictures and so the pilot passed them to his elder brother who published a specialist magazine. The archaeological world went wild. I was still a student at the time and my imagination was certainly fired.

"Every university in the country made a bid to get a team in here, but despite all the pressure brought to bear on him, the late Sir Peter remained adamant. Nobody was allowed onto his land. He kept armed gamekeepers here for a few years and I think that quite a number of eminent men found themselves picking shot out of their backsides.

"Of course, all that was a long time ago, and eventually most of the archaeology departments gave it up as a lost cause and forgot about it. I never did. I kept tabs on the place through the years, even taking the trouble to research into Sir Peter's family so that I knew who his heir was. As soon as the old boy snuffed it, I had a cablegram on the way to Australia. Anyway, come along both of you and see for yourselves."

As we neared "Dad," I noticed that the lower slopes were thickly covered not only with the short, scrubby olive-colored grass common to the southern chalklands but also with a profusion of gorse, brambles and wild flowers. I expected our ascent to be heavy going.

And then Wayt pointed out a well-beaten pathway of hard-packed, dusty earth. With young Porter leading the way and Wayt bringing up the rear, we began to climb. The path was as firm underfoot as any concrete pavement.

"Now this is peculiar," mused Calloway. "Here's a place supposedly banned to outsiders for God knows how long, and apparently avoided by the locals, yet this pathway is so well established that it's completely devoid of plant growth."

"Very peculiar," agreed Wayt. "I think that this path is hundreds, if not thousands, of years old. On the other hand, it hadn't been used for many years before our arrival. When we came here, the path was invisible, well camouflaged by interwoven grasses and brambles. All the way to the treeline you can see where we had to cut the growth back. We found the path quite by accident. We were nosing around, trying to find the easiest way up, and one of the students stumbled across it.

"From the shape of the brambles along the edge of the path, I'm disposed to think that they were not the result of random growth but that they were purposely trained to cover the path. Probably the work of the misanthropic Sir Peter."

Although the rise was not excessively steep, our conversation died away as we trudged higher. At last we reached the upper limit of the grass cover where the path disappeared into the lower edge of the forest. We halted for a breather.

"You'll have to take it easy going through here," warned Ken Porter, "the tree growth is very thick."

He was right. It was apparent as we entered into their shade that the woods had completely escaped the predations of man. From bright daylight we found ourselves suddenly enclosed in green-shadowed dimness, and we constantly ducked and weaved to avoid the weighty solidity of ancient limbs. The path itself was now much softer to walk upon, being carpeted with the mulch of countless years of dead leaves. And then almost as quickly as we had entered the forest we reached the crest of the hill and were dazzled as we moved out into the bright sunlight.

The downward slope on this side was much more gentle and only about one-third of the height we had just climbed. To east and west, long arms of land inclined gradually down to a cliff edge, forming from the plateau between them a natural, horseshoe-shaped amphitheatre. Beyond the ragged brink where the land finished, the dark brown-green swell of the English Channel crawled towards the horizon. In the distance, to the west, I could see a misty patch which I guessed was Beachy Head jutting out into the sea.

The stone "circle" was more of an oval, the barrow a prominent wen in the center. All around were signs of excavation and a number of young men and women worked at a variety of tasks, digging, scraping, sieving, cleaning. Even from where we stood we could hear the pleasant hum of good-humored conversation punctuated by occasional shouts of laughter.

"They're happy in their work," I observed.

"I'm an easy taskmaster," said Wayt. "They're all volunteers and if they're contented I get far more out of them. Come on, let's go down."

As we reached the bottom of the incline, one of the students called out to Wayt and our host excused himself. Calloway ambled away towards the far end of the circle and I tagged along.

"Don't go too near the edge," yelled Wayt. "It could be unsafe and it's several hundred feet to the beach."

Calloway waved a placatory hand and continued on to the flat slab at the point of the oval. Its surface was not truly flat but gently convex, worn and pitted and mossy and with deep channels gouged into the sides and the head.

"I think Wayt's right about this. Sacrificial stone." He cupped his hands to light a cigarette. "The grooves are evidently to drain away blood."

"Human, I suppose."

Calloway shrugged. "Depends on how big a favor the priests would want from the gods," he opined. He waved again to Wayt. "Our friend's anxious for us to take a look at his tomb."

As we sauntered back, I looked with interest at the standing stones. They were not large, say about the size of those at Avebury in Wiltshire although fewer in number, but that notwithstanding each must have been an immense weight. One could only marvel at the ancient men who had labored to bring such columns over immense distances and nigh-impossible terrain.

"Didn't mean to sound like a nursemaid," Wayt apologised as we joined him. "Erosion is a serious problem along this part of the coast. Some of the cliffs nearer to Hastings are losing several feet each year with rockfalls. That's another reason I was always so keen to get to this place. I wanted to uncover its secrets before it goes crashing into the sea."

He took a large flashlight offered by one of the students and we trailed after him as he went down into the dug-out barrow. The entrance was low and we crouched down as we went through. I felt for Calloway who was not built for such exercise. It was no better inside, for we had to squat and shuffle along. After five or six yards of a thigh-stretchingly painful journey we were stopped by the great rock which blocked the way into the tomb. It was still intact despite the signs of hard work to clear the dirt packed in around it.

"You can see that we haven't managed to breach this yet," said Wayt. "But we'll get there sooner or later." He swivelled the torch's beam to one side. "And this is one of the sculptures you know of, Calloway."

The photographs could not possibly have conveyed the skill of the mason who had carved the figure. In the torchlight, limned by black shadows, that stone image seemed imbued with strange life and I half expected it to struggle and scream upon its cross.

"It's . . . disturbing," I said. Wayt smiled, pleased with my reaction.

Calloway reached out and placed a gentle hand on the carving. "Extraordinary," he murmured.

Wayt directed the torch at the opposite jamb, onto the identical figure carved there. "Right, Calloway, you're the expert on strange things—have you any idea what these carvings signify?"

"Never seen anything like them before," lied Calloway.

"I see." Wayt sounded disappointed. "There's something else," he said, flicking the beam onto the lintel. "Since I sent you those photographs we've been able to clean away the dirt from up there. It now looks fairly certain that the tomb itself is Roman."

Chiselled deeply into the lintel were the words: "HIC JACET PRISCVS."

"I know a lot about Roman Britain," said Wayt. "But the name of Priscus isn't familiar to me. And yet he must have been of some importance to merit a tomb like this."

"Perhaps a common soldier," I suggested. "His importance being symbolic, even if his name is unknown to historians. You know, the eternal warrior, the universal soldier."

Wayt shook his head. "No, Father Shea, the Romans would not have honored their common soldiery by giving them distinctive tombs, not even concealed tombs such as this. Nor would they have bothered to record a common soldier's name on his tomb."

"A pity," I said. "Great occasions in history belong to ordinary people as well as the eminencies. I think we should know more of history's bit players. For instance, I would like to know the name of the centurion at Calvary."

"It was Ducus Waynus," muttered Calloway, who had a taste for bad epic films. To Wayt he said in a bored voice, "This could be some sort of battle standard, I suppose, perhaps belonging to a mercenary legion. Now I am getting out of here before my legs lock and you have to summon a bull-dozer to extricate me."

We wriggled our way out of the barrow and spent long minutes gingerly easing aching leg muscles. I wondered how a miner felt at the end of an eight-hour shift. Calloway took out his cigarette case and lit up. "Sorry that I can't help you, Wayt. Thanks for the chance to see the tomb, though; it's been interesting. We'll have to leave now, we've a long drive ahead of us."

The archaeologist smiled ruefully. "Ah well, the most enjoyable mysteries are those which take a lot of solving. You'll excuse me if I don't see you off personally. I'll stick around and see how my team's been doing today. Ken will take you to your car." He shook hands and turned away.

When we gained the ridge I looked back. Wayt was already hard at work, and apparently giving a lecture to a rapt audience as he labored. I guessed that he would make a good teacher.

While I was unlocking the Land Rover's door, Calloway said to Porter, "You think a lot of Wayt?"

"We all do."

Calloway took a card from his pocket and handed it to the young American. "I'm not happy about this dig," he said. "That's where you can reach me. I want you to contact me if anything on this site, anything at all, gives you cause to worry. If I'm not around, leave a message. But don't mention this to Wayt. I don't want to give him any cause for concern."

"Are you expecting something to go wrong?" I asked as I turned the vehicle.

"Perhaps." He lit another flat Turkish cigarette.

My friend smoked in silence for some minutes then said, "At least I now know what happened to Priscus."

"Not a common soldier?" I asked.

Calloway wound down the window and threw out his cigarette stub. "Far from common."

I waited for more, then grew impatient. "You'd better tell me what you know."

Calloway nodded. "In the first century AD, during the reign of Vespasian, the family Priscus was wiped out along with all retainers and slaves, and their names were expunged from the records, even from those archives going back to the early Republic. And all because of Vitellius Priscus, whom I believe to be the occupant of that tomb back there.

"If any professional historian has heard of Priscus, it will only be as an unsubstantiated legend. But within certain occult circles his story is well known.

"Vitellius Priscus was a patrician and a high-ranking army officer. He was a good soldier and unlike many of his class he chose not to linger in the decadence that was Rome. He loved to campaign in distant lands, he loved to see action. He had a reputation as a scholar, too, and was once a protege of Petronius Arbiter, although he sensibly ended that friendship when Petronius fell foul of Nero.

"As long as he could avoid offending any of the more insane Caesars, his future was assured. In time, he was awarded an assistant governorship in Egypt.

"It was there that Priscus changed. His scholarship and natural curiosity led him into a study of the occult. He fell in with a strange and clandestine sect of Egyptian priests and became their most willing pupil. It is said that his was one of those rare talents that climbs swiftly and without hindrance into the highest occult grades. And like most who experience this effortless rise, he chose to follow the path of evil.

"His occult legacy is *The Twenty-one Essays*, in which he claimed to have lived and experienced abominations repellent even to the most jaded of Roman voluptuaries. The book was proscribed and further military advancement curtailed. At the time, his family still had influence sufficient to ensure his survival, but Priscus was banished to Britain.

"Simultaneously, there was gossip about Priscus, whispers that he was changing physically, becoming a 'demon.'

"The last thing that's known for certain is that Priscus arrived in Britain. He was never heard of again and his family was eliminated.

"With what we have seen today, this is what I think must have happened. Somehow, while in Egypt, Priscus had become infected with an alien strain, just like the Innsmouth people. Priscus was crucified and interred in that barrow—I imagine that the Romans and the druids colluded to destroy what both saw as a menace.

"And there you have it. Now, Roderick, if you don't mind, I am going to have a nap. Wake me when we get to Southdown."

I went away after that for a couple of months, going to a monastery in France to aid an independent investigation into certain alleged malpractices.

I returned home one afternoon, weary and looking forward to a few days of relaxation. My immediate plans included a hot bath and an early supper, followed by an evening in my favorite armchair with *The Pickwick Papers* and a glass of The Glenlivet. I pondered taking a few days off, perhaps to go fishing, for I had worked hard while in France. My curates were able men and could well carry on without me.

I had barely started to unpack when there was a sharp rap at my door and in stalked the housekeeper.

Mrs. Byrne's usually jovial face was compressed with vexation.

"It's himself! Professor Calloway!" she announced. "Demanding to see you and will not take no for an answer."

"Not busy, are you Roderick?" boomed Calloway as I walked into the study. "I'm sure you can spare me a few days, three or four at the most."

"Really, Reuben," I protested. "I've only just returned from France. I have a parish to run and I can't go dashing off again." My conscience nudged me, a reminder that I had intended to do exactly that.

"Rubbish!" snapped my friend. "Young Father What's-his-name, or the other one, they've managed all this time without you. They'll cope for a little longer."

"It's hardly fair to them . . ." my voice tailed off as my guilty conscience again reminded me of my intentions.

"Look, I'll just go and wait in the Rolls while you pack a few things," said Calloway, knowing that he had won with very little trouble. "Keep it simple and casual. Oh, and dark and hard-wearing."

Minutes later I climbed in beside Calloway and threw my small holdall onto the back seat, where there was already a compact bundle.

"Thank you, Roderick," said Calloway, as he attempted to steer onto the main road and light one of his dreadful cigarettes at the same time. "It's good to have someone with me whom I can trust."

"Where are we going?"

"Oh, didn't I say? We're going to Lower Bedhoe."

"Something has happened at the dig," I said.

He nodded. "Last week I had a call from that American lad, Porter. He's not at the dig any more and he's anxious about what might be going on there. I got Porter to come and see me and I recorded what he had to say. Listen."

Calloway loaded an audio cassette into the car's unit and pressed the play button. Ken Porter's voice came from the speakers, hesitant at first as if unused to speaking into a microphone, then gaining in confidence as he proceeded.

"It was about a month after your visit that we broke through into the tomb," Porter started. "That may seem a long time to a layman, but in archaeological work you must go carefully so that you don't damage anything important.

"The earth was packed solidly around the boulder which sealed the tomb and when we had cleaned all the dirt away we found that the gap between the stone and the portal was sealed with some form of cement which was in good condition and very hard.

"It was decided to concentrate at first on removing a small section of the seal, perhaps about five or six inches. Once we had broken through that we should be able to see if there was any danger of damaging the tomb's contents. If the area behind the seal seemed to be clear, then we could remove the remainder with more vigor.

"When we started to chip away, we found that the cement was quite thick. It took several of us, working in relays, a couple of days to get through. You have been in that cramped, stuffy place and so you can probably guess what it was like. Doctor Wayt stuck it out well, staying down there most of the time to supervise.

"At last we judged that there was the thinnest layer of the seal left to remove. We all agreed that the honor of the final breakthrough should go to Doctor Wayt. He demurred, but it was his dig, which his persistence had made possible, and so we persuaded him.

"As many of us as possible huddled into that confined space before the sepulchre, all waiting eagerly for the great moment, while the remainder crowded about the entrance to the barrow.

"Wayt took a hammer and chisel and carefully tapped round the edges of the remaining piece of the barrier. It gave and fell into the tomb and there was a small crashing sound as it shattered on the inside ground. 'Sounds like they must have gone to the trouble of constructing a stone floor in there,' Doctor Wayt told us. 'Somebody pass me a flashlight and I'll take a look.'

"He held the light high and to the right and put his face as close to the freshly-opened gap as was possible. Then we heard a sort of puffing or hissing noise and Wayt cried out before falling back in a swoon. There were a few startled shouts and some muted panic, and I heard someone say, 'He must have inhaled bad air!'

"Now here is a strange thing, Professor Calloway, which I cannot explain. I was to Doctor Wayt's left, crouched inside the door's frame, and I had a good view of his torchlit profile as he leaned forward to that gap. It looked to me as if something gushed out from that hole in the seal and settled itself all over Doctor Wayt's face. He made a choking noise as if he had inhaled it.

"I don't know what it was, if anything. It seemed to be a black, drifting, shadowy mass, like a cloud of dust or cobwebs. But when we got him into the daylight, there were no traces of anything around his nose and mouth other than the sweat and grime one would have expected.

"Perhaps it was some kind of optical illusion; the darkness, the cramped conditions, the narrow beam of the flashlight, all of these could have contributed to what I thought I saw.

"I started to tell one of the kids to go for a doctor but just about then Wayt recovered a little and countermanded my order. He said something about a fainting fit caused by heat and cramp and that he would just rest in his tent until he felt well again.

"He stayed there all night and in the morning he seemed recovered although rather subdued. Doctor Wayt was always an ebullient man and the change was very marked. He suggested that as we had all worked hard recently, that we take a couple of days off. I queried this—after all, since I'd known him he'd been quite a workaholic. He told me with some asperity that the tomb had been there for a couple of thousand years, that it would wait a bit longer for us.

"He just lazed around for several days, then he extended our holiday and asked me if I would mind taking him to London on my motorbike. Said he wanted to do some research at the British Museum Library. Turned out that we were in London for four days. I was able to lodge with some friends but I don't know where Wayt stayed.

"Then when we got back to the dig, the Doctor, in effect, fired the lot of us. Well, not quite the lot of us, he kept several people on. Wasn't much that we could do, so we all upped our tents and went.

"But I wasn't happy, the whole thing felt wrong to me. During those few days in London, Doctor Wayt changed a lot. He became unpleasant in manner and acted kind of furtive. Then . . . it was odd about those he kept on."

"Odd in what way?" interjected Calloway's voice.

"Well, for a start they were the least experienced of the students. Then they were all foreigners—by that I mean that there were no British or Americans or any other native English speakers. There were two girls from mainland China and a Ugandan guy. Yeah, and something else funny, they were the smallest and skinniest kids there, none of them much use for heavy work.

"Don't know why, I felt kind of . . . creepy about it. I went back one night to have a mooch around. There was nobody there, there was *nothing* there save for Wayt's big, old-fashioned tent. Then I heard some noises, distant like they came from over the hill."

"What kind of noises?" Calloway again.

"I don't know. Weird, kinda like chanting."

"Did you investigate?"

"Hell, no!" Porter gabbled. "I suddenly got real scared, lit out of there. Then I remembered what you said about calling you."

The voice stopped and there was the hiss of blank tape. I reached out to switch the machine off.

"Have you done anything yet?" I asked Calloway.

"I called a friend at the Museum and found out what Wayt was doing there. He was consulting the *Al Azif* and some other hideous books."

Calloway had once told me about the *Al Azif*. I turned to look at him. His face was grim. "And that worries you," I said.

He fumbled with his cigarette case. "And that worries me," he agreed.

We drove straight through Lower Bedhoe without stopping. I don't think that anyone paid attention to us but it had been some time and two men in a battered old Rolls-Royce probably look totally different from two men in a battered old Land Rover. Instead of driving directly to the camp-site, Calloway drove the Rolls into the small car park at the rear of the youth hostel.

We climbed out of the car and Calloway stretched his huge frame until I thought that his scruffy grey suit would come apart at the seams. "A pleasant summer's evening, Roderick," he said. "Just the right kind of evening for a stroll up that hill. Of course, we'll have to detour slightly. It's better that Wayt doesn't know we're here until we call on him a bit later."

Without bothering to ascertain my feelings about this suggestion, Calloway set off at an astonishing pace for such a grossly-built man. We clambered over a wooden fence and approached the "Dad" hill from the west side. "We won't have the benefit of that excellent path, I'm afraid," said Calloway. "I hope that I don't damage my suit on the brambles." I kept my uncharitable opinion to myself.

As it happened, the climb was less arduous than I expected, the slope being more gentle from this approach. The brambles were a bit vicious but we were able to avoid the worst patches. Soon we were through the woods and looking down upon the stone circle. "Almost there," Calloway grunted.

As soon as our feet touched the level turf of the amphitheatre, Calloway dashed over to the flat stone and began to examine the ground. "Come here, Shea," he called. When I reached him, he was indicating small patches where the grass had been trampled and crushed.

"There's been a struggle here," I said.

"Yes, and look at that . . . and there . . . and again there . . ." Calloway pointed to a number of ominous brown stains on the flattened grass and on the altar stone itself. Comment was unnecessary. I crossed myself and muttered a quiet prayer, for whom or what I wasn't sure.

"One more thing." Calloway led me to the barrow and we squeezed our way in, illumination provided by the flicker of his cigarette lighter. The huge rock was still in its place sealing the tomb of Priscus. The jambs' carvings goggled at us, looking even more lifelike in the dancing glow shed by the tiny flame. Calloway jerked his head towards the entrance and we crawled out.

"No more work done," I said, brushing the dirt from my trousers. My friend stood tapping a Turkish cigarette on his thumbnail and then for the first time since I had known him, replaced it in his case unlit.

"Let's go and have a word with Wayt," he said quietly.

We went back through the woods and this time down by the beaten path. We circled the solitary marquee, sole remnant of the camp which had been here, and approached from the front. Despite the warmth of the evening the flap was closed, and yet muted noises from within told us that the huge tent was not unoccupied.

"Hello in there!" called Calloway.

"*What's that!* Who's there?" The startled voice was that of Wayt but there was something different about it. It was coarser somehow, as if he was in the early stages of laryngitis.

"It's Calloway."

"What do you want? How dare you come here without permission!"

Calloway had been toying with the tent-flap and now he threw it open. "It would be better if we could talk face-to-face," he said.

The evening light did not penetrate very far into the marquee. From where I stood behind Calloway, part of the trestle table was visible, enough for me to see that it was covered with notebooks and sheets of paper, many of them illustrated with geometric patterns and scribed with copious notes. There was a hand resting on the table, a hand which was snatched back with some haste as the light poured in.

I had a glimpse only, but I saw that there was something wrong with that hand. I had an impression of some unpleasant skin disease, psoriasis perhaps. The area beyond the table was heavily shaded and I could see only the faintest outline of a seated figure.

"*Get out!*" Wayt screamed.

Calloway's voice was affable. "But I came here to offer more help," he purred. "I thought that if we worked together we could solve the riddle of those weird carvings."

There was a bark of laughter from inside the tent. "You fool, Calloway! I don't need your help! I don't want your help! I've found the answer to that riddle already. I know exactly what those carvings mean. It's something too immense for your peasant intellect, so go away and leave me be. I have important work to do."

"Of course," soothed Calloway. "I'm sorry to have disturbed you." He beckoned me away and we trudged back to the road. My friend was full of surprises this evening. First the unlighted cigarette and now this uncharacteristic capitulation.

"Did you notice Wayt's hand?" I asked.

"Yes," said Calloway. "Interesting, wasn't it?"

We reached the Rolls and I said, "Now what?"

Calloway had been gazing around at the landscape and now he pointed to a gentle rise about one-third of a mile back towards Lower Benhoe. "I think that would make a good camping site," he said.

"Camping site?"

Calloway reached into the back of the car and took out my holdall together with the second bundle I had noticed earlier. Handing me the latter, he said, "That's your tent. I've got a box of supplies for you and I'm leaving you a good pair of night-glasses."

"Calloway, would you mind telling me what is going on?"

Reuben Calloway looked at me as if I were simple. "Why, you're going to keep an eye on Wayt while I go to London to check on a few things. I also want to have a word with a certain occultist. I think that he will be able to lend me something very important."


Calloway was right. The rise did make a good camping spot, giving me an advantageous overview of Wayt's tent while remaining unseen myself. Calloway must have searched hard for the small tent which he had forced upon me, for its color blended perfectly with the surrounding vegetation.

I had protested against Calloway's presumption to no avail. Confident of his rightness, he would hear no argument. I agreed at last, for I knew that he was quite capable of presenting a *fait accompli* by leaping into the Rolls and leaving me stranded if I persisted in opposing his wishes.

"I'm sure that you won't have to worry about the daylight hours," he told me. "If my suspicions are correct, Wayt won't venture out while it's light for fear of being observed. So you'll be able to rest during the day and watch him at night. I am equally sure that nothing will happen for at least the next two nights by which time I should be back here. And Roderick, be careful. You're an observer. No action of any kind except as a final resort."

As a priest I try to practise tolerance and charity. As a human being I sometimes resent both Calloway's arrogance and his propensity to be right so often. We are good friends but I can appreciate why many find him intolerable.

During the day I rested. When I ate and drank, it was cold tinned food and bottled mineral water, for I did not want to risk a fire or cooking smells which could attract Wayt's attention. At night I dressed in denims, sweater and windcheater, all black, and lurked amidst the undergrowth with the binoculars trained on Wayt's tent.

Either Wayt, too, rested in the day or else he could tolerate darkness far more comfortably than most, for it was not until the darkest hours that any light would show in the tent. Then I would see his shadow, distorted by the feeble glow and the canvas walls, moving about or crouched over his table all night.

I almost missed his exit from the marquee on the third night. It was well after midnight and bright with stars, so much more clear and plentiful there in the countryside, but the moon had not yet appeared. I was becoming bored and every now and then, for a few moments, I would turn the binoculars to the night sky, enchanted with God's universe. I turned back just in time to see the light extinguished. The night-glasses to my eyes, I strained to see what was happening.

I glimpsed a slight movement, the flap of the tent being lifted, I presume, and then a patch of shadow moving towards the far side of the smaller hill where it turned towards the road.

Despite Calloway's promise, he had not yet returned. I felt obliged to do what he would have done. I jumped to my feet and began to run towards the road, caution abandoned. I hoped that Wayt would have no reason to turn back and that if he did, he would not see me.

I reached the fence, hauled myself over and squatted in the shallow ditch by the verge. With great care I lifted my head, binoculars at the ready and fixed on the road. I did not know which direction Wayt would take but thought that I could give him a few minutes to come my way before setting off in pursuit.

Then, black against the light metalled surface of the road, I could see a dark figure drawing near. I was sure that it could only be Wayt, and yet there was something disturbing about the archaeologist's appearance. He was swathed in a cloak and hood of dark material, his body was huddled over and he moved with a peculiar, quasi-hopping gait. I wriggled further down into the ditch, expecting momentary discovery, but he turned suddenly into the grounds of the youth hostel.

As Wayt moved out of sight, I hurried along until I was opposite the hostel and then again took cover. Within moments my quarry reappeared, this time bearing a large, well-wrapped burden which he handled with ease. He turned back the way he had come and having given him sufficient time to get well ahead, I followed.

Wayt retraced his steps but instead of returning to the marquee, he went directly to the larger hill and started up the path. I followed him with the binoculars until he vanished into the treeline.

Clipping the glasses to my belt, I moved rapidly up the path and plunged into the claustrophobic darkness of the woods. The going was not easy but I believed that I had good enough recall of the way the path ran. Foolishly, I put on a burst of speed and I think that I was almost trotting when a blow to the head knocked me flat on my back. Badly dazed, I could only wait for the *coup de grace*.

Nothing happened. I'm not sure how long it was that I lay there but probably no more than seconds. It became apparent that I had not been assaulted but had run into a heavy lower limb protruding from one of those immense old trees. I crawled to its base and hauled myself up, disorientated and struggling against nausea.

I leaned against the bole and raised a hand to my head. There was a swelling above my right eye, very tender to the touch, with wetness on my brow and cheek. Blood, no doubt, from abraded skin. I set off again in what I thought was the right direction, only more slowly this time, holding my arms out before me to fumble a way through the murk and tangle of branches and bushes, taking great care not to suffer further disaster.

I became aware of a strange noise ahead. It sounded like a monotonous, wordless chant, interrupted every few notes by a chilling wail, a high-pitched ululation which dried my mouth and knotted my stomach. This might have been what young Porter heard when he came to investigate. I understood now why he had felt panic, for it took all of my willpower to carry on.

The forest began to thin out and the darkness to lessen, and suddenly I emerged into the open. By some good fortune I was more or less where I had intended to be, near to the head of the track leading down to the tomb of Priscus. There was no need for immediate concealment, it being unlikely that my black-garbed figure would be visible against the gloomy backdrop of trees.

Cold stars glittered and almost in front of me a full moon shone. Although yet very low in the sky, it had risen sufficiently to cast a wide ribbon of light over the calm surface of the sea, creating a motley of silver and jet and ultramarine. The glow spilled onto the land, turning the amphitheatre with its stone circle into a gleaming bowl. Below me on the hillside, his singular gait unmistakable, was the misshapen figure of the archaeologist.

He reached the foot of the hill and turned with his burden to the altar stone. I started to follow, and as I did so I saw that in that strip of white light upon the sea there had appeared two or three black silhouettes, looking for all the world like immense flat heads. As I watched, another surfaced and then another. Despite the distance, there was something about those featureless shadows which made me shiver. I reached for the night-glasses but they were no longer at my belt. I must have lost them when I had my accident.

Then I realised that the weird chanting and the intermittent wailing were coming from far out at sea and were getting closer.

My approach down the slope was made more easy by the moonlight. I concentrated on stealth, but I think that Wayt was so intent upon his own business as to be oblivious to all else.

At the bottom I lowered myself onto my stomach and wriggled forward until I was safe within the shadow of a menhir. From the direction of the sea, in addition to the throbbing chant, I could now hear some splashing and there were other sounds, a medley of indistinguishable mutterings interspersed with an occasional coughing croak. Although not necessarily abnormal in themselves, in that place and at that time these new noises made the hair on my neck stiffen.

I peered out from behind my hiding place. Wayt was huddled over the altar stone, his body concealing from my eyes what he had there. His movements suggested that he was arranging something, and I had a morbid mental picture of a mortuary technician laying out a corpse.

There was a slight noise from somewhere behind me, a nocturnal animal or bird, perhaps, up there in the woods. Wayt whirled. His face was fully concealed beneath that heavy hood but I could sense his suspicion. His head swung from side to side as if he were *snuffling* out prey. Despite my conviction that he could not detect me within the shadow cast by the stone, I pressed my body closer to the ground.

The noise was not repeated and Wayt seemed to relax. For an instant he stood away from the altar and I could see what it was that lay there. Stretched out on that sinister slab, pinioned wrist and ankle, was the naked form of a young woman. She, then, was the burden Wayt had carried, the reason for his detour to the youth hostel. No doubt she was an innocent hiker or cyclist who, if travelling alone, would not be missed as quickly as a local person. She was still and quiet and I guessed that she was either drugged or in a trance. I recalled Calloway's admonition to do nothing unless and until absolutely necessary.

Wayt turned back to the altar and held both arms out to the heavens. Throwing back his head he commenced to chant some kind of prayer or ritual. It was in no language known to me and it occurred to me that what I could hear was not even of human origin, so bizarre did it sound. I would not even attempt to reproduce those alien syllables. Each time that Wayt paused in his dirge, so there were echoing croaks from the sea, becoming louder as they went on.

Abruptly there was silence and Wayt's arms fell to his sides. He lowered his head briefly, as if in obeisance, then raised his right arm once more. Now the moonlight flashed on a long, curved blade.

An involuntary cry was torn from me. *"No-o-o-o!"*

I was on my feet and running hard, covering the short distance between us more quickly than I would have believed myself capable of doing. With both hands I snatched at Wayt's wrist to prevent that wicked knife from descending.

It may have been that the recent blow to my head had weakened me, but I found myself thwarted by what seemed to be an unnatural strength in that sinewy limb. We grappled for a few seconds and then the knife was flung to one side. Wayt twisted about in my grasp and the cowl flew back from his head, exposing his face to the mocking light of the full moon. I cried out in horror and my grip loosened.

It was Wayt's face, right enough, but humanity was vestigial. The abhorrent visage into which I stared was bestial, a vile melding of man and amphibian and fish. Black eyes with horizontal yellow irises bulged from surrounding tissue which was covered with scales and warty excrescences; flattened and ridged nostrils flared; and a wide, lipless mouth slobbered at me. Little remained of his beautiful white hair save for a few ropy strands dangling from a scabrous scalp. With an almost casual backhanded cuff the thing knocked me to the rough turf.

"Hah! It's the priest!" While the words were spat out in understandable English, the guttural voice was throaty and phlegm-filled as if straining to form impossible sounds. "Hardly a worthy opponent for one such as I. Come here, priest!" He reached down with hands which were showing signs of webbing and claw development, seized my collar and lifted me to my feet.

I am a solidly-built man, no lightweight, and yet the man-thing ran me to the cliff's edge as if I had been a child. I could feel loose soil crumbling beneath my feet and I thought that his intention was to heave me over. Under my breath I muttered a final prayer, preparing to meet a shattering death on the boulders and shingle below.

Instead, Wayt held me firmly with one hand and pointed to the sea with the other. "Look, priest, look there!" he commanded. "See the future and marvel!"

There were now many dozens of those anomalous black shapes in the sea. Some had advanced as far as the shallows and were standing upright so that the water lapped at their knees and waists. Others wallowed in and out of the wavelets on their bellies, grisly travesties of porpoises. It was from all of them that the chanting and ghastly wailing was emanating.

As Wayt dragged me into sight, the cacophony died away until at last there was only an occasional croak from among their ranks. Mostly they just stood, staring in silence.

"My true brethren!" grunted the thing which held me. "Soon, when I have completed the requisite number of sacrifices, I will be fully changed, freed from the limitations of this pitifully short-lived human shell, and I will take my rightful place with them in the bosom of the eternal ocean.

"Imagine, priest, when you and that fat oaf Calloway and all those other pitiful . . . midgets . . . are ancient dust forgotten even by your impotent God, I will yet live. I will be here amongst the faithful when the stars are right for the final coming. I will witness the rising of the incomparable Green City from the blackest depths. I will be here to fall in worship when He . . . *He!* . . . emerges from durance in all of his terrible splendor to rule in glory for evermore! *Oh mightiest of fathers, hear your servant's cry!*"

He pulled me back from the cliff and towards the altar stone, maintaining that immovable grip, and stared at me thoughtfully. "Yes . . ." he mused. "Yes, you may be of use to me. Perhaps the offering of a Christian priest will hasten the desired metamorphosis. But first, to finish what I had started with the female!" He cast me aside with ease and bent to retrieve the sacrificial knife.

I fumbled in the pocket of my windcheater to find my crucifix. Overcoming dread and holding the cross aloft, I advanced upon the hideous creature. "In the name of God almighty, stop!" I commanded.

Wayt stared at me, astonished, and then emitted a coughing guffaw. Stepping forward, he again felled me with one of those careless slaps. Kneeling, he snatched the cross from my hand and buckled it in his fingers.

"You fool," he croaked. "To imagine that your feeble symbol of holiness could deter me."

"The crucifix won't," said a quiet, familiar voice. "But this certainly will." A huge hand, holding a star-shaped object, thrust between my line of vision and Wayt's frightening face. Wayt let out a yell of fear and fury and recoiled. He scrambled to his feet and made a dash for the hillside, only to cringe back and run to the precipice. Again, somehow, he was thwarted.

Calloway was helping me to my feet. "Sorry I'm late, Roderick," he said. "It took a little time to assemble my army. We almost gave away our approach when some damned fool stumbled up on the hill."

I looked around and saw that Calloway was not alone. There were men with him, ten or more, and all were holding the same star-shaped artefact. They had formed a circle about the monstrous Wayt who was now cowering on the ground, whimpering. I recognised some of the men: there was the farm laborer who had directed us and the aggressive blacksmith. I saw the wrinkled shopkeeper and the surly publican. All the others were villagers from Lower Bedhoe.

"You know what to do with him, men," said Calloway.

"Careful, Reuben, he's very strong," I warned.

"Not any more," said my friend. "These star-stones will ensure that."

I pulled Calloway to the precipice and pointed out at the sea where the grim multitude waited, now in menacing silence. "Look at those!"

"I've seen them," said Calloway, his voice reassuring. "There's not much that they can do against us. This cliff is too high and too frangible for them to scale with ease, and despite their numbers they would be powerless against our amulets."

He gestured again to the now helpless Wayt.

Several men, including the blacksmith, moved to lay hands on him while the remainder concentrated the strange power of the stones. He was acquiescent as they seized him and then I saw what was intended for him.

With a shocked cry I lunged forward to stop the enormity about to take place, but was restrained by Calloway's bulk.

"Stop it, Calloway, stop it!" I shouted. "You must stop it! *It's blasphemy!*"

"No," he growled, his powerful arms holding me immobile. "It's a cleansing."

Several more villagers had staggered slowly into view, hampered by the weight of their burden. It was a solid wooden beam with a six-foot crosspiece. They laid it on the ground in front of the tomb and then one man with a pick and a spade began to hack a deep, narrow slot in the sod.

Wayt's captors spreadeagled him upon the cross and his upper arms were securely lashed to the horizontal beam. The blacksmith knelt by the supine Wayt and with several savage blows from a small sledge drove six-inch nails through the creature's wrists.

Gasping with the effort, the men maneuvered the foot of the cross into the prepared slot, struggling to lift it clear of the ground. As it rose by several inches, long ropes were passed beneath the bar for them to haul upon. At last the cross was heaved into position, its base dropping with a thud into the hole. The smith hammered in wedges until satisfied that the cross could stand alone, firm and unwavering.

Throughout this ordeal, Wayt had remained still and mute, his stoicism unfathomable. The pounding of those long nails, the bone-jerking haul to the perpendicular, the sickening lurch as the crucifix settled, all of these must have caused him shrieking agony. But now, with obvious difficulty, he lifted his head and strained to look at the sky. His breath rasped audibly in his throat and chest as he managed to find voice. His shouted appeal was a dreadful parody of another crucifixion.

*"Father!"* he cried. "Dread Father from the stars and from the depths! Punish them! Punish them for what they do to your disciple!" The effort proved too much and with his breath a long, whistling exhalation, the grotesque head collapsed, the maw open and slack.

My head throbbed with a dull pain from my earlier accident and I felt a sombre cloak of depression settle about me. I lowered my face into hands which shook. It was extraordinary, but I could feel something, compassion of a kind, I suppose, for the monster on the cross. In that last cry there had been a spiritual suffering which transcended the physical. Wayt had become evil, perhaps; aberrant and frightening, certainly; but all of these changes were by human criteria. He remained a sentient being, capable of needs and longings, alien to us though the standards of his emotions might be.

"Put him out of his misery," ordered Calloway. "Then finish it the way I told you."

The blacksmith nodded, swung his hammer and cracked the man-thing's skull. Wayt shuddered once and was still. I saw that there were more people coming down from the hill and onto the plateau. I wondered if the whole of Lower Bedhoe was somehow involved.

Most of the newcomers were bearing bundles of dead branches, gleaned from the woods, which they piled about the foot of the cross. Someone splashed liquid onto the kindling and I caught the strong smell of petrol. A rag was ignited and tossed onto the pyre which exploded into fiery life, filling the air with a furnace wind and the crackling sound of burning wood. Villagers hurried to fuel the conflagration and whitening flames reached higher and higher to conceal and consume the remains of Alaric Wayt.

There were women there, too, covering the comatose girl with blankets and carrying her from the scene.

I sighed and Calloway gripped my shoulders, shaking me gently. "It was a cleansing, Roderick," he repeated softly. He took a hip-flask from his jacket and offered it to me. I sipped the brandy and then I took another, longer, swallow. It didn't help much. I returned the flask to my friend.

"What happened?" I asked. "What caused this?"

It was Calloway's turn to sigh. "Ken Porter's story, and what we ourselves witnessed, made me suspect that Wayt was undergoing something like an Innsmouth change. I was sure that nothing would happen until tonight, I just wasn't able to get back as soon as I had hoped. *Al Azif* instructs that a sacrifice must take place at each important phase of the moon. That must have been the fate of those three foreign students, last full moon, new moon and half moon. Tonight was the next full moon in the cycle.

"While I left you here to keep watch, I went to see a fellow who has had a lot to do with fighting the Ancient Ones and their acolytes. I knew that Titus had a supply of the star-stones and I begged their use for tonight. I also stopped off to make certain enquiries which gave me half-expected answers.

"There were four leading families in Innsmouth, all of them associating with the Deep Ones: the Marshes, Gilmans, Eliots and Waites, the last name being spelt in the common way. I told you all those months ago that some Innsmouth dwellers probably escaped the federal dragnet. There were quite a few children unaccounted for. He—" nodding at the burning cross from which there was now an abominable stench "—he was the offspring of a Waite. He was brought to this country, a babe in arms, by a distant cousin, a member of the British branch of the family. Wayt was legally adopted and his surname altered to an archaic spelling.

"We'll never know whether it was the Romans or Britons or both that destroyed Vitellius Priscus. Whoever, I think they failed to put the body to the flames and an essence—Porter's black shadow—was therefore able to survive in that sepulchre, waiting through long centuries for a new host.

"But the tradition of keeping outsiders away from this place survived from generation to generation. The reason may have been forgotten but the various landowners remained steadfast to the custom, despite all the turbulence of history, until Sir Peter died and the title passed to someone born and resident in a far land.

"I don't know what would have happened had any person other than Alaric Wayt opened the tomb. Much the same, I expect, although I think that his antecedents made him uncommonly susceptible. It's even possible that his ancestry was the reason for his determination to excavate the site—a racial memory. The tomb shadow must have triggered the instinct to make contact with his hideous kin, very likely in dreams, which is the way the Innsmouth dwellers did it. They goaded him to make the sacrifices necessary to speed his transformation and he researched the *Al Azif* for the essential rites. He chose the students who remained for two reasons: all were small and would minimise effort until his strength grew, and all were from lands where they were unlikely to be missed for a long time if at all. The rest you know."

"How do we explain Wayt's disappearance?" I asked.

"An accident," said Calloway. "His tent will catch fire and will be so thoroughly incinerated as to leave little to investigate. Witnesses will testify to his growing eccentricities, his insistence on staying alone in his tent with only an oil-lamp and the fuel supplies. The local coroner is a Bedhoe man and a verdict of accidental death will be returned."

"What about the girl?"

"She's in a simple trance. Wayt's first sacrifices were carried out the hard way but he soon discovered the secrets of hypnosis. I have enough knowledge to right matters. She'll be told that she was found on the road, sleepwalking."

I searched for other objections. "How do you know this won't re-cur?" I said. "Others may be given permission to dig here. Some residue of the horror may remain to infect them."

Calloway lit a cigarette. "I think not," he answered. "I have been calling in some favors. I'm sure the land will be found to be contaminated with anthrax and the Ministry of Agriculture will seal the area off in perpetuity."

The moon was high by now and the surface of the Channel was silvered to the horizon. It was clear save for the harlequin dappling of small waves.

"They've gone," I said.

"For now," said Calloway. "They'll be back, sometime, somewhere. We haven't won a war or even a battle here tonight. We've won a skirmish, a skirmish so insignificant as to be meaningless."

I could not help feeling bitter as I glanced at the consuming flames behind us. "Then why was this necessary?"

"Stop thinking like a priest for a moment," said Calloway. "If he hadn't been stopped, how many innocents would have died to achieve his purpose? Agreed that he had gone a long way into his transfiguration, but he was nowhere near changed enough to take his place in the sea."

Calloway tossed the stub of his cigarette over the cliff and I watched its glimmer trailing down to diminish in an effervescent cascade of sparks on the rocks below.

"You know," he went on. "It's my opinion that we will never win this hidden war. It has been said, time and again, that the Ancient Ones will return 'when the stars are right.' Think about it, Roderick, when will the stars be right and from whose vantage point?"

He stared at the night sky. "The universe is infinite, and at every point in that infinity the pattern of stars will be different. And from every point in that infinity the patterns will appear to change every few millennia. Given the present limits of human mind and thought, the scales of distance and time are so vast as to be inconceivable, unacceptable even.

"In astronomical terms, however, those scales are nothing but a step, but an instant. From somewhere out there, the stars could be right for the Ancient Ones tomorrow; or the due time could be so remote as for mankind to have become extinct. I hope the latter. For all our sakes, I hope the latter.

"No, we'll never conquer the Ancient Ones or their multitudinous servants. You see, they have time on *their* side."

# The Innsmouth Heritage

## Brian Stableford

The directions which Ann had dictated over the phone allowed me to reach Innsmouth without too much difficulty; I doubt that I would have fared so well had I been forced to rely upon the map printed on the end-papers of her book or had I been forced to seek assistance along the way.

While descending from the precipitous ridge east of the town I was able to compare my own impressions of Innsmouth's appearance with the account given by Ann in her opening chapter. When she spoke to me on the phone she had told me that the book's description was "optimistic" and I could easily see why she had felt compelled to offer such a warning. Even the book had not dared to use the word "unspoiled," but Ann had done her best to imply that Innsmouth was full of what we in England would call "old world charm." Old the buildings certainly were, but charming they were not. The present inhabitants—mostly "incomers" or "part-timers," according to Ann—had apparently made what efforts they could to redeem the houses from dereliction and decay, but the renovated facades and the new paint only succeeded in making the village look garish as well as neglected.

It proved, mercifully, that one of the principal exceptions to this rule was the New Gilman House, where a room had been reserved for me. It was one of the few recent buildings in the village, dating back no further than the sixties. The lobby was tastefully decorated and furnished, and the desk-clerk was as attentive as one expects American desk-clerks to be.

"My name's Stevenson," I told him. "I believe Miss Eliot reserved a room for me."

"Best in the house, sir," he assured me. I was prepared to believe it—Ann owned the place. "You sound English, sir," he added, as he handed me a reservation card. "Is that where you know the boss from?"

"That's right," I said, diffidently. "Could you tell Miss Eliot that I'm here, do you think?"

"Sure thing," he replied. "You want me to help you with that bag?"

I shook my head, and made my own way up to my room. It was on the top floor, and it had what passed for a good view. Indeed, it would have been a very good view had it not been for the general dereliction of the waterfront houses, over whose roofs I had to look to see the ocean. Out towards the horizon I could see the white water where the breakers were tumbling over Devil Reef.

I was still looking out that way when Ann came in behind me. "David," she said. "It's good to see you."

I turned round a little awkwardly, and extended my hand to be shaken, feeling uncomfortably embarrassed.

"You don't look a day older," she said, hypocritically. It had been thirteen years since I last saw her.

"Well," I said, "I looked middle-aged even in my teens. But you look wonderful. Being a capitalist obviously suits you. How much of the town do you own?"

"Only about three-quarters," she said, with an airy wave of her slender hand. "Uncle Ned bought the land for peanuts back in the thirties, and now it's worth—peanuts. All his grand ambitions to 'put the place back on the map' came to nothing. He got tenants for some of the properties he fixed up, but they're mostly week-enders who live in the city and can't afford authentic status symbols. We get a few hundred tourists through during the season—curiosity-seekers, fishermen, people wanting to get away from it all, but it's hardly enough to keep the hotel going. That's why I wrote the book—but I guess I still had too much of the dry historian in me and not enough of the sensational journalist. I should have made more of all those old stories, but I couldn't get my conscience past the lack of hard evidence."

"That's what a university education does for you," I said. Ann and I had met at university in Manchester—the real Manchester, not the place to which fate and coincidence had now brought me—when she was studying history and I was studying biochemistry. We were good friends—in the literal rather than the euphemistic sense, alas—but we hadn't kept in touch afterwards, until she discovered by accident that I was in New Hampshire and had written to me, enclosing her book with news of her career as a woman of property. I had planned to come to see her even before I read the book, and found the excuse which made the prospect even more inviting.

As she watched me unpack, the expression in her grey eyes was quite inscrutable. Politeness aside, she really did look good—handsome rather than pretty, but clear of complexion and stately in manner.

"I suppose your coming over to the States is part of the infamous Brain Drain," she said. "Was it the dollars, or the research facilities which lured you away?"

"Both," I said. "Mostly the latter. Human geneticists aren't worth *that* much, and I haven't published enough to be regarded as a grand catch. I'm just a foot-soldier in the long campaign to map and understand the human genome."

"It beats being chief custodian of Innsmouth and its history," she said, so flatly as to leave no possibility of a polite contradiction.

I shrugged. "Well," I said, "if I get a paper out of this, it will put

Innsmouth on the scientific map, at least—though I doubt that the hotel will get much business out of it. I can't imagine that there'll be a legion of geneticists following in my trail."

She sat down on the edge of the bed. "I'm afraid it might not be so easy," she said. "All that stuff in the book about the Innsmouth look is a bit out of date. Back in the twenties, when the population of the town was less than four hundred it may well have been exactly the kind of inbred community you're looking for, but the post-war years brought in a couple of thousand outsiders, and despite the tendency of the old families to keep to themselves the majority married out. I've looked through the records, and most of the families that used to be important in the town are extinct—the Marshes, the Waites, the Gilmans. If it hadn't been for the English branch, I guess the Eliots would have died out too. The Innsmouth look still exists, but it's a thing of the past—you won't see more than a trace of it in anyone under forty."

"Age is immaterial," I assured her.

"That's not the only problem. Almost all of those who have the look are shy about it—or their relatives are. They tend to hide themselves away. It won't be easy to get them to co-operate."

"But you know who they are—you can introduce me."

"I know who some of them are. But that doesn't mean that I can help you much. I may be an Eliot, but to the old Innsmouthers I'm just another incomer, not to be trusted. There's only one person who could effectively act as an intermediary for you, and it won't be easy to persuade him to do it."

"Is he the fisherman you mentioned over the phone—Gideon Sargent?"

"That's right," she said. "He's one of the few lookers who doesn't hide himself away, though he shows the signs more clearly than anyone else I've seen. He's saner than most—got himself an education under the G.I. Bill after serving in the Pacific in '45—but he's not what you might call talkative. He won't hide, but he doesn't like being the visible archetype of the Innsmouth look—he resents tourists gawping at him as much as anyone would, and he always refuses to take them out to Devil Reef in his boat. He's always very polite to me, but I really can't say how he'll react to you. He's in his sixties now—never married."

"That's not so unusual," I observed. I was unmarried; so was Ann.

"Maybe not," she replied, with a slight laugh. "But I can't help harbouring an unreasonable suspicion that the reason he never married is that he could never find a girl who looked fishy enough."

I thought this a cruel remark, though Ann obviously hadn't meant it to be. I thought it even crueller when I eventually saw Gideon Sargent, because I immediately jumped to the opposite conclusion: that no girl could possibly contemplate marrying him, because he looked too fishy by half.

The description which Ann had quoted in her book was accurate enough detail by detail—narrow head, flat nose, staring eyes, rough skin and baldness—but could not suffice to give an adequate impression of the eerie whole. The old man's tanned face put me in mind of a wizened koi carp, though I could not tell at first—because his jacket collar was turned up—whether he had the gill-like markings on his neck which were the last and strangest of the stigmata of the Innsmouth folk.

Sargent was sitting on a canvas chair on the deck of his boat when we went to see him, patiently mending a fishing-net. He did not look up as we approached, but I had no doubt that he had seen us from afar and knew well enough that we were coming to see him.

"Hello, Gideon," said Ann, when we were close enough. "This is Dr. David Stevenson, a friend of mine from England. He lives in Manchester now, teaching college."

Still the old man didn't look up. "Don't do trips round the reef," he said, laconically. "You know that, Miss Ann."

"He's not a tourist, Gideon," she said. "He's a scientist. He'd like to talk to you."

"Why's that?" he asked, still without altering his attitude. " 'Cause I'm a freak, I suppose?"

"No," said Ann, uncomfortably, "of course not . . ."

I held up my hand to stop her. "Yes, Mr. Sargent," I said. "That is why, after a manner of speaking. I'm a geneticist, and I'm interested in people who are physically unusual. I'd like to explain that to you, if I may."

Ann shook her head in annoyance, certain that I'd said the wrong thing, but the old man didn't seem offended.

"When I were a young'un," he commented, abstractedly, "there was a man offered Ma a hunnerd dollars for me. Wanned t'put me in a glass tank in some kinda sideshow. She said no. Blamed fool—hunnerd dollars was worth summin then." His accent was very odd, and certainly not what I'd come to think of as a typical New England accent. Though he slurred common words he tended to take more trouble over longer ones, and I thought I could still perceive the lingering legacy of his education.

"Do you know what 'genetics' means, Mr. Sargent?" I asked. "I really would like to explain why it's important that I talk to you."

At last he looked up, and looked me in the eye. I was ready for it, and didn't flinch from the disconcerting stare.

"I know what genes are, Doc," he said, coolly. "I bin a little curious myself, y'know, to fin' out how I got to be this way. You gonna tell me? Or is that what y'wanner figure out?"

"It's what I want to figure out, Mr. Sargent," I told him, breathing a slight sigh of relief. "Can I come aboard?"

"Nope," he replied. " 'Taint convenient. You at the hotel?"

"Yes I am."

"See y'there t'night. Quarter of eight. You pay f'r the liquor."

"Okay," I said. "Thanks, Mr. Sargent. I appreciate it."

"Don' mention it," he said. "An' I *still* don' do trips to the reef. Or pose f'r Jap cameras—you mind me, now, Miss Ann."

"I mind you, Gideon," she answered, as we turned away.

As soon as we were out of earshot, she said: "You're honored, David. He's never come to the hotel before—and not because no one ever offered to buy him a drink before. He still remembers the old place, and he doesn't like what Uncle Ned put up in its place any more than he likes all the colonists who moved in when the village was all-but-dead in the thirties."

We were passing an area of the waterfront which looked like a post-war bomb-site—or one of those areas in the real Manchester where they bulldozed the old slums but still haven't got round to building anything else instead.

"This is the part of the town that was torched, isn't it?" I said.

"Sure is," she replied. "Way back in '27. Nobody really knows how it happened, though there are plenty of wild stories. Gang warfare can be counted out—there was no substantial bootlegging here-abouts. Arson for arson's sake, probably. It's mostly mine now—Uncle Ned wanted to rebuild but never could raise the finance. I'd sell the land to any developer who'd take it on, but I'm not hopeful about my chances of getting rid of it."

"Did the navy really fire torpedoes into the trench beyond the reef?" I asked, remembering a story which she'd quoted in her book.

"Depth charges," she said. "I took the trouble to look up the documents, hoping there'd be something sensational behind it, but it seems that they were just testing them. There's very deep water out there—a crack in the continental shelf—and it was convenient for checking the pressure-triggers across the whole spectrum of settings. The navy didn't bother to ask the locals, or to tell them what was going on; the information was still classified then, I guess. It's not un-natural that the wacky stories about sea-monsters were able to flourish uncontradicted."

"Pity," I said, looking back at the crumbling jetties as we began to climb the shallow hill towards Washington Street. "I rather liked all that stuff about the Esoteric Order of Dagon conducting its hideous rites in the old Masonic Hall, and Obed Marsh's covenant with the forces of watery evil."

"The Esoteric Order of Dagon was real enough," she said. "But it's hard to find out what its rituals involved, or what its adherents ac-tually believed, because it was careful not to produce or keep any records—not even sacred documents. It seems to have been one of a group of crazy quasi-gnostic cults which made a big thing about a book called the *Necronomicon*—they mostly died out at about the time the first fully-annotated translation was issued by the Miskatonic University Press. The whole point of being an esoteric sect is lost when your core text becomes exoteric, I guess.

"As for old Obed's fabulous adventures in the South Seas, almost all the extant accounts can be traced back to tales that used to be told by the town character back in the twenties—an old lush named Zadok Allen. I can't swear that every last detail originated in the dregs of a whisky bottle, but I'd be willing to bet my inheritance that Captain Marsh's career was a good deal less eventful than it seemed once Zadok had finished embroidering it."

"But the Marshes really did run a gold refinery hereabouts? And at least *some* of the so-called Innsmouth jewellery is real?"

"Oh sure—the refinery was the last relic of the town's industrial heyday, which petered out mid–nineteenth century after a big epidemic. I've looked at the account-books, though, and it did hardly any business for thirty-five or forty years before it closed down. It's gone now, of course. The few authentic surviving examples of the old Innsmouth jewellery are less beautiful and less exotic than rumor represents, but they're interesting enough—and certainly not local in origin. There are a couple of shops in town where they make 'genuine imitations' for tourists and other interested parties—one manufacturer swears blind that the originals were made by pre-Columbian Indians, the other that they were found by Old Obed during his travels. Take your pick."

I nodded, sagely, as if to say that it was what I'd suspected all along.

"What are you looking for, David?" she asked, suddenly. "You don't really think that there's anything in Zadok Allen's fantasies, do you? You surely can't seriously entertain the hypothesis that the old Innsmouthers were some kind of weird crossbreed with an alien race!"

I laughed. "No," I reassured her, with complete sincerity. "I don't believe that—nor do I believe that they're some kind of throwback to our phantom aquatic ancestors. You'd better sit in tonight when I explain the facts of life to old Gideon; the reality is likely to be far more prosaic than that, alas."

"Why *alas*?" she asked.

"Because what I'm looking for will only generate a paper. If the folklore quoted in your book were even half-true, it would be worth a Nobel Prize."

Gideon Sargent presented himself at the hotel right on time. He was dressed in what I presumed was his Sunday best, but the ensemble included a roll-neck sweater which kept the sides of his neck concealed. There were half a dozen people in the bar, and Gideon drew a couple of curious glances from the out-of-towners, but he was only a little self-conscious. He was used to carrying his stigmata.

He drank neat bourbon, but he drank slowly, like a man who had no intention of getting loaded. I asked a few questions to find out exactly how much he did know about genes, and it turned out that he really was familiar with the basics. I felt confident that I could give him a reasonably full explanation of my project.

"We've already begun the business of mapping the human genome," I told him. "The job will require the collective efforts of thousands of people in more than a hundred research centres, and even then it will take fifteen or twenty years, but we have the tools to do it. While we're doing it, we hope to get closer to the answers to certain basic problems.

"One of these problems is that we don't know how genes collaborate to produce a particular physical form. We know how they code for the protein building blocks, but we don't know much about the biochemical blueprint which instructs a growing embryo how to develop into a man instead of a whale or an ostrich. Now this may seem odd, but one of the best ways of figuring out how things work is to study examples which have gone wrong, to see what's missing or distorted. By doing that, you can build up a picture of what's necessary in order for the job to be done properly. For that reason, geneticists are very interested in human mutations—I'm particularly interested in those which cause physical malformation.

"Unfortunately, physical mutants usually fall into a few well-defined categories, mostly associated with radical and fairly obvious disruptions of whole chromosomes. There are very few viable human variations which operate on a larger scale than changing the color of the skin, or the epicanthic fold which makes Oriental eyes distinctive. That's not entirely surprising, because those which have arisen in the past have mostly been eliminated from the gene-pool by natural selection, or diluted out of existence by hybridization. It's one of the ironies of our trade that while molecular genetics was becoming sophisticated enough to make them significant, the highly inbred communities of the world were disappearing. All we have in America is a handful of religious communities whose accumulations of recessive genes aren't for the most part very interesting. As soon as I read Ann's book I realised that Innsmouth must have been a real genetic treasure-trove back in the twenties. I hope that there still might be time to recover some vital information."

Gideon didn't reply immediately, and for a moment or two I thought he hadn't understood. But then he said: "Not many people got the look any more. Some don' show it 'til they're older, but I don' see much sign of it comin' thru in anyone I see. Ain't no Marshes or Waites any more, and the only Eliots"—he paused to look at Ann—"are distant cousins o' the ones that settled here in the old days."

"But there are a few others, besides yourself, who show some of the signs, aren't there?" Ann put in.

"A few," Gideon admitted.

"And they'd co-operate with Dr. Stevenson—if you asked them to."

"Mebbe," he said. He seemed moodily thoughtful, as though something in the conversation had disturbed him. "But it's too late to do *us* any good, ain't it, Doc?"

I didn't have to ask what he meant. He meant that whatever understanding I might glean from my researches would only be of theoretical value. I wouldn't be able to help the Innsmouthers look normal.

It was, in any case, extremely unlikely that my work would lead to anything which could qualify as a "cure" for those afflicted with the Innsmouth stigmata, but really, there was no longer any need for that.

The Innsmouthers had taken care of the problem themselves. I remembered what I'd said about gross malformations being eliminated from the gene-pool by natural selection, and realised that I'd used the word "natural" in a rather euphemistic way—as many people do nowadays. The selective pressure would work both ways: the incomers who'd recolonized Innsmouth after the war would have been just as reluctant to marry people who had the Innsmouth look as people who had the Innsmouth look would have been to pass it on to their children.

Gideon Sargent was certainly not the only looker who'd never married, and I was sure that he wouldn't have, even if there'd been a girl who looked like he did.

"I'm sorry, Gideon," I said. "It's a cruel irony that your ancestors had to suffer the burden of ignorance and superstition because genetics didn't exist, and that now genetics does exist, there's not much left for you to gain from a specific analysis of your condition. But let's not underestimate the value of understanding, Gideon. It was because your forefathers lacked a true understanding that they felt compelled to invent the Esoteric Order of Dagon, to fill the vacuum of their ignorance and to maintain the pretence that there was something to be proud of in Innsmouth's plight. And that's why stories like the ones Zadok Allen used to tell gained such currency—because they provided a kind of excuse for it all. I'm truly sorry that I'm too late to serve your purposes, Gideon—I only hope that I'm not too late to serve mine. Will you help me?"

He looked at me with those big saucery eyes, so uncannily frightening in their innocence.

"Is there *anythin'* y' can do, Doc?" he asked. "Not about the bones, nor the eyes—I know we're stuck wi' *them*. But the dreams, Doc—can y'do anythin' about the dreams?"

I looked sideways at Ann, uncertainly. There *had* been something in her book about dreams, I recalled, but I hadn't paid much attention to it. It hadn't seemed to be part of the problem, as seen from a biochemist's point of view. Obviously Gideon saw things differently; to him they were the very heart of the problem, and it was because of them that he'd consented to hear me out.

"Everybody has dreams, Gideon," said Ann. "They don't mean anything."

He turned round to stare at her, in that same appalling fashion. "Do *you* have dreams, Miss Ann?" he asked, with seemingly tender concern.

Ann didn't answer, so I stepped into the breach again. "Tell me about the dreams, Gideon," I said. "I don't really know how they fit in."

He looked back at me, obviously surprised that I didn't know everything. After all, I was a doctor, wasn't I? I was the gene-wizard who knew what people were made of.

"All of us who got the look are dreamers," he said, in a painstakingly didactic fashion. " 'Taint the bones an' the eyes as kills us in the end—'tis the dreams which call us out to the reef an' bid us dive into the pit. Not many's as strong as me, Doc—I know I got the look as bad as any, an' had it all the time from bein' a kid, but us Sargents was allus less superstitious than the likes o' the Marshes, even if Obed's kin *did* have all the money 'fore it passed to Ned Eliot. My granpa ran the first motor-bus out o' here, tryin' to keep us connected to Arkham after the branch-line from Rowley was abandoned. It's the ones that *change* goes mad, Doc—they're the ones as starts *believin'.*"

"Believing what, Gideon?" I asked, quietly.

"Believin' as the dreams is true . . . believin' in Dagon an' Cthulhu an' Pth'thya-l'yi . . . believin' as how they c'n breathe through their gills'n dive all the way to the bottom of the ocean to Y'ha-nthlei . . . believin' in the Deep Ones. That's what happens to the people wi' the look, Doc. Natural selection—ain't that what y'called it?"

I licked my lips. "Everyone with the look has these dreams?" I queried. If it was true, I realised, it might make the Innsmouth enigma more interesting. Physical malformation was one thing, but specific associated psychotropic effects was quite another. I was tempted to explain to Gideon that one of the *other* great unsolved questions about the way the genes worked was how they affected mind and behaviour *via* the chemistry of the brain, but that would have meant taking the discussion out into deeper water than he could be expected to handle. There was, of course, a simpler and more probable explanation for the dreams, but in confrontation with Gideon's quiet intensity I couldn't help but wonder whether there might be something more profound here.

"The dreams allus go wi' the look," he insisted. "I had 'em all my life. Real horrors, sometimes—unearthly. Can't describe 'em, but take my word for it, Doc, you don' ever want to meet 'em. I'm way past carin' about the look, Doc, but if you could do summin 'bout the dreams . . . I'll dig up the others f'r ye. Every last one."

It would mean widening the tests, I knew, but I could see that it might be worth it. If the dreams were significant at the biochemical level, I could have something really hot. Not a Nobel Prize, but a real reputation-maker. The implications of discovering a whole new class of hallucinogenics were so awesome that I had difficulty pulling myself back down to earth. *First catch your hare,* I reminded myself, carefully.

"I can't make any promises, Gideon," I told him, trying hard to give the impression that I was being overly modest. "It's not easy to locate abnormal DNA, let alone map it and figure out exactly what it's doing. And I have to say that I have my reservations about the possibility of finding a *simple* answer which will lend itself to some kind of straightforward treatment. But I'll do the best I can to find an explanation of the dreams, and once we have an explanation, we'll be able to see what might be done to banish them. If you can get these people to agree to my taking blood and tissue-samples, I'll certainly do what I can."

"I c'n do it," he promised me. Then he stood up, obviously having said what he came to say, and heard what he'd hoped to hear. I put out my hand to shake his, but he didn't take it. Instead, he said: "Walk me to the shore, will y'Doc?"

I was almost as surprised by this as Ann was, but I agreed. As we went out, I told her that I'd be back in half an hour.

At first, we walked down the hill in silence. I began to wonder whether he really had anything to say to me, as I'd assumed, or

317

whether it was just some curious whim which had inspired him to ask me to go with him. But when we were within sight of the seafront he suddenly said: "You known Miss Ann a long time?"

"Sixteen years," I told him, figuring that it wasn't worth wasting time on an explanation of the fact that we hadn't communicated at all for twelve-and-a-half out of the last thirteen.

"You marry her," he said, as though it were the most natural instruction in the world for one stranger to give another. "Take her to Manchester—or back to England, even better. Innsm'th's a bad place f'r them as owns it, even if they ain't got the look. Don' leave it to y'r kids . . . will it to the state or summin. I know you think I'm crazy, Doc, you bein' an educated man 'n' all, but I know Innsm'th—I got it in th' bones, th' blood an' th' dreams. 'Taint worth it. Take her away, Doc. Please."

I opened my mouth to answer, but he'd timed his speech to preclude that possibility. We were now in one of the narrow waterfront streets which had survived the great fire, and he was already pausing before one of the shabby hovels, opening the door.

"Can't invite y'in," he said, tersely. " 'Taint convenient. G'night, Doc."

Before I could say a single word, the door closed in my face.

Gideon was as good as his word. He knew where to find the remaining Innsmouthers who had the look, and he knew how to bully or cajole them into seeing me. A few he persuaded to come to the hotel; the rest I was permitted to visit in their homes—where some of them had been virtual prisoners for thirty years and more.

It took me a week to gather up my first set of samples and take them back to Manchester. Two weeks after that I returned with more equipment, and took a further set of tissue specimens, some from the people I'd already seen, others—for the sake of comparison—from their unafflicted kinfolk. I threw myself into the project with great enthusiasm, despite that I still had a good deal of routine work to do, both as a research worker and in connection with my teaching. I made what passes in my business for rapid headway, but it wasn't rapid enough for the people of Innsmouth—not that there was ever any real possibility of making good my promise to find a way to banish their evil dreams.

Three months after our first meeting Gideon Sargent died in a freak storm which blew up unexpectedly while he was fishing. His boat was smashed up on Devil Reef, and what was left of it was later recovered—including Gideon's body. The inquest confirmed that he had died of a broken neck, and that the rest of his many injuries had been inflicted after death while the boat was tossed about on and around the reef.

Gideon was the first of my sample to die, but he wasn't the last. As the year crept on I lost four more, all of whom died in their beds of very ordinary causes—not entirely surprisingly, given that two were in their eighties and the others in their seventies.

There were, of course, a few unpleasant whispers which said (arguing *post hoc, ergo propter hoc,* as rumors often do) that my taking the tissue samples had somehow weakened or over-excited the people who died, but Gideon had done some sterling work in persuading the victims of the look that it was in their interests to co-operate with me, and none of the others shut me out.

I had no one left whose appearance was as remarkable as Gideon's. Most of the survivors in my experimental sample showed only partial stigmata of an underdeveloped kind—but they all reported suffering from the dreams now and again, and they all found the dreams sufficiently horrific to want to be rid of them if they could. They kept asking me about the possibility of a cure but I could only evade the question, as I always had.

While I was travelling back and forth from Innsmouth on a regular basis I naturally saw a lot of Ann, and was happy to do so. We were both too shy to be overly intrusive in questioning one another, but as time went by I began to understand how lonely and isolated she felt in Innsmouth, and how rosy her memories of university in England now seemed. I saw why she had taken the trouble to write to me when she learned that I had joined the faculty at Manchester, and in time I came to believe that she wanted to put our relationship on a more formal and permanent basis.

But when I eventually plucked up enough courage to ask her to marry me, she turned me down.

She must have known how hurt I was, and what a blow to my fragile pride I had suffered, because she tried to let me down very gently—but it didn't help much.

"I'm really very sorry, David," she told me, "but I can't do it. In a way, I'd like to, very much—I feel so lonely sometimes. But I can't leave Innsmouth now. I can't even go to Manchester, let alone back to England, and I know you won't stay in the States forever."

"That's just an excuse," I contended, in martyred fashion. "I know you own a great deal of real estate here, but you admit that it's mostly worthless, and you could still collect the rents—the world is full of absentee landlords."

"It's not that," she said. "It's . . . something I can't explain."

"It's because you're an Eliot, isn't it?" I asked, resentfully. "You feel that you can't marry for the same reasons that Gideon Sargent felt that he couldn't. You don't have a trace of the Innsmouth look about you, but you have the dreams, don't you? You nearly admitted as much to Gideon, that night when he came to the hotel."

"Yes," she said, faintly. "I have the dreams. But I'm not like those poor old mad people who locked themselves away until you came. I *know* that you won't find a cure for them, even if you can find an explanation. I understand well enough what can come of your research and what can't."

"I'm not sure that you do," I told her. "In fact, I'm not sure that you understand your own condition. Given that you don't have a trace of the look, and given that you're not directly descended from any of the Eliots of Innsmouth, what makes you think that your nightmares are anything more than just that: nightmares? As you said to Gideon when he raised the issue, everyone has dreams. Even I have dreams." In the circumstances, I nearly said *had,* but that would have been too obvious a whine.

"You're a biochemist," she said. "You think that the physical malformation is the real issue, and that the dreams are peripheral. Innsmouthers don't see it that way—for them, the dreams are the most important thing, and they've always seen the look as an effect rather than a cause. I'm an Innsmouther too."

"But you're an educated woman! You may be a historian, but you know enough science to know what the Innsmouth look *really* is. It's a genetic disorder."

"I know that the Esoteric Order of Dagon and Obed Marsh's adventures in the South Seas are just a myth," she agreed. "They're stories concocted, as you said to Gideon, to explain the dreams and excuse an inexplicable affliction caused by defective genes. But it might as easily have been the Eliots who imported those genes as anyone else, and they might easily have been in the family for many generations—England used to have its inbred populations too, you know. I know that you only took tissue-samples from me for what you called purposes of comparison, but I've been expecting all along that you would come to me and tell me that you'd found the rogue gene responsible for the Innsmouth look, and that I have it too."

"It doesn't matter," I said, plaintively. "It really doesn't matter. We could still get married."

"It matters to me," she said. "And we can't."


I suppose that incident with Ann should have redoubled my determination to trace the DNA-complex which was responsible for the Innsmouth syndrome, in order that I could prove to her that she wasn't afflicted, and that her dreams were only dreams. In fact, it didn't; I was hurt by her rejection, and depressed. I continued to work as hard as I ever had, but I found it increasingly difficult to go to Innsmouth, to stay in the hotel where she lived, and to walk through the streets which she owned.

I began to look for someone else to soothe my emotional bruises, while Ann and I drifted steadily apart. We were no longer good friends in any real sense, though we kept up some kind of a pretence whenever we met.

In the meantime, the members of my experimental sample continued to die. I lost three more in the second year, and it became even more obvious that whatever I discovered wasn't going to be of any practical import to the people whose DNA I was looking at. In a way, it didn't matter that much to the programme—the DNA which Gideon and all the rest had provided still existed, carefully frozen and stored away. The project was still healthy, still making headway.

In the third year, I finally found what I was looking for: an inversion on the seventh chromosome, which trapped seven genes, including three oddballs. In homozygotes like Gideon the genes paired up and were expressed in the normal way; in heterozygotes like most of my sample—including all of the survivors—the chromosomes could only pair up if one of them became looped around, stopping several of the genes from functioning. I didn't know what all of the genes did, or how—but my biochemical analyses had given me a partial answer.

I drove to Innsmouth the next day, in order to tell Ann the news. Although our relationship had soured and fallen apart, I still owed her as much of an explanation as I could now give.

"Do you know what Haeckel's law is?" I asked her, while we walked beside the Manuxet, past the place where the Marsh refinery had once been located.

"Sure," she said. "I read up on the whole thing, you know, after we got involved. Haeckel's law says that ontogeny recapitulates phylogeny—that the embryo, in developing, goes through a series of stages which preserve a kind of memory of the evolutionary history of an organism. It's been discredited, except as a very loose metaphor. I always thought that the Innsmouth look might turn out to have something to do with the fact that the human embryo goes through a stage where it develops gills."

"Only the ghosts of gills," I told her. "You see, the same embryonic structures which produce gills in fish produce different structures in other organisms; it's called homology. Conventional thinking, muddied by the fact that we don't really understand the business of blueprinting for physical structure, supposes that when natural selection works to alter a structure into its homologue—as when the fins of certain fish were modified by degrees into the legs of amphibians, for instance, or the forelimbs of certain lizards became the wings of birds—the blueprint genes for the new structure replace the blueprint genes for the old. But that's not the only way it could happen. It may be that the new genes arise at different loci from the old ones, and that the old ones are simply switched off. Because they aren't expressed any more in mature organisms they're no longer subject to eliminative natural selection, so they aren't lost, and though they may be corrupted by the accumulation of random mutations—which similarly aren't subject to elimination by natural selection—they may remain within the bodies of descendant species for millions of years. If so, they *may* sometimes be expressed if there's a genetic accident of some kind which prevents their being switched off in a particular organism."

She thought about it for a few moments, and then she said: "What you're saying is that human beings—and, for that matter, all mammals, reptiles and amphibians—may be carrying around some of the blueprint genes for making fish. These are normally dormant—untroublesome passengers in the body—but under certain circumstances, the switching mechanism fails and they begin to make the body they're in *fishy.*"

"That's right," I said. "And that's what I shall propose as the cause of the Innsmouth syndrome. Sometimes, as with Gideon, it can happen very early in life, even before birth. In other instances it's delayed until maturity, perhaps because the incipient mutations are suppressed by the immune system, until the time when aging sets in and the system begins to weaken."

I had to wait a little while for her next question, though I knew what it would be.

"Where do the dreams fit in?" she asked.

"They don't," I told her. "Not into the biology. I never really thought they did. They're a psychological thing. There's no psychotropic protein involved here. What we're talking about is a slight failure of the switching mechanism which determines physical structure. Ann, the nightmares come from the same place as the Esoteric Order of Dagon and Zadok Allen's fantasies—they're a response to fear and anxiety and shame. They're infectious in exactly the same way that rumors are infectious—people hear them, and reproduce them. People who have the look *know* that the dreams come with it, and knowing it is sufficient to make sure that they do. That's why they can't describe them properly. Even people who don't have the look, but fear that they might develop it, or feel that for some eccentric reason they *ought* to have it, can give themselves nightmares."

She read the criticism in my words, which said that I had always been right and she had always been wrong, and that she had had no good cause for rejecting my proposal. "You're saying that my dreams are purely imaginary?" she said, resentfully. People always are resentful about such things, even when the news is good, and despite the fact that it isn't their fault at all.

"You don't have the inversion, Ann. That's quite certain now that I've found the genes and checked out all the sample traces. You're not even heterozygous. There's no possibility of your ever developing the look, and there's no reason at all why you have to avoid getting married."

She looked me in the eye, as disconcertingly as Gideon Sargent ever had, though her eyes were perfectly normal, and as grey as the sea.

"You've never seen a *shoggoth*," she said, in a tone profound with despair. "I have—even though I don't have the words to describe it."

She didn't ask me whether I was renewing my proposal—maybe because she already knew the answer, or maybe because she hadn't changed her own mind at all. We walked on for a bit, beside that dull and sluggish river, looking at the derelict landscape. It was like the set for some schlocky horror movie.

"Ann," I said, eventually, "you do believe me, don't you? There really isn't a psychotropic element in the Innsmouth syndrome."

"Yes," she said. "I believe you."

"Because," I went on, "I don't like to see you wasting your life away in a place like this. I don't like to think of you, lonely in self-imposed exile, like those poor lookers who shut themselves away because they couldn't face the world—or who were locked up by mothers and fathers or brothers and sisters or sons and daughters who couldn't understand what was wrong, and whose heads were filled with stories of Obed Marsh's dealings with the devil and the mysteries of Dagon.

"That's the *real* nightmare, don't you see—not the horrid dreams and the daft rites conducted in the old Masonic Hall, but all the lives which have been ruined by superstition and terror and shame. Don't be part of that nightmare, Ann; whatever you do, don't give in to that. Gideon Sargent didn't give in—and he told me once, though I didn't quite understand at the time, that it was up to me to make sure that you wouldn't, either."

"But they got him in the end, didn't they?" she said. "The Deep Ones got him in the end."

"He was killed in an accident at sea," I told her, sternly. "You know that. Please don't melodramatise, when you know you don't believe it. You must understand, Ann—*the real horrors aren't in your dreams, they're in what you might let your dreams do to you.*"

"I know," she said, softly. "I do understand."

I understood too, after a fashion. Her original letter to me had been a cry for help, though neither of us knew it at the time—but in the end, she'd been unable to accept the help which was offered, or trust the scientific interpretation which had been found. At the cognitive level, she understood—but the dreams, self-inflicted or not, were simply too powerful to be dismissed by knowledge.

And that, I thought, was yet another *real* horror: that the truth, even when discovered and revealed, might not be enough to save us from our vilest superstitions.

I didn't have any occasion to go back to Innsmouth for some time, and several months slipped past before I had a reason sufficient to make me phone. The desk-clerk at the hotel was surprised that I hadn't heard—as if what was known to Innsmouthers ought automatically to be known to everyone else on earth.

Ann was dead.

She had drowned in the deep water off Devil Reef. Her body had never been recovered.

I didn't get any sort of prize for the Innsmouth project, and despite its interesting theoretical implications it wasn't quite the reputation-maker I'd hoped it would be. As things turned out, it was only worth a paper after all.

# The Homecoming

## Nicholas Royle

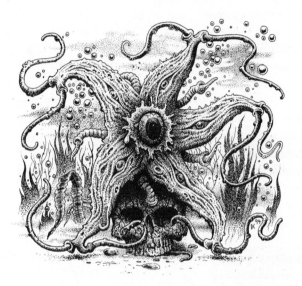

Belgrade's Danube railway station was cold and dark, its staff unhelpful. Daniela had to suppress a desire to turn back and return to her little room off Yuri Gagarin Boulevard. But she had taken the decision and there was no going back on it.

Belgrade had been comfortable—the standard of living far higher than anywhere in Romania—but never quite home. Her grasp of Serbo-Croat just about allowed her to order a beer and buy a bus ticket. It was with the help of other Romanian exiles that she had been able to find a room and furnish it with a large sofa and an old TV.

When reports of the Timisoara massacre first leaked out of Romania she stayed indoors round the clock waiting for further news. She was watching bleary-eyed from lack of sleep when the crowds massed in central Bucharest ostensibly to demonstrate support for

President Ceausescu. She couldn't believe what she was seeing. The Berlin Wall had crumbled and the Czech communists had been ousted only weeks before. And the Romanians were going to let the Ceausescu regime get away with the slaying of thousands of people in Timisoara, not to mention the subjugation of the entire country for the last twenty-four years.

The people in the square waved their banners and listened while Ceausescu droned from his balcony. Then the unthinkable appeared to be happening. Daniela tensed on her sofa, hardly daring to breathe in case she missed anything. Parts of the crowd had thrown down their banners and begun to berate their president. More joined in and Ceausescu became confused. He believed the people loved him because his sycophants assured him of it daily. He began a chopping, sweeping motion with his arm as if he wanted to brush the trouble-makers aside or erase them like an error committed in haste.

That night, troops from the ranks of the Securitate—the hated secret police—reacted with force. Dozens died but the spirit of the people was not broken. At eleven the next morning state television reported that the defence minister was a traitor and had committed suicide. The crowd sensed it as a turning point and attacked the central committee building.

Daniela was crouching on the floor, her mouth alternately dry and filling up with the juices of fear and excitement. Her whole body vibrated like a tightly coiled spring.

Ceausescu was still in the building when the revolutionaries gained access and began to rampage through it. The TV pictures showed him taking off in a helicopter at the same time as the revolutionaries swarmed on to the roof.

Daniela spat at the screen, pleaded with God to let the helicopter crash.

She watched the feared Securitate fight their desperate counter-revolution and was still watching on Christmas Day when the Ceausescus were shown lying dead on the ground after their summary trial and execution by firing squad.

She sat so close her nose touched the screen. There he was, the *Conducator*, the President of the Socialist Republic of Romania, the

Grand Leader of the Peoples of Romania, the despot who had bled the country dry with his insane obsession to pay off all foreign debt, so that his people queued for bread at 5 a.m. and considered chicken's feet a feast. The paranoid tyrant, who had his toilet seat scrubbed with alcohol before and after use and sent anyone making a joke about him to jail for two years, lay in the dirt, his collar tightly fastened, his grey old face puffy, his eyes closed forever.

She clasped the television set to her and rolled on to her back.

Two months later in Belgrade-Danube railway station she was thinking of reneging on her decision to go back home to Romania. No, she couldn't. She climbed on board the train. The guard wanted her to pay in US dollars for a sleeper. She offered him ten. He shook his head.

"How much?" she asked him.

"Thirty," he muttered sourly.

It was Daniela's turn to shake her head. "No way," she snorted and stalked off to find a seat. The problem with Romanian Railways was that you acquired a seat reservation at the same time as you bought your ticket. But only if your journey started inside Romania. She couldn't reserve a seat in Belgrade. When they crossed into Romania people would board the train at Timisoara with reservations for unmarked seats and Daniela could find herself with nowhere to sit. But she wasn't paying $30 for a sleeper. It was a disgrace and hardly in the spirit of the revolution.

The train rolled through northern Serbia, through the province of Vojvodina, and Daniela grew bored of the unchanging scenery. She felt tense and nervous about returning to Romania.

Several weeks had passed since the revolution. The counter-revolution had been put down inside a week, after which time Securitate agents were smoked out of the ruins and either killed or sent for trial. So she had nothing to fear. On the contrary: she was excited to be going back. But excitement always smelt a little like fear.

The motion of the train lulled her to sleep.

She dreamt pictures from the revolution. They were things she'd seen on television but now without the protection of the screen. Tanks rumbled through the streets of Bucharest belching exhaust fumes and shelling buildings indiscriminately. Automatic fire scored deep scratches in the plaster finishes of rundown apartment buildings. The muzzle of a gun appeared at a window, followed by a face and immediately a burst of fire directed at the street. A soldier fired back from behind the tank. He hit his target and the man fell back into the room while his gun toppled to the street. The tank's gun turret swivelled thirty degrees and shelled the building. Masonry and glass shattered like toys and flames blew out of several blackened windows. The gun twisted further round and shelled the next building, and the next.

It was a kind of purging process, she realised dimly. An exorcism by mortar and fire of the city's evil presence.

She woke up worrying about the tunnels. Apparently a secret network of tunnels existed underneath Bucharest accessible only to the Securitate. But with terrified agents scampering like rabbits for cover, the hiding places could not have remained inviolable.

She fell asleep again. Border guards woke her. They impinged on her exhausted senses as uniformed automata. Sleep took her once more. At Timisoara there was a mighty scuffling and shambling of feet and bodies as denizens of the persecuted town crammed on to the train. "Reservat! Reservat" they protested in a flat, toneless whine, but she snored louder and they died away.

Bucharest was still several hours distant. Daniela slid in and out of sleep as if it were a bath full of tepid, scummy water. She confused glimpses of the forlorn compartment and its huddled occupants with snatches of dreams. At one point she jumped when she thought she saw Ceausescu and his wicked wife slumped in the opposite seats, their faces puffed up and pockmarked by sooty bullet wounds, their jaws collapsed.

At some indeterminate stage in her dreams, Daniela became aware of natural light. Early-morning light the colour of dishwater was smeared across the window, streaked by thicker cloud as if applied unevenly with a cloth. Two of her fellow passengers were already awake: a stubble-faced old man stuffed into a shabby trilby, and a sallow boy no more than eighteen or nineteen. Their complexions reflected the mood of the morning and none of the revolutionary zeal she had expected.

Once she had woken up there was no going back to sleep. For one thing the dreams were too disturbing. She peered through the grimy glass hoping to see some feature of the presumed landscape loom out of the fog. But nothing emerged. The longer she stared the more she became dissociated from reality. Maybe Romania had vanished, replaced by this almost sea-like fog. She half expected to glimpse the flick of a fish's tail or to meet the mournful gaze of some fantastic creature of the deep.

She must have drifted back to sleep because all of a sudden she was looking out of the window at the outskirts of Bucharest. The fog had lifted but still hung above the rooftops, below the sky; more a mist now than a fog, but one polluted by soot and grit.

The train passed over a level crossing and Daniela caught sight of figures loitering at various points down a dusty street. One of the Dacias parked in a long row beneath the skeletal trees was a charred wreck. She supposed there would be the odd one or two scattered about.

But the train rattled on deeper into the city. She'd only been away a year and in that time things had changed. In the last decade most of the city's old buildings, churches first and foremost, had come under threat of demolition. It was no idle threat. The train passed a section of waste ground peppered with weeds that Daniela realised with a pang had been the site of one of the city's oldest Catholic churches.

With a jolt from the locomotive as it braked round the last curve, the line of dirty green carriages visible ahead through the window see-sawed into the Gara de Nord.


The station was the same as she remembered it. As ugly as sin itself. Eager for impressions she walked out into the streets. They smelt the same as they had before, of spoilt and rotten fruit. Since fresh fruit had rarely been freely available in Bucharest, Daniela had always believed the drains to be responsible. It depressed her that the revolution had not left its own scent on the city. She looked for signs of the fighting she'd watched on the television news. There were potholes in the middle of the road, but there always had been. The people she passed looked much as they had done before: unhealthy, paranoid, defeated. There was none of the joy of liberation in their eyes, no spark of defiance. The burden appeared not to have been lifted from them.

She wandered bewildered away from the railway station and its satellite cheap hotels and prostitutes. One street crossed another and turned into a new one. But they all looked the same. She passed a lot of broken and boarded-up windows. Doors were tightly locked and where shutters protected windows still further, they were snapped shut.

When she stopped walking she fancied she could hear movement behind the sightless windows and obstructed doorways. But the susurrant nature of the noise she heard put her more in mind, once more, of the city's drains.

On the corner was a dingy grocery store. She peered inside but could make nothing out of the huge shadows and shafts of dusty reflected light. Behind her the street whispered and she felt unaccountably anxious. She looked round. Three young children stood over a mound of fur on the opposite corner. Daniela looked closer and saw that the animal was a dog. Fixed in a rictus, its jaw was caked with blood and its legs stuck out stiffly. The children stared at Daniela with wide but uncurious eyes. One of them kicked the dog's belly with a bare foot. The dead animal scraped against the gritty pavement. Daniela hurried into the grocery store.

She became instantly lost in a maze of shelves. They held nothing but dust so thick it looked like stacks of dead mice. She turned into a dead end and frightened a spider. As big as a bunch of keys it clattered on to the floor and scuttled under the bottom shelf.

Sweat began to run in the dust on her forehead and her breathing became tight. She whirled round looking for the exit. An aisle looked promising, but when she turned the corner she found herself by the counter. She would have fled but a man materialised from shadows which hung like curtains and twitched.

"What do you want?" he asked her in a friendly voice. She wondered if it might be a trap.

"The shelves are empty," she whispered hoarsely.

He pointed to a selection of pickles and preserves in jars on a shelf behind the counter. He explained that stocks were low. His manner seemed not unfriendly and Daniela felt that if she couldn't trust him she couldn't trust anyone in this godforsaken city.

"I've been away," she said. "I saw everything on television. And now it looks the same as before."

The man shrugged his shoulders beneath his grubby shopcoat.

"Why are people still afraid?" she demanded crossly. "The Securitate are finished, aren't they?"

At this the man's brows knitted and he raised a yellowed finger to his lips. They parted to release a sound which reminded her of the boarded-up windows. She noticed that the man's finger also seemed to be pointing at the wall above his head. When she squinted through the gloom she recognised beneath trails of dusty cobwebs a photograph frame.

Daniela turned and ran. She couldn't deny that the frame had enclosed the shiny button eyes and hamster cheeks of the executed dictator. Why hadn't the photograph been destroyed? She collided with a shelf and coughed and spluttered when the dust flew in her face like a cloud of flies.

She was relieved to reach the door but distressed to see the three children across the street knelt down around the dog, plunging their large bony hands into its split carcass.

Weakened by her experience in the shop, Daniela felt unable to intrude on the depravity. She turned her back and at the next junction headed down the street that looked least threatening. There were still shuttered windows and patches of broken glass in the road but she began to feel reassured by certain signs. There were more shops and queues of people emerging from their doors. At an intersection she turned down a major boulevard towards the city centre.

Here the scars of civil war were plentiful. Burnt-out and overturned cars, entire tenement blocks destroyed by fire, craters in the road. Only the Intercontinental Hotel appeared untouched, where foreign journalists and newsmen would no doubt have stayed. Daniela drifted into a couple of stores. The photographs of Ceausescu had been taken down and left bleached rectangles on the wall. There was little to buy apart from the ubiquitous jars of pickled fruit and slabs of sweaty cheese.

She wandered further into the commercial district. Window-shoppers thronged the narrow lanes. Daniela couldn't help comparing the shops and goods to those available in Belgrade. In truth, there was no comparison.

She turned her attention to the shoppers themselves. They were, for the most part, dowdy and introspective. Before the revolution, one in four citizens was reckoned to be an informer. Consequently no one spoke, making Bucharest an aural city of shuffled footsteps. Even now few words were exchanged, as if the facility had deserted the people.

Unless . . .

Unless there were still good reason to be fearful of speaking.

Daniela's stomach flipped over. Her heart raced. The Securitate's unofficial uniform had consisted of tracksuits and leather jackets.

All around her in the street were men dressed this way. She had got used to seeing expensive leisure wear in Belgrade and thinking nothing of those inside it. But in Bucharest these clothes *meant* something.

A dark, swarthy man in jeans and a leather jacket carrying a shopping bag filled with jars and potatoes approached Daniela. Her legs went elastic. He looked at her eyes as he passed and she felt her soul bristle.

Across the street a middle-aged man wearing a tracksuit stood looking in a shoe-shop window. A woman in a long black coat came out of the shop and took his arm.

Two young men shared a joke as they sauntered down the middle of the street. At whose expense? she wondered as she eyed their leather jackets.

She couldn't remember if there had been so many tracksuits and jackets before. But maybe they didn't mean anything. They would be easier to get hold of after the revolution. And anyway, the Securitate had been eliminated. The National Salvation Front had seen to that.

Her head was in a whirl because she didn't know what to believe. She recalled the thought she'd had upon waking up in the train, about the tunnels. There were tunnels under the street where she stood, and secret passages in the Central Committee Building and the People's Palace. Was it possible that the Securitate had burrowed so deep beneath the city and into the nation's psyche, that they had become ingrained, indelible, immortal?

*The Deep Ones.*

Thrown off balance by panic, she began to run up the street, skidding to a halt outside shop doorways to look in. People stopped and stared. Men in leather jackets, women wearing fur hats, young men in tracksuits. At one doorway she grabbed hold of the doorposts and hurled herself into the shop's interior. It was a clothing store. To right and left hung cheap blouses and poor-quality jeans. Customers and staff stared open-mouthed as she dashed between the racks, brushing against the blouses and sending metal hangers spinning. She ground to a halt in a room at the back of the store furthest from the street. The carpet was reedy and worn and the floorboards sagged beneath her feet. The carpet smelt too, but the reek of leather was stronger. Around the room on rails suspended from the ceiling hung leather jackets. There were hundreds of them. In the middle of the room rails carrying tracksuits had been pushed together to squeeze in as many as possible. She caught a glimpse of a figure slipping out of the room by way of a narrow doorway between two thick curtains of leather and buckles and zip fasteners.

Her instinct was to run and grab the man from behind and force him to look at her. But she was immobilised by fear. The abundance of expensive gear should have relieved her anxiety—the inference being that this stuff was now widely available—but the effect was the reverse. She felt scrutinized. As if the jackets and cotton trousers had already been filled by the ever-watchful sharp-eared agents of the Securitate. She remembered mentioning Ceausescu's name in a factory canteen and the entire row of tables falling silent. One out of four of her fellow workers was bending an ear for a whispered criticism, the other three too scared to air their views. A week later she was rapped across the knuckles and slapped by a supervisor for failing to meet her quota, where normally a verbal chastisement would have been expected. She never had proof that the two incidents were related. But in a country where terror and paranoia reigned, proof was irrelevant.

She didn't need to worry any more, she told herself. Ceausescu and Elena were dead. She'd seen their bodies on television. They were the *Old Ones* now. They were history.

The garments surrounding her were just harmless threads inhabited by nothing more than twisted pieces of wire.

They were like shrouds enclosing ghosts.

*Or swaddling clothes wrapped around newborn terrors.*

The paranoia was a cancer. You thought you'd got rid of it. Then it sprang up again.

Daniela shivered and walked towards the doorway. She brushed against a jacket and the hanger jangled like the spider in the grocery store. The leather touched her cheek and she jumped away: it felt cold as a dead fish. Taking affright, she hared out of the shop.

The street was no haven. Her fellow citizens thronged the narrow streets and lanes and none could be trusted. She snaked through the queues of shoppers and escaped the commercial district for the wide boulevards where she could breathe easier. The people here were as few as the denuded trees under which they walked. Awkward adolescents in ill-fitting polyester suits stood guard in particular doorways as if the revolution had been a dream or a film made for television.

At the next intersection two police motorbikes roared into the boulevard, resounding against the canyon walls formed by massive apartment blocks. Following the police bikes came two smart black Dacias. Another escort was two seconds behind. The cavalcade gained speed, moving down the wide thoroughfare away from Daniela.

She felt an icy hand grip her insides and squeeze. Why did the country's new leaders ride around with a police escort? The National Salvation Front *was* the revolution. They didn't need protecting from the people. They *were* the people. She resumed her stride. Maybe they feared the Securitate like she did. With the Ceausescus dead the former secret police had nothing to lose, so might be even more dangerous than before.

*The tunnels, the tunnels . . .*

She imagined she could hear them susurrating in the dark labyrinth, feeling their way beneath the city, behind the façade, like grubs in a rotten apple. It smelt as bad.

She had noticed that passersby had slunk into the shadows of the buildings when the black Dacias came into view. Now they came out again like slow-witted, sightless creatures from beneath stones.

She stepped into the road and crossed to the other side. Cutting through an area of light industry she aimed for the district where she had lived, before deciding she'd had enough and hiking through the mountains south of Resita, where the frontier was traversable in the early hours of the morning. She patted her pocket and felt reassured by the bulge the keys made.

The devastation got worse as she veered south-east. Entire blocks were destroyed or the lower floors were knocked out and the upper storeys abandoned. Where people clung to their past existences, shreds of curtains were tousled by the breeze through jagged holes in the glass. A face peered down into the street. Its complexion hinted at a lifetime spent hundreds of fathoms beneath daylight. Daniela watched to see if the eyes would follow her as she passed by the building. They did not. She felt queerly light-headed and wondered if the detached aspect of the face was more than just an impression. It looked bloodless enough to have been severed, possibly weeks before.

Disappointment awaited her when she reached the building that had been hers. The upper floors had been demolished and the debris had trickled down to fill the apartments nearer the ground. Daniela had lived within four cracked, peeling walls on the third floor. She could still make out her room. It resembled a ruined tooth in which caries had festered for years.

Tears stung her eyes. She tried to knuckle them back. Instead of wanton destruction, it was a sacrifice in the name of the people. The Old Ones were dead, the Deep Ones bereft of leadership. All she had lost was a place to sleep. She took the keys from her pocket and flung them into the rubble at the base of the building. Wiping at her tears with a sleeve, she walked away, wondering glumly where to seek shelter.

At the back of her mind since returning to the city had been her brother and his apartment in the south-west quarter. It was fifteen years at least since they had seen each other and she had never visited him at home, but she had the address.

She headed back towards the city centre, wrinkling her nose at the ripe stench that blew up side roads from abandoned buildings and stagnant sewers. Among pedestrians once more she watched them slyly, but too many gibbous eyes met hers. They were observing her. She diverted her gaze to the pavement, where it existed, and the pitted road where it did not. She wondered if her clothes, acquired in Belgrade, aroused suspicion. But they were dull compared to items she could have bought.

She saw a bus and thought about crossing town in one to save time: soon it would be getting dark. It stopped at a red light and she frowned at its broken windows and dented panels. A skin of grime had been pulled tight over the whole bus. Disembodied heads bobbed behind the thick aquarium glass as it lunged away from the intersection.

Daniela shuddered at the thought of stepping into such a bus and the concertina doors flapping shut behind her like sentient accomplices of the dubious folk already on board. She would feel like a defendant confronted by her jurors and judges. Guilty until proven innocent. Sentenced and executed right there in court. Which, after all, was what the people had done to the Ceausescus. So now the Securitate would take their revenge. Suddenly everyone in the city was in the service of the Securitate and she was their quarry.

Another bus had pulled up at the side of the road and its doors folded back. Daniela turned and fled into the next side street. She didn't look back, but crossed the street and turned out of it as soon as she could. At the next corner she looked behind. There was nothing to see. Just the same random patterns of broken glass and boarded-up windows, machine-gun scratches and shell craters. She kept walking in what she hoped was the right direction, but had lost heart. She glanced up cross-streets, having developed the irrational fear that the bus might be following her on a parallel track.

Before long she was completely lost and her teeth had begun to chatter with the cold. Dusk obscured the nature of everything within her field of vision. Street lighting, part of the Old Ones' legacy, was the merest glimmer. Like a torch swung in a shuttered house, it only served to make it seem darker than it was. Daniela strained to read the name of the hundredth identical street she'd turned into. She was about to give up when the shadows smudging the letters cleared for a moment and she read: Gheorghe Street.

That was the street. It had to be.

Excitedly she dug a folded piece of paper out of her coat pocket and scrutinized it. The street name was the same.

With a lighter step she moved down the street trying to read the numbers. When she reached the right building she stepped back and gazed up at it. Nothing distinguished the building from its neighbours. The sky above the roofs was rapidly losing its colour. She ran up three flights of stairs, dodging lumps of masonry and piles of household rubbish. The door to her brother's flat was ajar. She knocked, expecting no reply, and gently pushed the door open. It was too dark to make anything out. She flicked a light switch and nothing happened.

Lurking on the threshold she became afraid, unable to enter or leave the apartment. There was no sound from the rest of the building, nothing stirring in the street. She couldn't even hear the sluicing of the drains. The flat smelt bad. Still she couldn't see anything, though her eyes had had time to adjust.

Having come so far, across borders real and imaginary, she couldn't just walk away. Something—maybe the same determination that helped her escape from the country in the first place—carried her into the apartment. She felt her way along the wall beyond the light switch. The plaster was clammy beneath her right hand. She moved slowly forward, her left arm extended in front of her. Suddenly the wall disappeared. She had reached an open doorway and peered through. Illumination from outside squeezed through cracks between boards nailed across the window frame. Three or four faint rods of light divined the room's secrets: a split mattress, stuffing and springs extruded, a smashed table, and an unresolvable jigsaw of broken glass.

A soft clunk came from somewhere behind her.

She froze and caught her breath. It was probably a bird trapped under the roof, or a rat. Or a man. A Securitate agent in hiding. A desperate man with nothing to lose.

She strained her ears for any kind of noise. The streets were as quiet as death. Then, as light as feathers falling on snow, she heard a pattering of tiny clawed feet.

Rats. She didn't mind rats. She preferred them to men.


There was no point staying at the apartment. Her brother was obviously long gone and without light she could neither search for clues to his whereabouts, nor clear a space to sleep. Gingerly she picked her way out of the apartment and down to street level. There was no one about. She crossed the street and walked to its end. There she turned right and headed in what she hoped was the direction of the city centre.

She was strangely comforted by the slushing of the drains when she noticed the noise had returned. There were passersby too. Some turned ostentatiously to watch her as she passed; others tended more to the shadows away from the piss-yellow streetlamps. A hotel sign flickered and buzzed. She asked for a single room. The assistant manager gave her forms to fill out and, after a brief, mumbled phone conversation, a key. She trudged up the stairs to the second floor and peered at the numbers on the doors, looking for 25. The lighting was meagre: every other bulb had been removed and those remaining leached no more than 20 watts of soupy ochre. She twisted the key and closed the door behind her. Only when she was confident no one had followed to listen outside the door did she begin to undress. She dropped her sweater on a plain wooden chair by the window. The moon was almost full. She beheld her image in a cracked mirror as she pulled off her shirt and unfastened her underwear. The moon-light fell on her pale body like a caul, making the number branded on her shoulder stand out: 20363.

She climbed into bed and hugged the blankets about her. She was trying to deny the regret she felt at coming back. Though the window was closed she could hear shuffling footsteps in the street. Within half an hour they had completely died away. She was drowsy and her limbs ached.

A sound outside her door made her jump and tingle with fright. She had heard footsteps. She listened but heard nothing. Maybe she'd dreamt it. Then, quite distinctly, she heard footsteps coming along the corridor, slowing down as they approached her room. Another set of footsteps came from the opposite direction and followed the same pattern. Voices muttered unintelligibly and were raised slightly as if in disagreement.

Suddenly the door rattled in its frame. The handle twisted and turned. A weight was pressed against it from outside and Daniela heard wood splinter.

They were getting in and she couldn't move: the blankets had pinioned her to the bed. She thrashed and grunted.

A long *craaaack* from the door.

She screamed.

And woke up, drenched in sweat and trembling with fear.

There was no sound in or outside her room. The hotel was as quiet as a morgue. She curled up into a ball underneath the bed clothes and tried to relax.

She was walking through the city again. Along nondescript streets battle-scarred from the revolution. With no aim in mind she just kept on walking. One street blended into another. She turned corners without being aware of changing direction. Her sense of smell, however, was active. The city stank of the drains which gurgled beneath the streets. And the smell was getting stronger. She walked on past darkened windows and barricaded doorways. The stench wafted up the street towards her in waves. At the end of the street she turned left into a wide boulevard as empty as it would have been in the early hours of the morning even though the sky was afternoon-bright. The boulevard broadened before her. A soft, persistent thrum could be felt beneath her feet. The old tenements had disappeared and been replaced by new buildings, huge and bland. She passed over a manhole cover and heard the rushing of something beneath. It smelt like sewage but sounded much thicker, almost corporeal. She wondered what vermin might be crawling around beneath the city.

She left the apartment blocks behind. In the middle of the boulevard now were fountains constructed out of plaster and false marble, and tall streetlamps twisted like grappling irons. These distractions melted away and she was suddenly engulfed by the stench of the drains. Like the sewage outfall pipes at Constanta, the smell reminded her also of the sea.

The boulevard had become a vast expanse stretching ahead of her to some kind of reef raised above it.

Then, in a flash, she saw the water. The entire boulevard between where she stood and the mysterious reef was covered with water. She stepped back in alarm for it was filthy water.

There was a haze above it which may have been steam or putrescence rising from the water. It was like a vast sea clogged with human issue. The stench became so bad she retched dryly. The reef shimmered in the haze and appeared about to reform its questionable geometry. Then it was solid again and peculiarly ugly and threatening, as before. If it was formed of rock, the surface was scored with holes and tunnels, like a maze. She wondered what foul creatures inhabited such a terrible place. The thought struck her that it might be a huge encrustation of waste fashioned by the tides into a rocky reef.

She noticed her legs were carrying her forward into the polluted shallows and screamed and screamed and screamed . . . until she woke up.

She sat up, her head throbbing from the horror of the dream and the din of her terror. Her screams echoed like ghosts on a tape recorder. Otherwise the hotel was quiet. No one came running to restrain the mad woman. Between two rags of curtains the morning fell into the room like a slab of unwashed concrete.

In her mind she kept replaying the stark image of the reef sticking out of the sea of vile waste. She imagined a myriad dirty parasites crawling all over their host.

The reef resembled nothing she'd seen in Bucharest, yet the stench of the drains and the random patterns of the street were an inextricable part of her new experience of the city.

She hauled her body out of bed, sensing it must be quite late in the morning. The tap in the bathroom at the end of the hall dribbled cold brown water, which only reminded her of her dream.

Downstairs the assistant manager watched her walk across the foyer, place her key on the desk counter and head for the exit. As she opened the door to the street she heard him pick up the phone and mutter a few words in a thick accent. She felt like an outsider, unable even to understand the language.


By day her brother's apartment building looked unremarkable. The gouts of trash littering the stairway offered no clues. She pushed open his door and stepped inside.

The apartment had been devastated, not by artillery, it seemed, for the walls and floors were intact, but by routine wreckers, obviously agents of the Securitate running amuck as they launched the counter-revolution; on the wall they had daubed in black paint the single word TRAITOR. Every item of furniture had been smashed. Even the three pieces of the bathroom suite had received sledgehammer blows. The bath had been holed, the toilet and washbasin had large chunks knocked out of them. She twisted one of the taps. Pipes groaned and water the same colour as her dream splashed her hand. She withdrew it instantly and wiped it on her trousers, shuddering. But she noticed, as it continued to run, that the brown disappeared and the water was soon clear. She switched off the tap, slightly encouraged.

Investigating the remaining rooms, she was surprised by the size of her brother's apartment. She wondered how he had come to live so well.

The headboard of his bed had been reduced to splinters but the base was still functional. She fetched the split mattress from the front room and placed it good-side-up on the bed. Maybe, if she could find sheets and a blanket, she wouldn't have to go back to the hotel.

She worked for two hours or more, piling rubbish in the corridor outside the apartment and salvaging what sticks of furniture she could. She tried removing some of the filth from the kitchen wall with tap water and rags from under the cleft sink. Driven by a determination to save what she could of her old life in the city, tenuous though she believed the link with her brother to be, she rubbed and scraped at the walls. Soon exhaustion calmed her efforts and she realised no progress would be made without proper materials. There was also the graffiti in the front room which she was determined to remove. Her brother was a patriot. She had no doubt he was out demonstrating at the moment his building was overrun. Though they had never been close, she felt a rush of protective love for him. *Let him be safe,* she prayed, as her mind conjured images of him lying crushed under masonry, dumped in a mass grave with another man's foot in his face, or crumpled at the base of a deeply scratched wall riddled with bullets, like the dead tyrant.

She left the flat to look for cleaning materials and to get some fresh air. She tried not to feel intimidated by the streets. She thought her personal efforts to eradicate the Securitate should strengthen her. Taking a new route which she hoped would lead to shops—there were none near the hotel—she jumped once when a car backfired in a neighbouring street.

The gloomy overcast of the morning had thinned only slightly. Nevertheless, when she turned into the boulevard it seemed brighter. For the middle of the afternoon the pavements were eerily quiet. The buildings were more modern and while they were less grim in their aspect, they were certainly more banal. She passed a row of elaborate fountains and stopped dead in her tracks.

Her heart, after missing a beat, thumped like a triphammer. Her mouth dried up and sweat sprang out on her hairline.

In front of her was the filthy sea of her dream and, shimmering, the reef.

She felt faint. Fear pooled in her mouth. Her skin prickled.

The mirage vanished, to be replaced by the New People's Palace, separated from her by an expanse of false marble. She recognised the Palace, Ceausescu's last folly, from television pictures filmed during its construction. This whole end of the city had been systematically razed and redeveloped as New Bucharest. She remembered now, the new buildings she'd passed were apartments for Securitate agents. It had been claimed that secret tunnels linked both the Palace and the new apartments to the existing tunnels under the city.

She looked at the Palace again. And screamed. It had changed back into the reef. The foul stench made her retch. She spewed bile into the sea lapping at her feet and scampered back from it.

But there was only false marble beneath her feet, discoloured by her involuntary disgust. The Palace, with its massive frontage, crenellated windows and deep-set archways bore a striking resemblance to the reef, as if she'd unknowingly modelled the dreamed edifice on this gleaming monstrosity.

She tore herself away to go in search of disinfectant and cloths. She settled instead for a bucket of thin white paint and a thick brush. As she set to work on the kitchen walls she was troubled by thoughts of the Palace and its inversion, the reef. She worried about the new apartment buildings and most of all the drains; the tunnels . . .

If Hell were to revisit the earth its denizens would come crawling up through the tunnels.

She dipped the brush and drew a broad swathe across the wall. *Cover-up,* she thought anxiously. But what she was doing felt more honest than that. A diseased branch had been severed and she was painting the stump to protect it. Maybe her brother would come back and be grateful for her efforts. For now, though, she was concerned on a practical level with making the apartment habitable. Though she could go back to Belgrade whenever she liked, she felt tied to Bucharest. She had come home. The only family she had in the world was here. Somewhere. She dipped the brush and stroked the wall. Dipped and stroked.

In the front room she obliterated the insult, TRAITOR. But when she stood back the word was still legible, so she slapped on several more layers. She stretched into corners and crouched down to the floor.

# Mother
# Hydra

Suddenly she stopped brushing. Something had caught her eye; a slanting graffito near the bottom of the wall. She rubbed away a smudge of dirt that had been obscuring it and read, "Daniela. 20363." Her heart jumped and she wasn't sure which emotion had kicked it. Love for her almost unknown brother, or fright at seeing her identity starkly represented on the wall? Had he scribbled it distracted by fear and excitement as the revolution gripped the city? Maybe he feared for her safety. Or was it, as it appeared, some kind of accusation or condemnation? Maybe the filth who had insulted her brother had intended to come after her next, not knowing she had fled the country a year before. But why would they write her name and number on the wall? And how would they even know of the number branded on her left shoulder?

It had to be her brother, desperate to help, unable to contact her. He would have seen the number when they were tiny children in Orphanage Number Six. Before they got separated. How he had committed the number to memory when so young was a mystery to her. But clearly he had. Tears stung her eyes as she wondered what their parents might have been like. They must have suffered and died so young. She had never known their names, nor seen their likeness, yet had always carried a dull ache for them which occasionally flared up, like a recurrent ulcer.

The terrible weight of self-pity now descended on her. No parents throughout her youth, no affection from the institutions that had raised her; and now no brother to share her grief. She left the brush in the paint and slunk into the bedroom where she curled up tightly on the cold, damp mattress.


The Deep Ones. The Old Ones.

The tunnels, the tunnels . . .

She couldn't clear her mind of anxiety before sleep stole from the darkest shadows of the room to claim her.

The reef stood proud of the stinking sea. The air shimmered but the reef stood firm as rock.

Her eye was hurting. She poked a finger and rubbed it, but the irritation didn't go away. She blinked furiously in an attempt to wash away the irritant. It failed to work. She noticed glints of light on the reef and wondered what on earth could have produced them. Maybe, if she had been right about the origin of the reef, it was infested with flies and the winter sun was catching in their wings.

She rubbed her eye again. There was a speck in it, something tiny and black. The sun flashed on another set of wings, dazzling her.

Still half asleep, she rubbed her eyes. They felt sore, as if they had been bathed in salt water. Something bright shone into them. She pressed her fingers into them again, feeling them yield horribly, and rubbed hard.

Then she realised where the light was coming from and, shielding her eyes, opened them. A narrow shaft of sunlight had sneaked in through the back window and fell across Daniela's face. She rolled on to her side away from the window. Her head was full of the reef, the flies crawling over it, and the sea of filth, but the sun warmed the back of her neck pleasantly and the horrific pictures lost some of their impact.

She reflected on the preceding day's whitewashing and wondered just what she hoped to achieve in Bucharest. Although it didn't feel like it, the city had changed irrevocably. The tyrants were dead—she'd seen their bullet-riddled bodies on television—and the country was free of their grip for the first time in twenty-four years. The sun moved from her neck over her head and struck the wall, revealing a patch of damp fungus. She had to carry on, she realised. The city was her home. Belgrade had just been a stopover. The sun crept towards the floor, picking out loose splinters from the floorboards. She thought briefly about her long-dead parents. The sun prised open a gap between two uneven floorboards and caught in something shiny trapped beneath the floor. Daniela watched curiously. As the sun fell a little deeper into the hole in the floor it glittered for a second then struck square and reflected into her face.

She uncurled her body and crawled on to the floor. Pulling one floorboard up to allow her hand entry, she reached in and grasped a plastic wallet. She eased it out through the gap and laid it on the floor.

Daniela's heart thudded. Her head buzzed with questions. She felt almost as if she were holding her lost brother's hand and he began speaking to her.

In the plastic folder were two photographs, a map of Bucharest with lines traced in ballpoint along particular streets and linking each other, and two letters addressed to her brother and signed Daniela.

She assumed her brother had formed some kind of an attachment to a woman who happened to bear her name. Until she began to read the first letter. Then it became clear that the letter purported to be from her, thanking him for writing. She was well and living in Constanta, the letter said. Employed in a fabrics factory, she earned sufficient money to keep her comfortable and was a member of the local Party.

The second letter added that she remembered her childhood with great fondness but was now so happy in Constanta that she didn't intend to visit Bucharest.

Obviously her brother had been taken in by the story and had asked to see her. They had put him off. She hadn't been to Constanta since her adolescence, when she was briefly transferred to an orphanage in the Black Sea port. The postmarks on the envelopes, however, dated them to the very recent past.

The letters upset her. The map she could only guess at. But the photographs. Where one might have expected to find treasured snapshots of beloved parents, Daniela found official-issue portraits of the executed dictator and his wife, both in blooming health.

As she stared at the tyrant's ever-youthful grin and his wife's peaceful, oval face, her stomach slowly tied itself into a knot.

Reluctantly her mind began to work, recalling the graffito, TRAITOR, from the front room, and completing simple equations of logic. She shouldn't have assumed that the word had been written by agents of the Securitate.

She walked through familiar streets and felt that at every window, even those boarded up, someone was watching her.

She had now remembered what the TV reporters had said at the time of the revolution. It had been revealed that many Romanian orphans were placed in special institutions where they were taught to honour and obey their country's leaders from the earliest possible age: as soon as they could recognise a simple photograph. They grew to love Nicolae and Elena as surrogate parents and their transformation into Ceausescu's crack personal bodyguard—"the blackshirts"—was merely the next step.

The last street turned into the boulevard and the new apartment buildings shone.

They became the most loyal and ruthless of all Securitate factions. So the TV reporters had claimed. And she knew better now than to doubt their revelations. TRAITOR. The family photographs of his adoptive parents. Her name and orphan's number scribbled on the wall.

The Palace gleamed beyond the fountains, sunlight glinting off the hundreds of windows. Her eye hurt. A speck intruded on her vision. She blinked, but kept walking, her head becoming gassy.

On television in Belgrade she had seen still video images of the Ceausescus lying bullet-riddled at the base of the wall.

She heard a soft throbbing noise.

*The tunnels, the tunnels . . .*

After the trial, the Ceausescus had been led outside by guards, and followed by the ad hoc team of observers and judges who had presided. The man with the television camera was at the back and still in the corridor when the shots rang out. Thus, he could only film the bodies, not the execution.

Or: a bit of connivance and make-up and the whole thing was a hoax.

The speck increased in size and the throb became a buzz in the ear. The Palace shimmered. The tunnels were quiet.

By the time the speck had grown into a helicopter and Daniela had worked out who was coming home, she had already begun to run across the dried-up sea of filth to the gleaming reef. As they climbed out of the machine on to the roof of the People's Palace, haggard and dishevelled but alive, Daniela reached the ground floor and started beating a tattoo on the first door she came to. Attracted and repelled, terrified and awed in equal measure, she demanded at the top of her voice to be let in.

The lord was back in his house and life, and death, could begin again.

# Deepnet

## David Langford

It was during the winter of 1990 that I pieced together ten years' hints, and almost wished I had not probed so deep. A shocking discovery about the world can be equally dismaying as a revelation of oneself. Perhaps committing these rough notes to disk will help clear my thoughts and even save me from the next step which seems so burningly inevitable.

My daughter . . .

The secret I think I know is centred on that small American port which I have never visited, although my late wife Janine once had an aunt there, or a cousin. (Too many years have slipped past for me to remember her every casual aside, though I very much wish I could.) All the same, the name is familiar enough in the industry, even though many software users never consciously note it. The title screen of every version of the Deepword word processor flashes up, just for a subliminal instant amid its wavy graphics, a copyright credit to Deepnet Communications Inc. of Innsmouth, MA.

I am using version 6.01 now. For all my new-found misgivings, I am used to its smooth, tranquil operation. We claim the industry is fast-moving and "at the cutting edge," but secretly most of my programming colleagues are creatures of tradition and ritual. Learn different keystrokes in order to make use of a far better program and save much precious time? There is no time for that.

Now I regret not taking time to listen to Janine when she talked about once visiting her small-town relative. Her image wavers in the seas of memory, somehow edited from liveliness to the stiff features of my one surviving picture (she always photographed badly). Her words . . . she made a humorous thing of it, but I was far away, thinking in program code. A derelict coastal town amid salt marshes, its few inhabitants straight out of *Cold Comfort Farm,* no doubt inbred for gnarled generations: *"Arrr,"* she quoted, *"I mind you do be a furriner in they durned high heels of Babylon, heh heh . . .* Something like that." If she had lived, it might have ceased to be a joke.

The publicity brochure prattles on about how empty houses filled when prosperity and the software industry came to Innsmouth in the early days of the small-computer boom. New freeways threaded the marsh. Through the '70s and '80s Deepnet grew into an amorphous multi-national whose tentacles extend everywhere. Those yokels and genetic casualties now only survive in the traditional humour of our trade newspapers; or so we all thought.

I pause here. Sara is telling me, in the thick, laboured voice I have learned to understand, that she wants to play a game on my backup computer. With her tenth birthday almost in sight, she will have to have her own machine soon. Janine wanted more children, but Sara is all I have. I love her very much.

Nevertheless I wish she reminded me even remotely of Janine, who was beautiful.

When the secret history of these times is properly written, I suspect that Janine should have a footnote of her own as one of the earliest recorded victims. Now and only now we are beginning to be told that pregnant women should beware of electromagnetic radiation, and in particular should stay well clear of computer VDUs. Beneath the world's rippling surface there is always some unsuspected horror, lurking as did thalidomide.

In those days of innocence, when the equipment was slower, cruder and doubtless lacking any screen against electromagnetic leakage, Janine and I were not well off. Her income from technical authorship was too important to us, and she stuck to the keyboard until almost the very end of her pregnancy. Worse, she was just a little short-sighted (which gave her grey eyes a fine faraway look), and liked to work up close to the VDU.

The software she used through those final months was Deepword 1.6.

I prefer not to compute just how many hours of that time we really shared. When I'd logged up my own overtime, Janine and I would all too often sit with vision blurred and mouths silenced by the sheer weight of fatigue, as though far underwater.

Of course I said I should be with her for the birth; as usual she read my real feelings and told me not to be a stupid bloody martyr. Even when too enormous to turn over in bed, Janine was kind-hearted and full of humour. The business took a very long time: for me, eleven hours in a grey waiting-room redolent with stale coffee and disinfectant, her last eleven hours. I had never seen a professionally comforting nurse sound so grim as the young one who let it slip that there was some question as to whether even the baby should be kept on life-support.

Before too many more years, I suppose, our tragedy will be seen to fit into the classical pattern of excessive EM field exposure during pregnancy, with its supposed pathogenic effects on tissue and especially young tissue. Miscarriage, for example, or infant leukaemia, or foetal abnormalities.

I was not shown Sara for some time. (I was not shown Janine at all.) Perhaps her soft bones had been twisted into some insupportable shape by the difficult birth, and later she relaxed as babies do into normality, or mostly so. No one explained to me the stitches on either side of her throat. I wish that first nurse had not looked so sick.

I will admit that Sara is excessively plain.

Watching her work with clumsy fingers at her Undersea Quest game reminds me that I have, in a way, visited the transatlantic home of Deepnet. The demonstration disk for their shoggoth high-resolution graphics design system is one long computerized special effect, a tour of the Innsmouth streets as though you were floating effortlessly along them.

Dominated by the vast squat blocks of the Deepnet complex, it appears as a place of strange contrasts. The stylized images of buildings feature one or two old-fashioned gambrel roofs, and a variety of antique brick and stone houses stand out quaintly from the sea of new development. To show the versatility of the 3-D software, several fanciful touches have been added. One of the monolithic factory structures is, like an Escher print, re-entrant and geometrically impossible; and I am fairly sure that the physical Innsmouth does not include a 250-foot pyramid in its central square, least of all one which slowly but inarguably rotates.

As with all software from these makers, there is something oddly addictive about the SHOGGOTH presentation. Perhaps it is a matter of light and shadow. Instead of whizzing you crudely through the simulated streets in video-game fashion, the ingenious programming team chose to unveil their creation at a lazy pace which, aided by a greenish wavering in the image, gives the subtle illusion of motion underwater.

"Rapture of the deep" was always Janine's phrase for when I lost myself in the depths of the computer terminal. It was a joke, but one which went sour on me when I looked back and thought of how little time we'd had together, how much of it I'd spent hacking out program code, enraptured.

Items notably not included in the SHOGGOTH demonstration are the jokey legends about Deepnet which surface from time to time in the trade papers. It was *Computer Weekly* which tried to make an amusing paragraph of the story that from their main development facility there runs a 45-inch cable of multichannel fibre-optic linkages which enters the nearby Manuxet estuary, heading seaward towards

Devil Reef, and never again emerges. The rival paper *Computing* had a running joke about inbred local workers, bulgy-eyed from endless hours at the VDU, who toil in the depths of the complex and likewise fail to emerge, or not at any rate during daylight.

I reserve my judgement on this gossip. Things very nearly as unlikely are said about DEC and IBM, or any clannish company.

All the same, there is a proverb about straws in the wind . . .

My suspicions weigh very heavily on me, like the pressure of deep water.

But am I suffering from insight or from insanity? Patterns which connect up too many things can be suspect (and here I remember that VDU radiation has also been *claimed* to induce brain tumours or suicidal depression). I freely admit that I do not possess anything like statistically reliable evidence. If I had more friends, I might be able to offer more examples than those of Janine, and of Jo Pennick, Helen Weir, and certain unknowns at a school near my Berkshire home.

I have spoken of Janine. The others came later.

We contract programmers lead a nomadic life, drifting from company to company, isolated from the permanent staff who resent our skills and high fees. Sometimes we exchange shop-talk in bars (we mostly drink too much). And so I came to hear . . .

Mrs. Pennick was a heavy user of Deepword 2.2, in the same condition and for much the same reasons as Janine. She died of complications soon after giving birth to her Peter. With Ms. Weir it was the Deepcalc 1.14 spreadsheet, a daughter called Rose, and unexplained suicide a month or so later. The unknowns remain unknown and I have no real right to guess at their software heritage. But a dreadful conviction washes over me whenever I see (as so frequently I do) these young children of the VDU age, who presumably have parents or a parent somewhere, and who strongly resemble the unrelated Sara and Peter and Rose. Very strongly indeed.

The polite word, I am told, is "exophthalmic."

I only advance a hypothesis. I dare not commit myself to admitting belief. Even the EM research is still very far from being conclusive. But suppose, just suppose . . . That little seaport in Massachusetts has long had an odd reputation, it seems. The term "inbreeding" was often used of its staring natives. Could this conceivably have been a result of deliberate policy?

"Deepnet," says a typical publicity flyer which comes to hand. "Time for your business to move out from the shallows. Take your computer projections below the surface, with software that goes a little deeper. Software from by the sea . . ."

Taking a hint from the eerie underwater imagery of so many Deepnet products (even their word processor's title screen is decorated with stylized waves), I find "inbreeding" shifting in my mind's eye to "breeding," and again to "breeding back," and I remember that all life arose in the sea. I also remember, unwillingly, the stitches that closed what might conceivably have been slits to left and right of the hours-old Sara's throat.

Very cautiously I allow myself to admit that the EM radiation pattern of a computer display must depend in part on the program driving that display; and to acknowledge that research into this radiation and its biological impact goes back thirty years; and to wonder whether, for twelve years or more, software from a certain source might not intentionally have had certain effects on pregnant users.

Are the children of Innsmouth growing up all around us?

"Deepnet. Great new applications from the old, established market leader. Software for the new generation. Talk to us on Internet at *innsmouth@deepnet.com.*"

One last niggling point concerns my daughter's "Undersea Quest," a best-selling computer game which has won many awards for excitement untainted with violence. Players learn to progress not by attacking but by co-operating with the huge, friendly and vaguely frog-like creatures which populate the game world. It is all very ecologically sound. A full virtual-reality version is promised before long.

Something in the watery glimmer of its graphics made me hunt out the instruction leaflet and look up the makers' name. PSP: Pelagic Software Products, a wholly owned subsidiary of Deepnet Communications Inc. Here is their message to the new generation.

At this point in my speculations I was struck with a vivid image of Janine telling me with her usual twinkle that I am just a thought-less, sexist beast. Fancy imagining all these terrible consequences for pregnant women, "the weaker vessel," while giving hardly a thought to my own very much longer hours working with Deepnet development software. Twelve years now, at least. Might there not be accumulated effects in *my* body, my brain?

I am terribly frightened that I may already know the answer to that question. In a few years, when the time comes, when her time comes, it will perhaps destroy me unless I first destroy myself. My hands and forehead are unpleasantly damp as I type these final sentences into the edit screen of Deepword 6.01.

"Deepnet. Bringing together the best of the old and new generations. The software family that rides the tide of tomorrow."

Breeding, and in-breeding. These insights come in a single hot moment. Turning to look again at Sara, I see those big protruding eyes fixed raptly on the screen, and her broad face tinged a soft, delicate green by its light. Overwhelmingly I can imagine the salt-sea smell of her, and I love her and I want her.

# To See the Sea

## Michael Marshall Smith

When the bus reached the top of the hill that finally brought the ocean into view, Susan turned to me and grinned.

"I can see the sea!" she said, sounding about four years old. I smiled back and put my arm round her shoulders, and we turned to look out of the window. Beyond the slight reflection of our own faces the view consisted of a narrow strip of light grey cloud, above a wide expanse of dark grey sea. The sea came up to meet a craggy beach, which was also grey.

The driver showed no sign of throwing caution to the winds and abandoning his self-imposed speed limit of thirty miles an hour, and so we settled ourselves down to wait. The ride had already involved two hours of slow meandering down deserted country lanes. Another thirty minutes wouldn't kill us.

We could at least now see what we had come for, and as we gazed benignly out of the window I could feel both of us relax. True, the sea didn't look quite as enticing as it might at, say, Bondi Beach, and the end of October was possibly not the best time to be here, but it was better than nothing. It was better than London.

In the four months Susan and I had been living together, life had been far from sweet. We both worked at the same communications company, an organisation run on panic and belligerence. It ought to have been an exciting job, but every day at the office was like wading through knee-high mud in a wasteland of petty grievances and incompetence. Every task the company undertook was botched and flawed: even the car park was a disaster. Built in the shape of a wedge, it meant that anyone at the far end had to get all those parked between them and the exit to come and move their cars before they could leave. About once a fortnight our car wouldn't start, despite regular visits to the world's least conveniently situated garage.

The flat we had moved into was beautiful, but prey to similar niggling problems. The boiler, which went out twice a day, was situated below the kitchen, so we had no hot water to wash up with. Lightbulbs in the flat went at forty minute intervals, each turning out to be some bizarre Somalian make which was unavailable in local stores. The old twonk who lived underneath us managed to combine a hardness of hearing that required his television to play at rock concert volume with a sensitivity that led him to shout up through the floor if we so much as breathed after eleven o'clock.

Up until Thursday, we'd been planning to spend the weekend at home, as we usually did. By the time the working week had ended we were too tired to consider packing bags, checking tyre pressures and hauling ourselves out of town. Perversely, the very fact that the car had packed up *again* on Friday evening had probably provided the impetus for us to make the trip. It had just been one thing too many, one additional pebble of grief on a beach that seemed to stretch off in all directions.

"Fuck it," Susan had snarled, when we finally made it back home. "Let's get out of town." The next morning we arose, brows furrowed, each grabbed a change of clothes, a toothbrush and a book, and stomped off to the tube station. And now, after brief periods on most of the trains that British Rail had to offer, we were there. Or nearly there, anyway.

As the bus clattered its elderly way down the coast, it passed a sign for Dawton, now allegedly only eight miles away. Judging by the state of the signpost, the village's whereabouts were of only cursory interest to the inhabitants of the surrounding countryside. The name was printed in black on an arrow that must once have been white, but was now grey and streaked with old rain tracks. It looked as though no-one had bothered to clean it for a while.

Virtually all of the minor annoyances which had been plaguing our every day were trivial in themselves. It was simply their volume and relentlessness which was getting us down. The result was a state of constant flinching, in which neither of us were fully ourselves. The paradoxical advantage of this was that we were getting to know each other very quickly, seeing sides of each other that would normally sit in obeisance for years. We found ourselves opening up to each other, blurting secrets as we struggled to find a new equilibrium.

One of these secrets, divulged very late one night when we were both rather tired and emotional, had involved Susan's mother. I already knew that her mother had carved her name in Susan's psyche by leaving her father when Susan was five, and by never bothering to get in touch again. A need for security was amongst the reasons that Susan had fallen into the clutches of her ridiculous ex-boyfriend. Before her mother had gone, however, it transpired that she had managed to instil a different kind of fear in her daughter.

In 1955, ten years before Susan was born and five before she married, Geraldine Stanbury went on a holiday. She was gone three weeks, touring around European ports with a couple of friends from college. On their return, the ship, which was called the *Aldwinkle*, was hugging the coast of England against a storm when a disaster occurred. The underside of the ship's hull was punctured and then ripped apart by an unexpected rock formation, and the boat went down. By an enormous stroke of good fortune an area within the ship remained airtight, and all three hundred and ten passengers and crew were able to hole up there until help arrived the next morning. In the end, not a single person was lost, which perhaps accounts for the fact that the wreck of the *Aldwinkle* has failed to become a well-known part of English disaster lore.

Susan's mother told her this story often when she was a child, laying great stress on what it had been like to be trapped under the water, not knowing whether help would come. As Susan told me this, sitting tensely on the rug in our flat, I was temporarily shocked out of drunkenness, and sat up to hold her hand. A couple of weeks previously we had come close to a small argument over where to take the holiday we had been looking forward to. Having been raised in a coastal town I love the sea, and had suggested St. Augustine, on the Florida coast. Susan had demurred, in an evasive way, and suggested somewhere more inland. The reasons for this now seemed more clear.

After Mrs. Stanbury had left, the story of her near death continued to prey on her daughter's mind, though in different ways. As she'd grown up, questions had occurred to her. Like why, for example, there had not been a light showing at that point in the coast, when dangerous rocks were under the water. And why no-one in the nearby village had raised an alarm until the following morning. The ship had gone down within easy view of the shore: was it really possible that no-one had seen its distress? And if someone had seen, what on earth could have compelled them to keep silent until it should have been too late?

The village in question was that of Dawton, a negligible hamlet on the west coast of England. As I held Susan that night, trying to keep her warm against the bewilderment which years of asking the same questions had formed, I suggested that we should visit the village some time, to exorcise the ghosts it held for her. For of course no-one could have seen the ship in distress, or an alarm would have been raised. And lighthouses sometimes fail.

When we got up for work the next morning, both more than a little hung over, such a trip seemed less important. In the next couple of weeks, however, during which we had two further nights on which the hardships of the day drove us to spend the evening in the pub, where we could not be contacted, the idea was mentioned again. It was a time for clearing out, in both our lives. One of the ways in which we were battling against the avalanche of trivia which still sometimes threatened to engulf us was by sorting out the things we could, by seeking to tidy away elements of our past which might have detrimental effects on our future together.

And so on the Friday when Susan finally demanded we get out of town, I suggested a pilgrimage to Dawton, and she agreed.


As the archaic bus drew closer to the village I noticed that Susan grew a little more tense. I was about to make a joke, about something, I'm not sure what, when she spoke.

"It's very quiet out here."

It was. We hadn't passed a car in the last ten or fifteen minutes. That was no great surprise: as the afternoon grew darker the weather looked set to change for the worse, and judging from its size on the map, there would be little to draw people to Dawton unless they happened to live there. I said as much.

"Yes, but still." I was about to ask her what she meant when I noticed a disused farm building by the side of the road. On its one remaining wall someone had painted a large swastika in black paint. Wincing, I pointed it out to Susan, and we shook our heads as middle-class liberals will when confronted with the forces of unreason.

"Hang on though," she said, after a moment. "Isn't it the wrong way round?" She was right, and I laughed. "Christ," she said. "To be that stupid, to do something so mindless, and still to get it *wrong . . .*"

Then a flock of seagulls wheeling just outside the window attracted our attention. They were scraggy and unattractive birds, and fluttered close to the window in a disorganised but vaguely threatening way. As we watched, however, I was trying to work out what the swastika reminded me of, and trying to puzzle out why someone should have come all this way to paint it. We were still two miles from Dawton. It seemed a long way to come to daub on a disused wall, and unlikely that such a small coastal town should be racked with racial tension.

Ten minutes later the bus rounded a final bend, and the village of

Dawton was in sight. I turned and raised my eyebrows at Susan. She was staring intently ahead. Sighing, I started to extricate our bag from beneath the seat. I hoped Susan wasn't building too much on this sleepy village. I don't know what I was expecting the weekend to bring: a night at a drab bed and breakfast, probably, with a quiet stroll down the front before dinner. I imagined that Susan would want to look out across the sea, to try to imagine the place where her mother had nearly lost her life, and that would be it. The next day we would return to London. To hope for anything more, for a kiss that would heal all childhood wounds, would be asking a little too much.

"You getting off, or what?"

Startled, we looked up to the front of the bus. The vehicle had stopped, apparently at random, fifty yards clear of the first dishevelled houses that stood on the land side of the road.

"Sorry?" I said.

"Bus stops here."

I turned to Susan, and we laughed.

"What, it doesn't go the extra hundred yards into the village?"

"Stops here," the man said again. "Make your mind up."

We clambered rather huffily down out of the bus onto the side of the road. Before the door was fully shut, the driver had the bus in reverse. He executed a three point turn at greater than his usual driving speed, and then sped off up the road away from the village.

"Extraordinary man," said Susan.

"Extraordinary git, more like." I turned and looked over the low wall we had been dumped beside. A stone ramp of apparent age led down to a stony strip of beach, against which the grey water was lapping with some force. "Now what?"

From where we stood the coast bent round to our left, enabling us to see the whole of the village in its splendour. Houses much like those just ahead accounted for most of the front, with a break about halfway along where there appeared to be some kind of square. Other dwellings went back a couple of streets from the front, soon required to cling to the sharp hills which rose less than two hundred yards from the shore. An air of gradual decay hung over the scene, of neg-

TO SEE THE SEA

ligent disuse. The few cars we could see parked looked old and haggard, and the smoke issuing thinly from a couple of chimneys only
helped to underline the general air of desertion. Susan looked con-
trite.

"I'm sorry. We shouldn't have come."

"Of course we should. The answering machine will be half-full of
messages already, and I'm glad it's listening to them and we're not."

"But it's so dismal." She was right. Dismal was the word, rather
than quiet. Anywhere can be quiet. Quiet just means that there isn't
much noise. Dawton was different. Noise wouldn't have been an im-
provement.

"Dawton's dismal," I said, and she giggled. "Come on. Let's find a
disappointing guest house that doesn't have a TV in each room, never
mind tea and coffee-making facilities."

She grabbed me by the hand, kissed my nose, and we turned to
walk. Just a yard in front of us, obscured by sand and looking much
older than the one on the wall we had seen, another swastika was
painted on the pavement. Again it was the wrong way round. I shook
my head, puzzled, and then walked over it on our way towards the
houses.


"We could try this one, I suppose."

"What d'you reckon?"

"It doesn't look any nicer than the other one."

"No."

We were standing at one corner of Dawton's square, outside the
village's second pub. We had already rejected one on the way from the
guest house. We weren't expecting a CD jukebox and deep-fried
camembert, but we'd thought we could probably find better. Now we
were beginning to doubt it.

Susan leant forward to peer through the window.

"We could go straight to a restaurant," I suggested.

"If there is one."

In the end we nervously decided to have a quick drink in the pub.

365

If nothing else the landlord should be able to tell us where the town restaurant was. Susan pushed the heavy wooden door, and I followed her in.

The pub consisted of a single bare room. Though it was cold no fire burned in the grate, and the predominance of old stained wood failed to bring any warmth to the ambience. A number of chairs surrounded the slab-like tables, each furnished with a tattered cushion for a seat. The floor was of much-worn boards, with a few faded rugs. There was no-one to be seen, either in the body of the room or behind the bar.

After a searching look at each other, we walked up to the bar, and I leant over. The area behind was narrow, almost like a corridor, and extended beyond the wall of the room we were in. By craning my neck I could see that there appeared to be another room on the other side of the wall. It could have been another bar except that it was completely dark, and there were no pumps or areas to store glasses. I pointed this out to Susan, and we frowned at each other. At the end of the bar area was a door, which was shut. After a pause, I shouted hello.

It wasn't much of a shout, because I was feeling rather intimidated by the sepulchral quiet of the room, but it rang out harshly all the same. We both flinched, and waited for the door at the end of the corridor to be wrenched open. It wasn't, and I said hello again, a little more loudly this time.

A faint sound, possibly one of recognition, seemed to come from behind the door. I say "seemed" because it was very faint, and appeared to come from a greater distance than you would have expected. Loath to shout again, in case we had already been heard, we shrugged and perched ourselves on two ragged barstools to wait.

The situation was strangely similar to that which we had encountered on entering the guest house in which we would be spending the night. We had only walked about ten houses down the line from where the bus had deposited us before we saw a sign nailed unceremoniously to the front of one of them, advertising rooms for the night. We'd entered, and loitered for a good few minutes in front of a counter before an elderly woman creaked out of a back room to attend to us.

The room we were shown was small, ill-favoured and faced away from the sea. Naturally it had neither a television nor drink-making facilities, and you could only have swung a cat in it if you had taken care to provide the animal with a crash helmet first. As the rest of the house seemed utterly deserted we asked the woman if we could have a room with a sea view instead, but she had merely shaken her head. Susan, fiendish negotiator that she is, had mused aloud for a moment on whether a little extra money could obtain such a view for us. The woman had shaken her head again, and said they were "booked."

I discovered a possible reason for this when down in the sitting room of the house, waiting for Susan to finish dressing for the evening. It was a dark and poky room, notwithstanding its large window, and I would not have chosen to spend much time there. The idea of simply sitting in it was frankly laughable. The chairs were lumpy and ill-fashioned, their archaic design so uncomfortable it seemed scarcely conceivable that they had been designed with humans in mind, and the window gave directly out onto a gloomy prospect of dark grey sea and clouds. I was there only because I had already seen enough of our small room, and because I hoped I might be able to source some information on likely eating places in the village.

At first I couldn't find anything, which was odd. Usually the guest houses of small towns on the coast are bristling with literature advertising local attractions, produced in the apparent hope that the promise of some dull site thirty miles away might induce the unwary into staying an extra night. The house we were staying in, however, clearly wished to be judged on its own merits, or else simply couldn't be bothered. Though I looked thoroughly over all the available surfaces, I couldn't find so much as a card.

I was considering without much enthusiasm the idea of tracking down the old crone to ask her advice when I discovered something lying on the sill in front of the window. It was a small pamphlet, photocopied and stapled together, and the front bore the words "Dawton

Festival." It also mentioned a date, the 30th of October, which happened to be the following day.

There was nothing by way of editorial on the Festival itself, bar the information that it would start at 3 o'clock in the afternoon. Presumably the unspecified festivities continued into the evening, hence the drabness of our berth. The guest house's more attractive rooms had obviously been booked for two nights in advance, by forthcoming visitors to what promised to be the west coast's least exciting event.

I couldn't glean much of interest from the booklet, which had been typeset with extraordinary inaccuracy, to the point where some of it didn't even look as if it was in English. Most of the scant pages were filled with small advertisements for businesses whose purposes remained obscure. There was no mention of a restaurant. The centre spread featured a number of terribly reproduced photographs purporting to show various notables of the town, including, believe it or not, a "Miss Dawton." Her photograph in particular had suffered from being badly photocopied too many times, and was almost impossible to make out. Her figure blended with the background tones, making her appear rather bulky, and the pale ghost of her face was so distorted as to appear almost misshapen.

I was about to shout again, this time audibly, when the door at the end of the bar seemed to tremble slightly. Susan started, and I stood up in readiness.

The door didn't open. Instead we both heard a very distant sound, like that of footsteps on wet pavements. It sounded so similar, in fact, that I turned to look at the outer door of the pub, half-expecting to see the handle turn as one of the locals entered. It didn't, though, and I returned to looking at the door. The sounds continued, getting gradually closer. They sounded hollow somehow, as if they were echoing slightly. Susan and I looked at each other, frowning once more.

The footsteps stopped on the other side of the door, and there was a long pause. I was beginning to wonder whether we wouldn't perhaps have been better off with the first pub we'd seen when the door suddenly swung open, and a man stepped out behind the bar.

Without so much as glancing in our direction he shut the door behind him and then turned his attention to the ancient till. He opened it by pressing on some lever, and then began to sort through the money inside in a desultory fashion.

I think we both assumed that he would stop this after a moment or so, despite the fact that he had given no sign of seeing us. When he didn't, Susan nudged me, and I coughed a small cough. The man turned towards us with an immediacy and speed which rather disconcerted me, and stood, eyebrows raised. After a pause I smiled in a way I hoped looked friendly rather than nervous.

"Good evening," I said. The man didn't move. He just stood, half turned towards us, with his hands still in the till and his eyebrows still in the air. He didn't even blink. I noticed that his eyes were slightly protuberant, and that the skin round his ears looked rough, almost scaly. His short black hair was styled as if for pre-war fashion, and appeared to have been slicked back with Brylcreem or something similar. A real blast from the past. Or from something, anyway.

After he'd continued to not say anything for a good ten seconds or so, I had another shot.

"Could we have two halves of lager, please?"

As soon as I started speaking again the man turned back to the till. After I'd finished there was a pause, and then finally he spoke.

"No."

"Ah," I said. It wasn't really a reply. It was just a response to the last thing I was expecting a publican to say.

"Don't have any beer."

I blinked at him.

"None at all?"

He didn't enlarge on his previous statement, but finished whatever he was doing, closed the till, and started moving small glasses from one shelf to another, still with his back to us. The glasses were about three inches high and oddly shaped, and I couldn't for the life of me work out either what one might drink from them or why he was choosing to move them.

"A Gin then," Susan's voice was fairly steady, but a little higher than usual, "with tonic?" She normally had a slice of lemon too, but I think she sensed it would be a bit of a long shot.

She got no reply at all. When all of the small glasses had been moved, the man opened the till again. Beginning to get mildly irritated, in spite of my increasing feeling of unease, I glanced at Susan and shook my head. She didn't smile, but just stared back at me, face a little pinched. I looked back at the man, and after a moment leant forward to see more closely.

His hair hadn't been slicked back, I realised. It was wet. Little droplets hung off the back in a couple of places, and the upper rim of his shirt was soaked. There had been a fine drizzle earlier on, enough to make the pavements damp. We'd walked most of the way from the guest house in it, and suffered no more than a fine dusting of moisture. So why was his hair so wet? Why, in fact, had he been out at all? Shouldn't he have been tending his (surprisingly beer-free) pumps?

He could have just washed it, I supposed, but that didn't seem likely. Not this man, at this time in the evening. And surely he would have dried it enough to prevent it dripping off onto his shirt, and running down the back of his neck? Peeking forward slightly I saw that his shoes were wet too, hence the wet footsteps we had heard. But where had he come from? And why was his hair wet?

Suddenly the man swept the till shut and took an unexpected step towards me, until he was right up against the bar. Taken aback, I just stared at him, and he looked me up and down as if I was a stretch of old and dusty wallpaper.

"Do you have *anything* we could drink?" I asked, finally. He frowned slightly, and then his face went blank again.

"Is there a place round here we can buy food?" Susan asked. She sounded half-way to angry, which meant she was very frightened indeed.

The man stared at me for a moment more, and then raised his right arm. I flinched slightly, but all he was doing, it transpired, was pointing. Arm outstretched, still looking at me, he was pointing in the opposite direction to the door. And thus, I could only assume, in the direction of somewhere we could buy some food.

"Thanks," I said. "Thank you." Susan slid off her stool and preceded me to the door. I felt the back of my neck tickle all of the way there, as if I was frightened that something might suddenly crash into it. Nothing did, and Susan opened the door and stepped out. I followed her, and turned to pull the door shut. The man was still standing, arm outstretched, but his face had turned to watch us go, his eyes on Susan. Something about the way the light fell, or about the strangeness of his behaviour, made me think that there might be something else about his face, something I hadn't really noticed before. I couldn't put my finger on what it might be.

When I stepped out onto the pavement the first thing I saw was that it had started to rain a little harder, a narrow slant of drizzle which showed in front of the few and dingy streetlights. The second thing was Susan, who was standing awkwardly, her body turned out towards the street, head and shoulders faced to me. She was staring upwards, and her mouth was slightly open.

"What?" I said, a little sharply. I wasn't irritated, just rather spooked. She didn't say anything. I took a step towards her and turned to see.

I never really notice pub signs. Most of the time I go to pubs I know, and so they're of no real interest to me. On other occasions I just, well I just fail to notice them. They're too high up, somehow, and not terribly interesting. So I hadn't noticed the one hanging outside this pub either, before we went in. I did now.

The sign was old and battered, the wood surround stained dark. A tattered and murky painting showed a clumsily rendered ship in the process of sinking beneath furiously slashing waves. Below there was a name. The pub was called The Aldwinkle.


Ten o'clock found us pushing plates away, lighting cigarettes, and generally feeling a little better. With nothing to go on apart from the publican's scarcely effusive directions, we'd wandered along the front for a while, coats wrapped tight around us and saying little. We were in danger of running out of front and considering turning back when we came upon a small house in which a light was glowing. The window had been enlarged almost the full width of the house, and inside we could see a few tables laid out. All the tables were empty.

We stood outside for a moment, wondering whether we could face any more of Dawton's version of hospitality, when a young man crossed the back of the room. He was tidily dressed as a waiter, and failed, at that distance, to give us any obvious reason for disquiet. His whole demeanour, even through glass, was so different from that which we had encountered so far that we elected to shoulder our misgivings and go in.

The waiter greeted us cordially and sat us, and the tension which, I realised belatedly, had been growing within us since the afternoon abated slightly. The young man was also the proprietor and cook, it transpired, and was moreover from out of town. He told us this when we observed, quite early into the meal, that he didn't seem like the other villagers we'd met. Soon afterwards the main course arrived and he disappeared into the kitchen to leave us to it.

We drank quite a lot during the meal. As soon as we sat down we knew we were going to, and ordered two bottles of wine to save time. We hadn't spoken much during the walk, not because we didn't feel there was much to say, but almost as if there was too much. Susan hadn't looked out over the sea, either, though there was once or twice when I thought she might be about to.

"Why would they call a pub that?"

Susan was still trembling slightly when she finally asked. Not a great deal, because it would take a lot to unseat her that much. But her hands are normally very steady, and I could see her fork wavering slightly as she waited for me to answer. I'd had time to think about it, to come up with what I hoped was a reasonable suggestion.

"I guess because it's the most interesting thing which ever happened here."

Susan looked at me and shook her head firmly, before putting another fork of the really quite passable lamb into her mouth. We'd looked for fish on the menu initially, assuming it would be the specialty of the house as in all small coastal towns, and were surprised to find not a single dish available. I'd asked the waiter about it, but he'd simply smiled vaguely and shaken his head.

"No," she said, finally. "That's not the reason."

I opened my mouth to press my claim, and then shut it again. I didn't believe it either. Perhaps it was just because of the behaviour of the publican, or the overall atmosphere of the town. Maybe it was just the colour of the sky, or the way the rain angled as it fell, but somehow I just didn't quite believe that there wasn't more to the pub's name than a simple remembrance. There'd been something about the painting, some aspect of its style or colours, that hinted at something else, some more confused or inexplicable element. To name a pub after a ship that sank in—possibly—dubious circumstances, and to put that ship's name up on a sign with a painting that seemed almost to have some intangible air of celebration about it, hardly seemed like amiable quaintness.

But such speculations weren't what we were here for, and I saw my job as being that of steering Susan away from them. Although there was something a little strange about the whole thing, it didn't mean that the villagers had tried to cause harm to the passengers of the *Aldwinkle* thirty-odd years ago. It simply didn't make sense: what could possibly have been in it for them? Either way I didn't want the weekend to compound Susan's suspicions. Her mother's blatherings had left her with more than enough distrust of the human race. We'd come here to try to undermine that, not provide documentary evidence to support it.

So I steered the conversation away from the sign, and focused on the publican. There was enough material for speculation and vitriol there to keep us going to the other side of dessert, by which time we were more than a little drunk and rambling rather. By the time the waiter came through with our coffees I thought Susan had left more disturbing thoughts behind.

I was wrong. As he stood at the end of the table she turned on him.

"What do you know about the *Aldwinkle?*" she said, challengingly. The waiter's hand paused for just a moment as he laid the milk jug down. Or maybe it didn't. Maybe I imagined it.

"It's a pub," he said. Susan tried again, but that was all he would say. As he'd observed, he was from out of town and only came to Dawton to work. He sat at an adjoining table as we finished our third bottle of wine, and we chatted a little. Business wasn't going well, it would seem, and we'd made it to the restaurant just in time. Within a few weeks he suspected that he would probably have to give up. There simply wasn't the custom, and we'd been his only patrons that evening.

We enquired as to what the locals did of an evening. He didn't know. As we talked I began to sense an air of unease about him, as if he would prefer to discuss something other than the town and its inhabitants. Probably simply paranoia on my part. I was starting to realise that we were going to have to leave this haven, and return to our room. The thought did not fill me with glee.

In the end we paid, bid him goodnight, and stepped out onto the front. The first thing that struck me was the realisation that I was extremely drunk. I tend to drink just about everything as I would beer, that is in the same sort of quantity. This approach doesn't work too well with wine. I'd probably had the better part of two bottles, and suddenly, as we stood swaying in the wind that whipped down the soulless stretch of the front, it felt like it.

Susan was a little the worse for wear too, and we stumbled in unison as we stepped off the curb to walk across the road to the front. Susan slipped her hand underneath my coat and looped her arm around my back and, not saying anything, we stepped up onto the ragged pavement on the other side of the road.

It was late now, but a sallow moon spread enough light for us to see what lay in front of us. Beyond the low wall a ramp of decaying concrete sloped down to the shore. The shore appeared to consist of puddled mudflats, and stretched at least a hundred yards out to where still water the colour of slate took over. In the distance we could just hear the sound of small waves, like two hands slowly rubbed together.

"Tide's out," I observed sagely, except that it came out more like "tie shout." I opened my eyes wide for a moment, blinked, and then fumbled in my pockets for a cigarette.

"Mn," Susan replied, not really looking. She was gazing vaguely at the wall in front of us, for some reason not letting her eyes reach any higher. She shook her head when I offered her a smoke, which was unusual. I put a hand on the cold surface of the wall, for something to lean against, and looked back out at the sea.

When I was a kid my family often used to go on holiday to St. Augustine. Actually the place where we stayed was just outside, a little further down Crescent Beach in the direction of, but thankfully a good ways from, Daytona Beach. I remember standing on the unspoilt beach as a child, probably no more than five or six, and slowly turning to look out at the sea from different angles, and I remember thinking that you can't ever really stand still when you're looking at the sea. There's nowhere you can stand and think "Yep, that's the view," because there's always more of it on either side.

In Dawton it was different. There was only one way you could see it. Perhaps it was because of the curve of the bay, or maybe it was something else. Your eye was drawn outwards, as if there was only one way you could see the view, only one thing you could see.

Suddenly Susan's arm was removed and she took a step forwards. Without looking at me she grabbed the wall purposefully with both hands and started to hoist herself over it.

"What're you doing?" I demanded, stifling a hiccup.

"Going to see the sea."

"But," I started, and then wearily reached out to follow her. Obviously the time had come for Susan to do her staring out across the water. The best I could do was tag along, and be there if she wanted to talk.

The concrete ramp was wet and quite steep, and Susan almost lost her footing on the way down. I grabbed her shoulder and she regained her balance, but she didn't say anything in thanks. She hadn't really said anything to me since we'd left the restaurant. Her tone when telling me where she was going had been distant, almost irritable, as if she was annoyed at having to account for her actions. I tried not to take it personally.

When we got to the bottom of the ramp I stopped, swaying slightly. I peered owlishly at the stinking mud in front of us. Clearly,

I thought, this was where the expedition ended. Susan felt otherwise. She stepped out onto the mud and started striding with as
much determination as the ground and her inebriation would allow. I stared after her, feeling suddenly adrift. She didn't seem herself, and I was afraid of something, of being left behind. Wincing, I
put a tentative foot onto the mud and then hurried after her as best
I could.

We walked a long way. The mud came in waves. For twenty yards
it would be quite hard, and relatively dry, and then it would suddenly
change and turn darker and wetter until, to be honest, it was like
wading through shit. The first time this happened I tried to find dryer
patches, to protect my shoes, but in the end I gave up. It was as much
as I could do to keep up with Susan, who was striding head down towards the sea.

I glanced back at one point, and saw how far we'd come. When
we'd stood on the front I'd thought the sea was a hundred yards or so
away, but it must have been much further. I couldn't see any lights in
the houses on the front, or any of the streetlights. For an awful moment I thought that something must have happened, that everyone
had turned their lights off so we wouldn't be able to find our way
back. I turned to shout to Susan but she was too far ahead to hear. Either that, or she ignored me. After another quick glance back I ran to
catch up with her.

She was still walking, but her head was up and her movements
were jerky and stilted. When I drew level with her I saw that she was
crying.

"Susan," I said. "Stop." She walked on for a few more yards, tailing off, and then stopped. I put my hands on her shoulders and she
held herself rigid for a moment, but then allowed herself to be folded
into me. Her hair was cold against my face as we stood, surrounded
by mud in every direction.

"What is it?" I said eventually. She sniffed.

"I want to see the sea."

I raised my head and looked. The sea appeared as far away as it
had when we'd been standing on the front.

"The tide must still be going out," I said. I'm not sure if I believed it. Susan certainly didn't.

"It's not letting me," she said, indistinctly. "And I don't know why."

I didn't know what to say to that, and just stared out at the water. I wondered how much further it was before the bay deepened, how much further to the crop of rocks where the *Aldwinkle* presumably still lay.

In the end we turned and walked back, Susan allowing me to keep my hand around her shoulders. She seemed worn out. I was beginning to develop a headache, while still feeling rather drunk. When we got back to the ramp we climbed halfway up it and then sat down for a cigarette. My shoes, I noticed belatedly, were ruined, caked about a centimetre thick in claggy mud. I took them off and set them to one side.

"This weekend isn't going quite as I thought it would," I said, eventually.

"No." I couldn't tell from Susan's tone whether she thought this was a good or a bad thing.

We looked out at the water for a while in silence. Now we were back it looked little more than a hundred yards away, two hundred at the most. It couldn't have moved. We simply can't have walked as far as we'd thought we had, which is odd, because it felt like we'd walked forever.

"How are you feeling?" I asked.

"It's out there somewhere," she said. I nodded. It wasn't a direct reply, but in another sense I guess it was.

"Was it the sea you wanted to see?" I ventured.

"I don't know," she said, and her head dropped.

A little later we stood up. I decided to leave my shoes where they were. They weren't an especially nice pair, and it seemed less troublesome to leave them there than to find some way of taking them home in their current state and then cleaning them. On a different evening, in a different mood, leaving them might have felt like a gesture of some kind, something wild and devil-may-care. Instead I just felt a little confused and sad, as well as vulnerable and exposed.

Susan warmed up a little on the walk back along the front, enlivened slightly by a stream of weak jokes from me. After a while I felt her cold hand seek out mine, and I grasped it and did my best to warm it up. The village we passed in front of seemed to have died utterly during the course of the evening. The streets were silent and not a single light showed in any of the windows. It was like walking beside a photograph of a ghost town.

Until we got closer to our guest house, that is. From a way off we could see that all the lights seemed to be on, though dimly, and as we approached we began to hear the sound of car doors slamming carried on the quiet air. About fifty yards away we stopped.

The street outside the house, which had been empty when we'd arrived, was lined both sides with cars. The lights *were* on, on all three floors. They looked dim because in each window a shade was pulled down. The other guests had evidently arrived.

As we looked, someone moved behind one of the upper windows. The angle of the light behind him or her cast a grotesquely shaped shadow on the blind, and I found myself shivering for no evident reason. Quietly, and to myself, I wished that we were staying somewhere else. Like London.

I was fumbling for our key on the doorstep when suddenly the door was pulled wide. Warm yellow light spilled out of the hallway and Susan and I looked up, blinking, to see the old lady proprietor standing in front of us. My first befuddled thought was that we must have transgressed some curfew and she was about to berate us for being late.

Far from it. The old crone's manner was bizarrely improved, and she greeted us with strange and twittering warmth before ushering us into the hallway. Once there she steered us into the sitting room before we'd even had time to draw breath, though we had no desire to go there. Susan entered the room first and glanced back at me. I opened my eyes wide to signal my bafflement. Susan shrugged, and we seemed to mutually decide that it would be easier to go along with it. The old woman flapped us towards some chairs in the centre of the room and offered us a cup of tea. My first impulse was to refuse—I was beginning to sag rather by then—but then remembered that our room didn't have so much as a kettle, and accepted. The woman clapped her hands together in apparent delight, and out of the corner of my eye I saw Susan glancing at me again. There was nothing I could tell her. None of it was making any sense to me either, and as soon as the woman left the room I turned to Susan and said so. I also observed that there seemed to be something gaudy and strange about the old woman. She looked different.

"She's wearing make-up," she said. "And that *dress*?"

The dress, made of some dark green material, was certainly not to my taste, and the make-up had been hastily applied, but it clearly spoke of some effort being made. Presumably it was the new guests, whoever they might be, who merited such a transformation. We looked round the room, feeling slightly ill at ease. On the table to one side of me I noticed something.

A pamphlet for the Dawton Festival lay next to the large glass ashtray. I looked across at the window sill and saw that the one I had consulted earlier was still there. For want of anything else to do I picked it up and showed it to Susan. Flicking through the pages a second time failed to furnish us with any more information on what the Festival might consist of. When we got to the centre pages I nudged Susan, looking forward to drawing her attention to the oddity of a Dawton Beauty contest. But when my finger was pointing at the photo I suddenly stopped.

I realised now what had struck me about the publican in The Aldwinkle, the aspect of his appearance which I hadn't been able to put my finger on. There had been something about the shape of his head, the ratio of its width to its depth, the bone structure and the positioning of the ears, which reminded me forcibly of the degraded photograph of "Miss Dawton." I couldn't believe that she actually looked like that, that I was seeing something other than the result of dark and badly reproduced tones blending into each other, but still the resemblance was there.

"It must be his daughter."

When Susan spoke I turned to her, startled.

"It's just the printing," I said. "She can't look like that." Susan shook her head firmly.

"It's his daughter."

The door slid quietly open and I quickly slipped the leaflet to one side, trying to hide it. I don't know why: it just seemed like a good idea. It didn't work.

"Will you be staying for the Festival?" the old woman croaked, laying two cups of brick-red tea down on the table. She addressed her comment to Susan, who said no. Our plan, as discussed in the restaurant, was to rise early the next morning and get the hell back to London. I was loath to question her too closely on what the Festival might involve, because I was aware that I was enunciating my words very carefully to keep the drunkenness out of my voice. On the few occasions when Susan spoke I heard her doing the same thing.

As we sat there, sipping our tea and listening to her rustling voice, I began to feel a curious mixture of relaxation and unease. If the Festival was such a draw, why wouldn't she tell us about it? And was it my imagination or did she cock her head slightly every now and then, as if listening for something?

A few moments later the second question at least seemed to be answered. We heard the sound of the front door being opened and then, after a long pause, being shut again. Still talking in her dry and uninformative voice the old crone slipped over towards the door to the sitting room and then, instead of going out, gently pushed it shut. She carried on talking for a few moments as Susan and I watched her, wondering what she was up to. Perhaps it was my tired mind, but her chatter seemed to lose cohesion for a while, as if her attention was elsewhere. After a couple of moments she came to herself again, and reopened the door. Then, with surprising abruptness, she said goodnight and left the room.

Coming at the end of a day which felt like it had lasted forever, the whole vignette was almost laughable: not because it was funny, but because it was odd in some intangible way that made you want to cover it with sound. Neither of us felt much like actually laughing, I suspect, as we levered ourselves out of the dreadfully uncomfortable chairs and made our way unsteadily upstairs.

I was especially quiet on the stairs, because I wasn't wearing any shoes. Strange, perhaps, that the old woman had either not noticed this or had chosen not to make any comment.

My memories of the next hour or so are confused and very fragmentary. I wish they weren't, because somewhere in them may lie some key to what happened afterwards. I don't know. This is what I remember.

We went upstairs to our room, passing doors under which lights shone brightly, and behind which low voices seemed to be murmuring. As we wove down the corridor I thought at first that a soft smoke was beginning to percolate down from the ceiling. It wasn't, of course. I simply wasn't seeing very well. I felt suddenly very drunk again: more drunk, in fact, than at any point in the evening. Susan, though only a pace or two in front of me, seemed a very long way ahead, and walking that short corridor seemed to take much longer than it should. A sudden hissing noise behind one of the doors made me veer clumsily to the other side of the corridor, where I banged into an opposite door. It seemed to me that some sound stopped then, though I couldn't remember what it had been. As I leant my head on the door to our room and tried to remember how you used a key I found myself panting slightly, my shoulders slumped and weak. Another wave of vagueness surged into my head and I turned laboriously to Susan, who was standing weaving by my side, and asked her if she felt alright. She answered by suddenly clapping her hands over her mouth and stumbling away towards the toilet.

I leaned in the direction she'd gone, realised or decided that I wouldn't be much help, and fell into our room instead. The light switch didn't seem important, either because of the weak moonlight filtering into the room or because I couldn't be bothered to find it. I flapped my way out of my coat with sluggish brutality and sat heavily on the bed. I started unbuttoning my shirt and then suddenly gave up. I simply couldn't do it.

As I sat there, slumped over, I realised that I was feeling even worse. I couldn't understand why I was feeling so bad, or even what exactly the problem was. It reminded me of a time when I'd had food poisoning after a dodgy seafood pizza. A few hours after the meal I'd started feeling . . . well, just odd, really, in a way I found difficult to define. I didn't feel particularly ill, just completely disconnected and altogether strange. I now felt roughly similar, though as if I'd drunk all the wine in the world and taken acid as well. The room seemed composed of dark wedges of colour which had no relation to objects or spaces, and if asked to describe it I wouldn't have known where to start.

Suddenly remembering that Susan was throwing up in the toilet I jerked my head up, wondering again if I should go to her aid, and then I passed out.

Susan's skin was warm and almost sweaty. We rolled and I felt myself inside her, with no idea of how I'd got there. I have images of the side of her chin, of one of her hands and of her hair falling over my face: but no memory of her eyes.

I think I felt wetness on my cheek at one point, as if she cried again, but all I really remember is the heat, the darkness, and not really being there at all.


The first thing I did when I woke was to moan weakly. I was lying on my side facing the window, and a weak ray of sun was shining on my head. My brain felt as if it had been rubbed with coarse sandpaper, and the last thing I needed was light. I wanted very much to turn away from it, but simply didn't have what it took. So I moaned instead.

After a few minutes I slowly rolled over onto my back, and immediately noticed that Susan wasn't beside me. I had a dim memory of her eventually coming to bed the night before, and so assumed that she must have woken first and be taking a shower. I rolled back over onto my side and reached pitifully out towards the little table by the bed. My cigarettes weren't there, which was odd. I always have a cigarette last thing before going to sleep. Except last night, by the look of it.

Suddenly slightly more awake, I levered myself into a sitting position. What had I done before going to bed? I couldn't really remember. My coat was lying in a tangle on the floor, and I experienced a sudden flashback of thrashing my way out of it. Reaching down I found my cigarettes and lighter in the pocket and distractedly lit up. As I squinted painfully round the room I noticed something out of place.

Susan's washing bag was on the chair by the window.

Looking back, I knew from that moment something was wrong. I went through the motions in the right order and with only gradually increasing speed, but I knew right at that moment.

Susan's washing bag was still here in the room. She hadn't taken it with her, which didn't make sense. Maybe she'd gone to the bathroom not to wash, but to be ill again. I clambered out of bed, head throbbing, and threaded myself into some clothes with about as much ease as pushing yarn through the eye of a needle. On the way out of the room I grabbed her washing bag, just in case.

The bathroom was deserted. There was no-one in the stalls, and both the bath and the shower cubicles were empty. Not only empty, but cold, and silent, and dry. I walked back to the room quickly, my head feeling much clearer already. Strangely clear, in fact: it generally takes an hour or so for my head to start recovering from a hangover. Hands on hips I looked around the room and tried to work out where she'd be. Then I noticed the shade of the clouds outside, and suddenly turned to look at my watch on the table.

It was twenty to four in the afternoon.

For a moment I had a complete sensation of panic, as if I'd overslept and missed the most important meeting of my life. Or even worse, perhaps, as if it were just starting, this minute, on the other side of town. The feeling subsided, but only slightly, as I scrabbled round the room for some more clothes. Normally I have to bathe in the mornings, will simply not enter company without doing so: which is part of why I say now that I already knew something was wrong. Perhaps something that had happened the night before, something that I had forgotten, told me that things were amiss. A bath didn't seem important.

It took five minutes to find the room keys where I'd dropped them, and then I locked the room and walked quickly down the corridor. I ducked my head into the bathroom again, but nothing had changed. As I passed one of the other doors I flinched slightly, expecting to hear some sound, but none came. I wasn't even sure what I was expecting.

The lower floor of the guest house was equally deserted. I checked in what passed as the breakfast room, although they would obviously have stopped serving by late afternoon. I stood in front of the desk and even rang the bell, but no-one appeared. Pointlessly I ran back upstairs again, checked the room, and even knocked timidly on one of the other doors. There was no response.

Downstairs again I wandered into the sitting room, wondering what to do. There was no reason for the increasing unease and downright fright I was feeling. Susan wouldn't have just left me. She must be out in town somewhere, with everyone else. It was Festival day, after all. Maybe she'd wanted to see it. Maybe she'd told me that last night, and I'd been too splatted to take it in.

The two cups we'd drunk tea out of the night before were still there, still sitting on the table next to the Festival pamphlet. Frowning, I walked towards them. Guest house landladies are generally obsessed with tidiness. And where *was* she, anyway? Surely she didn't just abandon her guest house because a poxy town Festival was on?

As I looked at the cups I experienced a sudden lurching in my stomach, which puzzled me. It was almost like a feeling I used to get looking through the window of a certain pizza chain, when I saw the thick red sauce that coated the pizzas on the plates of the people inside. When you've seen and felt that same sauce coming out of your nose while you're buckled up over a toilet in the small hours, you tend not to feel too positive about it in the future. The reaction has nothing to do with your mind, but a lot to do with the voiceless body making its warning clear in the only way it can.

A feeling of nausea. Why should I feel that about tea?

I moved a little closer to the table and peered into the cups. One had a small amount left in the bottom, which was to be expected: Susan never quite finished a cup. My cup was empty. At the bottom of the cup, almost too faintly to be seen, the pottery sparkled slightly, as if something there was irregularly reflecting the light. Feeling as if I'd been punched in the stomach without warning, I kneeled beside the table to take a closer look.

I hadn't had sugar in my tea last night. I never do. I gave it up three years ago and lost over half a stone, and I'm vain enough to want to keep it that way. But there was something in the bottom of the cup. I picked the other cup up and tilted it slightly. The small puddle of tea rocked to reveal a similar patch on the bottom. It was less defined than in my cup, but it was still there.

Something had been put in our tea.

I looked up suddenly at the door, sure that it had moved. I couldn't see any difference, but I stood up anyway. I stood up and I ran out of the house.

As I walked quickly down the front towards the square I tried to make sense of what I'd found. To a degree it added up. I'd felt very, very strange when I'd gone upstairs the night before, strange in a way I'd never experienced through alcohol before. I'd hugely overslept too, which also made sense, and the hangover I'd woken up with had passed differently to usual.

As I approached the square I slowed down a little. I realised that I'd been expecting lots of people to be gathered there, celebrating this benighted village's Festival. There was no-one. The corner of the square I could see was as empty as it had been the night before.

Susan, on the other hand, had got up early. Which also made sense: she'd thrown up immediately after we'd drunk the tea. Less of it would have made it into her bloodstream, and she'd not have experienced the same effects. That made sense. That was fine.

But two things weren't fine, and didn't make sense whichever way I added them up.

First, most obviously, why had someone put something in our tea? This wasn't a film, some Agatha Christie mystery: this was a small village on the English coast. Who would want to drug us, and why?

The second question was less clear-cut, but bothered me even more. Susan had an iron constitution, and could hold her drink. She could drink like a fish, to be honest. So why had she thrown up, so long after drinking, when I hadn't?

Perhaps she was supposed to. Perhaps the drug, whatever it was, had different effects on different people.

The square was completely deserted. I stood still for a moment, trying to work out what to do next. There was no bunting, no posters, nothing to suggest a town event was in progress. I turned round slowly, feeling the hairs on the back of my neck rise. It was unnaturally quiet in that rotten, decomposing square, abnormally empty and silent. It didn't just feel as if no-one was there. It felt like the fucking Twilight Zone.

I walked across to The Aldwinkle and peered in through the window. The pub was empty and the lights were off, but I tried the door anyway. It was open. Inside I stood at the bar and shouted, but no-one came. Something had happened in the pub after we had been there last night. Some of the chairs had been shunted to the side of the room, and others put in their place. They looked like the chairs in the guest house, ugly and misshapen. Their occupants had obviously had better luck when trying to buy a drink: a few of the small glasses lay scattered on one of the tables. One of the Festival pamphlets lay there too, and I irritably swatted it aside. It fluttered noisily to the floor and fell open, displaying its ridiculous inaccuracies. "R'lyeh iä fhtagn!," for example. What the fuck was that supposed to mean?

It did at least make me think more clearly. The Festival had started at three o'clock. I knew that. What I didn't know was *where* it had started. Presumably it took the form of a procession, which began at one end of the town and ended at another, possibly in the square. Perhaps I was here too early. I was now hopping from foot to foot with anxiety over Susan, and felt that anything had to be worth trying. If the Festival wouldn't come to me, I'd bloody well go and find it.

I launched myself out of the pub, slamming the door shut behind me, and ran off towards the opposite corner of the square. I carried on up the little road, past yet more dilapidated houses, casting glances down narrow side roads. When the road began to peter out into cliff-side I turned and went another way. And another. And another.

It didn't take long for the streets to sap what little courage I'd injected myself with. It was like running through a dream where the horror you fear round each corner turns out to be the horror of nothing at all. No-one leant on their fences, passing the time of day. No-one was hanging out washing. No little children ran carelessly through the streets or up the cobbled alleys. No-one, in short, was doing anything. All there was to see was rows of dirty houses, many with upper windows which seemed to have been boarded up. It was a ghost town.

And then I found something. Or thought I did.

I was moving a little more slowly by then, fifteen years of cigarettes taking their toll. To be absolutely honest I was bent over near a street corner, hands on my knees, vigorously coughing my guts up. When the fit subsided I raised my head and thought I heard something. A piping sound.

Jerking myself upright, I snapped my head this way and that, trying to determine where the sound was coming from. I thought it might be from back the way I'd come, perhaps in a parallel road, and jogged up the street. I couldn't hear anything there, but I ducked into the next side road anyway. There I heard the sound again, a little louder, and something else: the rustle of distant conversation. Casting a fearful glance up at the darkening sky I pelted down the road.

I turned the corner cautiously. There was nothing there, but I knew there had been. I'd just missed it. I ran along the road to the next corner and listened, trying to work out which way the procession had gone. I chose left and soon heard noise again, louder this time: an odd tootling music, and the babble of strange voices. The sound made me pause for a moment, and another fragment of the previous evening slipped into my head. Was it a noise like that, an unwholesome and hateful gurgling, which I had heard behind one of the guest house doors?

Suddenly the sounds seemed to be coming from a different direction, and I whirled to follow them. Then, quite by chance, I happened to be looking over the abandoned garden of one of the houses I was passing when I saw something through the gap between it and its neighbour. Three sticks, about a foot apart, moving in the opposite direction to me. As they progressed they appeared to rock slightly, and it was that which made the connection. They weren't just sticks. I couldn't be certain, because it was now fairly dark. But to me they looked like little masts.

I'd thought I couldn't run any faster, that my lungs would surely protest and perhaps burst. But I doubled back on myself and sprinted up the street, taking the corner on the slide. The street was empty but this time I was sure I saw the flicker of someone's ankle as they disappeared around the corner, and I pelted down the road towards it.

I don't know what made me glance at the house at the end. It was almost certainly just an accident, something for my head to do while my body did all the running. Just before I reached the end my eyes drifted across the filthy pane of its main window, and what I saw—or thought I saw—terrified me into losing my balance and falling. I seemed to take a long time to fall, and my mind insists that this is what I saw as I did.

A face, almost merged with the shadows of the room behind the window. A face that started off as something else, something unrecognisable and alien, something which slid and twitched into a normal face faster than the eye could see. A normal face that looked a little like the publican's, and a little like Miss Dawton's. And like, I realised, that of the old crone from the guest house, especially when we'd returned last night. It wasn't simply make-up which had made the difference, far from it. If I hadn't been so drunk I think I would have realised at the time. I think the make-up had been put on to hide something else.

And there was one more thing about the face. It looked a little bit like my mother.

All that passed through my head in the time it took me to fall, and was smacked out of it when my head cracked into a curbstone.

My knee felt badly grazed and twisted, but I was up on my feet immediately, backing hurriedly away from the house. There was nothing to see in the window. No-one was there. Maybe they never had been. Nevertheless I turned and ran away.

It started to rain then, at first drizzling, but then settling into a steady downpour. I plodded down one street after another, sometimes thinking I heard something, sometimes hearing nothing but water. My head hurt by then, and blood ran down the side of my face, mingling with the falling rain and running down into my shirt. At the slightest sound I started and whirled around, but too sluggishly to make any difference. I couldn't seem to think in straight lines. It didn't feel like it had the night before. It just felt as if I was terribly, miserably frightened.

In the end I gave up and headed towards the square as best I could, limping my way down the tangled streets. It should have occurred to me sooner I suppose, after all, I'd had the right idea in the beginning. I should have stayed where the procession might end. In retrospect I'm glad I was too stupid to realise that, but at the time I wearily cursed myself.

It didn't make any difference. The square was still deserted. But they'd been there. That much was clear from the very atmosphere, from the feeling of recently emptied space. It was also obvious from the scraps of paper lying in gutters, which hadn't been there before. I squatted to pick one or two of the sodden pieces up. They were from the pamphlet, as I might have expected. "Yogsogo . . ." one fragment said. ". . . thulu mw'yleh iä . . ." read another. Late, far too late, I wondered if it all meant something, if it was something more than a local idiosyncrasy or the result of a blind typist. I don't think I can be blamed for not suspecting that earlier. All I'd wanted was a weekend out of London. I wasn't expecting anything else.

Looking back up through the slanting rain I noticed something. From where I was it looked as if the door to the pub was now open. I got up and walked towards it, taking occasional paranoid glances into the darkness at the other corners of the square.

No light was showing, but the door was open. The publican had left his pub. The landlady had abandoned her guest house. Were these people so trusting, or did they simply not care? My face in an unconscious wince of tension, I carefully pushed the door open a little further. No sound came from the room, and when I poked my head cautiously within I saw it was completely empty. I stepped in. The room looked much as it had when I'd last been there, except at the bar. The flap which allowed access to the bar area had been lifted up and left that way, and the door behind was also open. I walked over and, wishing I had a God or religion to invoke, stepped behind the bar.

The first thing I did was to peer into the gloom of the second room, the one you could just see when standing at the bar. I couldn't see much except chairs, all of the unusual shape. Then I turned and looked through the other door. The wall beyond was panelled with dark wood, and the narrow corridor it formed a part of stopped just past the door. I stepped through and looked to the left. Stone steps led down into darkness. I felt around for a light but couldn't find one. Even if I had I doubt I would have had the courage to use it.

I thought for a moment before starting down. I wondered about running back to the guest house, checking if Susan had returned. Perhaps the Festival had ended, and she was waiting impatiently in the sitting room, wondering where I was.

I don't know why I didn't believe that was the way things were. I simply didn't, and I went down the steps instead.

There were a good number of them, and they went straight down. It was pitch dark almost from the top, and I walked down with a hand braced against the walls on each side of me. My head was still hurting, indeed it seemed to be getting worse. When I shut my eyes it felt almost as if a small light were beginning to glow in my temple, so I kept them open, little difference though it made to my progress.

Eventually I ran into a wall, and turned left. I walked a little way down another corridor and then realised that I could see a slightly lighter patch in front of me, and hear the sound of distant waves. Not only that.

I could hear piping, and I started to run.

Of course, I thought, as I panted my way towards the end, of course the procession would end on the beach. And of course, perhaps, it would go there by way of a pub that had been called The Aldwinkle, a pub whose name celebrated the night they'd found their chance to emerge. Susan had been right. The name wasn't simply a souvenir of a bygone event. It meant something to the village, as did the wreck itself, along with R'yleh and everything else. It meant something horrible, celebrated a disastrous opportunity which had been taken advantage of. The piping grew stronger as I approached the end of the tunnel, and when I emerged breathless onto the beach I saw them.

They were walking in pairs, slowly and in a peculiar rhythm. In the middle of the column a model of a boat bobbed and swayed, held up by a multitude of hands. Soon it would have a chance to see if it could float, because they were walking into the sea.

As I watched, rooted to the spot, the figures at the front of the procession took their first steps into the choppy waters. They did so confidently, without any fear, and I thought finally I understood. I lurched forward without thinking, shouting Susan's name. The column was a long way away, maybe two hundred yards or more across the mud, but I shouted very loudly, and I thought I saw a figure at the back of the procession turn. It was too dark to even be sure that it happened, but I think it did. I think she turned and looked.

I broke into a run and got maybe five yards before something crashed into the side of my head. As my vision faded to black I thought I saw the thing that had been hiding look at me to check I was done, before shambling quickly to join the others.


I came back to London two days later, and I'm still here. For the time being. All of Susan's stuff is in boxes under the stairs. Having it lying around was too painful, but I can't get rid of it. Not until I know what I'm going to do.

I regained consciousness, after about three hours stretched on my face in the mud, to find the beach completely deserted. I started to stumble towards the water, mind still programmed as it had been before I was knocked out, but then I changed my mind. I walked crying back up the slope and called the police from a public phone booth, and then I slumped down to the ground and passed out. I was taken to hospital eventually, where they found two concussions. But before that I talked to the police, and told them what I knew. I ranted a great deal apparently, about a coastal town where they didn't eat the fish, about the meaning of inverted swastikas, and about monstrous villagers who could disguise their true nature and look like normal people.

In the end the police brought the heavy squad in. They had to. An empty village where doors have been left open and belongings abandoned is more than local plod can handle. The city cops weren't terribly interested in my ramblings, and I can't say that I blame them. But before they arrived I thought one of the local police, an old sergeant who lived in a nearby village, took what I said very seriously.

He must have done. Because on the following day, as I sat shivering in the sitting room of the empty guest house, I saw police divers head out towards the sea. No-one knows about this, and they won't. The press never got wind of the story, and various powers will make sure they never do. I'm not going to tell anyone. It's better that no-one knows. The only question in my mind is what I should do, whether I can forget enough not to act on my knowledge. Time will tell.

I brought my shoes back to London in the end, which was a gesture of a kind. The police found them on the front, and I identified them as mine. Deep in one toe I found a note. "Goodbye, my dear," it said.

That she went with them I know, and I'm glad she lost her fear of the sea. Perhaps it had never been real fear, but a denial of something else. When I remember the last hour we spent together I wonder now whether it was a tear I felt on my cheek, or whether her hair was wet. Because when the divers returned they'd made a discovery, something that will never be known. More divers arrived an hour later, and for the next day the beach was crawling with them as they returned to the water again and again.

They found the *Aldwinkle,* and something inside. The skeletons of three hundred and ten people, to be precise. By the jewellery round her neck and the remains of her passport, one was identified as Geraldine Stanbury.

# Dagon's Bell

## Brian Lumley

### I: DEEP KELP

It strikes me as funny sometimes how scraps of information—fragments of seemingly dissociated fact and half-seen or -felt fancies and intuitions, bits of local legend and immemorial myth—can suddenly connect and expand until the total is far greater than the sum of the parts, like a jigsaw puzzle. Or perhaps not necessarily *funny* . . . odd.

Flotsam left high and dry by the tide, scurf of the rolling sea; a half-obliterated figure glimpsed on an ancient, well-rubbed coin through the glass of a museum's showcase; old-wives tales of hauntings and hoary nights, and the ringing of some sepulchral, sunken bell at the rising of the tide; the strange speculations of sea-coal gatherers supping their ale in old North-East pubs, where the sound of the ocean's wash is never far distant beyond smoke-yellowed bull's-eye window panes. Items like that, apparently unconnected.

But in the end there was really much more to it than that. For these things were only the *pieces* of the puzzle; the picture, complete, was far vaster than its component parts. Indeed cosmic . . .

I long ago promised myself that I would never again speak or even think of David Parker and the occurrences of that night at Ket-tlethorpe Farm (which formed, in any case, a tale almost too grotesque for belief); but now, these years later . . . well, my promise seems rather redundant. On the other hand it is possible that a valuable warning lies inherent in what I have to say, for which reason, despite the unlikely circumstance that I shall be taken at all seriously, I now put pen to paper.

My name is William Trafford ("Bill"), which hardly matters, but I had known David Parker at school—a Secondary Modern in a colliery village by the sea—before he passed his college examinations, and I was the one who would later share with him Kettlethorpe's terrible secret.

In fact I had known David well: the son of a miner, he was never typical of his colliery contemporaries but gentle in his ways and lacking the coarseness of the locality and its guttural accents. That is not to belittle the North-Easterner in general (after all, I became one myself!) for in all truth they are the salt of the earth; but the nature of their work, and what that work has gradually made of their environment, has moulded them into a hard and clannish lot. David Parker, by his nature, was not of that clan, that is all; and neither was I at that time.

My parents were Yorkshire born and bred, only moving to Harden in County Durham when my father bought a newsagent's shop there. Hence the friendship that sprang up between us, born not so much out of straightforward compatibility as of the fact that we both felt outsiders. A friendship which lasted for five years from a time when we were both eight years of age, and which was only rejoined upon David's release from his studies in London twelve years later. That was in 1951.

Meanwhile, in the years flown between . . .

My father was now dead and my mother more or less confined, and I had expanded the business to two more shops in Hartlepool, both of them under steady and industrious managers, and several smaller but growing concerns much removed from the sale of magazines and newspapers in the local colliery villages. Thus my time was mainly taken up with business matters, but in the highest capacity, which hardly consisted of back-breaking work. What time remained I was pleased to spend, on those occasions when he was available, in the company of my old school friend.

And he too had done well, and would do even better. His studies had been in architecture and design, but within two short years of his return he expanded these spheres to include interior decoration and landscape gardening, setting up a profitable business of his own and building himself an enviable reputation in his fields.

And so it can be seen that the war had been kind to both of us. Too young to have been involved, we had made capital while the world was fighting; now while the world licked its wounds and rediscovered its directions, we were already on course and beginning to ride the crest. Mercenary? No, for we had been mere boys when the war started and were little more than boys when it ended.

But now, eight years later . . .

We were, or saw ourselves as being, very nearly sophisticates in a mainly unsophisticated society—that is to say part of a very narrow spectrum—and so once more felt drawn together. Even so, we made odd companions. At least externally, superficially. Oh, I suppose our characters, drives and ambitions were similar, but physically we were poles apart. David was dark, handsome and well-proportioned; I was sort of dumpy, sandy, pale to the point of pallid. I was not unhealthy, but set beside David Parker I certainly looked it!

On the day in question, that is to say the day when the first unconnected fragment presented itself—a Friday in September '53, it was, just a few days before the Feast of the Exaltation, sometimes called Roodmas in those parts, and occasionally by a far older name—we met in a bar overlooking the sea on old Hartlepool's headland. On those occasions when we got together like this we would normally try to keep business out of the conversation, but there were times when it seemed to intrude almost of necessity. This was one such.

I had not noticed Jackie Foster standing at the bar upon entering, but certainly he had seen me. Foster was a foreman with a small fleet of sea-coal gathering trucks of which I was co-owner, and he should not have been there in the pub at that time but out and about his work. Possibly he considered it prudent to come over and explain his presence, just in case I *had* seen him, and he did so in a single word.

"Kelp?" David repeated, looking puzzled; so that I felt compelled to explain.

"Seaweed," I said. "Following a bad blow, it comes up on the beach in thick drifts. But—" and I looked at Foster pointedly, "—I've never before known it to stop the sea-coalers."

The man shuffled uncomfortably for a moment, took off his cap and scratched his head. "Oh, once or twice ah've known it almost this bad, but before your time in the game. It slimes up the rocks an' the wheels of the lorries slip in the stuff. Bloody arful! An' stinks like death. It's lyin' feet thick on arl the beaches from here to Sunderland!"

"Kelp," David said again, thoughtfully. "Isn't that the weed people used to gather up and cook into a soup?"

Foster wrinkled his nose. "Hungry folks'll eat just about owt, ah suppose, Mr. Parker—but they'd not eat this muck. We carl it 'deep kelp.' It's not unusual this time of year—Roodmas time or thereabouts—and generally hangs about fair a week or so until the tides clear it or it rots away."

David continued to look interested and Foster continued:

"Funny stuff. Ah mean, you'll not find it in any book of seaweeds—not that ah've ever seen. As a lad ah was daft on nature an' arl. Collected birds eggs, took spore prints of mushrooms an' toadstools, pressed leaves an' flowers in books—arl that daft stuff—but in arl the books ah read ah never did find a mention of deep kelp." He turned back to me. "Anyway, boss, there's enough of the stuff on the beach ta keep the lorries off. It's not that they canna get onto the sands, but when they do they canna see the coal for weed. So ah've sent the lorries south ta Seaton Carew. The beach is pretty clear down there, ah'm told. Not much coal, but better than nowt."

My friend and I had almost finished eating by then. As Foster made to leave, I suggested to David: "Let's finish our drinks, climb down the old sea wall and have a look."

"Right!" David agreed at once. "I'm curious about this stuff."

Foster had heard and he turned back to us, shaking his head concernedly. "It's up ta you, gents," he said, "but you won't like it. Stinks, man! *Arful!* There's kids who play on the beach arl the live-long day, but you'll not find them there now. Just the bloody weed, lyin' there an' turnin' ta rot!"

## II: A WEDDING AND A WARNING

In any event, we went to see for ourselves, and if I had doubted Foster then I had wronged him. The stuff *was* awful, and it *did* stink. I had seen it before, always at this time of year, but never in such quantities. There had been a bit of a blow the night before, however, and that probably explained it. To my mind, anyway. David's mind was a fraction more inquiring.

"Deep kelp," he murmured, standing on the weed-strewn rocks, his hair blowing in a salty, stenchy breeze off the sea. "I don't see it at all."

"What don't you see?"

"Well, if this stuff comes from the deeps—I mean from really deep down—surely it would take a real upheaval to drive it onto the beaches like this. Why, there must be thousands and thousands of tons of the stuff! All the way from here to Sunderland? Twenty miles of it?"

I shrugged. "It'll clear, just like Foster said. A day or two, that's all. And he's right: with this stuff lying so thick, you can't see the streaks of coal."

"How about the coal?" he said, his mind again grasping after knowledge. "I mean, where does it come from?"

"Same place as the weed," I answered, "most of it. Come and see." I crossed to a narrow strip of sand between waves of deep kelp. There I found and picked up a pair of blocky, fist-sized lumps of ocean-rounded rock. Knocking them together, I broke off fragments. Inside, one rock showed a greyish-brown uniformity; the other was black and shiny, finely layered, pure coal.

"I wouldn't have known the difference," David admitted.

"Neither would I!" I grinned. "But the sea-coalers rarely err. They say there's an open seam way out there," I nodded toward the open sea. "Not unlikely, seeing as how this entire county is riddled with rich mines. Myself, I believe a lot of the coal simply gets washed out of the tippings, the stony debris rejected at the screens. Coal is light and easily washed ashore. The stones are heavy and roll out—downhill, as it were—into deeper water."

"In that case it seems a pity," said David. "—That the coal can't be gathered, I mean."

"Oh?"

"Why, yes. Surely, if there is an open seam in the sea, the coal would get washed ashore with the kelp. Underneath this stuff, there's probably tons of it just waiting to be shovelled up!"

I frowned and answered: "You could well be right . . ." But then I shrugged. "Ah, well, not to worry. It'll still be there after the weed has gone." And I winked at him. "Coal doesn't rot, you see."

He wasn't listening but kneeling, lifting a rope of the offensive stuff in his hands. It was heavy, leprous white in the stem or body, deep dark green in the leaf. Hybrid, the flesh of the stuff was—well, fleshy—more animal than vegetable. Bladders were present everywhere, large as a man's thumbs. David popped one and gave a disgusted grunt, then came to his feet. "God!" he exclaimed, holding his nose. And again: *"God!"*

I laughed and we picked our way back to the steps in the old sea wall.

And that was that: a fragment, an incident unconnected with

anything much. An item of little real interest. One of Nature's periodic quirks, affecting nothing a great deal. Apparently . . .

It seemed not long after the time of the deep kelp that David got tied up with his wedding plans. I had known, of course, that he had a girl—June Anderson, a solicitor's daughter from Sunderland, which boasts the prettiest girls in all the land—for I had met her and found her utterly charming; but I had not realised that things were so advanced.

I say it did not seem a long time, and now looking back I see that the period was indeed quite short—the very next summer. Perhaps the span of time was foreshortened even more for me by the suddenness with which their plans culminated. For all was brought dramatically forward by the curious and unexpected vacancy of Kettlethorpe Farm, an extensive property on the edge of Kettlethorpe Dene.

No longer a farm proper but a forlorn relic of another age, the great stone house and its outbuildings were badly in need of repair; but in David's eyes the place had an Olde Worlde magic all its own, and with his expertise he knew that he could soon convert it into a modern home of great beauty and value. And the place was going remarkably cheap.

As to the farm's previous tenant: here something peculiar. And here too the second link in my seemingly unconnected chain of occurrences and circumstances.

Old Jason Carpenter had not been well liked in the locality, in fact not at all. Grey-bearded, taciturn, cold and reclusive—with eyes grey as the rolling North Sea and never a smile for man or beast—he had occupied Kettlethorpe Farm for close on thirty years. Never a wife, a manservant or maid, not even a neighbour had entered the place on old Jason's invitation. No one strayed onto the grounds for fear of Jason's dog and shotgun; even tradesmen were wary on those rare occasions when they must make deliveries.

But Carpenter had liked his beer and rum chaser, and twice a week would visit The Trust Hotel in Harden. There he had used to sit in the smokeroom and linger over his tipple, his dog Bones alert under the table and between his master's feet. And customers had used to fear Bones a little, but not as much as the dog feared his master.

And now Jason Carpenter was gone. Note that I do not say dead, simply gone, disappeared. There was no evidence to support any other conclusion—not at that time. It had happened like this:

Over a period of several months various tradesmen had reported Jason's absence from Kettlethorpe, and eventually, because his customary seat at The Trust had been vacant over that same period, members of the local police went to the farm and forced entry into the main building. No trace had been found of the old hermit, but the police had come away instead with certain documents—chiefly a will, of sorts—which had evidently been left pending just such a search or investigation.

In the documents the recluse had directed that in the event of his "termination of occupancy," the house, attendant buildings and grounds "be allowed to relapse into the dirt and decay from which they sprang"; but since it was later shown that he was in considerable debt, the property had been put up for sale to settle his various accounts. The house had in fact been under threat of the bailiffs.

All of this, of course, had taken some considerable time, during which a thorough search of the rambling house, its outbuildings and grounds had been made for obvious reasons. But to no avail.

Jason Carpenter was gone. He had not been known to have relatives; indeed, very little had been known of him at all; it was almost as if he had never been. And to many of the people of Harden, that made for a most satisfactory epitaph.

One other note: it would seem that his "termination of occupancy" had come about during the Roodmas time of the deep kelp . . .

And so to the wedding of David Parker and June Anderson, a sparkling affair held at the Catholic Church in Harden, where not even the drab, near-distant background of the colliery's chimneys and cooling towers should have been able to dampen the gaiety and excitement of the moment. And yet even here, in the steep, crowd-packed streets outside the church, a note of discord. Just one, but one too many.

For as the cheering commenced and the couple left the church to be showered with confetti and jostled to their car, I overheard as if they were spoken directly into my ear—or uttered especially for my notice—the words of a crone in shawl and pinafore, come out of her smoke-grimed miner's terraced house to shake her head and mutter:

"Aye, an' he'll take that bonnie lass ta Kettlethorpe, will he? Arl the bells are ringin' now, it's true, but what about the *other* bell, eh? It's only rung once or twice arl these lang years—since old Jason had the house—but now there's word it's ringin' again, when nights are dark an' the sea has a swell ta it."

I heard it as clearly as that, for I was one of the spectators.

I would have been more closely linked with the celebrations but had expected to be busy, and only by the skin of my teeth managed to be there at all. But when I heard the guttural imprecation of the old lady I turned to seek her out, even caught a glimpse of her, before being engulfed by a horde of Harden urchins leaping for a handful of hurled pennies, threepenny bits and sixpences as the newlyweds' car drove off.

By which time summer thunderclouds had gathered, breaking at the command of a distant flash of lightning, and rain had begun to pelt down. Which served to put an end to the matter. The crowd rapidly dispersed and I headed for shelter.

But ... I would have liked to know what the old woman had meant ...

### III: GHOST STORY

*"Haunted?"* I echoed David's words.

I had bumped into him at the library in Hartlepool some three weeks after his wedding. A voracious reader, an "addict" for hard-boiled detective novels, I had been on my way in as he was coming out.

"Haunted, yes!" he repeated, his voice half-amused, half-excited. "The old farm—haunted!"

The alarm his words conjured in me was almost immediately relieved by his grin and wide-awake expression. Whatever ghosts they were at the farm, he obviously didn't fear them. Was he having a little joke at my expense? I grinned with him, saying: "Well, I shouldn't care to have been your ghosts. Not for the last thirty years, at any rate. Not with old man Carpenter about the place. That would be a classic case of the biter bit!"

"Old Jason Carpenter," he reminded me, smiling still but less brilliantly, "has disappeared, remember?"

"Oh!" I said, feeling a little foolish. "Of course he has." And I followed up quickly with: "But what do you mean, haunted?"

"Local village legend," he shrugged. "I heard it from Father Nicholls, who married us. He had it from the priest before him, and so on. Handed down for centuries, so to speak. I wouldn't have known if he hadn't stopped me and asked how we were getting on up at the farm. If we'd seen anything—you know—odd? He wouldn't have said anything more but I pressed him."

"And?"

"Well, it seems the original owners were something of a fishy bunch."

"Fishy?"

"Quite literally! I mean, they *looked* fishy. Or maybe froggy? Protuberant lips, wide-mouthed, scaly-skinned, popeyed—you name it. To use Father Nicholls' own expression, 'ichthyic.'"

"Slow down," I told him, seeing his excitement rising up again. "First of all, what do you mean by the 'original' owners? The people who built the place?"

"Good heavens, no!" he chuckled; and then he took me by the elbow and guided me into the library and to a table. We sat. "No one knows—no one can remember—who actually built the place. If ever there were records, well, they're long lost. God, it probably dates back to Roman times! It's likely as old as the Wall itself—even older. Certainly it has been a landmark on maps for the last four hundred and fifty years. No, I mean the first *recorded* family to live there. Which was something like two and a half centuries ago."

"And they were—" I couldn't help frowning, "—odd-looking, these people?"

"Right! And odd not only in their looks. That was probably just a case of regressive genes, the result of indiscriminate inbreeding. Anyway, the locals shunned them—not that there were any real 'locals' in those days, you understand. I mean, the closest villages or towns then were Hartlepool, Sunderland, Durham and Seaham Harbour. Maybe a handful of other, smaller places—I haven't checked. But this country was wild! And it stayed that way, more or less, until the modern roads were built. Then came the railways, to service the pits, and so on."

I nodded, becoming involved with David's enthusiasm, finding myself carried along by it. "And the people at the farm stayed there down the generations?"

"Not quite," he answered. "Apparently there was something of a hiatus in their tenancy around a hundred and fifty years ago; but later, about the time of the American Civil War, a family came over from Innsmouth in New England and bought the place up. They, too, had the degenerate looks of earlier tenants; might even have been an offshoot of the same family, returning to their ancestral home, as it were. They made a living farming and fishing. Fairly industrious, it would seem, but surly and clannish. Name of Waite. By then, though, the 'ghosts' were well established in local folklore. *They* came in two manifestations, apparently."

"Oh?"

He nodded. "One of them was a gigantic, wraithlike, nebulous figure rising from the mists over Kettlethorpe Dene, seen by travellers on the old coach road or by fishermen returning to Harden along the cliff-top paths. But the interesting thing is this: if you look at a map of the district, as I've done, you'll see that the farm lies in something of a depression directly between the coach road and the cliffs. Anything seen from those vantage points could conceivably be emanating from the farm itself!"

I was again beginning to find the nature of David's discourse disturbing. Or if not what he was saying, his obvious *involvement* with the concept. "You seem to have gone over all of this rather thoroughly," I remarked. "Any special reason?"

"Just my old thirst for knowledge," he grinned. "You know I'm never happy unless I'm tracking something down—and never happier than when I've finally got it cornered. And after all, I do live at the place! Anyway, about the giant mist-figure: according to the legends, it was half-fish, half-man!"

"A merman?"

"Yes. And now," he triumphantly took out a folded sheet of rubbing parchment and opened it out onto the table—"*Ta-rah!* And what do you make of that?"

The impression on the paper was perhaps nine inches square; a charcoal rubbing taken from a brass of some sort, I correctly imagined. It showed a mainly anthropomorphic male figure seated upon a rock-carved chair or throne, his lower half obscured by draperies of weed bearing striking resemblance to the deep kelp. The eyes of the figure were large and somewhat protuberant; his forehead sloped; his skin had the overlapping scales of a fish, and the fingers of his one visible hand where it grasped a short trident were webbed. The background was vague, reminding me of nothing so much as cyclopean submarine ruins.

"Neptune," I said. "Or at any rate, a merman. Where did you get it?"

"I rubbed it up myself," he said, carefully folding the sheet and replacing it in his pocket. "It's from a plate on a lintel over a door in one of the outbuildings at Kettlethorpe." And then for the first time he frowned. "Fishy people and a fishy symbol . . ."

He stared at me strangely for a moment and I felt a sudden chill in my bones—until his grin came back and he added: "And an entirely fishy story, eh?"

We left the library and I walked with him to his car. "And what's your real interest in all of this?" I asked. "I mean, I don't remember you as much of a folklorist?"

His look this time was curious, almost evasive. "You just won't believe that it's only this old inquiring mind of mine, will you?" But then his grin came back, bright and infectious as ever.

He got into his car, wound down the window and poked his head out. "Will we be seeing you soon? Isn't it time you paid us a visit?"

"Is that an invitation?"

He started up the car. "Of course—any time."

"Then I'll make it soon," I promised.

"Sooner!" he said.

Then I remembered something he had said. "David, you mentioned two manifestations of this—this ghostliness. What was the other one?"

"Eh?" he frowned at me, winding up his window. Then he stopped winding. "Oh, that. The bell, you mean . . ."

"Bell?" I echoed him, the skin of my neck suddenly tingling. "What bell?"

"A ghost bell!" he yelled as he pulled away from the kerb. "What else? It tolls underground or under the sea, usually when there's a mist or a swell on the ocean. I keep listening for it, but—"

"No luck?" I asked automatically, hearing my own voice almost as that of a stranger.

"Not yet."

And as he grinned one last time and waved a farewell, pulling away down the street, against all commonsense and logic I found myself remembering the old woman's words outside the church: "What about the *other* bell, eh?"

What about the other bell, indeed . . .


## IV: "MIASMA"

Half-way back to Harden it dawned on me that I had not chosen a book for myself. My mind was still full of David Parker's discoveries; about which, where he had displayed that curious excitement, I still experienced only a niggling disquiet.

But back at Harden, where my home stands on a hill at the southern extreme of the village, I remembered where once before I had seen something like the figure on David's rubbing. And sure enough it was there in my antique, illustrated two-volume Family Bible; pages I had not looked into for many a year, which had become merely ornamental on my bookshelves.

The item I refer to was simply one of the many small illustrations in Judges XIII: a drawing of a piscine deity on a Philistine coin or medallion. Dagon, whose temple Samson toppled at Gaza.

Dagon . . .

With my memory awakened, it suddenly came to me where I had seen one other representation of this same god. Sunderland has a fine museum and my father had often taken me there when I was small. Amongst the museum's collection of coins and medals I had seen . . .

"Dagon?" the curator answered my telephone inquiry with interest. "No, I'm afraid we have very little of the Philistines; no coins that I know of. Possibly it was a little later than that. Can I call you back?"

"Please do, and I'm sorry to be taking up your time like this."

"Not at all, a pleasure. That's what we're here for."

And ten minutes later he was back. "As I suspected, Mr. Trafford. We do have that coin you remembered, but it's Phoenician, not Philistine. The Phoenicians adopted Dagon from the Philistines and called him Oannes. That's a pattern that repeats all through history. The Romans in particular were great thieves of other people's gods. Sometimes they adopted them openly, as with Zeus becoming Jupiter, but at other times—where the deity was especially dark or ominous, as in Summanus—they were rather more covert in their worship. Great cultists, the Romans. You'd be surprised how many secret societies and cults came down the ages from sources such as these. But . . . there I go again . . . lecturing!"

"Not at all," I assured him, "that's all very interesting. And thank you very much for your time."

"And is that it? There's no other way in which I can assist?"

"No, that's it. Thank you again."

And indeed that seemed to be that . . .

I went to see them a fortnight later. Old Jason Carpenter had not had a telephone, and David was still in the process of having one installed, which meant that I must literally drop in on them.

Kettlethorpe lies to the north of Harden, between the modern coast road and the sea, and the view of the dene as the track dipped down from the road and wound toward the old farm was breathtaking. Under a blue sky, with seagulls wheeling and crying over a distant, fresh-ploughed field, and the hedgerows thick with honeysuckle and the droning of bees, and sweet smells of decay from the streams and hazelnut-shaded pools, the scene was very nearly idyllic. A far cry from midnight tales of ghouls and ghosties!

Then to the farm's stone outer wall—almost a fortification, reminiscent of some forbidding feudal structure—which encompassed all of the buildings including the main house. Iron gates were open, bearing the legend "Kettlethorpe" in stark letters of iron. Inside . . . things already were changing.

The wall surrounded something like three and a half to four acres of ground, being the actual core of the property. I had seen several rotting "Private Property" and "Trespassers Will Be Prosecuted" notices along the road, defining Kettlethorpe's exterior boundaries, but the area bordered by the wall was the very heart of the place.

In layout: there was a sort of geometrical regularity to the spacing and positioning of the buildings. They formed a horseshoe, with the main house at its apex; the open mouth of the horseshoe faced the sea, unseen, something like a mile away beyond a rise which boasted a dense-grown stand of oaks. All of the buildings were of local stone, easily recognizable through its tough, flinty-grey texture. I am no geologist and so could not give that stone a name, but I knew that in years past it had been blasted from local quarries or cut from outcrops. To my knowledge, however, the closest of these sources was a good many miles away; the actual building of Kettlethorpe must therefore have been a Herculean task.

As this thought crossed my mind, and remembering the words of the curator of Sunderland's museum, I had to smile. Perhaps not Herculean but something later than the Greeks. Except that I couldn't recall a specific Roman strong-man!

And approaching the house, where I pulled up before the stone columns of its portico, I believed I could see where David had got his idea of the age of the place. Under the heat of the sun the house was redolent of the centuries; its walls massive, structurally Romanesque. The roof especially, low-peaked and broad, giving an impression of strength and endurance.

What with its outer wall and horseshoe design, the place might well be some strange old Roman temple. A temple, yes, but wavery for all its massiveness, shimmering as smoke and heat from a small bonfire in what had been a garden drifted lazily across my field of vision. A temple—ah!—but to what strange old god?

And no need to ponder the source of *that* thought, for certainly the business of David's antiquarian research was still in my head; and while I had no intention of bringing that subject up, still I wondered how far he had progressed. Or perhaps by now he had discovered sufficient of Kettlethorpe to satisfy his curiosity. Perhaps, but I doubted it. No, he would follow the very devil to hell, that one, in pursuit of knowledge.

"Hello, there!" he slapped me on the back, causing me to start as I got out of my old Morris and closed its door. I started . . . reeled . . .

. . . He had come out of the shadows of the porch so quickly . . . I had not seen him . . . My eyes . . . the heat and the glaring sun and the drone of bees . . .

"*Bill!*" David's voice came to me from a million miles away, full of concern. "What on earth . . . ?"

"I've come over queer," I heard myself say, leaning on my car as the world rocked about me.

"Queer? Man, you're pale as death! It's the bloody sun! Too hot by far. And the smoke from the fire. And I'll bet you've been driving with your windows up. Here, let's get you into the house."

Hanging onto his broad shoulder, I was happy to let him lead me staggering indoors. "The hot sun," he mumbled again, half to me, half to himself. "And the honeysuckle. Almost a miasma. Nauseating, until you get used to it. June has suffered in exactly the same way."

## V: THE ENCLOSURE

"Miasma?" I let myself fall into a cool, shady window seat.

He nodded, swimming into focus as I quickly recovered from my attack of—of whatever it had been. "Yes, a mist of pollen, invisible, born on thermals in the air, sweet and cloying. Enough to choke a horse!"

"Is that what it was? God!—I thought I was going to faint."

"I know what you mean. June has been like it for a week. Conks out completely at high noon. Even inside it's too close for her liking. She gets listless. She's upstairs now, stretched out flat!"

As if the very mention of her name were a summons, June's voice came down to us: "David, is that Bill? I'll be down at once."

"Don't trouble yourself on my account," I called out, my voice still a little shaky. "And certainly not if you don't feel too well."

"I'm fine!" her voice insisted. "I was just a little tired, that's all."

I was myself again, gratefully accepting a scotch and soda, swilling a parched dryness from my mouth and throat.

"There," said David, seeming to read my thoughts. "You look more your old self now."

"First time that ever happened to me," I told him. "I suppose your 'miasma' theory must be correct. Anyway, I'll be up on my feet again in a minute." As I spoke I let my eyes wander about the interior of what would be the house's main living-room.

The room was large, for the main part oak-panelled, almost stripped of its old furniture and looking extremely austere. I recalled the bonfire, its pale flames licking at the upthrusting, worm-eaten leg of a chair . . .

One wall was of the original hard stone, polished by the years, creating an effect normally thought desirable in modern homes but perfectly natural here and in no way contrived. All in all a charming room. Ages-blackened beams bowed almost imperceptibly toward the centre where they crossed the low ceiling wall to wall.

"Built to last," said David. "Three hundred years old at least, those beams, but the basic structure is—" he shrugged, "—I'm not sure, not yet. This is one of five lower rooms, all about the same size. I've cleared most of them out now, burnt up most of the old furniture; but there were one or two pieces worth renovation. Most of the stuff I've saved is in what used to be old man Carpenter's study. And the place is—will be—beautiful. When I'm through with it. Gloomy at the moment, yes, but that's because of the windows. I'm afraid most of these old small-panes will have to go. The place needs opening up."

"Opening up, yes," I repeated him, sensing a vague irritation or tension in him, a sort of urgency.

"Here," he said, "are you feeling all right now? I'd like you to see the plate I took that rubbing from."

"The Dagon plate," I said at once, biting my tongue a moment too late.

He looked at me, stared at me, and slowly smiled. "So you looked it up, did you? Dagon, yes—or Neptune, as the Romans called him. Come on, I'll show you." And as we left the house he yelled back over his shoulder: "June—we're just going over to the enclosure. Back soon."

"Enclosure?" I followed him toward the mouth of the horseshoe of buildings. "I thought you said the brass was on a lintel?"

"So it is, over a doorway—but the building has no roof and so I call it an enclosure. See?" and he pointed. The mouth of the horseshoe was formed of a pair of small, rough stone buildings set perhaps twenty-five yards apart, which were identical in design but for the one main discrepancy David had mentioned—namely that the one on the left had no roof.

"Perhaps it fell in?" I suggested as we approached the structure.

David shook his head. "No," he said, "there never was a roof. Look at the tops of the walls. They're flush. No gaps to show where roof support beams might have been positioned. If you make a comparison with the other building you'll see what I mean. Anyway, whatever its original purpose, old man Carpenter filled it with junk: bags of rusty old nails, worn-out tools, that sort of thing. Oh, yes— and he kept his firewood here, under a tarpaulin."

I glanced inside the place, leaning against the wall and poking my head in through the vacant doorway. The wall stood in its own shadow and was cold to my touch. Beams of sunlight, glancing in over the top of the west wall, filled the place with dust motes that drifted like swarms of aimless microbes in the strangely musty air. There was a mixed smell of rust and rot, of some small dead thing, and of . . . the sea? The last could only be a passing fancy, no sooner imagined than forgotten.

I shaded my eyes against the dusty sunbeams. Rotted sacks spilled nails and bolts upon a stone-flagged floor; farming implements red with rust were heaped like metal skeletons against one wall; at the back, heavy blocks of wood stuck out from beneath a mould-spotted tarpaulin. A dead rat or squirrel close to my feet seethed with maggots.

I blinked in the hazy light, shuddered—not so much at sight of the small corpse as at a sudden chill of the psyche—and hastily withdrew my head.

"There you are," said David, his matter-of-fact tone bringing me back down to earth. "The brass."

Above our heads, central in the stone lintel, a square plate bore the original of David's rubbing. I gave it a glance, an almost involuntary reaction to David's invitation that I look, and at once looked away. He frowned, seemed disappointed. "You don't find it interesting?"

"I find it . . . disturbing," I answered at length. "Can we go back to the house? I'm sure June will be up and about by now."

He shrugged, leading the way as we retraced our steps along sunsplashed, weed-grown paths between scrubby fruit trees and dusty, cobwebbed shrubbery. "I thought you'd be taken by it," he said. And, "How do you mean, 'disturbing'?"

I shook my head, had no answer for him. "Maybe it's just me," I finally said. "I don't feel at my best today. I'm not up to it, that's all."

"Not up to what?" he asked sharply, then shrugged again before I could answer. "Suit yourself." But after that he quickly became distant and a little surly. He wasn't normally a moody man, but I knew him well enough to realize that I had touched upon some previously unsuspected, exposed nerve; and so I determined not to prolong my visit.

I did stay long enough to talk to June, however, though what I saw of her was hardly reassuring. She looked pinched, her face lined and pale, showing none of the rosiness one might expect in a newly-wed, or in any healthy young woman in summertime. Her eyes were red-rimmed, their natural blue seeming very much watered-down; her skin looked dry, deprived of moisture; even her hair, glossy-black and bouncy on those previous occasions when we had met, seemed lackluster now and disinterested.

It could be, of course, simply the fact that I had caught her at a bad time. Her father had died recently, as I later discovered, and of course that must still be affecting her. Also, she must have been work-ing very hard, alongside David, trying to get the old place put to rights. Or again it could be David's summer "miasma"—an allergy, perhaps.

Perhaps ...

But why any of these things—David's preoccupation, his near-obsession (or mine?) with occurrences and relics of the distant past; the old myths and legends of the region, of hauntings and misty phantoms and such; and June's queer malaise—why any of these things should concern me beyond the bounds of common friendship I did not know, could not say. I only knew that I felt as if somewhere a great wheel had started to roll, and that my friend and his wife lay directly in its path, not even knowing that it bore down upon them ...

### VI: DAGON'S BELL

Summer rolled by in warm lazy waves; autumn saw the trees shame-lessly, mindlessly stripping themselves naked (one would think they'd keep their leaves to warm them through the winter); my businesses presented periodic problems enough to keep my nose to the grind-stone, and so there was little spare time in which to ponder the strangeness of the last twelve months. I saw David in the village now and then, usually at a distance; saw June, too, but much less frequently. More often than not he seemed haggard—or if not haggard, hagridden, nervous, agitated, *hurried*—and she was . . . well, spectral. Pale and willow-slim, and red-eyed (I suspected) behind dark spectacles. Married life? Or perhaps some other problem? None of my business.

Then came the time of the deep kelp once more, which was when David made it my business.

And here I must ask the reader to bear with me. The following part of the story will seem hastily written, too thoughtlessly prepared and put together. But this is how I remember it: blurred and unreal, and patterned with mismatched dialogue. It happened quickly; I see no reason to spin it out . . .


David's knock was urgent on a night when the sky was black with falling rain and the wind whipped the trees to a frenzy; and yet he stood there in shirt-sleeves, shivering, gaunt in aspect and almost vacant in expression. It took several brandies and a thorough rub-down with a warm towel to bring him to a semblance of his old self, by which time he seemed more ashamed of his behaviour than eager to explain it. But I was not letting him off that lightly. The time had come, I decided, to have the thing out with him; get it out in the open, whatever it was, and see what could be done about it while there was yet time.

"Time?" he finally turned his gaze upon me from beneath his mop of tousled hair, a towel over his shoulders while his shirt steamed before my open fire. "*Is* there yet time? Damned if I know . . ." He shook his head.

"Well then, *tell* me," I said, exasperated. "Or at least try. Start somewhere. You must have come to me for something. Is it you and June? Was your getting married a mistake? Or is it just the place, the old farm?"

"Oh, come on, Bill!" he snorted. "You know well enough what it is. Something of it, anyway. You experienced it yourself. Just the place?" the corners of his mouth turned down, his expression souring. "Oh, yes, it's the place, all right. What the place was, what it might be even now . . ."

"Go on," I prompted him; and he launched into the following:

"I came to ask you to come back with me. I don't want to spend another night alone there."

"Alone? But isn't June there?"

He looked at me for a moment and finally managed a ghastly grin. "She is and she isn't," he said. "Oh, yes, yes, she's there—but still I'm alone. Not her fault, poor love. It's that bloody awful place!"

"Tell me about it," I urged.

He sighed, bit his lip. And after a moment: "I think," he began, "—I think it was a temple. And I don't think the Romans had it first. You know, of course, that they've found Phoenician symbols on some of the stones at Stonehenge? Well, and what else did the ancients bring with them to old England, eh? What did we worship in those prehistoric times? The earth-mother, the sun, the rain—the sea? We're an island, Bill. The sea was everywhere around us! And it was bountiful. It still is, but not like it was in those days. What's more natural than to worship the sea—and what the sea brought?"

"Its bounty?" I said.

"That, yes, and something else. Cthulhu, Pischa, the Kraken, Dagon, Oannes, Neptune. Call him—it—what you will. But it was worshipped at Kettlethorpe, and it still remembers. Yes, and I think it comes, in certain seasons, to seek the worship it once knew and perhaps still . . . still . . ."

"Yes?"

He looked quickly away. "I've made . . . discoveries."

I waited.

"I've found things out, yes, yes—and—" His eyes flared up for a moment in the firelight, then dulled.

"And?"

"*Damn it!*" he turned on me and the towel fell from his shoulders. Quickly he snatched it up and covered himself—but not before I had seen how thin mere months had made him. "Damn it!" he mumbled again, less vehemently now. "Must you repeat everything I

415

say? God, I do enough of that myself! I go over everything—Over and over and over . . ."

I sat in silence, waiting. He would tell it in his own time.

And eventually he continued. "I've made discoveries, and I've heard . . . things." He looked from the fire to me, peered at me, ran trembling fingers through his hair. And did I detect streaks of grey in that once jet mop? "I've heard the bell!"

"Then it's time you got out of there!" I said at once. "Time you got June out, too."

"I know, I *know!*" he answered, his expression tortured. He gripped my arm. "But I'm not finished yet. I don't know it all, not yet. It lures me, Bill. I have to know . . ."

"Know what?" It was my turn to show my agitation. "What do you need to know, you fool? Isn't it enough that the place is evil? You know *that* much. And yet you stay on there. Get out, that's my advice. Get out now!"

"*No!*" his denial was emphatic. "I'm not finished. There has to be an end to it. The place must be cleansed." He stared again into the fire.

"So you do admit it's evil?"

"Of course it is. Yes, I know it is. But leave, get out? I can't, and June—"

"Yes?"

"She *won't!*" He gave a muffled sob and turned watery, searching eyes full upon me. "The place is like . . . like a magnet! It has a *genius locus*. It's a focal point for God-only-knows-what forces. Evil? Oh, yes! An evil come down all the centuries. But I bought the place and I shall cleanse it—end it forever, whatever it is."

"Look," I tried reasoning with him, "let's go back, now, the two of us. Let's get June out of there and bring her back here for the night. How did you get here anyway? Surely not on foot, on a night like this?"

"No, no," he shook his head. "Car broke down half-way up the hill. Rain must have got under the bonnet. I'll pick it up tomorrow." He stood up, looked suddenly afraid, wild-eyed. "I've been away too long. Bill, will you run me back? June's there—alone! She was sleeping when I left. I can fill you in on the details while you drive . . ."

## VII: MANIFESTATION

I made him take another brandy, threw a coat over his shoulders, bustled him out to my car. Moments later we were rolling down into Harden and he was telling me all that had happened between times. As best I remember, this is what he said:

"Since that day you visited us I've been hard at work. Real work, I mean. Not the other thing, not delving—not all of the time, anyway. I got the grounds inside the walls tidied up, even tried a little preliminary landscaping. And the house: the old windows out, new ones in. Plenty of light. But still the place was musty. As the summer turned I began burning old Carpenter's wood, drying out the house, ridding it of the odour of centuries—a smell that was always thicker at night. And fresh paint, too, lots of it. Mainly white, all bright and new. June picked up a lot; you must have noticed how down she was? Yes, well she seemed to be on the mend. I thought I had the—the 'miasma'— on the run. *Hah!*" he gave a bitter snort. "A 'summer miasma,' I called it. Blind, blind!"

"Go on," I urged him, driving carefully through the wet streets.

"Eventually, to give myself room to sort out the furniture and so on, I got round to chucking the old shelves and books out of Carpenter's study. That would have been okay, but . . . I looked into some of those books. That was an error. I should have simply burned the lot, along with the wormy old chairs and shreds of carpet. And yet, in a way, I'm glad I didn't." I could feel David's fevered eyes burning me in the car's dark interior, fixed upon me as he spoke.

"The *knowledge* in those books, Bill. The dark secrets, the damnable mysteries. You know, if anyone does, what a fool I am for a mystery. I was hooked; work ceased; I had to know! But those books and manuscripts: the *Unter-Zee Kulten* and *Hydrophinnae*. Doorfen's treatise on submarine civilizations and the *Johansen Narrative* of

417

1925. A great sheaf of notes purporting to be from American government files for 1928, when federal agents 'raided' Innsmouth, a decaying, horror-haunted town on the coast of New England; and other scraps and fragments from all the world's mythologies, all of them concerned with the worship of a great god of the sea."

"Innsmouth?" my ears pricked up. I had heard that name mentioned once before. "But isn't that the place—?"

"—The place which spawned that family, the Waites, who came over and settled at Kettlethorpe about the time of the American Civil War? That's right," he nodded an affirmative, stared out into the rain-black night. "And old Carpenter who had the house for thirty years, he came from Innsmouth, too!"

"He was of the same people?"

"No, not him. The very opposite. He was at the farm for the same reason I am—now. Oh, he was strange, reclusive—who wouldn't be? I've read his diaries and I understand. Not everything, for even in his writing he held back, didn't explain too much. Why should he? His diaries were for him, aids to memory. They weren't meant for others to understand, but I fathomed a lot of it. The rest was in those government files.

"Innsmouth prospered in the time of the clipper ships and the old trade routes. The captains and men of some of those old ships brought back wives from Polynesia—and also their strange rites of worship, their gods. There was queer blood in those native women, and it spread rapidly. As the years passed the entire town became infected. Whole families grew up tainted. They were less than human, amphibian creatures more of the sea than the land. Merfolk, yes! Tritons, who worshipped Dagon in the deeps: 'Deep Ones,' as old Carpenter called them. Then came the federal raid of '28. But it came too late for old Carpenter.

"He had a store in Innsmouth, but well away from the secret places—away from the boarded-up streets and houses and churches where the worst of them had their dens and held their meetings and kept their rites. His wife was long dead of some wasting disease, but his daughter was alive and schooling in Arkham. Shortly before the raid she came home, little more than a girl. And she became—I don't know—lured. It's a word that sticks in my mind. A very real word, to me.

"Anyway, the Deep Ones took her, gave her to something they called out of the sea. She disappeared. Maybe she was dead, maybe something worse. They'd have killed Carpenter then, because he'd learned too much about them and wanted revenge, but the government raid put an end to any personal reprisals or vendettas. Put an end to Innsmouth, too. Why, they just about wrecked the town! Vast areas of complete demolition. They even depth-charged a reef a mile out in the sea . . .

"Well, after things quieted down Carpenter stayed on a while in Innsmouth, what was left of it. He was settling his affairs, I suppose, and maybe ensuring that the evil was at an end. Which must have been how he learned that it wasn't at an end but spreading like some awful blight. And because he suspected the survivors of the raid might seek haven in old strongholds abroad, finally he came to Kettlethorpe."

"Here?" David's story was beginning to make connections, was starting to add up. "Why would he come here?"

"Why? Haven't you been listening? He'd found something out about Kettlethorpe, and he came to make sure the Innsmouth horror couldn't spread here. Or perhaps he knew it was already here, waiting, like a cancer ready to shoot out its tentacles. Perhaps he came to stop it spreading further. Well, he's managed that these last thirty years, but now—"

"Yes?"

"Now he's gone, and I'm the owner of the place. Yes, and I have to see to it that whatever he was doing gets finished!"

"But what *was* he doing?" I asked. "And at what expense? Gone, you said. Yes, old Carpenter's gone. But gone where? What will all of this cost you, David? And more important by far, what will it cost June?"

My words had finally stirred something in him, something he had kept suppressed, too frightened of it to look more closely. I could tell by the way he started, sat bolt upright beside me. "June? But—"

"But nothing, man! Look at yourself. Better still, take a good look at your wife. You're going down the drain, both of you. It's something that started the day you took that farm. I'm sure you're right about the place, about old Carpenter, all that stuff you've dredged up—but now you've got to forget it. Sell Kettlethorpe, that's my advice—or better still raze it to the ground! But whatever you do—"

"*Look!*" he started again and gripped my arm in a suddenly claw-hard hand.

I looked, applied my brakes, brought the car skidding to a halt in the rain-puddled track. We had turned off the main road by then, where the track winds down to the farm. The rain had let up and the air had gone still as a shroud. Shroudlike, too, the milky mist that lay silently upon the near-distant dene and lapped a foot deep about the old farm's stony walls. The scene was weird under a watery moon—but weirder by far the morbid *manifestation* which was even now rising up like a wraith over the farm.

A shape, yes—billowing up, composed of mist, writhing huge over the ancient buildings. The shape of some monstrous merman—the ages Evil shape of Dagon himself!

I should have shaken David off and driven on at once, of course I should have, down to the farm and whatever waited there; but the sight of that figure mushrooming and firming in the dank night air was paralysing. And sitting there in the car, with the engine slowly ticking over, we shuddered as one as we heard, quite distinctly, the first muffled gonging of some damned and discordant bell. A tolling whose notes might on another occasion be sad and sorrowful, which now were filled with a menace out of the eons.

"The bell!" David's gasp galvanized me into action.

"I hear it," I said, throwing the car into gear and racing down that last quarter-mile stretch to the farm. It seemed that time was frozen in those moments, but then we were through the iron gates and slew-ing to a halt in front of the porch. The house was bright with lights, but June—

While David tore desperately through the rooms of the house, searching upstairs and down, crying her name, I could only stand by the car and tremblingly listen to the tolling of the bell; its dull, sepulchral summons seeming to me to issue from below, from the very earth beneath my feet. And as I listened so I watched that writhing figure of mist shrink down into itself, seeming to glare from bulging eyes of mist one final ray of hatred in my direction, before spiralling down and disappearing—into the shell of that roofless building at the mouth of the horseshoe!

David, awry and babbling as he staggered from the house, saw it too. "There!" he pointed at the square, mist-wreathed building. "That's where it is. And that's where she'll be. I didn't know she knew . . . she must have been watching me. Bill—" he clutched at my arm, "—are you with me? Say you are, for God's sake!" And I could only nod my head.

Hearts racing, we made for that now ghastly edifice of reeking mist—only to recoil a moment later from a figure that reeled out from beneath the lintel with the Dagon plate to fall swooning into David's arms. June, of course—but how could it be? How could *this* be June?

Not the June I had known, no, but some other, some revenant of that June . . .

## VIII: "THAT PLACE BELOW . . ."

She was gaunt, hair coarse as string, skin dry and stretched over features quite literally, shockingly altered into something . . . different. Strangely, David was not nearly so horrified by what he could see of her by the thin light of the moon; far more so after we had taken her back to the house. For quite apart from what were to me undeniable alterations in her looks in general—about which, as yet, he had made no comment—it then became apparent that his wife had been savaged and brutalized in the worst possible manner.

I remember, as I drove them to the emergency hospital in Hartlepool, listening to David as he cradled her in his arms in the back of the car. She was not conscious, and David barely so (certainly he was oblivious to what he babbled and sobbed over her during that nightmare journey) but my mind was working overtime as I listened to his crooning, utterly distraught voice:

"She must have watched me, poor darling, must have seen me going to that place. At first I went for the firewood—I burned up all of old Jason's wood—but then, beneath the splinters and bits of bark, I found the millstone over the slab. The old boy had put that stone there to keep the slab down. And it had done its job, by God! Must have weighed all of two hundred and forty pounds. Impossible to shift from those slimy, narrow steps below. But I used a lever to move it, yes—and I lifted the slab and went down. Down those ancient steps—down, down, down. A maze, down there. The earth itself, honeycombed! . . .

". . . What were they for, those burrows? What purpose were they supposed to fulfill? And who dug them? I didn't know, but I kept it from her anyway—or thought I had. I couldn't say why, not then, but some instinct warned me not to tell her about . . . about that place below. I swear to God I meant to close it up forever, choke the mouth of that—that *pit!*—with concrete. And I'd have done it, I swear it, once I'd explored those tunnels to the full. But that millstone, June, that great heavy stone. How did you shift it? Or were you helped?

"I've been down there only two or three times on my own, and I never went very far. Always there was that feeling that I wasn't alone, that things moved in the darker burrows and watched me where I crept. And that sluggish stream, bubbling blindly through airless fissures to the sea. That stream which rises and falls with the tides. And the kelp all bloated and slimy. Oh, my God! My God! . . ."

. . . And so on. But by the time we reached the hospital David had himself more or less under control again. Moreover, he had dragged from me a promise that I would let him—indeed help him—do things his own way. He had a plan which seemed both simple and faultless, one which must conclusively write *finis* on the entire affair. That was to say *if* his fears for Kettlethorpe and the conjectural region he termed "that place below" were soundly based.

As to why I so readily went along with him—why I allowed him to brush aside unspoken any protests or objections I might have entertained—quite simply, I had seen that mist-formed shape with my own eyes, and with my own ears had heard the tolling of that buried and blasphemous bell. And for all that the thing seemed fantastic, the conviction was now mine that the farm was a seat of horror and evil as great and maybe greater than any other these British Isles had ever known . . .

We stayed at the hospital through the night, gave identical, falsified statements to the police (an unimaginative tale of a marauder, seen fleeing under cover of the mist toward the dene), and in between sat together in a waiting area drinking coffee and quietly conversing. Quietly now, yes, for David was exhausted both physically and mentally; and much more so after he had attended that examination of his wife made imperative by her condition and by our statements.

As for June: mercifully she stayed in her traumatic state of deepest shock all through the night and well into the morning. Finally, around 10:00 p.m. we were informed that her condition, while still unstable, was no longer critical; and then, since it was very obvious that we could do nothing more, I drove David home with me to Harden.

I bedded him down in my guest-room, by which time all I wanted to do was get to my own bed for an hour or two; but about 4:00 p.m. I was awakened from uneasy dreams to find him on the telephone, his voice stridently urgent. As I went to him he put the 'phone down, turned to me haggard and red-eyed, his face dark with stubble. "She's stabilized," he said, and: "Thank God for that! But she hasn't come out of shock—not completely. It's too deep-seated. At least that's what they told me. They say she could be like it for weeks . . . maybe longer."

"What will you do?" I asked him. "You're welcome to stay here, of course, and—"

"Stay here?" he cut me short. "Yes, I'd like that—afterwards."

I nodded, biting my lip. "I see. You intend to go through with it. Very well—but there's still time to tell the police, you know. You could still let them deal with it."

He uttered a harsh, barking laugh. "Can you really imagine me telling all of this to your average son-of-the-sod Hartlepool bobby? Why, even if I showed them that . . . the place below, what could they do about it? And should I tell them about my plan, too? What!— mention dynamite to the law, the local authorities? Oh, yes, I can just see that! Even if they didn't put me in a straight-jacket it would still take them an age to get round to doing anything. And meanwhile, if there is something down there under the farm—and Bill, we know there is—what's to stop it or them moving on to fresh pastures?"

When I had no answer, he continued in a more controlled, quieter tone. "Do you know what old Carpenter was doing? I'll tell you: he was going down there in the right seasons, when he heard the bell ringing—going down below with his shotgun and blasting all hell out of what he found in those foul black tunnels! Paying them back for what they did to him and his in Innsmouth. A madman who didn't know what he wrote in those diaries of his? No, for we've *seen* it, Bill, you and I. And we've heard it—heard Dagon's bell ringing in the night, summoning that ancient evil up from the sea.

"Why, that was the old man's sole solitary reason for living there: so that he could take his revenge! Taciturn? A recluse? I'll say he was! He lived to kill—to kill *them!* Tritons, Deep Ones, amphibian abortions born out of a timeless evil, inhuman lust and black, alien nightmare. Well, now I'll finish what he started, only I'll do it a damn sight faster! It's my way or nothing." He gazed at me, his eyes steady now and piercing, totally sane, strong as I had rarely seen him. "You'll come?"

"First," I said, "there's something you must tell me. About June. She—her looks—I mean . . ."

"I know what you mean," his voice contained a tremor, however tightly controlled. "It's what makes the whole thing real for me. It's proof positive, as if that were needed now, of all I've suspected and discovered of the place. I told you she wouldn't leave the farm, didn't I? But did you know it was her idea to buy Kettlethorpe in the first place?"

"You mean she was . . . lured?"

"Oh, yes, that's exactly what I mean—but by what? By her blood, Bill! She didn't know, was completely innocent. Not so her forebears.

Her great-grandfather came from America, New England. That's as far as I care to track it down, and no need now to take it any further. But you must see why I personally have to square it all away?"

I could only nod.

"And you will help?"

"I must be mad," I answered, nodding again, "—or at best an idiot—but it seems I've already committed myself. Yes, I'll come."

"Now?"

"Today? At this hour? That *would* be madness! Before you know it, it'll be dark, and—"

"Dark, yes!" he broke in on me. "But what odds? It's *always* dark down there, Bill. We'll need electric torches, the more the better. I have a couple at the farm. How about you?"

"I've a good heavy-duty torch in the car," I told him. "Batteries, too."

"Good! And your shotguns—we'll need them, I think. But we're not after pheasant this time, Bill."

"Where will you get the dynamite?" I asked, perhaps hoping that this was something which, in his fervor, he had overlooked.

He grinned—not his old grin but a twisted, vicious thing—and said: "I've already got it. Had it ever since I found the slab two weeks ago and first went down there. My gangers use it on big landscaping jobs. Blasting out large boulders and tree stumps saves a lot of time and effort. Saves money, too. There's enough dynamite at the farm to demolish half of Harden!"

David had me, and he knew it. "It's now, Bill, now!" he said. And after a moment's silence he shrugged. "But—if you haven't the spit for it—"

"I said I'd come," I told him, "and so I will. You're not the only one who loves a mystery, even one as terrifying as this. Now that I know such a place exists, of course I want to see it. I'm not easy about it, no, but . . ."

He nodded. "Then this is your last chance, for you can be sure it won't be there for you to see tomorrow!"

## IX: DESCENT INTO MADNESS

Within the hour we were ready. Torches, shotguns, dynamite and fusewire—everything we would need—all was in our hands. And as we made our way from the house at Kettlethorpe along the garden paths to the roofless enclosure, already the mists were rising and beginning to creep. And I admit here and now that if David had offered me the chance again, to back out and leave him to go it alone, I believe I might well have done so.

As it was, we entered under the lintel with the plate, found the slab as David had described it, and commenced to lever it up from its seatings. As we worked, my friend nodded his head toward a very old and massive millstone lying nearby. "That's what Jason Carpenter used to seal it. And do you believe June could have shifted that on her own? Never! She was helped—must have been helped—from below!"

At that moment the slab moved, lifted, was awkward for a moment but at our insistence slid gratingly aside. I don't know what I expected, but the blast of foul, damp air that rushed up from below took me completely by surprise. It blew full into my face, jetting up like some noxious, invisible geyser, a pressured stench of time and ocean, darkness and damp, and alien things. And I knew it at once: that tainted odour I had first detected in the summer, which David had naively termed "a miasma."

Was this the source, then, of that misty phantom seen on dark nights, that bloating spectre formed of fog and the rushing reek of inner earth? Patently it was, but that hardly explained the shape the thing had assumed . . .

In a little while the expansion and egress of pent-up gasses subsided and became more a flow of cold, salty air. Other odours were there, certainly, but however alien and disgusting they no longer seemed quite so unbearable.

Slung over our shoulders we carried part-filled knapsacks which threw us a little off balance. "Careful," David warned, descending ahead of me, "it's steep and slippery as hell!" Which was no exaggeration.

The way was narrow, spiralling, almost perpendicular, a stairwell through solid rock which might have been cut by some huge and eccentric drill. Its steps were narrow in the tread, deep in the rise, and slimy with nitre and a film of moisture clammy as sweat. And our powerful torches cutting the way through darkness deep as night, and the walls winding down, down, ever down.

I do not know the depth to which we descended; there was an interminable sameness about that corkscrew of stone which seemed to defy measurement. But I recall something of the characters carved almost ceremoniously into its walls. Undeniably Roman, some of them, but I was equally sure that these were the most recent! The rest, having a weird, almost glyphic angularity and coarseness—a barbaric simplicity of style—must surely have predated any Roman incursion into Britain.

And so down to the floor of that place, where David paused to deposit several sticks of dynamite in a dark niche. Quickly he fitted a fuse, and while he worked so he spoke to me in a whisper which echoed sibilantly away and came rustling back in decreasing susurrations. "A long fuse for this one. We'll light it on our way out. And at least five more like this before we're done. I hope it's enough. God, I don't even know the extent of the place! I've been this far before and farther, but you can imagine what it's like to be down here on your own . . ."

Indeed I could imagine it, and shuddered at the thought.

While David worked I stood guard, shotgun under my arm, cocked, pointing it down a black tunnel that wound away to God-knows-where. The walls of this horizontal shaft were curved inward at the top to form its ceiling, which was so low that when we commenced to follow it we were obliged to stoop. Quite obviously the tunnel was no mere work of nature; no, for it was far too regular for that, and everywhere could be seen the marks of sharp tools used to chip out the stone. One other fact which registered was this: that the walls were of the same stone from which Kettlethorpe Farm—in what original form?—must in some dim uncertain time predating all memory, myth and legend have been constructed.

And as I followed my friend, so in some dim recess of my mind

I made note of these things, none of which lessened in the slightest degree the terrific weight of apprehension resting almost tangibly upon me. But follow him I did, and in a little while he was showing me fresh marks on the walls, scratches he had made on previous visits to enable him to retrace his steps.

"Necessary," he whispered, "for just along here the tunnels begin to branch, become a maze. Really—a maze! Be a terrible thing to get lost down here . . ."

My imagination needed no urging, and after that I followed more closely still upon his heels, scratching marks of my own as we went. And sure enough, within a distance of perhaps fifty paces more, it began to become apparent that David had in no way exaggerated with regard to the labyrinthine nature of the place. There were side tunnels, few at first but rapidly increasing in number, which entered into our shaft from both sides and all manner of angles; and shortly after this we came to a sort of gallery wherein many of these lesser passages met.

The gallery was in fact a cavern of large dimensions with a domed ceiling perhaps thirty feet high. Its walls were literally honeycombed with tunnels entering from all directions, some of which descended steeply to regions deeper and darker still. Here, too, I heard for the first time the sluggish gurgle of unseen waters, of which David informed: "That's a stream. You'll see it shortly."

He laid another explosive charge out of sight in a crevice, then indicated that I should once more follow him. We took the tunnel with the highest ceiling, which after another seventy-five to one hundred yards opened out again onto a ledge that ran above a slow-moving, blackly-gleaming rivulet. The water gurgled against our direction of travel, and its surface was some twenty feet lower than the ledge; this despite the fact that the trough through which it coursed was green and black with slime and incrustations almost fully up to the ledge itself. David explained the apparent ambiguity.

"Tidal," he said. "The tide's just turned. It's coming in now. I've seen it fifteen feet deeper than this, but that won't be for several hours yet." He gripped my arm, causing me to start. "And look! Look at the kelp . . ."

Carried on the surface of the as yet sluggish stream, great ropes of weed writhed and churned, bladders glistening in the light from our torches. "David," my voice wavered, "I think—"

"Come on," he said, leading off once more. "I know what you think—but we're not going back. Not yet." Then he paused and turned to me, his eyes burning in the darkness. "Or you can go back on your own, if you wish . . . ?"

"David," I hissed, "that's a rotten thing to—"

"My *God*, man!" he stopped me. "D'you think you're the only one who's afraid?"

However paradoxically, his words buoyed me up a little, following which we moved quickly on and soon came to a second gallery. Just before reaching it the stream turned away, so that only its stench and distant gurgle stayed with us. And once more David laid charges, his actions hurried now, nervous, as if in addition to his admitted fear he had picked up something of my own barely subdued panic.

"This is as far as I've been," he told me, his words coming in a sort of rapid gasping or panting. "Beyond here is fresh territory. By my reckoning we're now well over a quarter-mile from the entrance." He flashed the beam of his torch around the walls, causing the shadows of centuries-formed stalactites to flicker and jump. "There, the big tunnel. We'll take that one."

And now, every three or four paces, or wherever a side tunnel opened into ours, we were both scoring the walls to mark a fresh and foolproof trail. Now, too, my nerves really began to get the better of me. I found myself starting at every move my friend made; I kept pausing to listen, my heartbeat shuddering in the utter stillness of that nighted place. Or was it still? Did I hear something just then? The echo of a splash and the soft *flop, flop* of furtive footsteps in the dark?

It must be pictured:

We were in a vast subterranean warren. A place hollowed out centuries ago by . . . by whom? By what? And what revenants lurked here still, down here in these terrible caverns of putrid rock and festering, sewage-like streams?

*Slap, slap, slap* . . .

And that time I definitely had heard something. "David—" my voice was thin as a reedy wind. "For God's sake—"

"*Shh!*" he warned, his cautionary hiss barely audible. "I heard it too, and they might have heard us! Let me just get the rest of this dynamite planted—one final big batch, it'll have to be—and then we'll get out of here." He used his torch to search the walls but could find no secret place to house the explosives. "Round this next bend," he said. "I'll find a niche there. Don't want the stuff to be found before it's done its job."

We rounded the bend, and ahead—

—A glow of rotten, phosphorescent light, a luminescence almost sufficient to make our torches redundant. We saw, and we began to understand.

The roofless building up above—the enclosure—that was merely the entrance. This place here, far underground, was the actual place of worship, the subterranean temple to Dagon. We knew it as soon as we saw the great nitre-crusted bell hanging from the centre of the ceiling—the bell and the rusted iron chain which served as its rope, hanging down until its last link dangled inches above the surface and centre of a black and sullenly rippling lake of scum and rank weed . . .

For all that horror might follow on our very heels, still we found ourselves pulled up short by the sight of that fantastic final gallery. It was easily a hundred feet wall to wall, roughly circular, domed over and shelved around, almost an amphitheater in the shape of its base, and obviously a natural, geological formation. Stalactites hung down from above, as in the previous gallery, and stalagmitic stumps broke the weed-pool's surface here and there, showing that at some distant time in our planet's past the cave had stood well above sea level.

As to the source of the pool itself: this could only be the sea. The deep kelp alone was sufficient evidence of that. And to justify and make conclusive this observation, the pool was fed by a broad expanse of water which disappeared under the ledge beneath the far wall, which my sense of direction told me lay toward the sea. The small ripples or wavelets we had noted disturbing the pool's surface could only be the product of an influx of water from this source, doubtless the flow of the incoming tide.

Then there was the light: that same glow of putrescence or organic decomposition seen in certain fungi, an unhealthy illumination which lent the cave an almost submarine aspect. So that even without the clean light of our electric torches, still the great bell in the ceiling would have remained plainly visible.

But that bell ... who could say where it came from? Not I. Not David. Certainly this was that bell whose sepulchral tolling had penetrated even to the surface, but as to its origin ...

In that peculiar way of his, David, as if reading my thoughts, confirmed: "Well, it'll not ring again—not after this lot goes off!" And I saw that he had placed his knapsack full of dynamite out of sight beneath a low, shallow ledge in the wall and was even now uncoiling a generous length of fuse wire. Finishing the task, he glanced at me once, struck a match and set sputtering fire to the end of the wire, pushing it, too, out of sight.

"There," he grunted, "and now we can get—" But here he paused, and I knew why.

The echo of a voice—a *croak?*—had come to us from somewhere not too far distant. And even as our ears strained to detect other than the slow gurgle of weed-choked waters, so there echoed again that damnably soft and furtive slap, slap, slap of nameless feet against slimy stone ...

## X: DEEP ONES!

At that panic gripped both of us anew, was magnified as the water of the pool gurgled more loudly yet and ripples showed which could *not* be ascribed solely to an influx from the sea. Perhaps at this very moment something other than brine and weed was moving toward us along that murky and mysterious watercourse.

My limbs were trembling, and David was in no better condition as, throwing caution to the wind, we commenced scramblingly to retrace our steps, following those fresh marks where we had scratched them upon the walls of the maze. And behind us the hidden fuse slowly sputtering its way to that massive charge of dynamite; and approaching the great pool, some entirely conjectural thing whose every purpose we were sure must be utterly alien and hostile. While ahead . . . who could say?

But one thing was certain: our presence down here had finally stirred something up—maybe many somethings—and now their noises came to us even above our breathless panting, the hammering of our hearts and the clattering sounds of our flight down those black tunnels of inner earth. Their *noises,* yes, for no man of the sane upper world of blue skies and clean air could ever have named those echoing, glutinous bursts of sporadic croaking and clotted, inquiring gurgles and grunts as speech; and no one could mistake the slithering, slapping, *flopping* sounds of their pursuit for anything remotely human. Or perhaps they were remotely human, but so sunken into hybrid degeneracy as to seem totally alien to all human expectations. And all of this without ever having seen these Deep Ones—"Tritons," as David had named them—or at least, not yet!

But as we arrived at the central gallery and paused for breath, and as David struck a second match to light the fuse of the charge previously laid there, that so far merciful omission commenced to resolve itself in a manner I shall never forget to my dying day.

It started with the senses-shattering gonging of the great bell, whose echoes were deafening in those hellish tunnels, and it ended . . . but I go ahead of myself.

Simultaneous with the ringing of the bell, a renewed chorus of croaking and grunting came to us from somewhere dangerously close at hand; so that David at once grabbed my arm and half-dragged me into a small side tunnel leading off at an angle from the gallery. This move had been occasioned not alone by the fact that the sounds we had heard were coming closer, but also that they issued from the very burrow by which we must make our escape! But as the madly capricious gods of fate would have it, our momentary haven proved no less terrifying in its way than the vulnerable position we had been obliged to quit.

The hole into which we had fled was no tunnel at all but an "L"-shaped cave which, when we rounded its single corner, laid naked to our eyes a hideous secret. We recoiled instinctively from a discovery grisly as it was unexpected, and I silently prayed that God—if indeed there was any good, sane God—would give me strength not to break down utterly in my extreme of horror.

In there, crumpled where he had finally been overcome, lay the ragged and torn remains of old Jason Carpenter. It could only be him; the similarly broken body of Bones, his dog, lay across his feet. And all about him on the floor of the cave, spent shotgun cartridges; and clasped in his half-rotted, half-mummied hand, that weapon which in the end had not saved him.

But he had fought—how he had fought! Jason, and his dog, too . . .

Theirs were not the only corpses left to wither and decay in that tomb of a cave. No, for heaped to one side was a pile of quasi-human—*debris*—almost beyond my powers of description. Suffice to say that I will not even attempt a description, but merely confirm that these were indeed the very monstrosities of David's tale of crumbling Innsmouth. And if in death the things were loathsome, in life they would yet prove to be worse by far. That was still to come . . .

And so, with our torches reluctantly but necessarily switched off, we crouched there in the fetid darkness amidst corpses of man, dog and nightmares, and we waited. And always we were full of that awful awareness of slowly burning fuses, of time rapidly running out. But at last the tolling of the bell ceased and its echoes died away, and the sounds of the Deep Ones decreased as they made off in a body toward the source of the summoning, and finally we made our move.

Switching on our torches we ran crouching from the cave into the gallery—and came face to face with utmost terror! A lone member of that flopping, frog-voiced horde had been posted here and now stood central in the gallery, turning startled, bulging batrachian eyes upon us as we emerged from our hiding place.

A moment later and this squat obscenity—this part-man, part-fish, part-frog creature—threw up webbed hands before its terrible face, screamed a hissing, croaking cry of rage and possibly agony, and finally hurled itself at us . . .

. . . Came frenziedly lurching, flopping and floundering, head-long into a double-barrelled barrage from the weapon I held in fingers which kept on uselessly squeezing the triggers long after the face and chest of the monster had flown into bloody tatters and its body was lifted and hurled away from us across the chamber.

Then David was yelling in my ear, tugging at me, dragging me after him, and . . . and all of the rest is a chaos, a madness, a nightmare of flight and fear.

I seem to recall loading my shotgun—several times, I think—and I have vague memories of discharging it a like number of times; and I believe that David, too, used his weapon, probably more successfully. As for our targets: it would have been difficult to miss them. There were clutching claws, and eyes bulging with hatred and lust; there was foul, alien breath in our faces, slime and blood and bespattered bodies obstructing our way where they fell; and always a swelling uproar of croaking and flopping and slithering as that place below became filled with the spawn of primal oceans.

Then . . . the Titan blast that set the rock walls to trembling, whose reverberations had no sooner subsided when a yet more ominous rumbling began . . . Dust and stony debris rained down from the tunnel ceilings, and a side tunnel actually collapsed into ruin as we fled past its mouth . . . but finally we arrived at the foot of those upward-winding stone steps in the flue-like shaft which was our exit.

Here my memory grows more distinct, too vivid if anything—as if sight of our salvation sharpened fear-numbed senses—and I see David lighting the final fuse as I stand by him, firing and reloading, firing and reloading. The sharp smell of sulphur and gunpowder in a haze of dust and flickering torch beams, and the darkness erupting anew in shambling shapes of loathsome fright. The shotgun hot in my hands, jamming at the last, refusing to break open.

Then David taking my place and firing point-blank into a mass of mewling horror, and his voice shrill and hysterical, ordering me to climb, climb and get out of that hellish place. From above I look down and see him dragged under, disappearing beneath a clawing, throbbing mass of bestiality; and their frog-eyes avidly turning upward to follow my flight . . . fangs gleaming in grinning, wide-slit mouths . . . an instant's pause before they come squelching and squalling up the steps behind me!

And at last . . . at last I emerge into moonlight and mist. And with a strength born of madness I hurl the slab into place and weight it with the millstone. For David is gone now and no need to ponder over his fate. It was quick, I saw it with my own eyes, but at least he has done what he set out to do. I know this now, as I feel from far below that shuddering concussion as the dynamite finishes its work.

Following which I stumble from the roofless building and collapse on a path between stunted fruit trees and unnaturally glossy borders of mist-damp shrubbery. And lying there I know the sensation of being shaken, of feeling the earth trembling beneath me, and of a crashing of masonry torn from foundations eaten by the ages.

And at the very end, sinking into a merciful unconsciousness, at last I am rewarded by a sight which will alone allow me, with the dawn, to come awake a sane, whole man. That sight which is simply this: a great drifting mass of mist, dissipating as it coils away over the dene, melting down from the shape of a rage-tormented merman to a thin and formless fog.

For I know that while Dagon himself lives on—as he has "lived" since time immemorial—the seat of his worship which Kettlethorpe has been for centuries is at last no more . . .

That is my story, the story of Kettlethorpe Farm, which with the dawn lay in broken ruins. Not a building remained whole or standing as I left the place, and what has become of it since I cannot say for I never returned and I have never inquired. Official records will show, of course, that there was "a considerable amount of pit subsidence" that night, sinkings and shiftings of the earth with which colliery folk the world over are all too familiar; and despite the fact that there was no storm as such at sea, still a large area of the ocean-fringing cliffs were seen to have sunken down and fallen onto the sands or into the sullen water.

What more is there to say? There was very little deep kelp that year, and in the years since the stuff has seemed to suffer a steady decline. This is hearsay, however, for I have moved inland and will never return to any region from which I might unwittingly spy the sea or hear its wash.

As for June: she died some eight months later giving premature birth to a child. In the interim her looks had turned even more strange, ichthyic, but she was never aware of it for she had become a happy little girl whose mind would never be whole again. Her doctors said that this was just as well, and for this I give thanks.

As well, too, they said, that her child died with her . . .

# Only the End of the World Again

## Neil Gaiman

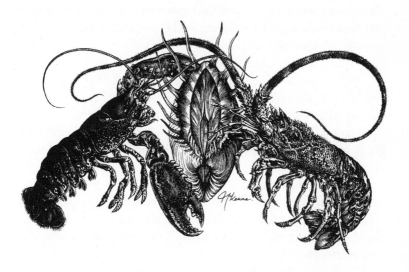

It was a bad day: I woke up naked in the bed, with a cramp in my stomach, feeling more or less like hell. Something about the quality of the light, stretched and metallic, like the colour of a migraine, told me it was afternoon.

The room was freezing—literally: there was a thin crust of ice on the inside of the windows. The sheets on the bed around me were ripped and clawed, and there was animal hair in the bed. It itched.

I was thinking about staying in bed for the next week—I'm always tired after a change—but a wave of nausea forced me to disentangle myself from the bedding, and to stumble, hurriedly, into the apartment's tiny bathroom.

The cramps hit me again as I got to the bathroom door. I held on to the door-frame and I started to sweat. Maybe it was a fever; I hoped I wasn't coming down with something.

The cramping was sharp in my guts. My head felt swimmy. I crumpled to the floor, and, before I could manage to raise my head enough to find the toilet bowl, I began to spew.

I vomited a foul-smelling thin yellow liquid; in it was a dog's paw—my guess was a Doberman's, but I'm not really a dog person; a tomato peel; some diced carrots and sweet corn; some lumps of half-chewed meat, raw; and some fingers. They were fairly small, pale fingers, obviously a child's.

"Shit."

The cramps eased up, and the nausea subsided. I lay on the floor, with stinking drool coming out of my mouth and nose, with the tears you cry when you're being sick drying on my cheeks.

When I felt a little better I picked up the paw and the fingers from the pool of spew and threw them into the toilet bowl, flushed them away.

I turned on the tap, rinsed out my mouth with the briny Innsmouth water, and spat it into the sink. I mopped up the rest of the sick as best I could with washcloth and toilet paper. Then I turned on the shower, and stood in the bathtub like a zombie as the hot water sluiced over me.

I soaped myself down, body and hair. The meagre lather turned grey; I must have been filthy. My hair was matted with something that felt like dried blood, and I worked at it with the bar of soap until it was gone. Then I stood under the shower until the water turned icy.

There was a note under the door from my landlady. It said that I owed her for two weeks' rent. It said that all the answers were in the Book of Revelations. It said that I made a lot of noise coming home in the early hours of this morning, and she'd thank me to be quieter in future. It said that when the Elder Gods rose up from the ocean, all the scum of the Earth, all the non-believers, all the human garbage and the wastrels and deadbeats would be swept away, and the world would be cleansed by ice and deep water. It said that she felt she ought to remind me that she had assigned me a shelf in the refrigerator when I arrived and she'd thank me if in the future I'd keep to it.

I crumpled the note, dropped it on the floor, where it lay alongside the Big Mac cartons and the empty pizza cartons, and the long-dead dried slices of pizza.

It was time to go to work.

I'd been in Innsmouth for two weeks, and I disliked it. It smelled fishy. It was a claustrophobic little town: marshland to the east, cliffs to the west, and, between the two, a harbour that held a few rotting fishing boats, and was not even scenic at sunset. The yuppies had come to Innsmouth in the '80s anyway, bought their picturesque fisherman's cottages overlooking the harbour. The yuppies had been gone for some years, now, and the cottages by the bay were crumbling, abandoned.

The inhabitants of Innsmouth lived here and there, in and around the town, and in the trailer parks that ringed it, filled with dank mobile homes that were never going anywhere.

I got dressed, pulled on my boots and put on my coat and left my room. My landlady was nowhere to be seen. She was a short, pop-eyed woman, who spoke little, although she left extensive notes for me pinned to doors and placed where I might see them; she kept the house filled with the smell of boiling seafood: huge pots were always simmering on the kitchen stove, filled with things with too many legs and other things with no legs at all.

There were other rooms in the house, but no-one else rented them. No-one in their right mind would come to Innsmouth in winter.

Outside the house it didn't smell much better. It was colder, though, and my breath steamed in the sea air. The snow on the streets was crusty and filthy; the clouds promised more snow.

A cold, salty wind came up off the bay. The gulls were screaming miserably. I felt shitty. My office would be freezing, too. On the corner of Marsh Street and Leng Avenue was a bar, "The Opener," a squat building with small, dark windows that I'd passed two dozen times in the last couple of weeks. I hadn't been in before, but I really needed a drink, and besides, it might be warmer in there. I pushed open the door.

The bar was indeed warm. I stamped the snow off my boots and went inside. It was almost empty and smelled of old ashtrays and stale beer. A couple of elderly men were playing chess by the bar. The barman was reading a battered old gilt-and-green-leather edition of the poetical works of Alfred, Lord Tennyson.

"Hey. How about a Jack Daniel's straight up?"

"Sure thing. You're new in town," he told me, putting his book face down on the bar, pouring the drink into a glass.

"Does it show?"

He smiled, passed me the Jack Daniel's. The glass was filthy, with a greasy thumb-print on the side, but I shrugged and knocked back the drink anyway. I could barely taste it.

"Hair of the dog?" he said.

"In a manner of speaking."

"There is a belief," said the barman, whose fox-red hair was tightly greased back, "that the *lykanthropoi* can be returned to their natural forms by thanking them, while they're in wolf form, or by calling them by their given names."

"Yeah? Well, thanks."

He poured another shot for me, unasked. He looked a little like Peter Lorre, but then, most of the folk in Innsmouth look a little like Peter Lorre, including my landlady.

I sank the Jack Daniel's, this time felt it burning down into my stomach, the way it should.

"It's what they say. I never said I believed it."

"What *do* you believe?"

"Burn the girdle."

"Pardon?"

"The *lykanthropoi* have girdles of human skin, given to them at their first transformation, by their masters in Hell. Burn the girdle."

One of the old chess-players turned to me then, his eyes huge and blind and protruding. "If you drink rain-water out of warg-wolf's paw-print, that'll make a wolf of you, when the moon is full," he said. "The only cure is to hunt down the wolf that made the print in the first place and cut off its head with a knife forged of virgin silver."

"Virgin, huh?" I smiled.

His chess partner, bald and wrinkled, shook his head and

croaked a single sad sound. Then he moved his queen, and croaked again.

There are people like him all over Innsmouth.

I paid for the drinks, and left a dollar tip on the bar. The barman was reading his book once more, and ignored it.

Outside the bar big wet kissy flakes of snow had begun to fall, settling in my hair and eyelashes. I hate snow. I hate New England. I hate Innsmouth: it's no place to be alone, but if there's a good place to be alone I've not found it yet. Still, business has kept me on the move for more moons than I like to think about. Business, and other things.

I walked a couple of blocks down Marsh Street—like most of Innsmouth, an unattractive mixture of eighteenth century American Gothic houses, late nineteenth century stunted brownstones, and late twentieth prefab grey-brick boxes—until I got to a boarded-up fried chicken joint, where I went up the stone steps next to the store and unlocked the rusting metal security door.

There was a liquor store across the street; a palmist was operating on the second floor.

Someone had scrawled graffiti in black marker on the metal: *just die,* it said. Like it was easy.

The stairs were bare wood; the plaster was stained and peeling. My one-room office was at the top of the stairs.

I don't stay anywhere long enough to bother with my name in gilt on glass. It was handwritten in block letters on a piece of ripped cardboard that I'd thumbtacked to the door.

LAWRENCE TALBOT
ADJUSTOR

I unlocked the door to my office and went in.

I inspected my office, while adjectives like *seedy* and *rancid* and *squalid* wandered through my head, then gave up, outclassed. It was fairly unprepossessing—a desk, an office chair, an empty filing cabinet; a window, which gave you a terrific view of the liquor store and the empty palmist's. The smell of old cooking grease permeated from the store below. I wondered how long the fried chicken joint had been boarded up; I imagined a multitude of black cockroaches swarming over every surface in the darkness beneath me.

"That's the shape of the world that you're thinking of there," said a deep, dark voice, deep enough that I felt it in the pit of my stomach.

There was an old armchair in one corner of the office. The remains of a pattern showed through the patina of age and grease the years had given it. It was the colour of dust.

The fat man sitting in the armchair, his eyes still tightly closed, continued, "We look about in puzzlement at our world, with a sense of unease and disquiet. We think of ourselves as scholars in arcane liturgies, single men trapped in worlds beyond our devising. The truth is far simpler: there are things in the darkness beneath us that wish us harm."

His head was lolled back on the armchair, and the tip of his tongue poked out of the corner of his mouth.

"You read my mind?"

The man in the armchair took a slow deep breath that rattled in the back of his throat. He really was immensely fat, with stubby fingers like discoloured sausages. He wore a thick old coat, once black, now an indeterminate grey. The snow on his boots had not entirely melted.

"Perhaps. The end of the world is a strange concept. The world is always ending, and the end is always being averted, by love or foolishness or just plain old dumb luck.

"Ah well. It's too late now: the Elder Gods have chosen their vessels. When the moon rises . . ."

A thin trickle of drool came from one corner of his mouth, trickled down in a thread of silver to his collar. Something scuttled down into the shadows of his coat.

"Yeah? What happens when the moon rises?"

The man in the armchair stirred, opened two little eyes, red and swollen, and blinked them in waking.

"I dreamed I had many mouths," he said, his new voice oddly small and breathy for such a huge man. "I dreamed every mouth was opening and closing independently. Some mouths were talking, some whispering, some eating, some waiting in silence."

He looked around, wiped the spittle from the corner of his mouth, sat back in the chair, blinking puzzledly. "Who are you?"

"I'm the guy that rents this office," I told him.

He belched suddenly, loudly. "I'm sorry," he said, in his breathy voice, and lifted himself heavily from the armchair. He was shorter than I was, when he was standing. He looked me up and down blearily. "Silver bullets," he pronounced, after a short pause. "Old-fashioned remedy."

"Yeah," I told him. "That's so obvious—must be why I didn't think of it. Gee, I could just kick myself. I really could."

"You're making fun of an old man," he told me.

"Not really. I'm sorry. Now, out of here. Some of us have work to do."

He shambled out. I sat down in the swivel chair at the desk by the window, and discovered, after some minutes, through trial and error, that if I swiveled the chair to the left it fell off its base.

So I sat still and waited for the dusty black telephone on my desk to ring, while the light slowly leaked away from the winter sky.

*Ring.*

A man's voice: *Had I thought about aluminum siding?* I put down the phone.

There was no heating in the office. I wondered how long the fat man had been asleep in the armchair.

Twenty minutes later the phone rang again. A crying woman implored me to help her find her five-year-old daughter, missing since last night, stolen from her bed.

The family dog had vanished too.

*I don't do missing children,* I told her. *I'm sorry: too many bad memories.* I put down the telephone, feeling sick again.

It was getting dark now, and, for the first time since I had been in Innsmouth, the neon sign across the street flicked on. It told me that Madame Ezekiel performed Tarot Readings and Palmistry. Red neon stained the falling snow the colour of new blood.

Armageddon is averted by small actions. That's the way it was. That's the way it always has to be.

The phone rang a third time. I recognised the voice; it was the aluminum-siding man again. "You know," he said, chattily, "transformation from man to animal and back being, by definition, impossible, we need to look for other solutions. Depersonalisation, obviously, and likewise some form of projection. Brain damage? Perhaps. Pseudoneurotic schizophrenia? Laughably so. Some cases have been treated with intravenous thioridazine hydrochloride."

"Successfully?"

He chuckled. "That's what I like. A man with a sense of humour. I'm sure we can do business."

"I told you already. I don't need aluminum siding."

"Our business is more remarkable than that, and of far greater importance. You're new in town, Mr. Talbot. It would be a pity if we found ourselves at, shall we say, loggerheads?"

"You can say whatever you like, pal. In my book you're just another adjustment, waiting to be made."

"We're ending the world, Mr. Talbot. The Deep Ones will rise out of their ocean graves and eat the moon like a ripe plum."

"Then I won't ever have to worry about full moons anymore, will I?"

"Don't try and cross us," he began, but I growled at him, and he fell silent.

Outside my window the snow was still falling.

Across Marsh Street, in the window directly opposite mine, the most beautiful woman I had ever seen stood in the ruby glare of her neon sign, and she stared at me.

She beckoned, with one finger.

I put down the phone on the aluminum-siding man for the second time that afternoon, went downstairs, and crossed the street at something close to a run; but I looked both ways before I crossed.

She was dressed in silks. The room was lit only by candles, and stank of incense and patchouli oil.

She smiled at me as I walked in, beckoned me over to her seat by the window. She was playing a card game with a Tarot deck, some version of solitaire. As I reached her, one elegant hand swept up the cards, wrapped them in a silk scarf, placed them gently in a wooden box.

The scents of the room made my head pound. I hadn't eaten any-thing today, I realised; perhaps that was what was making me light-headed. I sat down, across the table from her, in the candle-light.

She extended her hand, and took my hand in hers.

She stared at my palm, touched it, softly, with her forefinger.

"Hair?" She was puzzled.

"Yeah, well. I'm on my own a lot." I grinned. I had hoped it was a friendly grin, but she raised an eyebrow at me anyway.

"When I look at you," said Madame Ezekiel, "this is what I see. I see the eye of a man. Also I see the eye of a wolf. In the eye of a man I see honesty, decency, innocence. I see an upright man who walks on the square. And in the eye of wolf I see a groaning and a growling, night howls and cries, I see a monster running with blood-flecked spittle in the darkness of the borders of the town."

"How can you see a growl or a cry?"

She smiled. "It is not hard," she said. Her accent was not American. It was Russian, or Maltese, or Egyptian perhaps. "In the eye of the mind we see many things."

Madame Ezekiel closed her green eyes. She had remarkably long eyelashes; her skin was pale, and her black hair was never still—it drifted gently around her head, in the silks, as if it were floating on distant tides.

"There is a traditional way," she told me. "A way to wash off a bad shape. You stand in running water, in clear spring water, while eating white rose petals."

"And then?"

"The shape of darkness will be washed from you."

"It will return," I told her, "with the next full of the moon."

"So," said Madame Ezekiel, "once the shape is washed from you, you open your veins in the running water. It will sting mightily, of course. But the river will carry the blood away."

She was dressed in silks, in scarves and cloths of a hundred dif-ferent colours, each bright and vivid, even in the muted light of the candles.

Her eyes opened.

"Now," she said. "The Tarot." She unwrapped her deck from the black silk scarf that held it, passed me the cards to shuffle. I fanned them, riffed and bridged them.

"Slower, slower," she said. "Let them get to know you. Let them love you, like . . . like a woman would love you."

I held them tightly, then passed them back to her.

She turned over the first card. It was called *The Warwolf*. It showed darkness and amber eyes, a smile in white and red.

Her green eyes showed confusion. They were the green of emeralds. "This is not a card from my deck," she said, and turned over the next card. "What did you do to my cards?"

"Nothing, Ma'am. I just held them. That's all."

The card she had turned over was *The Deep One*. It showed something green and faintly octopoid. The thing's mouths—if they were indeed mouths and not tentacles—began to writhe on the card as I watched.

She covered it with another card, and then another, and another. The rest of the cards were blank pasteboard.

"Did you do that?" She sounded on the verge of tears.

"No."

"Go now," she said.

"But—"

"*Go*." She looked down, as if trying to convince herself I no longer existed.

I stood up, in the room that smelled of incense and candle-wax, and looked out of her window, across the street. A light flashed, briefly, in my office window. Two men, with flashlights, were walking around. They opened the empty filing cabinet, peered around, then took up their positions, one in the armchair, the other behind the door, waiting for me to return. I smiled to myself. It was cold and inhospitable in my office, and with any luck they would wait there for hours until they finally decided I wasn't coming back.

So I left Madame Ezekiel turning over her cards, one by one, staring at them as if that would make the pictures return; and I went downstairs, and walked back down Marsh Street until I reached the bar.

The place was empty, now; the barman was smoking a cigarette, which he stubbed out as I came in.

"Where are the chess-fiends?"

"It's a big night for them tonight. They'll be down at the bay. Let's see: you're a Jack Daniel's? Right?"

"Sounds good."

He poured it for me. I recognised the thumb-print from the last time I had the glass. I picked up the volume of Tennyson poems from the bar-top.

"Good book?"

The fox-haired barman took his book from me, opened it and read:

*"Below the thunders of the upper deep;*
*Far, far beneath in the abysmal sea,*
*His ancient dreamless, uninvaded sleep*
*The Kraken sleepeth . . ."*

I'd finished my drink. "So? What's your point?"

He walked around the bar, took me over to the window. "See? Out there?"

He pointed toward the west of the town, toward the cliffs. As I stared a bonfire was kindled on the cliff-tops; it flared and began to burn with a copper-green flame.

"They're going to wake the Deep Ones," said the barman. "The stars and the planets and the moon are all in the right places. It's time. The dry lands will sink, and the seas shall rise . . ."

"For the world shall be cleansed with ice and floods and I'll thank you to keep to your own shelf in the refrigerator," I said.

"Sorry?"

"Nothing. What's the quickest way to get up to those cliffs?"

"Back up Marsh Street. Hang a left at the Church of Dagon, till you reach Manuxet Way and then just keep on going." He pulled a coat off the back of the door, and put it on. "C'mon. I'll walk you up there. I'd hate to miss any of the fun."

"You sure?"

"No-one in town's going to be drinking tonight." We stepped out, and he locked the door to the bar behind us.

It was chilly in the street, and fallen snow blew about the ground, like white mists. From street level I could no longer tell if Madame Ezekiel was in her den above her neon sign, or if my guests were still waiting for me in my office.

We put our heads down against the wind, and we walked.

Over the noise of the wind I heard the barman talking to himself: *"Winnow with giant arms the slumbering green,"* he was saying.
*"There hath he lain for ages and will lie*
*Battening upon huge seaworms in his sleep,*
*Until the latter fire shall heat the deep;*
*Then once by men and angels to be seen,*
*In roaring he shall rise . . ."*

He stopped there, and we walked on together in silence, with blown snow stinging our faces.

*And on the surface die,* I thought, but said nothing out loud.

Twenty minutes' walking and we were out of Innsmouth. The Manuxet Way stopped when we left the town, and it became a narrow dirt path, partly covered with snow and ice, and we slipped and slid our way up it in the darkness.

The moon was not yet up, but the stars had already begun to come out. There were so many of them. They were sprinkled like diamond dust and crushed sapphires across the night sky. You can see so many stars from the sea-shore, more than you could ever see back in the city.

At the top of the cliff, behind the bonfire, two people were waiting—one huge and fat, one much smaller. The barman left my side and walked over to stand beside them, facing me.

"Behold," he said, "the sacrificial wolf." There was now an oddly familiar quality to his voice.

I didn't say anything. The fire was burning with green flames, and it lit the three of them from below; classic spook lighting.

"Do you know why I brought you up here?" asked the barman,

and I knew then why his voice was familiar: it was the voice of the man who had attempted to sell me aluminum-siding.

"To stop the world ending?"

He laughed at me, then.

The second figure was the fat man I had found asleep in my office chair. "Well, if you're going to get eschatological about it . . ." he murmured, in a voice deep enough to rattle walls. His eyes were closed. He was fast asleep.

The third figure was shrouded in dark silks and smelled of patchouli oil. It held a knife. It said nothing.

"This night," said the barman, "the moon is the moon of the Deep Ones. This night are the stars configured in the shapes and patterns of the dark, old times. This night, if we call them, they will come. If our sacrifice is worthy. If our cries are heard."

The moon rose, huge and amber and heavy, on the other side of the bay, and a chorus of low croaking rose with it from the ocean far beneath us.

Moonlight on snow and ice is not daylight, but it will do. And my eyes were getting sharper with the moon: in the cold waters men like frogs were surfacing and submerging in a slow water-dance. Men like frogs, and women, too: it seemed to me that I could see my landlady down there, writhing and croaking in the bay with the rest of them.

It was too soon for another change; I was still exhausted from the night before; but I felt strange under that amber moon.

"Poor wolf-man," came a whisper from the silks. "All his dreams have come to this; a lonely death upon a distant cliff."

*I will dream if I want to,* I said, *and my death is my own affair.* But I was unsure if I had said it out loud.

Senses heighten in the moon's light; I heard the roar of the ocean still, but now, overlaid on top of it, I could hear each wave rise and crash; I heard the splash of the frog people; I heard the drowned whispers of the dead in the bay; I heard the creak of green wrecks far beneath the ocean.

Smell improves, too. The aluminum-siding man was human, while the fat man had other blood in him.

And the figure in the silks . . .

I had smelled her perfume when I wore man-shape. Now I could smell something else, less heady, beneath it. A smell of decay, of putrefying meat, and rotten flesh.

The silks fluttered. She was moving towards me. She held the knife.

"Madame Ezekiel?" My voice was roughening and coarsening. Soon I would lose it all. I didn't understand what was happening, but the moon was rising higher and higher, losing its amber colour, and filling my mind with its pale light.

"Madame Ezekiel?"

"You deserve to die," she said, her voice cold and low. "If only for what you did to my cards. They were old."

"I don't die," I told her. *"Even a man who is pure in heart, and says his prayers by night.* Remember?"

"It's bullshit," she said. "You know what the oldest way to end the curse of the werewolf is?"

"No."

The bonfire burned brighter now, burned with the green of the world beneath the sea, the green of algae, and of slowly-drifting weed; burned with the colour of emeralds.

"You simply wait till they're in human shape, a whole month away from another change; then you take the sacrificial knife, and you kill them. That's all."

I turned to run, but the barman was behind me, pulling my arms, twisting my wrists up into the small of my back. The knife glinted pale silver in the moonlight. Madame Ezekiel smiled.

She sliced across my throat.

Blood began to gush, and then to flow. And then it slowed, and stopped . . .

    —The pounding in the front of my head, the pressure in the back.

    All a roiling change a how-wow-row-now change a red wall coming towards me from the night

      —i tasted stars dissolved in brine, fizzy and distant and salt

> —my fingers prickled with pins and my skin was
> lashed with tongues of flame my eyes were topaz I
> could taste the night

My breath steamed and billowed in the icy air. I growled involuntarily, low in my throat. My forepaws were touching the snow. I pulled back, tensed, and sprang at her. There was a sense of corruption that hung in the air, like a mist, surrounding me. High in my leap I seemed to pause, and something burst like a soapbubble . . .

*I was deep, deep in the darkness under the sea, standing on all fours on a slimy rock floor, at the entrance to some kind of citadel, built of enormous, rough-hewn stones. The stones gave off a pale glow-in-the-dark light; a ghostly luminescence, like the hands of a watch.*

*A cloud of black blood trickled from my neck.*

*She was standing in the doorway, in front of me. She was now six, maybe seven feet high. There was flesh on her skeletal bones, pitted and gnawed, but the silks were weeds, drifting in the cold water, down there in the dreamless deeps. They hid her face like a slow green veil.*

*There were limpets growing on the upper surfaces of her arms, and on the flesh that hung from her ribcage.*

*I felt like I was being crushed. I couldn't think any more.*

*She moved towards me. The weed that surrounded her head shifted. She had a face like the stuff you don't want to eat in a sushi counter, all suckers and spines and drifting anemone fronds; and somewhere in all that I knew she was smiling.*

*I pushed with my hind-legs. We met there, in the deep, and we struggled. It was so cold, so dark. I closed my jaws on her face, and felt something rend and tear.*

*It was almost a kiss, down there in the abysmal deep . . .*

I landed softly on the snow, a silk scarf locked between my jaws.

The other scarves were fluttering to the ground. Madame Ezekiel was nowhere to be seen.

The silver knife lay on the ground, in the snow. I waited on all fours, in the moonlight, soaking wet. I shook myself, spraying the brine about. I heard it hiss and spit when it hit the fire.

I was dizzy, and weak. I pulled the air deep into my lungs.

Down, far below, in the bay, I could see the frog people hanging on the surface of the sea like dead things; for a handful of seconds they drifted back and forth on the tide, then they twisted and leapt, and each by each they plop-plopped down into the bay and vanished beneath the sea.

There was a loud noise. It was the fox-haired bartender, the pop-eyed aluminum-siding salesman, and he was staring at the night sky, at the clouds that were drifting in, covering the stars, and he was screaming. There was rage and there was frustration in that cry, and it scared me.

He picked up the knife from the ground, wiped the snow from the handle with his fingers, wiped the blood from the blade with his coat. Then he looked across at me. He was crying. "You bastard," he said. "What did you do to her?"

I would have told him I didn't do anything to her, that she was still on guard far beneath the ocean, but I couldn't talk any more, only growl and whine and howl.

He was crying. He stank of insanity, and of disappointment. He raised the knife and ran at me, and I moved to one side.

Some people just can't adjust even to tiny changes. The barman stumbled past me, off the cliff, into nothing.

In the moonlight blood is black, not red, and the marks he left on the cliff-side as he fell and bounced and fell were smudges of black and dark grey. Then, finally, he lay still on the icy rocks at the base of the cliff, until an arm reached out from the sea and dragged him, with a slowness that was almost painful to watch, under the dark water.

A hand scratched the back of my head. It felt good.

"What was she? Just an avatar of the Deep Ones, sir. An eidolon, a manifestation, if you will, sent up to us from the uttermost deeps to bring about the end of the world."

I bristled.

"No, it's over, for now. You disrupted her, sir. And the ritual is most specific. Three of us must stand together and call the sacred names, while innocent blood pools and pulses at our feet."

I looked up at the fat man, and whined a query. He patted me on the back of the neck, sleepily.

"Of course she doesn't love you, boy. She hardly even exists on this plane, in any material sense."

The snow began to fall once more. The bonfire was going out.

"Your change tonight, incidentally, I would opine, is a direct result of the selfsame celestial configurations and lunar forces that made tonight such a perfect night to bring back my old friends from Underneath . . ."

He continued talking, in his deep voice, and perhaps he was telling me important things. I'll never know, for the appetite was growing inside me, and his words had lost all but the shadow of any meaning: I had no further interest in the sea or the clifftop or the fat man.

There were deer running in the woods beyond the meadow: I could smell them on the winter night's air.

And I was, above all things, hungry.


I was naked when I came to myself again, early the next morning, a half-eaten deer next to me in the snow. A fly crawled across its eye, and its tongue lolled out of its dead mouth, making it look comical and pathetic, like an animal in a newspaper cartoon.

The snow was stained a fluorescent crimson where the deer's belly had been torn out.

My face and chest were sticky and red with the stuff. My throat was scabbed and scarred, and it stung; by the next full moon it would be whole once more.

The sun was a long way away, small and yellow, but the sky was blue and cloudless, and there was no breeze. I could hear the roar of the sea some distance away.

I was cold and naked and bloody and alone; ah well, I thought: it happens to all of us, in the beginning. I just get it once a month.

I was painfully exhausted, but I would hold out until I found a deserted barn, or a cave; and then I was going to sleep for a couple of weeks.

A hawk flew low over the snow toward me, with something dangling from its talons. It hovered above me for a heartbeat, then dropped a small grey squid in the snow at my feet, and flew upward. The flaccid thing lay there, still and silent and tentacled in the bloody snow.

I took it as an omen, but whether good or bad I couldn't say and I didn't really care any more; I turned my back to the sea, and on the shadowy town of Innsmouth, and began to make my way toward the city.

# Afterwords:
# Contributors' Notes

RAMSEY CAMPBELL is the most respected living British horror writer. He is a multiple winner of the Bram Stoker Award, the World Fantasy Award and the British Fantasy Award—more awards for horror fiction than any other writer. After working in the civil service and public libraries, he became a full-time writer in 1973. The editor of a number of anthologies (including the first five *Best New Horror* series with Stephen Jones), he has also written hundreds of short stories (most recently collected in *Ghosts and Grisly Things*) and the novels *The Doll Who Ate His Mother, The Face That Must Die, The Parasite, The Nameless, The Claw, Incarnate, Obsession, The Hungry Moon, The Influence, Ancient Images, Midnight Sun, The Count of Eleven, The Long Lost* and *Pact of the Fathers*. " 'The Church in High Street' is more of a collaboration between me and August Derleth than his

HPL 'collaborations' were," observes the author. "The first book of Lovecraft's I read made me into a writer. I read it in a single malingering day off school, and for a year or more I thought H. P. Lovecraft was not merely the greatest horror writer of all time, but the greatest writer I had ever read. I wrote my Lovecraftian tales for my own pleasure: the pleasure of convincing myself that they were as good as the originals. It was only on the suggestion of two fantasy fans that I showed them to August Derleth at Arkham House. Derleth told me to abandon my attempts to set my work in Massachusetts and in general advised me in no uncertain terms how to improve the stories. I suspect he would have been gentler if he'd realised I was only fifteen years old. I was still in the process of adopting his suggestions when he asked me to send him a story for an anthology he was editing. Delighted beyond words, I sent him the rewritten 'The Tomb-Herd,' which he accepted under certain conditions: that the title should be changed to 'The Church in the High Street' (though he later dropped the latter article) and that he should be able to edit the story as he saw fit. The story as published, there and here, therefore contains several passages that are Derleth's paraphrases of what I wrote. Quite right too: as I think he realised, it was the most direct way to show me how to improve my writing, and selling the story was so encouraging that I completed my first book a little over a year later."

DAVE CARSON has received the British Fantasy Award for Best Artist on five occasions. He is most widely recognised for his Lovecraftian illustrations, which have appeared on T-shirts, posters and art prints around the world, and he has contributed to such publications as *Dagon, Fear, Interzone, White Dwarf* and many others. His artwork has also been published in *The Encyclopedia of Horror, The Best Horror from Fantasy Tales,* Brian Lumley's *Mad Moon of Dreams* and *The Clock of Dreams, Beneath Nightmare Castle, The Anthology of Fantasy & the Supernatural,* the *Fantasy Tales* and *Dark Voices* series, and *H. P. Lovecraft's Book of Horror,* which he co-edited with Stephen Jones. When asked on a convention panel why he became an artist, he replied "I just like to draw monsters." It shows.

ADRIAN COLE sold his first short story in 1973, since then he has published more than fifty tales of horror, sword and sorcery, fantasy and science fiction. His first novels were The Dream Lords trilogy (1976–77), followed by four science fiction books, including the humourous space opera *Wargods of Ludorbis* and two "young adult" novels, *Moorstones* and *The Sleep of Giants*. More recently, he has seen publication on both sides of the Atlantic with *A Place Among the Fallen, Throne of Fools, The King of Light and Shadows* and *The Gods in Anger*, which comprise the Omaran Saga, a mixture of heroic fantasy and horror; and his subsequent Star Requiem series, which includes *Mother of Storms, Thief of Dreams, Warlord of Heaven* and *Labyrinth of Worlds* and he describes as "even more of an hybrid—fantasy, space opera and horror." His novel *Blood Red Angel* blurs the sub-genres even more than his earlier works. "I discovered HPL when I was sixteen," explains the writer, "working in my school holidays in a hotel in Newquay, Cornwall, for a summer season. In the many bookshops of Newquay I picked up *The Lurking Fear* and found therein the wonderful 'The Shadow over Innsmouth'—its impact on me was instant and long-lasting. (I've spent years perfecting the Innsmouth squint.) The image of the New England town stayed in my mind and when I moved to North Devon in 1976, I was stunned to find myself living a few miles from what I took to be the English equivalent of Innsmouth, namely Appledore. Now, don't get me wrong—I wouldn't dream of insulting the good people of Appledore, even when they squint at me, but its atmosphere, its close-set houses, its setting so close to the sea (estuary, to be accurate) readily call up the feel of Innsmouth. And at certain times of night, when the tide is right and the moon rises across the water . . . well. But it's no problem for me. As I said, I live a couple of miles away. Bideford is nothing like Appledore—bigger quayside, steeper hills, narrower side roads, more houses, older . . . next door is the old charnel house. But none of this has influenced me. I only swim up and down to the estuary at night to be sociable. Doesn't everyone?"

BASIL COPPER has written over eighty books and was described by the *Los Angeles Herald-Examiner* as "the best writer in the genre since

H. P. Lovecraft." He corresponded with August Derleth for six years, until the latter's untimely death in 1971, gaining much information and insight into Lovecraft's character and strange lifestyle. A journalist and editor of a local newspaper before becoming a full-time writer in 1970, his first sales in the horror field were to the *Pan Book of Horror Stories* in the mid-1960s, and his short fiction has been collected in several volumes. Besides writing two non-fiction studies of the vampire and werewolf, his novels of the macabre and gaslight gothic include *The Great White Space, The Curse of the Fleers, Necropolis, House of the Wolf* and *The Black Death.* The latter is published by Fedogan & Bremer, as are two collections of Sherlock Holmes pastiches based on the character created by August Derleth, *The Exploits of Solar Pons* and *The Recollections of Solar Pons.* With "Beyond the Reef," the author explains, he ". . . wanted the atmosphere to be of a 'faded twenties variety' as in HPL's original tales, but without being too much of a pastiche or derivative in any way."

NEIL GAIMAN is only mentioned in passing in the works of H. P. Lovecraft, in the Lovecraft-Derleth story "The Survivor," in which it is revealed that the mysterious Dr. Charriere has a recognisable drawing of Gaiman on his wall, along with certain caballistic charts, and pictures of large reptiles. He has, however, a bust of Lovecraft on his windowsill (the 1991 World Fantasy Award for Best Short Story), and lives in a remarkably Lovecraftian house, somewhere a long way from the sea. He is the most critically acclaimed British graphic novel writer of today, with such volumes as the Sandman series, *Black Orchid, The Books of Magic, Violent Cases* and *Signal to Noise* to his credit. He co-wrote the bestselling novel *Good Omens* (with Terry Pratchett), is the author of *Neverwhere* and *American Gods,* co-devised the Temps series, and co-edited *Ghastly Beyond Belief* (with Kim Newman) and *Now We Are Sick* (with Stephen Jones). His latest collection of short fiction is *Smoke and Mirrors.* The story in this volume is dedicated to the late Fritz Leiber.

DAVID LANGFORD was born in 1953 and some eleven years later discovered that he could borrow all H. P. Lovecraft's books from the library if he assured his mother they were "nice detective stories." One vivid memory, of eating porridge while reading of his first Shoggoth, is best not shared. He has since become a freelance writer, critic and software consultant, dividing his creative endeavours between books and science fiction fandom (winning the Hugo Award eighteen times). His novels include *The Leaky Establishment, The Space Eater, The Wilderness of Mirrors,* and *Earthdoom* (the latter co-written with John Grant), while a collection of pastiches appeared under the title *The Dragonhiker's Guide to Battlefield Covenant at Dune's Edge: Odyssey Two. Irrational Numbers* is a booklet of tales published by Necronomicon Press, and his short fiction has often been selected for *The Year's Best Horror Stories.* He spends too much time fiddling with eldritch intricacies for his own doomed software company Ansible Information Ltd, and has never really regained the taste for porridge.

D. F. LEWIS had two of his stories rejected in 1968 by August Derleth for being "pretty much pure grue," since then he has had more than one thousand tales published in small press magazines and anthologies on both sides of the Atlantic. Described variously as "the Lovecraft of this era" and "either a genius graced with madness (or) a madman cursed with genius," he cites H. P. Lovecraft, Lord Dunsany, Robert Aickman and Philip K. Dick amongst his disparate literary influences. Various magazines have devoted special issues to his fiction, *The Best of D. F. Lewis* appeared from Tal Publications in 1993, and his stories have been reprinted in *Best New Horror* and *The Year's Best Horror Stories.*

H. P. LOVECRAFT is acknowledged as a master of modern horror and a mainstream American writer second only to Edgar Allan Poe. Born in 1890, poor health as a child led him to read voluminously, and the stories of Poe, Dunsany and Machen inspired his own writing career. He remained a studious antiquarian and virtual recluse until his premature death in 1937. Two years later August Derleth and Donald Wandrei established their own imprint, Arkham House, to publish a posthumous collection, *The Outsider and Others,* and eventually bring all Lovecraft's work back into print. Today his relatively small body of work has influenced countless imitators and formed the basis of a world-wide industry of books, games and movies based on his concepts.

BRIAN LUMLEY was born just nine months after the death of H. P. Lovecraft, but he claims that's just a coincidence. His first books were published by Arkham House in the mid-1970s, while he was still serving in the British army. His early stories, many involving the Cthulhu Mythos, appeared in the collections *The Caller of the Black* and *The Horror at Oakdene*, while he continued Lovecraft's themes in such books as *Beneath the Moors*, *The Burrowers Beneath*, *The Transition of Titus Crow*, *Spawn of the Winds*, *The Clock of Dreams*, *In the Moons of Borea*, *Elysia*, *The Compleat Crow*, and the *Dreams* trilogy. Other novels have included *The House of Doors*, *Demogorgan*, *Psychomech*, *Psychosphere*, *Psychamok*, the best-selling five-part Necroscope series and its sequels, and the Vampire World trilogy: *Blood Brothers*, *The Last Aerie* and *Bloodwars*. His short fiction has been collected in *Fruiting Bodies and Other Fungi* (including the British Fantasy Award–winning title story) and *Return of the Deep Ones and Other Mythos Stories*.

MARTIN MCKENNA first had his artwork published when he was sixteen (including Brian Lumley's "Return to Arkham" in *Dagon*). Since then he has appeared in such publications as *Warlock*, *White Dwarf* and *Interzone* (for which he was voted best illustrator two years running). He has contributed artwork to many Games Workshop books, including *Drachenfels*, *Zaragoz*, *Wolf Riders* and *Ignorant Armies*, and also illustrated such volumes as *Daggers of Darkness*, *Vault of the Vampire*, *Curse of the Vampire*, *Dead of Night*, *Legend of the Shadow Warriors*, *Moonrunner*, *Return to Firetop Mountain*, *Legend of Zagor*, *The Mammoth Books of Vampires*, *Zombies*, *Werewolves*, and *Frankenstein*, *The Anthology of Fantasy and the Supernatural*, the Fantasy Tales series, *Northern Chills* and *Voyages into Darkness*. His artwork has also graced a variety of board games, role-playing games and trading cards. "Innsmouth, with its air of wormy decay and its sinister folk with their unwholesome relationship with the sea, is particularly visually evocative," observes the artist. "Many strong images come to mind, such as the jagged skyline of sagging gambrel roofs and rotten streets with unnaturally shaped residents loping through the gloom. It's doing justice to it all that's the problem. I particularly wanted to portray some of the Innsmouth folk at various stages of their degeneration. I also wanted to use certain ordinary marine creatures in some of the illustrations, as I find many of these can appear fairly alarming in themselves. When we first came up with the notion of collaborating on some Lovecraftian artwork, I knew I wanted to have a go at portraying Cthulhu. Both Jim and Dave have dealt with Him in the past, and although I've tackled a few fairly eldritch things I've never had the opportunity to approach this subject before now. The finished collaboration recently hung in a convention art show where I overheard one viewer remark that it was 'absolutely disgusting,' which made it seem all the more worthwhile."

BRIAN MOONEY has been contributing short stories to magazines and anthologies for nearly thirty years, although he has never been prolific. His first professional appearance was in *The London Mystery Selection* in 1971, since then his fiction has appeared in *The Pan Book of Horror Stories, Dark Voices, Dark Detectives, The Mammoth Book of Werewolves, The Mammoth Book of Frankenstein, Final Shadows, Fantasy Tales, Dark Horizons,* and *Fiesta,* amongst other titles. About his protagonist in "The Tomb of Priscus," he explains: "Like many of us, when I first started writing I toyed with Lovecraftian tales. Reuben Calloway made his first appearance as a minor character in a Mythos story which I have never bothered to rewrite. Then his name is mentioned in 'The Guardians of the Gates,' published in the second issue of *Cthulhu: Tales of the Cthulhu Mythos.* His first appearance in his own right, with his amanuensis, Father Roderick Shea, was in 'The Affair at Durmamnay Hall,' published in *Kadath* No. 5. Calloway is by himself in a werewolf story in *The Anthology of Fantasy and the Supernatural.* I see him as being something of a scruffy Orson Welles with all the arrogance but without the charm."

KIM NEWMAN is a freelance writer, film critic, broadcaster and former semi-professional kazoo-player. A playwright whose works include the gruesome thriller *My One Little Murder Can't Do Any Harm* and the musical *The Gold Diggers of 1981,* his non-fiction includes the critically acclaimed film studies *Nightmare Movies* and *The BFI Companion to Horror,* and he is the co-editor of *Ghastly Beyond Belief* (with Neil Gaiman), the Bram Stoker Award–winning *Horror: 100 Best Books* (with Stephen Jones) and the anthology *In Dreams* (with Paul J. McAuley). His short fiction appears regularly in various anthologies and magazines and has recently been collected in *Seven Stars* and *Unforgivable Stories.* He is the author of the novels *The Night Mayor, Bad Dreams, Jago, The Quorum, Anno Dracula* and its sequels, *The Bloody Red Baron* and *Judgment of Tears.* "Like everyone in the field, I went through a period, at about thirteen, reading H. P. Lovecraft," he reveals. "His Cthulhu Mythos (actually worked into something systematic by August Derleth) is one of the pervasive ideas of horror and science fiction. With a last line in the tradition of Lovecraft disciple Robert Bloch, my story is a fond homage to one of my favourite HPL stories, 'The Shadow over Innsmouth.' 'One for My Baby (and One More for the Road),' by Johnny Mercer and Harold Arlen, was introduced in 1943, not by Sinatra (who sang it in 1958 on the *Only the Lonely* album) but by Fred Astaire in the otherwise forgettable movie *The Sky's the Limit.* I apologise for mutating the song."

JIM PITTS made his debut as an illustrator in David Sutton's *Bibliotheca: H. P. Lovecraft* and Jon Harvey's *Balthus* in 1971. Over the past three decades, his artwork has appeared extensively in British, European and American publications such as *Fantasy Tales, Whispers, Shadow* and numerous British Fantasy Society publications, including *Dark Horizons* and *Chills.* He has also illustrated various hardcover and paperback collections such as Michel Parry's *Savage Heroes* and *Spaced Out,* and Brian Lumley's *The Compleat Khash: Volume One.* Other aspects of his work include paperback covers, a record sleeve and the odd sculpture. He was awarded the Ken McIntyre Award in the early 1970s, and after years of being nominated, he received the British Fantasy Award for Best Artist in both 1991 and 1992. Influences he acknowledges include the *Weird Tales* artists such as Virgil Finlay, Lee Brown Coye and, more importantly, Hannes Bok, without whose inspiration he admits things could have turned out very differently. "The stories of Howard Phillips Lovecraft have always been an enthusiasm of mine," reveals the artist, "and having the opportunity to join forces with Dave Carson and Martin McKenna, two of the best illustrators working in the British fantasy scene today, to work on this book was a dream come true. Our first collaboration sprang independently of this project in 1993 at a convention in Scarborough on England's north east coast (curiously enough, a region well known for its fishing industry). Within a couple of months, Martin came up with the central figure of Cthulhu, I then took the bottom centre and left side and Dave completed the bottom right and upper right side. Hopefully our efforts to capture the wormy, crumbling buildings and degenerate fishy folk of Innsmouth will be worthy of Lovecraft's wonderful story and so justify the long hours the three of us have spent at the drawing boards."

NICHOLAS ROYLE won the 1991 British Fantasy Award for his anthology *Darklands*, and he made it a double the following year by picking up awards for both *Darklands 2* and his story "Night Shift Sister" from *In Dreams*. He has sold more than one hundred short stories to periodicals in Britain, Europe and the USA, including *Ambit, Interzone, Fear, Gorezone, Skeleton Crew, Chills, Peeping Tom, New Socialist* and *Reader's Digest*. His fourth novel, *The Director's Cut*, was published in 2000, and he has been anthologised in such volumes as *Dark Terrors, Dark Voices, The Mammoth Book of Zombies* and *Werewolves, Narrow Houses, The Sun Rises Red, Suger Sleep, Cutting Edge, Book of the Dead, Interzone: The Fifth Anthology, Final Shadows, The Anthology of Fantasy and the Supernatural, The Year's Best Fantasy and Horror* and consecutive editions of *Best New Horror* and *The Year's Best Horror Stories*. About his story in this book, he recalls: "I travelled widely in Eastern Europe between 1987 and 1989, and pre-revolutionary Bucharest remains the most depressing place I have ever visited. With its tangible atmosphere of fear and paranoia it was like something out of a nightmare. I was not lucky enough to set eyes on the reviled dictator Nicolae Ceausescu, but then I lived in London for eight years and I never saw Margaret Thatcher either. Come the revolution."

GUY N. SMITH is incredibly prolific, with more than sixty best-selling horror books to his credit and worldwide sales of over three million. A farmer, bookseller and author of ecological/countryside books (with such titles as *Ratting and Rabbiting for Amateur Gamekeepers* and *Moles and Their Control*), his first horror novel was *Werewolf by Moonlight* in 1974. He gave up his job in banking the following year to become a full-time writer, producing a string of lively novels with such colourful titles as *The Sucking Pit, The Slime Beast, Satan's Snowdrop* and *The Festering*, along with his popular crustacean series: *Night of the Crabs, Killer Crabs, Origin of the Crabs, Crabs on the Rampage, Crab's Moon* and *Crabs: The Human Sacrifice*. The Guy N. Smith Fan Club was formed in 1992, and his recent books include *The Knighton Vampires, The Plague Chronicles*, and two children's novels, *Badger Island* and *Rak*.

MICHAEL MARSHALL SMITH won the British Fantasy Award for Best Short Fiction two years running—for "The Man Who Drew Cats" in 1991 (the same year he was also presented with the Icarus Award as Best Newcomer), and "The Dark Land" in 1992. His stories have appeared in *Dark Terrors, Dark Voices, Best New Horror, Darklands, Darklands 2, Touch Wood, The Mammoth Book of Zombies, The Mammoth Book of Werewolves, The Mammoth Book of Frankenstein, The Year's Best Fantasy and Horror Sixth Annual Collection* and *The Anthology of Fantasy and the Supernatural*, amongst others. His Philip K. Dick Award–winning first novel, *Only Forward*, was published by HarperCollins in 1994. "As regards me and Lovecraft," he admits, "there's probably not much of interest. 'The Shadow over Innsmouth' is certainly up there in my favourites of his, along with 'The Dream-Quest of Unknown Kadath' and 'The Colour out of Space.' One of my all-time favourite phrases comes from the latter: '. . . and the bloodworts grew insolent in their chromatic perversity.' Top of the list is *At the Mountains of Madness*, which—and this is going to sound massively pretentious—I religiously read on transatlantic flights, timing it so that the plane is over Newfoundland or similarly bleak and arctic-looking territories for the climax of the story. As for 'To See the Sea,' there's not much to say, except that (a) it leapt full-grown into my head and (b) I'm glad to finally have got my feelings about a particular car-park I know off my chest."

BRIAN STABLEFORD is an author, critic and academic who worked for twelve years as a lecturer in Sociology at the University of Reading before becoming a full-time writer. He has contributed to many reference books on the science fiction and fantasy fields, and is the author of more than fifty novels, including *The Empire of Fear, Young Blood, Serpent's Blood,* and the trilogy *The Werewolves of London, The Angel of Pain* and *The Carnival of Destruction.* His short fiction is collected in *Sexual Chemistry: Sardonic Tales of the Genetic Revolution,* and he has edited a number of anthologies for Dedalus, for whom he also translates Decadent novels under the pseudonym "Francis Amery."

DAVID SUTTON has been writing and editing in the fantasy and horror genres for nearly thirty-five years. A winner of the World Fantasy Award and twelve-time recipient of the British Fantasy Award, his fiction has been published in a wide range of small press publications and anthologies on both sides of the Atlantic. His short fiction has appeared in *Best New Horror, The Mammoth Book of Werewolves, The Mammoth Book of Zombies, Final Shadows, Cold Fear, Taste of Fear, Ghosts and Scholars, Gothic* and *Skeleton Crew,* amongst many others. He has edited two volumes of *New Writings in Horror and the Supernatural, The Satyr's Head and Other Tales of Terror* and, more recently, is co-compiler of *The Best Horror from Fantasy Tales, The Anthology of Fantasy and the Supernatural,* and the Dark Terrors, Dark Voices and Fantasy Tales series. He says about this volume: "When the editor told me he was putting together an anthology based around a single H. P. Lovecraft story, I immediately thought it might be 'The Colour out of Space,' or 'The Dunwich Horror,' or 'The Shunned House.' The story he chose is one of the author's major yarns, but I wouldn't have pegged it as the focus for the present book. However, re-reading 'The

Shadow over Innsmouth' after quite a number of years, its stature for me has grown. It is a deeply disturbing story, full of ideas from which to draw another tale. Lovecraft's blending of the Federal raid on Devil Reef, the weird religious Dagon sect, the attention to historical detail, the resonance of the Cthulhu Mythos and the grim half-humans and Deep Ones, all make this a wonderfully creepy story."

PETER TREMAYNE has been acknowledged as "one of Britain's leading horror-fantasy writers" and the *Asbury Park Press* declared that he "weaves no less engrossing tales than Edgar Allan Poe." He has written more than twenty-five books in the fantasy and horror field, including *Dracula Unborn, The Ants, The Curse of Loch Ness, Zombie!, Swamp!, Angelus!* and *Snowbeast.* He has also edited *Masters of Terror: William Hope Hodgson* and *Irish Masters of Terror,* and has published over a score of short stories (collected in *My Lady of Hy-Brasil* and *Aisling and Other Irish Tales of Terror*), most of them utilising his unparalleled knowledge of Irish folktales and recorded mythology. His story in this volume expertly links Lovecraft's Cthulhu Mythos to Irish legends, so it should come as no surprise to learn that "Peter Tremayne" is one of a number of pseudonyms used by bestselling Celtic scholar Peter Berresford Ellis, who offers the following observations: "The Irish language contains Europe's third oldest literature with a mythology second to none. While H. P. Lovecraft (in his seminal essay 'Supernatural Horror in Literature') tended to dismiss Irish horror tales as 'more whimsically fantastic than terrible,' he had to rely for his judgment on translators of Irish folklore such as Yeats, Synge, Lady Gregory, etc. who were not primarily concerned with the cosmic horror of the weird tale. Lovecraft made the mistake of thinking of Irish writers of the true weird, such as Charles Maturin, Sheridan Le Fanu, Fitzjames O'Brien and Bram Stoker, as 'British' and not Irish. In Irish myth there appear the ancient gods of evil known as the Fomorii (Dwellers under the Sea) and an ancient synonym for these beings is Daoine Domhain—the Deep Ones. Could the terrible clashes between the Irish deities of Light and Darkness have been carried to the New World by Irish immigrants to be picked up as Lovecraft's tales of the Deep Ones? My story is inspired by some local

Cork traditions about the O'Driscoll clan who dwelt on the now mainly deserted islands off the mainland Irish port of Baltimore (*Baile an Tigh Moir*—the town of the big house), whose name was also taken to the New World by Irish migrants."

JACK YEOVIL is an amnesiac who took his name from the West Country town in which he was found in 1989. He has no recollection of his previous life. He has written for *Empire* and *Good Times* magazines, contributed stories to the GW Books anthologies *Ignorant Armies, Wolf Riders, Red Thirst* and *Route 666*, all edited by David Pringle, and has written the novels *Drachenfels, Demon Download, Krokodil Tears, Comeback Tour, Beasts in Velvet* and *Genevieve Undead.* His greatest literary influences are Robert Faulcon, Harry Adam Knight, Carl Dreadstone and Jack Martin, and he describes his story in this book as "a tribute to two great authors, awkward outsiders, who used a despised genre to make a genuine contribution to English and American letters. If you write in their genre, you must be influenced by them, and if you're a reader who seeks a way into the genre, you could do no better than start with them: Howard Phillips Lovecraft and Raymond Chandler. It occurred to me that Chandler and Lovecraft had a lot in common. Born in 1888 and 1890 respectively, they lived unhappily in America but dreamed of a lost and imaginary England. Awkward outsiders, they were often beset with financial troubles and began their writing careers in pulp magazines. Their visionary, challenging work was first presented alongside lurid dross, though they later came to be recognised as central to separate movements within their chosen genres, hard-boiled crime and weird horror. Married strangely to older wives, they distrusted and feared women, often presenting cruel, almost inhuman female characters. Some of their greatest work is set in seaside towns whose physical corruption has an almost philosophical dimension. Since their deaths, they have become the most imitated and influential writers in their fields and are capable of inspiring entire collections devoted to their characters and themes, not to mention many of the bestselling novelists in their categories. Personally, I found the love of Chandler's prose which I developed in my late teens helped cure habits I'd picked up through an earlier interest in Lovecraft. With 'The Big Fish,' I wanted to bring a touch of Lovecraft's Innsmouth to Chandler's Bay City, fusing elements from 'The Shadow over Innsmouth' and *Farewell, My Lovely*. If its narrator isn't quite Philip Marlowe, he certainly would like to be. I see him as more like Dick Powell than Humphrey Bogart. The stylistic tangle the story can't resolve has something to do with the disparity between a Lovecraft protagonist, who is always overwhelmed by his hostile world, and a Chandler hero, who somehow shrugs it off. The other set of cross-generic twins of the period are Robert E. Howard and Cornell Woolrich, a pair of mother-dominated paranoid miseries whose vision of a hostile universe makes Lovecraft's cosmic horror seem quite sunny; but I can't envision a story in which Conan Wears Black, though a chance meeting in a diner with Bob and Cornell comparing photographs of their mothers has some horrific possibility."

# ABOUT THE EDITOR

STEPHEN JONES lives in London, England. He is the winner of two World Fantasy Awards, three Horror Writers Association Bram Stoker Awards and two International Horror Guild Awards, as well as a thirteen-time recipient of the British Fantasy Award and a Hugo Award nominee. A former television producer/director and genre movie publicist and consultant (the first three *Hellraiser* movies, *Night Life, Nightbreed, Split Second, Mind Ripper, Last Gasp*, etc.), he is the co-editor of *Horror: 100 Best Books, The Best Horror from Fantasy Tales, Gaslight & Ghosts, Now We Are Sick, H. P. Lovecraft's Book of Horror, The Anthology of Fantasy & the Supernatural, Secret City: Strange Tales of London, The Mammoth Book of Best New Horror,* and the Dark Terrors, Dark Voices and Fantasy Tales series. He has written *Creepshows: The Illustrated Stephen King Movie Guide, The Essential Monster Movie Guide, The Illustrated Vampire Movie Guide, The Illustrated Dinosaur Movie Guide, The Illustrated Frankenstein Movie Guide,* and *The Illustrated Werewolf Movie Guide,* and compiled *The Mammoth Book of Terror, The Mammoth Book of Vampires, The Mammoth Book of Zombies, The Mammoth Book of Werewolves, The Mammoth Book of Frankenstein, The Mammoth Book of Dracula, The Mammoth Book of Vampire Stories by Women, Shadows over Innsmouth, Dancing with the Dark, Dark of the Night, Dark Detectives, White of the Moon, Exorcisms and Ecstasies* by Karl Edward Wagner, *The Vampire Stories of R. Chetwynd-Hayes, Phamtoms and Fiends* by R. Chetwynd-Hayes, *James Herbert: By Horror Haunted, The Conan Chronicles* by Robert E. Howard (two volumes), *Clive Barker's A-Z of Horror, Clive Barker's Shadows in Eden, Clive Barker's The Nightbreed Chronicles* and *The Hellraiser Chronicles.* You can visit his Web site at www.herebedragons.co.uk/jones.